I0656778

EXODUS
FROM
YANGANA

EXODUS FROM YANGANA

By
Angel F. Rojas

Translated from the Spanish

by

Robert C. Hewick

© Copyright 2007, María Elena Rojas de Ratinoff

All Rights Reserved.

No part of this book may be reproduced, stored in a retrieval system, or transmitted by any means, electronic, mechanical, photocopying, recording, or otherwise, without written permission from the author.

ISBN: 978-0-6151-7841-7

TABLE OF CONTENTS

Page

Translator's Introduction..ix

Robert C. Hewick

PRELUDE xvii

A Strange Sound is Heard in Palanda

PART ONE 1

The Flight of a Collectively Condemned

INTERLUDE 122

The Drunken Hymn to the Seeds

PART TWO...133

Yangana In Its Age of Innocence

INTERLUDE 233

The Ballad of Sad Euphoria

PART THREE..248

The Last Merrymaking in Yangana

EPILOGUE 441

The Horizon of a New Tomorrow

ACKNOWLEDGEMENTS

Finally it is here!

The English version of *Exodus from Yangana* has been published!

This translation was done by our beloved friend Roberto Hewick, an Englishman who loved our native Ecuador. He finished the translation in 1981, and the manuscript has been dormant for 26 long years!

Our most sincere thanks to Dr. Carlos Lopez Urrutia, whose enthusiasm and perseverance was instrumental in the publishing of the English version of *Exodus from Yangana.*

Recognition and sincere expressions of gratitude are due to Jacobo Ratinoff who first suggested the idea of publishing the translation of the novel to Carlos López and whose support and encouragement was invaluable in carrying out this project.

We also want to thank Dr. Rolando Hamilton and his wife, the poet Celia Correas, for their suggestions.

Gratefully.

The heirs of Angel F. Rojas

TRANSLATOR'S INTRODUCTION

Thirty-two years ago *Exodo de Yangana* made its first splash in Ecuador. Ripples soon spread through Latin America and later traveled to Europe. Now an established classic, another edition came out in Colombia last year. The present volume, however, is its first appearance in English. It should fascinate American readers and help them to understand the causes of the present turmoil in Latin America.

Partly a documentary, partly a chronicle in the oral storytelling tradition, partly a novel filled with lively personalities caught up in romances and tragedies, the book gives a life-size picture of society in a remote Andean village. The factual time for the action is about 50 years ago, but the sociological time was the just pre-industrial era.

The residents of Yangana were exceedingly articulate and spoke with rich vocabularies in spite of their meager educations. They ate well and often, specializing in bizarre-to-us dishes like soups and stews composed of cows' feet, cassava, crushed bones and cobs of corn topped with roasted peanuts. They gossiped day and night about love, infidelity and the follies of their neighbors. They drank much—both men and women—on any occasion like a birth, a death, a harvest, a marriage, a saint's day. They were cruel, compassionate, subtle and courageous, vain, humble and cynical. They had many, many skills and accomplishments, some of which are now strange to the modern world. Above all they were confirmed individuals and staunchly independent.

I first met Angel F. Rojas, the author of this remarkable tale, in the little provincial capital of Machala in southwestern Ecuador near the Peruvian border where I had lived for over 6 years as representative of an American banana company. Before that I had lived for 23 years in remote rural areas of Honduras—sometimes so remote as to be almost primitive—not only as an employee of a banana company but also for eight years as the owner of my own little banana farm.

During these years I had married a Honduranian, had three bilingual sons and formed a deep and lasting affection for Latin America, its people and the Spanish language.

All this was the subject of later conversations with Angel Rojas—sometimes lying in our respective hammocks and sometimes walking together. He was and still is a well-known Guayaquil lawyer and political figure who at that time owned a banana farm near Machala which he visited from time to time. We found that we shared a common interest in social history and literature and we could talk endlessly about the way different peoples thought and lived under different circumstances and at different times. As for me, I had been born in England and educated at Oxford and Harvard, specializing in the history of the United States. In the general disillusionment following the First World War, I had rebelled against the empire-building tradition of my family and eventually found myself in the American tropics instead of in India or Africa.

On one of Rojas' visits to Machala he gave me a copy of the first edition of his *Exodo* which had been published in Buenos Aires in 1949. When I read the book I found it gave an extraordinarily true and vivid picture of life in small isolated rural villages such as I had known and lived in both in Honduras and Ecuador. On re-reading it two years ago, in the third and latest edition, I was again impressed by the knowledgeable firsthand description of daily life—almost a documentary of all kinds of arts and crafts performed in traditional ways. Equally striking was the sensitive understanding of the problems of human behavior in a society at once intensely traditional and intensely individualistic.

Parts of the story—some of the most vivid—employ the technique of oral storytelling in the tradition of Homer or Boccaccio, a tradition that was still flourishing when I first went to Latin America. In isolated villages such as Yangana there was of course no TV, no radio; books and newspapers were scarce. It was a self-contained pre-industrial society. Storytelling was the established evening entertainment and was tremendously enjoyed.

The details of daily work of all kinds in and around the village are fully described—plowing, sowing and harvesting; tobacco planting and curing; rum distilling; sugar, candle and soap making; harness and saddle making; butchering; tanning; brick, tile and adobe making. How Papá Toro cast a new bell for the village church is particularly memorable.

Don Vicente, the local scholar and philosopher with his beloved library the merchant, the parish priest, the prostitute, the cobbler, the potter, the herb doctor, the midwife, the inventor-mechanic, the tree-planter all come alive in unforgettable vignettes.

The effect on the traveling botanist from the USA of this spectacle of an almost Utopian self-contained world is touchingly related in the Gringo Spark's own words. No wonder he was astonished by the extraordinary ingenuity and resourcefulness shown by men with no mechanical background, living in places where there were no workshops and no spare parts. Froilán Zapata the inventor-mechanic is a prime example of this. I myself have seen Mocha, my car driver, eleven thousand feet up on deserted mountain roads, plug leaking gas tanks with soap, repair worn wiring contacts with foil from cigarette packs, and replace lost brake fluid with raw rum. And Mocha was a man who only a few years before had been a barefoot boy driving oxen.

One basic theme runs through the story of Yangana. It is the cause and effect of the struggle over ownership and use of land. Just as in 18th Century England expanding markets, new agricultural methods and safer and quicker transport made land infinitely more valuable and desirable to those who could look ahead, the same results followed all through Latin America during the second half of the 19th Century and the beginning of the Twentieth.

Large or powerful landowners used political influence, legal or quasi-legal pretexts, or downright force to expropriate for their own use the ancestral communal lands of their poorer neighbors. This was carried out with the connivance and often the open support of the provincial or national governments. The whole process is admirably and faithfully described in the book. The resentment of the dispossessed has smoldered ever since and erupted in sporadic rural revolts in many countries. Now it is exploding. A related theme in the story is the patience and resignation of people of all classes when faced by the common sufferings of human life, by natural disasters of all kinds, and by the cruelty, corruption and oppression of government at all levels. All these evils, up to a point, were accepted as an inevitable part of life. It was only when goaded by unbearable injustice and deprivations, and inflamed by drink, that the people of Yangana finally rebelled.

Robert C. Hewick
Cotuit, Cape Cod
February, 1981

"Who killed the Overlord?
Fuenteovejuna, my lord.
And who is Fuenteovejuna?
All of us."

Lope De Vega (1563–1635) "Fuenteovejuna"

PRELUDE

A Strange Sound is Heard in Palanda

"What's happening?" wondered Joaquín Reinoso for the hundredth time in his isolated refuge in Palanda. "What on earth is going on?"

Ever since noon he had been uneasy. During the siesta hours while the steaming jungle was asleep his senses were awake, keeping the same nervous watch that they had kept for the past two years and now he thought he could feel a vague vibration in the earth coming gently and discreetly from far away. That was the first message.

He stopped work, resting his slashing machete. Everything was quiet. In the silence he listened, straining his nerves, trying to perceive and differentiate.

He knew that in the deep shadows of the forest there are always intermittent mutterings of a language which a man familiar with them understands perfectly. A breaking branch, or a tree which has been slowly falling for days while its roots and intertwined limbs give way one by one. A herd of wild pigs passing by, a troop of tapirs pursued by a puma, a band of chattering monkeys, a flock of frightened birds taking wing. The voice of the wind, the noise of the river, even the soundless coming of the mist, the convulsion in the treetops from a distant thunderstorm.

The knowledgeable man can interpret all these sounds and can by intuition calculate their distance. It is not unusual for him to experience a mysterious organic condition of hair-raising panic. When this happens the expense of nervous energy is so great that he is momentarily exhausted, only to regain later, as though in compensation, a resplendent ancestral vigor.

During these periods of apparently morbid excitement the whole body is converted into a great and delicate receptacle which reacts over all its surface to the changes in the world outside. It resembles one vast and total sense, formed by the fusion of all five. This strange integration acquires an unbelievable power of perception. It can on occasion foresee future events and not only hear faraway sounds, but identify exactly from what direction and from what distance they are coming.

Joaquín felt, however, that in this case he had to sort out his impressions as thoroughly as he could, since the first facts transmitted to his senses seemed unbelievable. He began by lying down with his ear, to the bare ground. No sooner done, than he, sprang up, startled by something threatening which for all his knowledge of the forest he could not understand. The earth was palpably shaking with the tread of animals, many animals. He could discern hoof-beats of a heard of horses, mules and donkeys and a multitude of human footsteps. Never before had the mysterious vibrations of the earth spoken to his senses in such a way.

As the afternoon sun moved toward the treetops of the western horizon, this sound and the unmistakable feelings which portend the presence of human beings grew closer and closer. After listening for the sixth time with his ear to the ground he could doubt no longer. He went back to his hut and confirmed to his wife what he had suspected since noontime.

"This sound, Rosa Elvira, that I have been hearing all afternoon," he said as he slowly climbed the bamboo ladder, "comes from people. I've just heard it quite clearly and it sounds like a lot of them, a whole crowd. And what's more, they are coming with animals, many animals. They're coming this way, the same way we did, looking for the river."

"Couldn't they be Jívaro Indians?" asked the woman in a soft musical voice, trying to appear calm.

"Jívaros with horses? Since when have they had horses? Jívaros with cattle? These are not Jívaros."

And after a long thoughtful silence, swinging in his hammock, hands clasped over his knees, "No, they are not Jívaros," he repeated.

Again he paused. "Nor can they be the police coming for me. Because these people are bringing cows with them and what would police be doing with cows? But why so many people? Why so much livestock?"

"Let's get ready. Better dig up the cartridges."

Man and wife set to work as they tried to understand the meaning of what was now clearly an invasion. An invasion of their solitary life in the dense forest. An invasion by a whole multitude heading straight for them.

"And suppose it really is the police?" again the man wondered aloud. There was no answer and he fell once more into anxious speculation. His child was sleeping there in the hut. He now had to defend a house, a woman, a son, a banana field and cassava. And above all, the freedom that had cost him so much.

The cartridges were found perfectly preserved in a deep bed of ashes. The couple got out their two rifles and made their plans. They would escape separately and meet later in a safe and secret place.

So Joaquín Reinoso, making a final determined vow to himself, set off gun in hand to explore the terrain traversed at that moment by unknown men coming with an unknown and perhaps sinister purpose.

PART ONE

The Flight of a Collectively Condemned

There may have been as many as 160 families on the march. A whole town was slowly and painfully moving through the arduous jungle like survivors of a shipwreck.

Nine days of walking, trepidation and watchfulness had left their mark on both men and beasts, but in spite of their weariness they struggled on. Hope seemed to buoy them up. Hope still gave them courage and drew them on while an equal force drove them from behind. For behind them they had just left something dreadful, for that reason they painfully bid farewell with no hope of returning.

On reaching the head of Caranango Gorge, the caravan stopped for two hours to look back at the lovely valley for the last time. The whole crowd broke into sighs and sobs. They believed they had been punished by fate. With one piercing voice they cried out their farewell.

The old people wept unashamedly; the younger men swallowed their tears and in strangled voices shouted to their wives and children to be quiet.

After crossing the pass at Caranango, the road began to drop. A few yards further on, and the people who had been looking back for a last lingering glimpse of the beloved countryside they were leaving behind to be remembered forever after with sweet nostalgia, could now see only the ancient wayside cross at the head of the Pass. The stragglers later told how "Curly" Ocampo—sunburned, sturdy and pock marked—bringing up the rear with rifle and cartridge belt slung over his shoulder, had stopped for an instant, looked at that weather beaten piece of wood, the final symbol of the world they were leaving, and shaken his fist at it in rage.

Perhaps 160 families were on the march.

Hardly a soul was missing. The whole town was again set in motion slowly slipping down the gentle slope, ever closer to the river. The line moved slowly but unfalteringly on course, like a drop of oil on a polished wall. It never slackened. It was powered by over 600 human wills.

(1)

First of them all marched Don Lisandro Fierro. Don Lisandro Fierro was the oldest one of all. Begetter of an almost biblical family, deaf as a post, as a young man he had been a personal friend of President Garcia Moreno. He was riding, wherever there was room on the road, mounted on a big trusty old gray mare. The old man's face was huge. His complexion at once high-colored and dark; he had been tanned by the sun when as a strong man he worked the fields—the same sun that until yesterday had warmed his declining years in the quiet mornings of his town. He had never used eyeglasses and the mischievous sparkle of those little eyes which had seen so much was half hidden by bushy eyebrows. He still spoke in a hoarse growl and since he could hear nothing, he shouted so loud that his venerable beard waved in the breeze. Little children were terrified of him.

As for his feet, in their broad shoes, they were safely set in a pair of old bronze stirrups. To cover his now shrunken thighs, he used an old Mexican sarape which doubled as a blanket. Whenever there was a halt on the road, the old man flung the sarape down on the ground and stretched out on it.

A favorite game in the region that these people had just abandoned was a traditional form of bingo called "quina." For hours at a time the players would listen, their elbows on the table and their eyes anxiously fixed on their numbered boards, waiting for the numbers to be called, and loudly they were called. The girls always blushed at the allusive names which designated certain numbers, but they understood them so well that they never failed to put their counters—grains of corn—on the proper squares.

The numbers called out were almost always ingeniously phrased to carry sexual allusions. Number One was a synonym for the phallus. Number Thirteen was called briefly, "Further In," Number Fourteen, "The Girl Dripping Gum," Number Fifteen, "The Gum Keeps Dripping" or "The Girl's in danger" and so on. And the highest of all, Number Ninety was naturally, "Don Lisandro!" since for all the young men of the town he was the symbol of Priapus the Procreator.

All these people loved the old man. He seemed to them something left over from another age, one of the fabled ancients, and some of them really believed he'd been made of superhuman stuff, of a clay that would never crumble.

He could remember with astonishing freshness the events of his youth and related them in exactly the same way whenever he had a chance. Those who were in a position to judge never considered him especially intelligent, but they all recognized him as an undisputed authority when he spoke of his long life and of those far off times. There were some who looked on him as a kind of oracle and learned by heart all his good advice as if his lips spoke with the wisdom of the ages. "The Devil knows more not because he's the Devil, but because he's so old," they would say.

But the general esteem in which he was held did not stop the lads of the town and especially those of his own family—his grandchildren and his great grandchildren— from making fun of the old man. The older and more sober-minded of his neighbors were shocked by this behavior and considered it another lamentable sign of the times, an

4

example of how the younger generation no longer respected the experience of the old or the lessons of the past.

But in spite of every reprimand, these mischievous unmannerly boys kept on teasing the old man. They called him an old iguana, an alligator, or copperhead snake. They said his ears would soon be long enough to wipe his nose with instead of as usual with his fingers. They imagined him riding off into the woods on his old mare to hold long shouted conversations with the Devil under the locust trees and cottonwoods all festooned with Spanish moss, while the wind from the hilltops whistled and swirled over the fields.

And so he came accompanied by his three daughters, all grandmothers with their children and grandchildren. Many of the girls of the family were notably handsome women with smooth white complexions, blue eyes and fair hair. This had always been taken as proof of the story that Don Lisandro's father had been a Spanish soldier who had settled in the neighborhood after the War of Independence. In any event, whether single, married or widowed, everyone of them had done her best to have children and all of these were on the march.

(2)

Next came the Mendieta brothers.

These Mendietas were the two best horsemen in town. They only had to "work over" a mule a few times to produce a docile mount with a gentle pace, answering smoothly to rein or spur. It made no difference how skittish the animal was to start with, the result was always the same. The elder of the brothers was perhaps the hardest drinker of the whole neighborhood. In fact he was always half drunk the first time he saddled an untamed animal. He used to say that mules could tell in a moment when a rider was drunk and the rougher the treatment the better they behaved, exactly the same as women did.

"It's true that I've suffered falls," he would explain, "but only when cold sober. When I'm 'fortified' no mule or horse or woman has ever thrown me off."

People who knew him and had seen him in action agreed that his boast was to some extent justified. But they laughed at him for one exception, the indomitable mother of his two children. This woman had for the last ten years resisted all his blandishments and sworn she would never again submit to such an abandoned drunk. He had made many futile attempts to tame the stubborn woman and finally took the two children away from her. They were on the road with him now—a cross-eyed boy and a little snot-nosed chit of a girl—riding good mules handsomely saddled and bridled.

Although the Mendieta brothers swore that they were full brothers, they did not look it. The elder was short, slight, with slant eyes, smooth face and straight black hair. The other was tall, with curling beard, light olive complexion and thick eyebrows. They shared only one physical feature, outrageously bowed legs.

To add to this portrait, since the younger Mendieta was much taller than his brother, his bowlegs were the more noticeable, so that the burden of jokes made about this family defect naturally fell upon him. People teased him, saying that when he stood up, an ox loaded with straw could pass between his legs and he'd never notice it.

The brothers had with them a string of frisky young mules that responded to the slightest touch, their ears twitching at every sound. They came in line, one after the other tied with long ropes. Every so often they stumbled or stuck in the mud, reared up and kicked out, laid back their ears and tried to bolt only to be brutally reined in. All this was accompanied by the blasphemous oaths of the riders.

The elder Mendieta's stormy old love—the mother of the cross-eyed boy and the snot-nosed little girl—was on the road, too, but far down the line of march.

He tried to keep her in sight and kept thinking that some day she would again be his. Like that time when he rode drunk into her house, on horseback, frightened her out of her wits and had his way with her. That had been the very last time: ten years ago.

(3)

Next came "The Virgin of the Wild Fig Tree," considered the most beautiful girl in all the countryside.

She was tall and slender with wide hips and narrow waist. People found it hard to describe adequately her great beauty—her sparkling eyes, her noble shoulders which she was not afraid to show when she bathed in the river, the lovely curves of her bosom, the marvelously straight line of her powerful legs, her tanned skin, cool and silky.

The very sight of her excited the boys, while grown up men lay awake thinking of her. She had evidently inherited from her mother the burning look in her eyes, at once innocent and coquettish, and a sweet almost silvery voice. Her presumed father, "Shameless Carlos," so-called for his many amorous conquests, had for his part left her an extraordinary power of attraction over the opposite sex. Many were the serenades sung at her window, not because she was tall and gracious, not because she was fresh and virginal, not because she smiled quickly and blushed easily, not because she dressed like a city girl and made her own clothes with her own sewing machine, but above all because there was something in her body and soul which drove the boys wild.

The neighbors figured that this something was even stronger since the girl was the double-distilled product of a volcanic, adulterous driving passion to say nothing of the evil spell cast by the huge tree, the wild fig under whose shadow she had spent her life.

This particular variety of wild fig tree was known throughout the province as a "heavy" or gloomy tree. It grew best on the edges of mountain streams where its thick foliage made the early nightfall even more somber. When the wind blew strong, its coarse leaves rustled mournfully, providing a funereal accompaniment to the sound of the rushing water. Nobody dared to rest under the sinister shade of the wild fig tree or let their mounts drink of the water running over its roots. Ghostly specters from the other world loved to pounce down from its overhanging branches. To live near these trees was to ask for trouble.

In spite of all this, or perhaps because of it, the girl's mother, Doña Pascuala had built her little house under the shade of a wild fig tree that grew beside the road a kilometer out of town. And there she brought up her daughter, baring her teeth so to speak, at all who approached. By the time the child was twelve she was already beautiful and people began to call her by that strange name, "The Virgin of the Wild Fig Tree." She seemed imbued with the bewitching power of the tree, and this produced an amorous malaise in all who came near her.

This unattainable goddess had nevertheless a sure defense against even the most determined suitors, those ready to run any risk, and that was the frightful viper—her mother. So it was that what with a terrible mother on one side and terrified lovers on the other, the girl could make her way calmly through the narrow streets of the town pursued only by lustful looks of crazy passion and hopeless love, just as a snake dares to swim across a river in flood.

Naturally she was accused of being proud. Her would-be lovers sighed at the thought that those full red lips, those lissome arms and restless hands were being reserved for some stranger, for the enjoyment of some delighted city-dweller who would carry her off to share a life of luxury.

The only time the young men of the town could touch her forbidden body was during Carnival. That was their one chance to enter the closed house where she lived, and they came by dozens. They doused her with colored water, rubbed her lovely firm cheeks with colored talcum powder—green, red, blue—as if crazed they threw her bodily into the nearby creek. They smeared her trembling bosom with crushed red cactus flowers leaving what looked like a blood stain on her dress and it drove the revelers to frenzy.

Even now, when the Virgin of the Wild Fig Tree was freed from its unholy protection; her body and soul still carried with them something of the mysterious attraction of those trees that growled in the wind on dark nights by the river bank.

Her mother, Doña Pascuala Bailón, that well-known harridan of the biting tongue, accompanied her on the march.

The terrible and terrifying Doña Pascuala, who in her better moments was so coaxing and soft-spoken, enjoyed a well-earned reputation as mistress of her art. At various times she had routed in debate the most virulent and imaginative speakers, the loudest-mouthed men and women. These contests in shouted abuse sometimes lasted for two or three hours, witnessed by a crowded and appreciative audience.

It was generally admitted that she had won her most famous victory some years before by silencing the most foul-mouthed man in Yangana, Big Mouth Camilo Isidro. This insolent, shameless character, finding himself pushed into a corner by Doña Pascuala's barrage of words, chose to let down his pants in front of his opponent. The story was that the ferocious and implacable woman, far from retreating, immediately drew profitable comparisons from the sight before her and drove the scoundrel from the field.

From that day forth Big Mouth was a changed man, but he never forgave Doña Pascuala for her sneering mockery of his manhood.

It was interesting that she was always polite to passers-by or people she met in the road, asking them how they did. This was, of course, the common courtesy of the place, but at times she would stay talking in the middle of the road and try in a way to explain or excuse her venomous rages.

"I have to protect my daughter," she would say. "I live all alone and she's a pretty girl. I am the thorn, she is the rose. What would the poor thing do if I didn't protect her?"

Everyone agreed with the reasoning and not just to please the famous tongue-lasher.

Next came Joaquín Torres, doctor and apothecary. He had a huge supply of medicinal herbs and an imposing array of dusty flasks. This enabled him to practice with confidence the complete art of healing all human ailments without exception, not only those sent by God in the course of nature, but also those caused by the evil spells of enemies.

Of mixed Spanish and Indian blood, this Don Joaquín was a skinny bald-headed old character stinking of all kinds of medicinal herbs—valerian, rue, wild cinnamon and heaven knew what else.

His invariable method of diagnosis was to study the patient's urine. He could then decide whether it was a matter of natural sickness or if an evil spell was involved. As was to be expected, most cases turned out to be the latter. Then again he made a further distinction: either the spell was a "fresh" one and therefore almost always susceptible to treatment, or else too much time had passed before seeking treatment.

"When the evil has passed a certain point," he would explain. "It's very hard to arrest it. The spell is gaining on us."

Such a case required special treatments every night for a week or more at a time, consisting of infusions of aguacolla leaves, the waving of wands and switches to scare off the evil spirit, and last of all the absorption of strong liquors poured into the nostrils from a snail shell. This was the last resort, always provided the moon was waning at the same time.

The townspeople had two theories about Don Joaquín Torres' medical knowledge. One version was that the old man was himself a wizard, double-distilled, worse than those who cast spells. That was the reason he could cure them.

"Not so," said the other group. "He is not a wizard, just a good honest herb doctor. If he were a wizard, he wouldn't threaten and lash out so at his fellow spirits. He knows his profession and heals the ills God sends us."

Carrying with him this ambiguous reputation, scorned by the healthy and sought after by the sick—dirty, smelly, cadaverous old herbalist that he was—Don Joaquín Torres had his place in the Caravan.

(6)

Next came Doña Petrona Alcocer, the queen of midwives. Sixty years old, she had practiced her profession for over thirty. She moved along slowly as if bearing the burden of her fabulous botanical knowledge and the weight of all the children she had ushered into the world.

It was said that for the last twenty years she had been able to tell from the third month on the sex of an unborn child and that she was always right.

When dealing with a first birth, she was deft, easy and quick in handling both mother and child. Retained after-birth was no problem: just three swallows of a herbal concoction known only to her did the trick.

Her large capable hands looked smaller than they were because she herself was so stout. Nor was her skill with these hands confined to fulltime normal births. Her knowledge encompassed all the art of massage and the use of Indian infusions to procure an early abortion. What was more, she managed these affairs so smoothly and discreetly that nobody ever knew of them.

And these patients of hers, now relieved of their burden no matter what stage it had reached, had only to take a good bath of mysterious leaves and roots and lo! they were well again. Free from fear, strengthened and toned up, they were soon back at their old games.

Doña Petrona Alcocer, star of all midwives, sturdy, wise and understanding, how many children and how many reputations owed their salvation to your huge forearms and rolled up sleeves!

(7)

Next came Fermín López, a man cursed by fate, condemned to suffer from fire all his life.

He was still young, barely thirty-four. His fine features and pale bearded race were lighted up by a smile which many people considered threatening or at least insolent. His eyes had the look of a doomed man; they seemed to have witnessed uncounted horrors and to have faced death itself many times. One of his arched eyebrows was higher than the other and bore the mark of his first scorching by fire.

The man had always gone barefoot and anybody could see at a glance the horrible way one of his legs had been scarred by fire. The big toe and the one next to it were fused together into one deformity. In fact he was covered all over with scars and those who knew his story could tell from their color more or less when he had got them, since López had been burned by accident more than once.

He was a ready talker and liked to speak of what might be called his fiery fate and nobody who listened doubted the truth of what he said. On the contrary, they even figured that López "The Match" must be a kind of messenger of Fire to the Earth. The frightful wounds on his body proved it.

Comments would run like this:—"I'd have thought that Fermín had been squirted by a skunk when he was a baby and that that's why he's so unlucky," said Anacleto Aliago, "if it weren't that the only liquids he had anything to do with are inflammable ones, and skunk urine stinks so that it would actually have helped him put out his fires. Nor can they truthfully think that there was something wrong with his mother's milk. Milk does not catch fire, on the contrary it can be used to put out a fire. I'll tell you what he is. He's a kind of detonator, a percussion cap, a fuse, a fellow made of gunpowder—that's what he is."

The tragic tale of The Flames of Fermín López ran thus:—

"Flames were Fermín López' foster mother. His parents and brothers all died when their house on the outskirts of Yangana burned down. Fermín was saved by one of those miracles that only the fire itself could have performed. The fire merely kissed the infant as it passed, blistering its forehead, scorching its eyelids and almost destroying its right eyebrow with the first rapturous embrace. The flames now knew the smell of Fermín López' flesh, roasted by their caress, and from then on they would never cease giving their burning gifts."

"When the boy reached the age of seven, it was time he learned his letters and a trade. The Fire Spirit realized that he needed a teacher and sent him to work in Don Augustín Vargas' cane mill. Before he had been there six months the mill burned down and his master's house with it. Fermín López, from now on known as The Match, emerged from the ashes with one leg out of joint and the naked foot trailing its skin like a half-off sock."

"Fermín López survived and grew to manhood, his beard grown, his Adam's apple and his voice strong and firm. Time for the flames to teach him yet another lesson, that when boys become men they no longer cry. So it was that he found himself the evening before the town's anniversary fiesta at the house of the Indian, Presentación Quille, the fireworks maker. Fermín was sitting at the kitchen door drinking from a gourd of fresh water held in both hands, when a spark from the fire fell on some gunpowder left over from the day's preparations. Fermín was found, naturally, among the survivors of the resulting explosion. A tongue of flame had scorched his chest and flung him out of doors senseless. His face was saved thanks to the gourd of water he had been drinking. His bare hands and arms were horribly burned and the pain was so dreadful that his whole face was twisted in agony. But he was eighteen years old and he must learn that he could no longer throw himself on his bed and cry like a child. So he did learn."

"For the next few years, López the Match lived a quiet life, enough time to know the meaning of happiness. He harvested two good crops and it really seemed as if his bad luck had forgotten its protegé."

"He devoted himself to his land during those peaceful years. He loved the look and feel of freshly turned earth, and to create a farm where before there had been only jungle. The sight of the first fragile sprouts of new corn pushing up through the clods filled him with joy, he never tired of watching his crops grow and ripen under the sun. He had built his little mud-walled thatched house a half hour out of town. He took care that it was far enough away from the farm to make sure, absolutely sure, that no spark from the yearly brush-burning could reach it."

"But one day our Fermín López, our Match, woke up with itching feet and set out at random. Before long he heard the distant sound of an ax. Following the sound, he came to a little fenced hut and behind the fence he saw something he would never forget. Yes, friends and people of Yangana—he saw a girl who, thinking she was alone, was relieving herself."

"As fate would have it, The Match's meeting with this young woman was to prove once again an encounter with the Fire Spirit. Unrelenting fire that this time would burn him slowly and sweetly and leave an invisible scar more terrible than any of the others. Once the girl had recovered from the embarrassment of their first meeting—not a very romantic first start to be sure—she, too, began to burn with the same flame. Before long, our gallant farmer no longer left an empty house behind him when he went to work."

"And they were happy, openly and unbelievably happy, while the child within her grew as a seed grows in newly planted ground. And they were still happy for four days after the child was born. Then the mother fell sick with a fever, a burning fever that lasted a month. The despairing husband clasped her hands day and night. Hands and wrists that grew thinner every day, a pulse that beat faster as if life were growing stronger and not ebbing slowly away as the Fire Spirit claimed another victim. The child lingered on for twelve days after the mother's death, kept alive with sugared water and corn,-:gruel, and then he followed her."

"And so López the Match finally gave up the struggle against the fiery fate to which he had been born. From first to last he had tried and failed. Never again would he do anything to free himself from his bondage to the flames."

"He could think of only one way to cheat the Fire Spirit that had harassed him for so long. He would hang himself from a tree. He set out resolutely for the woodland, turned for one last look at his fields and his hut, but at that instant it struck him that the little house he was leaving behind was still intact. No! he couldn't leave it like that, the little house where he had so loved his wife and son, never! He would save himself from the fire, but not his little house. He ran back with a bundle of lighted straw in his hand and in a moment the thatched roof was in flames, while he himself looked on calmly from a safe distance. It seemed ironical that for once the flames were circling their favorite child without scorching him."

"The fatal lure of the Fire Spirit now took a sentimental turn. López the Match suddenly remembered that the silk shawl he had given his wife when they were courting would be lost in the fire. He had wrapped its cool soft folds around her poor fevered shoulders when she was dying. Not for anything in the world would he leave this last reminder of his lost one to go up in flames. That could never be. He needed it to twist and twist in his hands and finally to shroud his head when he'd be hanging from the highest limb of some tree. He shut his eyes and spurred by an irresistible impulse sprang into the bonfire. He was found at sundown lying unconscious at the edge of his corn field, still clutching a piece of scorched cloth."

"What would he have gained?" concluded the tale, "by insisting on killing himself with a rope? He had to get that idea out of his head, he had to shrink from death by hanging and once again to wish to live until his master the Fire Spirit should grant him eternal peace."

And so López the Match had his place in the line of march, perhaps a little afraid that his bad luck would still haunt even this collective enterprise of a whole community. Perhaps, too, he had a vague feeling of having been some kind of unwitting accomplice in the dreadful conflagration that had totally destroyed Yangana. But his companions on the road thought otherwise. They actually felt that in a way he was some sort of insurance, a savior and protector who personally bore the brunt of all the hatred of the Gods. They thought of him as a kind of lightning conductor or condenser which neutralized all those elemental furies which would otherwise annihilate everyone else. Just as Torres, the herb doctor protected them from the sicknesses sent by God and by the Devil, so López the Match, the official victim of bad luck, the spoiled child of the crop-destroying fire, would protect them from the wrath of the elements.

(8)

Then came the widow of Don Patricio Aldeán, unquestionably the most distinguished lady of the community.

Fortyish, stout and slow moving, very much a sociable person, full of gestures and grimaces, she was intelligent and a gracious and agreeable talker. When visitors came from the city she was the soul of the party, and who but she was always chosen to organize the annual play which for three hundred years had been performed in honor of Our Lord of Good Fortune, the patron saint of the town, the town they had just burned to the ground.

She directed all the rehearsals herself, cast the actors for all the parts, and on opening night served as prompter too, her voice clear and warm.

She wore city clothes and was herself an accomplished dressmaker familiar with fashion plates and dress forms. She could make a dress in any style so easily that it never failed to astonish all her friends.

As for food, she was famous for setting a good table. Anybody who dined at her house could be sure of fine fare and was expected to do it full justice. Her larder was the best stocked in town, since Doña Patrocinio or Mama Patrocinio as she was usually called, loved not only to cook the most delicious dishes but to enjoy them herself. Food was almost a passion with her. There were cheeses from the upland dairies, rich salty yellow cheeses; great strips of fat sun-dried meat stretched on a cord from one side of the room to the other; salted and pickled fish from Peru; long strings of sausages hanging from the beams of the loft; and a chest lined with fresh leaves where she kept her rich spiced bread kneaded and baked with her own hands twice a week.

The barnyard behind the house was full of poultry of all kinds, and always a pig fattening in his sty. All under the widow's watchful and gluttonous eye. At the first light of dawn, when the hens were flapping down from their roosting trees, the old lady's three servant-girls began their usual uproarious pursuit of the particular bird destined for that day's dinner.

In general, the widow was highly respected by everybody in the town.

Proof of this was the fact that she was the only person who could persuade a father, no matter how strict or jealous or old fashioned, to allow his daughter or daughters to act in a local comedy. There was an established and recognized ritual for the negotiation. First the girl's parents roundly refused the request of the organizing committee. Next Doña Patrocinio put in her word, answered by messenger an hour later to the effect that they consented, but only out of personal consideration for her. Then a second visit from Doña Patrocinio to thank them for so kindly making an exception for her. At the same time, she presented a list of the dresses that would be needed for the heroine and the chorus and the colors and lengths of material to make them.

Was it any wonder that the whole town felt that if Mother Patrocinio could overcome such obstacles she deserved their gratitude?

Then came Don Vicente Muñoz, the most learned man in Yangana. He was said to be of aristocratic descent and it was certainly true that when he was in high school in the city, his companions had been the sons of upper class parents. There was talk of an unhappy romance, of a broken love affair which led him to abandon the city for good. This disappointment was the only explanation his neighbors could give for his crazy and ridiculous love of books and book learning. They affectionately called him "The Spaniard," because he looked to them like a Spanish gentleman of bygone days.

He was tall and thin with a slight stoop. His complexion was a pallid white, his high forehead like alabaster. He had allowed his reddish-yellow beard to grow out thick and curly, making a perfect frame for the long ascetic face with its sunken cheeks. His bristly eyebrows seemed to contradict the gentleness of his blue eyes.

He was now riding along, guiding his horse with the sure touch of his long, bony hands on the reins. But when these same hands were stretched out straight, they trembled ever so slightly in contrast to his strong hairy wrists. His breath smelled of tobacco, his deep sonorous voice sounded a little hoarse.

His books were packed in huge saddlebags, the kind used for carrying plantains. This must have been the most extraordinary journey of books in the century. Four strong mules bore on their backs what their master considered the most precious cargo in the world.

He really was in his own way a genuine bibliophile. Many of his books had been purchased very cheaply before the First World War. His house in Yangana may have been a humble one but it was clean and well kept. One of the rooms had a large window looking on the street and was full of the fragrance of cedarwood, for it was here on tightly packed shelves of the finest quality cedar that he kept his books.

Adjoining this aromatic little retreat of learning, the owner kept another simple room always ready for guests. How many friends came there! Across the years how many unknown strangers, finding themselves in a town where there was no hotel or inn or rooming house, had dismounted in the quiet street, held the reins with one hand and knocked at that hospitable door with the travel-stiff knuckles of the other! How many transient guests had sat down at the simple table to share the learned recluse's frugal meals!

His after dinner conversation, as soon as his youngest daughter had cleared the table, was gentle and discreet. He never talked about himself, instead he showed a courteous interest in the needs and comfort of the traveler.

When referring to books that he had read and reread, he spoke of them with disconcerting assurance. He was a bit of a free thinker and loved to quote Juan Montalvo since he was one of the few Ecuadorians who had known Don Juan personally. His great weakness was romantic novels. Gifted with a remarkable memory he would, on the rare occasions when he felt talkative, recite to a spellbound audience whole chapters from "The Count of Monte Cristo" or "The Three Musketeers."

He did a little writing from time to time, being the local correspondent of the paper published weekly in the provincial capital. In his articles he took no side in party politics although he would sometimes make a discreet reference to the corrupt practices of greedy politicians. And he would always make a speech when he thought it necessary, or rather he wrote the speeches that others delivered at fiestas and important public occasions in Yangana, such as theatrical performances, the opening of a bridge, a school prize giving, or the funeral of some well-known person. He wrote verse freely and easily and was much sought after to compose realistic and topical scripts for the situation comedies which were put on at least once a year. For Yangana was a town where theatrical performances were almost fanatically appreciated.

As he rode along followed by his little family and surrounded by his books, he seemed sunk in thought. True that he was entitled to every consideration, nevertheless his slender hands seemed to shake more than usual.

Some of his companions on the march thought that the cause of this might be a feeling of responsibility for taking part in what had just happened in Yangana, or perhaps it was simply a yearning for the quiet life he had left behind, for the smell of cedarwood shelves in his old house and the hours spent over his beloved books.

(10)

Next in line were three noted musicians, Ignacio Gordillo, Elías Gómez and Benjamín Betancur with their respective instruments—a fiddle, a bamboo flute, two holes of which had been bored with a hot iron poker, and a guitar. The fiddler was a thin, bony, potbellied carpenter who had made his fiddle with his own hands. He always wore shoes, his feet had rather a bad smell and he had admirable endurance in swinging the ax or adze.

Benjamín Betancur, the guitar player, was a handsome ruddy cheeked fellow and an excellent singer. He made the most of his good looks and was expert at getting free drinks. All this enabled him to achieve the most sensational amorous conquests. He often boasted when in his cups, to the effect that more than once he had been paid by lovesick neighbors to sing serenades for them in the hope of winning the heart of some girl, only to have the maiden decide in favor of the singer himself. His excuses to the frustrated lover would go like this, "You're mistaken, my poor fellow, in your case there was no need ever to think of deceiving you, since I had already triumphed."

Elías Gómez completed the trio of musicians, setting his thick lips to the seven blackened holes of his flute. He too had fashioned it with his own hands, slowly and carefully trimming both ends of the wooden cylinder with a thin sharp blade. To give it a really good tone he would also, when offered a drink before playing, pour it through his flute instead of down his own throat so that the instrument smelled of rum while the, player stayed sober. Those who appreciated music always wondered how that wide mouth and those full lips could breathe so delicate an air, so winning and so tuneful, a thread of sound that passed through his moving fingers to become ever sweeter, richer and more joyous.

(11)

Next came Jacinto Peñaflor, the cobbler, known behind his back as Jacinto Picuita.

He suffered with these two names. The first one was what he chose to call himself and liked to be called by; the other he despised as vulgar, harsh sounding and above all an uncivilized name suitable for half-breeds, but which as it happened, was in his case legally correct.

More a shoemender than a shoemaker, he loved cockfighting, but his real Sunday sport was to give his wife a good beating. On Monday morning his neighbors would say to one another, "Looks as if Don Picuita has stitched a black patch on his wife's eye."

This happened so routinely that when for some reason or other he forgot the weekly thrashing, the neighbors had nothing to talk about and felt cheated out of their usual gossip. They felt they had a right to expect that every Monday Picuita's wife would come out with a black eye. They were angry at the man for slackness and neglecting his duty.

(12)

Next came the old solder Ulpiano Arévalo. During his army career he had risen to the rank of sergeant and become not only a first class marksman but also a good cook. He had been drafted in the provincial capital at the age of seventeen and fought in the Esmeraldas Campaign of 1914. Years later, now a strong resolute man of few words, he had deserted, but never lost the look of a soldier with his boots and lively martial air. No wearing a poncho for him. His trousers were held up with an army belt and he had managed to keep his old rifle and plenty of cartridges.

He was considered a tricky wrist-and-elbow wrestler. On Sunday mornings and on holidays the strongest men in town used to meet in Vicente Orozco's barber shop to bet on their skill and strength. The most noted rivals, not counting Don José Toro—a regular Hercules with whom it was useless to compete—were this deserter Ulpiano Arévalo and "Toad" Labanda, the blacksmith. With their elbows on a heavy yellow table, face to face, the middle fingers of their right hands interlocked, they strained until they bled in the effort to bend each other's wrists, while the next contenders waiting their turn cheered them on.

At the time of the march Arévalo was the man in charge of the armed contingent, reporting directly to the head of the whole convoy. His rifle was his pride, kept bright after years of weekly oiling, all the parts clean and working smoothly, the muzzle plugged with a rag stopper.

For a man who had apparently lived the rough and bloody life of a fighter, Arévalo was totally lacking in imagination and knew nothing of how to tell a story. The only person who could draw him out and get him to speak in complete connected sentences was Don Vicente Muñoz, on the few occasions when they were talking undisturbed in his patio. Arevalo's answers to Don Vicente's questions were straightforward and coherent and in this way it was possible to learn his story piece by piece. After a barrage of questions about such and such an episode, Don Vicente could get a fair picture of what had actually happened. He would then retell it to the storyteller himself who listened to it as if astonished and with childlike fascination, while respectfully correcting any little error in the account.

These stories of Arévalo's life, drawn from him so painfully and laboriously by Don Vicente's almost obstetrical skill, showed him as never having attached any importance to his own bravery. He had obviously been quite unaware of it and had borne himself in battle without any posturing or vainglory.

What he did lack was intelligence and the gift of command. He obeyed to the letter the orders of his chief, Curly Ocampo. It had probably never entered his thick head that orders from a superior officer could be disobeyed.

(13)

Next came José Vallejo, alias the Chino, carpenter by trade.

He owed his nickname to his slant eyes and sallow complexion. He enjoyed a well deserved reputation as a skilled carpenter and cabinetmaker who had made most of the furniture in the better houses of Yangana. And, of course, it was he who had carved—and it took him two years—the fine work on the church altar and reredos, to say nothing of Don Vicente Muñoz's famous cedarwood bookcases.

He was never far from his beautiful but slatternly wife— "La Cabezona" or "The Disheveled One,"—who was a living proof that even the grimiest treasure must be watched over. Many were the married men in the town who envied the Chino and desired his wife for her hot beauty and her provocative sexual appeal. "If only," they thought, "we could steal that lusty figure of a woman, with her white skin and dirty ragged clothes from that wretched Chino, that yellow-faced Chino, that disgusting Chino." She seemed to them to be one of those fortuitous, unearned and undeserved gifts which fate sometimes bestows on the most miserable individuals. They wished they could take her away, enjoy her ecstatically, give her clothes worthy of her, give her shoes and persuade her at least once in a while to comb her lovely auburn curls.

(14)

Next came José Clemente Piedra, the soccer player.

He accompanied the ill-assorted couple just described, since he was a relative of La Cabezona and a character who had to be watched over since he had not yet recovered from a monumental drunk which had knocked him out during the fiesta, days ago.

He was on foot and wearing the strangest assortment of clothes, starting with soccer shoes which he himself had reinforced with studs, cleats and double soles. Above were thick high socks turned down just below his knees to display the national flag in three colors woven into the stockings. Loose olive colored shorts, a long-sleeved jersey and a bandana round his head completed the outfit. An outrageous bulge in his hip pocket betrayed a bottle.

However unusual his clothes may have seemed, it was even stranger that he should have chosen the route he was following. The fact was that when he had decided to join the march he hardly knew what he was doing. He had come quite a distance to attend the fiesta, partly to visit his beautiful kinswoman and partly as one of a team of soccer players made up on the spur of the moment as an excuse for a good time. With neither discipline nor team spirit, they had separated as soon as they reached Yangana, each one going his own mischievous way.

So it was that José Clemente Piedra, the soccer player, being in any case an outsider in the town, could not remember what exactly had led up to decisive events of the Fiesta. He had a vague recollection of sitting in a sleazy eating house with his boon companion Joaquín Gordillo the dropout agronomist, enjoying a delicious meal of roasted goat's flesh well spiced with hot pepper and onions, and drinking the most marvelous cold home brew. The pair were just warming up and felt ready for anything when the conflagration broke out. Before their half focused eyes a parade of crazy people seemed to be passing—people with savage faces, wild looks and blazing torches held on high. The two men were deafened by the accompanying outcry, the hoarse shouts of anger, the screams of fright, the howling of dogs and the roar of flames. José Clemente Piedra's mind became blank.

Hours later when he came to his senses, still half-drunk, hiccupping and stumbling, hawking and spitting a thick sticky phlegm, he clutched the arm of the ex-student of agronomy and gasped out, "I, too, my friend, am going with the rest of you."

(15)

Next came the aforesaid Joaquín Gordillo, ex-student of agronomy and another outsider.

He too had come from the city and been caught up and carried away in the avalanche of rioters. He was now happily marching along with the others, half tipsy, half asleep and full of jokes and wisecracks. Finding himself up to the neck in a totally unexpected adventure, he never for a moment thought of escaping. As for his family back home in the city, let them say what they liked! Didn't they know that he was a crazy good-for-nothing? Anyway, he could surely be of some help to this community of farmers. Inspired by this vague drunken hope, that perhaps for once he might be taken seriously and be of some use to somebody, he had not hesitated to join the caravan.

Although there were times when he felt discouraged, not knowing what he had let himself in for nor what was ahead of him, the presence of the soccer player by his side gave him fresh confidence. It was enough just to look at his big shoes, his chin thrust out and a ferocious scowl on his face. For the hundredth time, he shrugged his shoulders and kept on.

Those nearest him were tolerant and helpful, taking him for what he was. Some of them gave him a drink from time to time to keep up his spirits, but only in sips since it was in short supply.

(16)

Next came Doña Liberata Jiménez, notoriously given to lawsuits.

Her face, her black hair, straight and coarse without a trace of gray, and her short stocky body, all showed her to be of pure Indian descent. She had inherited with her Indian blood a stubborn habit of taking people to court on the slightest provocation.

People remembered that she had once spent two years in a suit to recover a useless old mare that had somehow fallen into somebody else's hands, no one seemed to know how. This lawsuit not only cost her every penny she had, but forced her to sell a really first class little coffee farm fenced in by a row of the sweetest orange trees ever planted in Yangana. In the end she had the satisfaction of winning her case. The mare was judged to belong to her, but the poor animal, worn out by old age added to a starvation diet while in custody of the court, died that very same day.

Women whose lives revolved around their households frowned on all of this and called her masculine because she adored cockfights and liked to play billiards and drink rum and was a notable gambler. They swore that she knew how to use her fists. Naturally, she was left-handed and always used that hand when making difficult cannon-shots or throwing dice. She was not afraid to go out alone at night wherever she fancied, and there were people who declared that they had seen her urinate standing up.

But, say what they liked, she had borne a daughter and was as her neighbors maliciously pointed out—the mother of her child, not the father.

This daughter whose mother—not father—was Doña Liberata, was a tall and skinny woman with very long arms and an unpleasantly pallid skin.

She was a poor creature whose lack of color made her almost an albino. In spite of looking like frozen fruit or a dead fly, she had unexpectedly and without a hint presented Doña Liberata with a grandson. The unlooked-for offshoot was received—according to those entitled to know—first with resounding fury and then later with passionate love expressed not in sweet words but in the most indecent terms possible. The sour ill-tempered she-wolf wanted to caress her grandson, but could only show her affection by surly growls. Her slaps and blasphemies filled the poor mother and her child with fright. From a distance the neighbors could hear the heavy woman's frenzied transports of tenderness accompanied by a coarse word, an affectionate slap, the piercing scream of a child followed by a hoarse burst of drunken laughter.

(17)

Next came Josefina Luna, the youngest of all the fat women in the caravan.

A nineteen year old girl who had been in elementary school with "The Virgin of the Wild Fig Tree," she looked like a woman of forty.

The bulk of her flabby flesh was already impressive. She wept easily and moved with great difficulty, being in no way a lively fat girl. Her neck was no longer distinguishable, smothered by the loose fat of her innumerable double chins. Yet her hands were very beautiful, and she knew it. They seemed by some miracle to have escaped the grossness which had overtaken her whole body and to have remained graceful and delicate, with a firm slightly dimpled texture. They moved freely with a natural elegance which imparted to the rest of the imposing mass a certain sprightly air, relieving it, so to speak, from a good part of its weight.

She had to change mounts twice a day and, needless to say, she could not get into the saddle unaided. A strong man had to help her. She ate heartily of her cold rations and wiped her face and neck continually with a large towel which she wrung out afterwards. Her father freshened up her face with cold water from every spring they passed on the road.

The young men amused themselves like boys with the time-worn diversion of assigning to her as lovers the thinnest men in town.

While assuming that in any case all precautions would be in vain, they used to say, "The Pretty Pretty Full Moon has to take the greatest care when she turns over in bed, Boas not to crush them under her weight." Or again, "The man who has the bad luck to falloff the top of a mountain is killed, etcetera, etcetera."

(18)

Next came Don José Toro', the bronze-and-iron smelter—a Hercules of a man.

Nobody knew his real name. Toro was the nickname he had earned on account of his extraordinary strength, in spite of his fifty years and drunken dissolute thriftless life. In the past there had been only one man in the town as strong as he—Don Lisandro, but that was another generation and another breed.

José Toro was a tall burly fellow. His bare arms, dark and muscular, laced by the knotty lines of his veins, looked like loaves of rye bread. His huge calloused hands were always burning hot. Much money had passed through those rough palms, since as a caster of bronze sugar-grinders he had always been well paid. But he had drunk it all up with his boon companions; it was no vain boast that he was the most serious drinking rival of the elder Mendieta.

His bull neck was as broad as his face and set on great rounded shoulders. His face, full of smirks and grimaces, was beginning to show wrinkles and creases. His eyelids were pouchy and his beard thick. His quick smile revealed large teeth with gaps between.

It was he who had cast the last bell for the church, the bell which the townspeople would never enjoy. It had barely been tried out the day of the Fiesta. It had remained high up in the belfry at Yangana among the smoking solitary ruins. Those silvery tones which so many future generations would have heard, remained silent inside that metal throat which perhaps would never speak again!

José Toro was certainly no sentimentalist, nevertheless he mourned the fact that the bell which he had made with his own hands had been abandoned. "Think of it! My bride was left at the church door. She was still a virgin," and he added, "Who will enjoy her?"

And he swallowed a lump in his throat, however much he managed to wink mischievously from a bloodshot eye and to show his yellow teeth in a cheerful smile.

He had acquired a tremendous reputation for physical strength.

Tales were told of how with just a twist of his wrists he could bend iron rods as if they were taffy candy. Of how he had dragged mules out of a mud hole—load, harness and all; had fought body to body with a puma in the hills; and could with one heave move a hundred gallon cask of rum.

There was never any argument about any of this. It was something the same as the longevity of Lisandro Fierro, the bad luck of Fermín López, the beauty of the "Virgin of the Wild Fig Tree," or the learning of Don Vicente Muñoz.

One or the other of José Toro's eyes was usually as red as a tomato. The cause of these almost chronic inflammations never varied—drunken sprees with those, great friends of his in which our Hercules stood treat and ended up passing out. Teasing the giant from a respectful distance would get things going, followed by a wild blow of his fist which hit nothing but threw him off balance. Finally the whole company fell on his recumbent body and gave his ribs a good pummeling, but even then they could not silence his raucous bellows.

(19)

Next came Carmen Valle, dedicated to the oldest feminine profession in the world.

She was slim and shapely, of medium height and with very white teeth. The important men of the town hated her by day and loved her by night. The silk lingerie that she wore, and the shameless delight with which she took it off, were a matter of the most private conversation among these austere personages who had, everyone of them in his turn and at so much a session, enjoyed those forbidden charms.

It was the city that had made her a sinner. She had gone there to study at the nuns' school. Nobody knew by what process she had left the convent to become what she now was, nor why she had had the audacity to return to her native town to continue the life she had begun in the city. Married women and girls who were about to marry looked askance at her with instinctive distaste. It irritated them to see her so elegantly dressed. Who could say what they felt, since they knew that she undressed with greedy impudence and from all appearances loved the exercise of her profession.

The soccer player was her traveling companion. They marched along gaily making loud joking remarks to each other and caring not one straw that the others left them severely alone. Nor were they troubled in the slightest by the looks cast in their direction by the more sanctimonious women of the caravan. One person did keep company with the couple—the daughter of blind Nicolás Bazarán—a young girl whose familiarity with the professional of the beautiful teeth could, in the opinion of the moralists among the travelers, lead to no good.

(20)

Next came the Vásquez brothers, all workers in clay.

Juan Vasquez was the potter, owner of a pottery workshop set up in an old shed originally used for a rum distillery, a man still young with a pale complexion, narrow chest and hands which were always cold. If one got close to him there was a noticeably unpleasant smell of urine, since he suffered from chronic incontinence which—according to the diagnosis of the herb doctor Torres—was directly connected with his trade of potter: he had to work all day handling wet clay, so that he was chilled to the very bone.

The blind man's daughter, the friend of Carmen Valle, may have been in love with him.

She often visited the miserable cold workshop and did not seem to mind that smell. The winsome girl was fascinated by the sight of the vessels taking shape as they rose from the wheel spun by the potter's foot. She marveled to see how with only a piece of wood and his colorless thumbs he gave the finishing touches to what would be beautiful pitchers, crocks, jugs, and plates while Vásquez kept glancing down at her with a kind of appraising interest.

"Stay and see how the pieces I made last Saturday are glazed," he would remark to her apparently just to say something. She would accept the invitation, come close to the oven and of her own accord throw in a few more sticks of firewood. Hours passed as she watched how the fragile vessels changed color and then, when they had cooled and were with exquisite care taken out of the oven, she liked to balance them on one hand close to her ear and tap them gently with the other hand to make sure that perfect firing had left them as resonant as glass.

And when, late in the afternoon, the blind man's daughter had left, without even the ghost of a smile from Vásquez, he would jump down away from his wheel and take out a statuette from behind a pile of clay—a statuette in the shape of a woman. And the tongue-tied potter would caress it between his hands saying very softly, "I expect you tomorrow Luz Perpetua. I love you. I love you. Don't forget to come. I'll have oranges for you and boiled corn, piping hot. And we'll glaze a lovely jug that I've made for you."

(21)

Roque, the most prosperous of all the brothers, owned a well-equipped tile and brick works where all his children were employed, sons and daughters. Two covered sheds—roofed with tiles, naturally—made it easier to handle the clay, already worked up for the first time in nearby pits and brought in on wheelbarrows. On the sandy floor the tiles and bricks fresh from the molds, were laid out to dry. At the edge of the slope outside stood the two kilns, each with a capacity of 800 bricks or 600 tiles. A yoke of oxen, covered with liquid mire up to their chests, spent the whole day going round and round in the pits, churning up the clay until it was sufficiently "cooked." The beasts' tails were completely smeared with muck and every so often they swished out and plastered the face of the youngest Vásquez who was standing at the edge of the pits urging on the oxen with shouts and whip lashes.

Well now, all this present and future wealth had been left behind on the outskirts of the town.

(22)

Miguel was the mason, an expert in mixing mud either for lath-and-mud walls or for adobe building blocks.

He could construct walls of these blocks with unbelievable speed after first laying an immense foundation of stones cemented with clay, all done by the book with level and plumb. The coat of plaster applied before the final whitewashing was made of a special very durable mix. In its preparation he used some rather dirty ingredients, such as cow dung. Making the mix took several weeks.

The third finger of his left hand was missing and he was harelipped. He was also the darkest of the brothers.

(23)

Ignacio was not really a mason, only a builder of mud walls. This one was a sturdy fellow, married to a very likeable woman by whom he had two sons. He found himself socially inferior to Miguel just as Miguel was lower in the scale than Roque, the most respected of the family. But Ignacio had not—at least in his own opinion—sunk to the level of his brother Juan, the potter. Juan, however, did not share this opinion and would not for the world have changed places with a wretched wall builder who was paid by the day.

Ignacio, the wall builder, had an assistant, a low-grade fellow or "cholo," Luis España. Together they could construct in a few weeks the very stoutest walls of well packed mud. As soon as the foundations were firmly set, the two men went to work to rig the forms for the wall, using heavy secured by bolts and strong cross-pieces. The next step was to fill the forms, pitching up shovelfuls of wet mud in perfect rhythm and then packing them down firmly with rammers. One consequence of his rough trade was that Ignacio Vásquez' chest muscles were enormously developed and the palms of his hands were like leather. The cholo España, being a thin, dried-up fellow had no appearance of strength, but once he got a rammer in his hands he was untiring.

(24)

Next came Eliseo Aliaga, the tree planter.

He was about fifty years old. His tanned skin was the color of tobacco, his face seemed to have been shaped with a knife—a large nose, high cheekbones, square cut beard, strong jaws. His neck was seamed like the bark of a tree. He had the powerful head of an Indian and long fingers like vine tendrils. His right leg was stiff so that it dragged when he walked. If he stood on that leg in a grove of trees and stretched out his arms, Don Eliseo Aliaga, sunburned, rugged and broad shouldered really seemed himself to be a tree with its roots deep in the ground. An imaginative onlooker could almost see the sap flowing through the body of the sturdy laborer, sap drawn up from the earth and absorbed by that one foot, as if it were the trunk of a tree.

He was in fact a kind of tree which had fathered almost all the trees still standing in Yangana when their owners left.

That was why, when they reached the pass at Cararango and turned to look back at the half-burned countryside that they were abandoning, Don Eliseo Aliaga, the one who had been most reluctant to leave, gave a great howl of grief.

"They are my trees," he cried, stretching out his arms in a gesture of despairing farewell, "I planted them and I've left them behind!"

He could not remember how old he had been when he planted his first tree. But as soon as he could move around independently he had begun to dig shallow holes with his little hands and plant the avocado seeds which his parents and brothers had thrown out in the patio at mealtimes to be licked by the hungry dogs.

Every day he would scratch the earth away from the holes and uncover the seeds. Until one day he saw with ecstatic delight that those beloved seeds had taken him seriously, had split into two fleshy halves and opened to send up a shoot.

Before very long the plants were as tall as the little planter and now, now that he was leaving them, they had grown to be such stout corpulent personages that he could barely stretch his arms around them during their daily conversations.

Such had been the beginning of a vocation cultivated for almost half a century.

He was also a natural born nurseryman with a gift for tending both wild and domesticated trees. He had forged a genuine friendship with wild trees brought from the most remote recesses of the forests. In his youth when his legs were sound and strong he had walked immense distances all through the great jungles of the Andes, clambering over their endless hillsides. The booty from his hunting trips included acorns, kernels and stones from strange fruits, fully opened seed-leaves found in some crack in the ground, little saplings pulled up roots and all, the small offsprings which had struggled so hard to take root at the foot of the big trees.

In his character of exacting tamer and loving master, Don Eliseo made all these plants obey him. There were some that had never known man, that had grown up in unexplored regions in the virgin forest, that all through their thousands of years had never felt the gentle touch of cultivation, the martyrdom of pruning, the stroke of the headsman's ax, or the tithes and taxes of harvest time.

Not even the most knowledgeable of woodsmen knew the names of many of these species, for they had never even seen them before. Whenever they came across a strange tree in the neighboring forest that they knew so well, a tree which seemed a botanical guest, they quoted a ready-made local phrase, "It must have been brought by Don Eliseo Aliaga."

He loved to make extremes meet, to turn curls into ringlets, to make fun of the rules and restrictions of subtropical ecology. The mountain palms with their knotty trunks were induced to live against their will in the suffocating heat which made life so sweet for the lowland palms of the tropics.

Pines, cherry trees, apple trees, peach trees flourished in the hot air, surprised to find themselves next door to plantains and sugar cane, and homesick for a cooler climate. Highlanders and lowlanders were lined up in close order, their helmets confronting the same sky, their tents pitched in the same burning heat. Hill and dale, cocoa and pears rubbed elbows in amazement. They were surrounded by quickset hedges, since Don Eliseo Aliaga would have looked on a fence of dead wood as treachery and contradiction.

The tight rows of thorns, of protecting piñones with their corrosive latex, made an impenetrable barrier.

"Not even a mosquito can get through this fence," he would say.

Within these living walls he carried out his experiments, handling and tending trees, crossing species, a strong and skillful man working his will on his docile and motley arboreal multitude like a botanical God.

All this was what made up Don Eliseo Aliaga's whole life, and the exodus had called on him to abandon it.

Nor would he have abandoned it if Curly Ocampo, who considered himself the leader and a good judge of human nature, had not managed to win him over by putting him in charge of transporting the seeds for the community.

This duty of taking the helpless seeds with him—seeds which were the beginnings of life, had roused all the protective instincts of this born planter. He was comforted in his grief at parting from the population of botanical adults left behind in the solitude of the scorched town and he took command of the immense load of seeds.

His second in command was to be the ex-student of agronomy Joaquín Gordillo—just as soon as his head was clear of rum. He had talked so much of his horticultural knowledge that he must be believed and given the chance to show his practical skill.

Nevertheless, when he looked from the height of Cararango at the splendid arboreal tribe he had left, the painful bitterness welled up again in the heart of the austere old man and he burst into tears like a child as he began to cross the gorge and start down the other slope.

(25)

Next came María De Los Angeles Zaragocín, bearing the burden of her shame.

She was a beautiful girl of sixteen with dark hair, greenish eyes and an air of sadness that never left her. Everybody knew that when she was only seven, she had been brutally raped at the annual Fiesta by two men, strangers to the town. Her father had searched in vain for the criminals, but nothing more was ever heard of them. The poor child was left shamed and humiliated, the whole town knew it and did not forget it. Nobody could have doubts about her lost virginity. Now that she was sixteen and menstruated every month she was said to weep bitterly when she remembered that as a child she had been brutally deflowered.

Mother Nature, however, never affected by sentiment, had in due course endowed her body with sensual curves. Her bust was high and firm, her legs powerful, the tread of her bare feet with their broad rosy heels was firm and elastic.

Some people said that she hated all men, including the father who had been unable to avenge her. Others held a different opinion—that it was not so much hate as anger against the men who despised her violated body; that it was the vile prejudice of men and boys alike; that beautiful as she was, nobody had yet asked her in marriage from fear of vulgar jokes and comments on the wedding night. She was the marked one, branded and accursed.

Notwithstanding her rancor, she was courteous, as was her mother. She seemed, however, to bear her mother an old grudge because she had never wanted to take her away, far from Yangana to some place where nobody would know about her terrible past, that past for which her tender years could not be blamed.

The men, however, who could have courted her, redeeming her from the tragic penance imposed for a crime committed by other men, did not think of it that way. So that María De Los Angeles Zaragocín, despised, impaired, branded: a broken vessel, a tasted fruit, an opened parcel, was also marching along with her heedless executioners.

(26)

Next came Víctor Zaruma, the tanner.

He owned a thriving tannery set up in the backyard of his house. There he had dug two vats, one for slaked lime and the other for powdered *huilco* bark. The hides delivered by José Manuel Medina, the slaughterhouse man, were first put, just as they were, into the lime wash until all the hair was gone. About a week later they were moved to the bark vat where they were cured by a kind of gradual osmosis. To insure uniform tanning, the edges of each hide were stitched up into pouches which were filled with fresh bark.

The revolting smell from the tannery, especially when the hides were taken from the vats and put out to dry, carried for many blocks and was an almost irresistible attraction for the buzzards. Twice a week the bark was changed in the vat and the soaking hides moved around.

The one who bore the brunt of this pestilential work, however, was not Víctor Zaruma, but his orphan son, the "Little Pouch." His father had raised him with a devotion that earned him the enthusiastic admiration of the neighbors. He adored the child, rubbing his beard on the infant's smooth skin, caressing his little face with dirty kisses smelling of leather and tobacco. For all this, no sooner was the little fellow able to walk than he was put to work.

There was no way on earth for him to get to school even for a day. The poor child was exploited by his father, toiling from dawn to dusk and he was not yet nine years old. Wringing wet and stained allover from head to foot with *huilco* juice, the skin of his feet cracked and burned by the lime, wearing a wretched cloth apron from waist to knees, the dethroned idol pounded the coffee-colored bark with a wooden mallet. The little workman was preparing huge mounds of material in the midst of which he was lost to sight, sometimes almost cheerful and sometimes sobbing with two streams of mucous dripping from nose to mouth.

The customers figured that Zaruma made good money and they of course thought him an infamous father. They calculated on paper to prove without a doubt that he got two sides of leather from each hide which meant 100% profit. Potential competitors for the lucrative business were not lacking. Yet up to the time that they all abandoned the town, Zaruma had remained unchallenged.

(27)

Next came Doña Francisca Aldeán, three times widowed.

She was famous for her conjugal ardor. Malicious gossip held that in a few weeks of unbridled honeymoon she had drained the marrow of her three successive partners even though the second of them had been as strong as a bear and could have been expected to resist the thirst of this insatiable vampire. After this there was not a man left in the town bold enough to risk being the fourth victim.

There was a quiet charm in the look of her dark eyes. She was slim, but with stout legs, wide hips and her hair was thick and curly. Her voice as full-toned, warm, passionate and a shade husky. She shook hands with a firm clasp. She always wore black. She had borne no children. Her flesh, which had sucked out the lives of three men, was still firm and elastic.

Some people believed that Doña Pancha Aldeán had killed her husbands not by dint of caresses, but by deliberate design, that she was a female Bluebeard, putting into effect a diabolical plan of elimination. In short, she was an assassin. This version, however, was not generally accepted since in none of the three cases had there been any property worth inheriting. Another and different story told of her wager with "Shameless Carlos," an event which over the years had given rise to exaggerated admiration, protests and exasperated comments among the neighbors.

The three times widow had challenged that fellow so famous for the thrust of his virility, and of course she was held to have come out the unruffled victor. The whole affair was apparently discovered later on to have been a fabrication on the part of Doña Pascuala who in her youth had cast eyes on the first of Doña Pancha Aldeán's bridegrooms and may have had occasional relations with Carlos.

On the other hand, Doña Pancha was proud of her reputation for being, quite apart from all this, the best baker of bread in the town. There was no need to worry about leftovers where her special partybread was concerned. The lads of the village had even made a play upon words about Doña Pancha Aldeán's good bread. They declared, of course, that it was not what was sold but what she kept that was so good, and they laughed ingenuously at the hidden pun.

(28)

Next came Carlos Alcocer, alias "Shameless Carlos," the Don Juan of Yangana.

An ugly fellow, he had spent a good part of his life on the Costa, working in the gold mines of Curipamba, and was by now beginning to suffer the effects of years of wear and tear and sundry hardships.

He had returned home six times. The first was when his mother, Doña Virginia Correa, who wept more easily than any woman who had ever lived, was still alive and he himself a lad with the faint down of a mustache on his lip. He was deeply attached to his birthplace and for the past two years or so he seemed to have lost his thirst for adventure. The once cocksure gallant was getting on in years and showed his discouragement by bitter silence when he watched the saucy girls trotting by so temptingly near the sniffing nostrils and thick lips of this born hunter.

One thing about those return trips was always related in the simple chronicles of Yangana. Each time he had come back home it was with a different woman, and how pretty they all looked!

The first one was a shrill-voiced Peruvian who was outspoken almost to the degree of insolence. She rolled her r's on her tongue with a long lively vibration which matched her brutal frankness and free gestures. She was dark and smooth-skinned. Her knees, the back of her neck and her elbows were almost black. People noticed in the streets that she seemed to have difficulty walking in high heeled shoes and this made them assume that her partner had given her her first pair of shoes when he brought her with him.

After two years of illicit union with Shameless Carlos, she found herself pregnant, whereupon she left him and married a fellow Peruvian who was courting her although he knew what kind of life she had been leading.

The second of Carlos' women was so shy that she always seemed on the point of blushing. She had very fair hair and curiously black eyes. At the time of their coming to Yangana, it was rumored that her blond head was not too strong since she had left a good inheritance in the province of El Oro to take up with the young gallant and that it was her money that the dashing couple threw around in the town during the short time that their visit lasted.

And this woman, too, who blushed to the tips of her fingers and hid her face under the edge of her shawl every time her lover looked deep into the process. Her health began to fail in the hairy arms of her lover. She was now going on for seventeen and at that age there was no arresting the course of the illness. From Chuquiribamba they came down to Yangana—she was feeling a little better now. She lingered in bed for six months, visibly losing weight and shrinking day by day, until she died.

His women had all left Carlos, one by one, each in her own way. He had earned in full measure the nickname he was taking with him to an unknown destiny.

The march had evidently caught him at a time when he was forsaken. He walked by himself. He had no compunction, however, in divulging his plans. He meant to take a permanent and definitive wife as soon as possible, the last of all, to whom he would give his name. In the Promised

Land of Canaan he would find rest for the sole of his, foot and for always.

This latest attitude on the part of Shameless Carlos was curious and perhaps in a way pathetic. He who had been the unrivalled Don Juan of Yangana, a scabrous fellow always chasing women, was now holding out his hands to the sky, wrists eager to be manacled with the final bond of marriage.

(29)

Next came Serafín Armijos, the hunter for buried treasure. Saint Ciprian's divining wands held no mysteries for him. He had used them to explore every little corner of earth that was promising either from its appearance or because of old tales or legends.

He had, for example, decided that hiding places likely to hold treasure would certainly be found in the following places:

1. At the end of the park just outside town, near the main irrigation ditch, where Don Pablo Cuenca's hens roosted. There could be no doubt about this, since Pablo Cuenca was known to be rich, very miserly, and gave every appearance of keeping his money in the ground.

2. Under the manger in the stable at Squire Valdivieso's country house which had originally belonged to Spaniards. It was an old house, very old—already old when Don Lisandro was a young man—and it was a proven fact that the colonial Spaniards liked to hide their riches underground in the least likely places.

3. Near the goat pen next to the León family's house. This treasure had a well established provenance. In the remote past the Leóns' house had belonged to a rich priest, together with the farm next to it where he preferred to spend his idle hours far from the town. Well now, legend had it that on sunny days he would, with the help of a deaf-mute servant, take out the gold pieces from their secret chests and count and recount them with an almost lustful avarice. After the counting, came the hiding away again in a place only

known to the two of them. In the course of time this particular spot became a goat pen and Serafín Armijos, himself, trembling with excitement, had heard the whole story through his magic wands.

In spite of all this, the inveterate smeller-out of treasure: had never found anything for himself. He was desperately poor. Just the same, he would be overcome with loquaciousness when given a chance to talk about the fortunes he had discovered for others. On these occasions he was full of details of -the how and the when and where of the find. Nobody, for sure, had ever got him to reveal the names of the lucky beneficiaries. For this reason, whenever one of the townspeople was seen to come up in the world from one day to another, without any clear clue as to the origin of this pecuniary success, the first reaction was to think that help had come from St. Ciprian's wands and the guiding hand of Serafín Armijos the intrepid treasure hunter and confirmed bachelor.

(30)

Next came Juanita Villalba, an ex-college student with a reputation as a venomous and skeptical atheist.

"A victim of today's pervasive impiety," was the opinion of Godoy, the merchant.

"A product of the bad teaching in those lay colleges where the holy fear of God is lost," according to the Señora Jesús Sarmiento.

"A masculine woman, a learned know-it-all, who detests everything because things went wrong in her life and she was left in the lurch with her head stuffed full of all kinds of crazy books," was the comparatively gentle judgment of Doña Pascuala.

"A most charming girl with whom it is a pleasure to talk and who combines the following original qualities: she is remarkably learned for her age and sex; she is as intelligent as she is pretty and as pretty as she is intelligent; and she belongs, in spite of being young and a woman, to the family of skeptics who are certainly not numerous among the fair sex." Such was the verdict of Don Vicente Muñoz who apparently felt a kind of fatherly affection for her, notwithstanding the often heated nature of their discussions.

"What does it all lead to, after all?" she would conclude with a kind of fine scorn. "Your opinion is as good as mine, even if they are contrary. If we are both right, why try to put one above the other?"

To which her severe questioner with a little impatient tap of his foot would answer, "Nothing can be done with you, you hopelessly skeptical young woman! For a whole hour you have been arguing in bad faith, to come up at the end with the impertinence that it's just as good to hold one opinion as another contrary to it!"

They both, however, loved their fierce duels from which she emerged more skeptical than ever but feeling a little easier in her mind, while he was more convinced that if he could only win her over to show some enthusiasm, even though it might be a hopeless task, it could be his greatest intellectual and professional triumph and in any case an outstanding event in his life. Furthermore, Don Vicente thought it necessary to cure Juanita for her own good of her systematized unbelief. He expressed himself thus: "It's a matter of conscience to throw a lifeline to this good girl. She must be made to believe in something. To believe in nothing at all is to be monstrously unhappy."

It infuriated him to hear her repeat her wearisome phrase, "And what would we gain by that?" An odious question for Don Vicente, a question both discouraged and discouraging, dashed like a stream of cold water on the liveliest youthful enthusiasms.

"And what do we gain by that?"

The girl was recognized as having artistic talents. On one occasion, for a bet, she played a part in the show at the annual Fiesta. Her performance was a genuine revelation and was still remembered as such by even the most critical among the audience. But when people said to her that she ought to go back to the city and cultivate her remarkable dramatic talents, she raised her eyebrows and interrupted them with her intolerable refrain, "And what would we gain by that?"

Years before, when movies with sound first came to the provincial capital, the more curious of the Yangana people made the trip to hear the voices of the performers. The film was a musical one. Juanita memorized all the lovely songs although she had heard them only once, and on the road going home she entranced her fellow travelers by singing them one after the other with astonishing fidelity.

Even then, when she was told that she had been born for music and should take advantage of her stupendous audial memory, she put a stop then and there to any warm enthusiasm with her burdensome litany, "And what would we gain by that?"

There was a story that when she was a third year student in the city she had fallen madly in love. The truth seemed to have been that the idyll was so tragic and stormy that she had to miss two years of college. This may have been the cause of the attitude which Don Vicente found so strange in a young woman and which was defense enough to keep the boldest gallants at arm's length. She aroused the deepest admiration but it remained silent because nobody dared to run the risk of being brought up short by a burst of laughter accompanied by the now famous chant, "And what would we gain by that?" The only exception which finally brought things to a head was to be the case of the gringo Spark.

Her health was delicate, but she never took care of herself. She said it was all the same to her whether she lived or died and the attentions of the doctor who visited her uninvited when she was sick, were fended off with the same stabbing question, "And what would we gain by that?" She denied the existence of God without paying the least attention to the shock that it gave to those who heard her, and calmly defended her point of view with the query, "And what would we gain by that?"

She had read every book in Don Vicente's library and since she had an extraordinarily retentive memory she remembered everything that she had read. On occasion she would quote certain passages with considerable warmth and vehemence—when they agreed with her feelings. A moment later the inner demon that froze all her emotional impulses forced her to arch her eyebrows and break out with her eternal repetition: "And what would we gain by that?"

Strange to say, her firmest friendship (and what would we gain by that?) was with Doña Patrocinio, the leader and tutelary spirit of the fiestas in Yangana. The two were often together, sometimes for weeks at a time, constituting what even the most unbiased observer could see was a living and vigorous antithesis both physical and intellectual: Doña Patrocinio, short, heavy and stout; Juanita Villalba tall, slender and long-limbed; the former hasty and warm in speech, the latter measured and almost toneless in conversation. They were like two opposing principles, something which in the opinion of Don Vicente himself, made this strange friendship a romantic one. There was fire on one side and ice on the other; here was enthusiasm and there was disillusion; performance, act and will in Doña Patrocinio, gloomy analysis, studied inhibition, indolence in Juanita Villalba. Lastly, once again, according to Don Vicente, there were times when they harbored real feelings of envy for one another. For example, when Doña Patrocinio was faced with particularly difficult problems in carrying some of her active social programs to completion; or when on a spring day Juanita Villalba's heart began to ring like a castanet and throb with a fleeting urge to plunge up to the shoulders into the joy of life.

Doña Patrocinio understood that her friend's tedious question, "And what would we gain by that?" saved her from many mistakes and rash projects, while Juanita was grateful to her stout friend for making her forget for a few moments that she had resolved to live her life as an Amazon spoiling for a fight.

"A strange soul for a simple town like ours!" concluded Don Vicente while he too denied her, to her face, the right to behave in a way unbecoming both to a young person and to a woman, something that collided violently with the patriarchal environment that he had found in Yangana.

(31)

Next came Melchor Celi, vagabond.

He was the head of a family, a numerous family. This had not prevented him from being the greatest wanderer in the whole province and from taking his wife and children along with him. Although not a gypsy by birth, he was incapable of settling down in anyone place for long. Traveling was his life, but there was a pattern to his movements. He cut a wide circle with his wanderings, and over the years returned regularly by the roads he had already traveled. This was the third time he had shown up in Yangana.

He always moved with his own beasts of burden and all his belongings. The youngest of his children traveled stowed up to the neck in pack saddles that were stretched tight as a drum, with the children's heads sticking out like flowers from a flower pot.

Once established with his family in some place, where he earned his living with no trouble by plying one of his seven trades, he would be more or less comfortable in a suitable house, develop good color and put on weight. Then a day would come when he would suddenly feel the first stirrings of a familiar itch. The urge to change his headquarters took possession of him. He was stifling. The horizon which two days ago he had found so kindly was now converted into a stern landowner scowling at him with hostile eyes and bidding him begone from his property. The same faces, the same voices, the same houses, all the picture that by now he knew by heart suddenly became unbearable.

The buzzards kept watch at a safe distance. They gazed at the blood-blackened ground with undisguised greed. But unceasing watch was also kept by the innumerable Medina family, one of the children was always on guard.

Oh stupendous country-style dried meat—you, too, were leaving the now deserted town of Yangana! You too were on the march, great piles of you, carrying with you your noble aroma—double-cured, fat, full-flavored—to venture forth on the so-called, highways of a province without roads, traveling in the bellies of saddlebags and provision baskets!

When the marching men and animals were obliged to rest, you allowed yourself to be roasted, sizzling and twisting, on makeshift fireplaces by the edges of mountain streams. Your rich, provocative smell mingled with the fragrance of black coffee boiling in a kettle hung between two forked sticks.

The butcher's daughters, rosy red-cheeked girls—all still single—moved in a close sunburned group. The youngest children, in somewhat the same style as those of "the tinker" Melchor Celi, came packed in great saddlebags, making another unusual load topped off at each cross strap by a ruddy head.

(33)

Next came Sebastián Japa, harnessmaker.

He had come to Yangana years ago with grown sons who learned their father's trade, dividing between them the work of making saddles and harness. They were so skilful that before long their products enjoyed a reputation reaching well beyond the confines of the province.

One of them devoted himself to making wooden saddle frames, the design, proportions and execution of which, done in strong seasoned wood, made them really beautiful pieces of craftsmanship.

Another was the one who worked on already tanned leather, treating it with oil and varnishes to leave it smooth, flexible, odorless, polished and shiny. He also did the tooling and edging, the high-relief patterns on saddle padding and saddle flaps, breast straps, cinches, cruppers and leather stirrup guards.

The third and last son was given the task of sewing. Every stitch was done by hand and had to be precisely and mathematically equal to all the others. He himself prepared the thread from tightly twisted fiber waxed and re-waxed with sweet smelling black cobbler's wax. He was also, when called for, a skilful maker and braider of reins—work which he hated and despised as unworthy of a master harnessmaker.

So it was not by accident that that harness and those trappings fully deserved the reputation they enjoyed. The saddles were so constructed and padded that they rubbed not a hair of the horse or mule. No matter how heavy the burden, the saddle and its pads fitted the anatomy of the animal so perfectly that there was no danger of chafing. The object of all this was purely practical—to provide good and efficient service.

But the aesthetic aspect was not neglected either in the excellent craftsmanship of the Japas. The proportions between saddle and leather-covered stirrups were precisely calculated. The tooling of the saddle flaps was never overloaded with ornamental figures. On the contrary, it was severely simple, consisting sometimes of only a few darker lines or grooves running parallel to the edges. The straps and thongs grew from the body of the saddle as naturally as fingers grow from a hand, a testimony to the unsurpassed perfection of the work.

All the leather had been cut with admirable precision of hand and eye. The hand-stitching followed a line of holes pierced with an awl, faithfully tracing the most difficult curves. And when the fittings and adornments were of silver, the effect was positively superb. In short, the perfection of the work began with the headstall, was lavished in turn on the cheek strap, the nose band, the brow band, the curb strap and the reins; it went on to the saddle pad, leaped to the stirrups, proceeded to the martingale, reached the girth, and ended up with the breeching and crupper. The whole outfit made a marvelous display of opulence.

(34)

Next came Papá Manuel Gustán, the polygamous old *cacique*.

He was the maker of coarse soap and tallow candles for the people of Yangana and the neighborhood. He needed active help for this work and had, devised a system which enabled him to live a quiet and easy life while satisfying his customers at the same time.

For a long while three women had kept him company: "the old woman," "the young woman," and "the *Chayona*,"—the Albino—known to all the townspeople by the collective name of "the candlemakers."

The way this family was constituted was really novel. The old Indian boss was lord and master of his servants and bedfellows who were Indians like himself. The first one to live with him was naturally the oldest. He had shown her how to make soap out of lye.

With this beginner Manuel Gustán, at that time young and strong, gave up being a sharecropper, settled in the town and set about making soap out of fat obtained from the butcher and other neighbors. While he was out looking for the raw material, the woman stayed home mixing the fat with the lye in a big copper pot which they had bought on credit. It was hard work for her and one afternoon when her partner returned from his rounds with a good load of fat and hardwood ashes in his saddlebags, he found a young woman in the house who spoke not one word of Spanish but who conversed perfectly well with the older one in Quichua.

The stranger appeared to be from Saraguro, since she wore a black *anacu* of thin cloth and a tattered old felt hat. In fact all her clothes were in very poor shape and smelled bad. Grinding his teeth, Papá Gustán had agreed much against his will to feed another mouth under his smoky roof. She was almost a beggar girl, but as time went on would become his second bedfellow. The man had to enlarge the bamboo platform that served as a bed for the original couple so as to make room for the now accepted intruder.

After a few weeks the task of boiling the pot of fat and lye, work that went on day and night, could now be shared by the two women in turn alike as were the nights of love.

It might have been thought that it was hard for the old one to get used to this, since she now saw herself displaced 'or at least shared. But in the middle of the night, when overcome by fatigue and sleep, she felt the warm body of the other woman lying on the bamboo bed, she knew there was someone to take over while she slept. She felt completely tranquil and placidly closed her eyes.

The third woman was Papá Gustán's niece, the daughter of a sister of his who had died four years before. Since the niece was left an orphan she had come to seek shelter with her uncle who was six days journey away. She arrived bearing the sad news and a little money which she had made by selling the few animals that had belonged to her mother. The old man was not at all displeased that his niece had showed such good sense. He made her welcome in his house, took care of the money she had so trustingly handed to him and perhaps he reflected that God was a good fellow.

That same afternoon he did not go out as usual to get fat for the soapworks. Instead, he cut three short forked stakes, made three holes with an iron bar in the floor of his hut and drove in the stakes with the forks uppermost. He had set them symmetrically five feet away from the edge of the platform. Then he replaced the old crosspieces with longer and stronger new ones, lashed them to the forked uprights with sisal fiber and wove an additional section of cane on to the crosspieces. Thus the width of the bed was increased by one-half.

Then when night fell, without the slightest protest from either of the other women, he stole his niece's virginity.

Now that he could count on three helpers he planned to enlarge his business. So, before long he undertook the making of tallow candles.

This meant getting another copper pot which he bought with his niece's money. A new task—the twisting of thread for the wicks—was introduced and a redistribution of chores had to be made among his assistants.

Number two, the Indian from Saraguro, a splendid hand spinner, took over the twisting of the hanks of cotton hung from her waist and at the same time watched over the smaller pot of tallow boiling on the fire. The old woman had charge of the larger pot which had to be kept at low heat. She stirred the contents with a stick, added stronger and stronger lye to make the boiling mass soapier, and carried fire wood from the pile nearby.

As for the niece, her job was to prepare the lye, choosing the best of the ashes brought in by her master and uncle, but more importantly, to fashion the tallow candles. It was quick and easy work once the wicks, strung by one end on long sticks, were ready for successive dippings in the boiling fat.

About once a year the priest who came to Yangana for the Fiesta, exhorted the backsliders among the congregation to approach the confessional and put their consciences in order. He made veiled references to certain stubborn characters and to those who ought to change their way of life. Papá Gustán, however, believed that his life was unquestionably in better order than anybody else's.

"Papá Gustán," people would say to him, "you go even farther than Shameless Carlos."

So he too was on the march, neither sorrowing nor rejoicing, accompanied by his three servants and following the customers for his soap and candles. He was riding a donkey and the three women were' of course on foot. They were keeping an eye on the safety of the copper pots and watching over the frail health and comfort of their lord and master.

(35)

Next came Agustín Labanda, the blacksmith.

He could not be called a strong man, although physical strength was traditionally associated with his trade. On the contrary, what he was most admired for was his prodigious memory. It was thanks to him, for example, that Don Vicente Muñoz' improvisations were remembered.

The sight of one eye had been impaired by a flying spark. Evidently, he was exceedingly mortified by this defect since he could not bear the slightest allusion to it.

His labors at forge and anvil filled many needs, principally the shoeing of horses and the making of the metal parts for sickles, axes, pickaxes, hoes, plowshares and branding irons.

His broad forehead was covered with sweat and soot from the forge. That wonderful memory, like a book in the hands of an illiterate, was of no use to him. "What a pity he has never been able to study!" people said, "What a great person he could have been!"

Some of the more enthusiastic champions of the town even went so far as to blame the evil fate of the whole community on the fact that it had not allowed the intellectual career of one of its most gifted sons to flower, perhaps to earn national fame and honor for them all.

"What a loss for the town that it could not profit from Agustín Labanda's power of memory!"

It irritated Don Vicente to hear reasoning of this sort, and he would cut short the useless laments of Labanda's admirers, "These good people cannot distinguish memory from intelligence!"

His listeners naturally attributed Don Vicente Muñoz's remarks to pure envy.

(36)

Next came Froilán Zapata, who also worked in metal, but as an inventor and mechanic.

He was not just another blacksmith, not even a better blacksmith. He was much more than that. He did not work for paying customers since he was in fact an amateur who did what he did for pure pleasure. He had inherited real estate including a house in the center of town which gave him enough rent to live comfortably. His great love was for precision-made firearms and intricate mechanical work. But in truth Yangana did not give him much opportunity to employ his talents fully. He spent most of his time adjusting a sewing machine that no longer sewed; repairing or making over a shotgun that had lost its trigger; mending a wall clock or a pocket watch; cleaning people's rifles and handguns; reloading cartridges in a machine of his own invention.

What generally happened was that the man spent most of his time inventing machines that had already been invented or devising traps for wild animals, using the most ingenious methods. And since Curly Ocampo was the proud possessor of a splendid rifle complete with telescopic sight, Don Froilán Zapata was so skilful that he managed, by picking up a part here and a part there, using file, hammer and anvil, threadcutter, nuts, bolts and screws—all with infinite patience—to make an identical copy. This, so said the experts, shot as accurately as the best foreign-made weapon.

For it was a fact that the people of Yangana firmly believed that everything mechanical, any machine, had been invented abroad, by gringos in particular. They, the people of Yangana, had an almost superstitious respect for gringos, those big ruddy-faced men who spoke in such a strange way and knew by instinct all the technical secrets of mechanics and machinery. They held that South Americans must be inferior beings because they had not yet given to the world one of those inventors who are the wonder of succeeding generations. They imagined that every gringo was a mechanical genius and were convinced that they had a natural aptitude and understanding for all that concerned mechanics and electricity.

Therefore, Don Froilán Zapata, a South American of mixed blood, short in stature with dark skin and straight hair seemed to be the exception that proved the rule—a native born man who was as good a mechanic as any gringo. He was considered capable of undertaking the most complex assignments, such as assembling or taking down an internal combustion engine or installing a radio station—things to be found only in the far away city where some of them had never been.

(37)

Next came a middle-aged pair, Vicente Orozco the barber and Rosa Pullaguari, the soup and stew maker. They walked close together although their kindly feelings towards one another had soured over the years.

Their combined trades had been well patronized in the neighborhood. The man owned some second hand razors of poor quality and two old forceps which he used to draw teeth. At the same time, when not otherwise occupied, he took care of his hat blocking shop. Living quarters, shop and soup kitchen were all in one small house, the principal room having its walls completely covered with palm fiber hats. After giving each hat a good scrubbing with a bristle brush and hard soap, the two of them ironed all the hats onto forms, gummed them lightly to set the shape, and smeared them with a coat of white lead.

The woman's chief occupation, however, was the preparation of really succulent food for sale. She cooked soup almost continuously, a soup based on cow's feet with cassava thrown in for thickening. She then added half-ripe plantains, milk, rice, pepper, oregano and cumin seed. The tendons and sinews stirred into the soup were converted into masses of gelatin that shook in the ladle. Yellow grease floated in the thick nourishing broth, its bubbles reflecting the ceiling like a thousand little eyes.

It was a long process and no wonder the woman was tired when it was finished. As soon as the beef bones—hooves, hocks and shins—were bought they were placed in hot ashes so as to singe the hair and scorch the hooves. When the revolting smell of charred hide and hair gave the signal, the next step was to scrape the scorched hide with a knife. The hooves were pried off with the knife point.

All that was left to do was to smash up the bones with an ax and throw them into the great pot where they boiled away happily hour after hour until the thick cow hide had turned into a glutinous mass. Meanwhile all the other ingredients were being added to make out of this powerful dish a massive and hypnotic food.

This couple, the hatter-barber and the tavern keeper-cook, were now in their late middle age and had had no children. The fact that such a broth, made from such knuckles and feet, had had no effect on Orozco was one of life's omissions that the local philosophers and chroniclers could never satisfactorily explain.

(38)

Next came Matías Puglla, the sugar maker.

He looked just what he was—the most stupid and most physically repulsive person imaginable. From head to foot he gave every evidence of a stupendous emptiness.

His unusually narrow forehead, crowned by a rebellious lock of graying hair, seemed encased by thick hollow walls. It was furrowed by two deep parallel wrinkles which reduced even more the narrow gap between the scalp and the heavy joined eyebrows. His nose was flat and twisted over to the left so that one nostril was bigger than the other. His moustache seemed to sprout out of these unequal cavities like a wire brush. He habitually kept his mouth open and his thick protruding lower lip was always wet. Saliva collected at the corners of his mouth in a white froth which inflamed the skin as if he was suffering from shingles. He moved wearily, dragging his great flat feet and he never bothered to notice whether his trousers were buttoned or not. When he put them on, all he remembered was that he must fasten the waist so that they wouldn't fall down. As a result, he had been the target of a hundred stupid and vulgar jokes when he sat down, jokes which nevertheless failed to produce the slightest sign of animation, not to say shame in his incredible simpleton's face. One of his shoulders was lower than the other and his arms were so short that they hardly reached his coat pockets.

Within this human wasteland, however, there was, according to his neighbors, something interesting and above all useful. He knew how to make white sugar. This was something he had learned during a long absence when he had wandered despised and rejected along the fertile slopes of Chaguarpamba.

Up to the time he returned home, the people of Yangana had always been firmly convinced that it was impossible to make refined sugar in their part of the world and that they. must confine themselves to making and consuming coarse brown sugar. The syrup from their cane would not do. They therefore recognized as a supreme virtue the fact that Matías Puglla had demonstrated the contrary and shown his fellow townsmen how to refine sugar, giving them with unselfish and simple-minded generosity the benefit of his practical sugar maker's knowledge acquired in Chaguarpamba. There, while spending many years planting rice and peanuts, he had also as a matter of local routine, learned how to convert coarse blocks of dark brown sugar to pure white loaves as hard as flint.

By refining sugar for the first time in Yangana he had earned the gratitude of the town. Once he had established himself on his cane field and started what was at that time a daring enterprise, the sugar from this valley became famous in the market of the provincial capital for its rocky hardness, its snowy color, its almost mineral dryness and its really delicious taste.

Needless to say, he had problems with skeptics at first. Many previous attempts had failed. Cane from these parts was only good for coarse brown sugar and rum. And as for the prospect of selling his product, the local people would never buy white sugar. They would always prefer the coarse blocks, and gave reasons for this: it had better food value, was cheaper and more "salty" than white sugar.

But the simple-minded fellow did not give up his project for objections like that. He just spat on his hands and went on with the job of setting up his mill.

A few weeks later smoke and steam could be seen coming up through the rafters of the makeshift roof. The smoke rose with its dark puffs of dense cloud while the white steam, fragrant and misty, rose trembling from the surface of the boiling juice and joined the smoke. And that stolid-looking, dull-witted man, with an enormous skimming spoon in his hand, happily stirred the syrup which boiled thicker and thicker in the evaporator. The bronze crusher ground its golden teeth as the cane stalks moaned between its jaws. The oxen panted and blew foam from their mouths, licking their distended nostrils from side to side. While all the time the men who operated the grinders and drove the oxen filled the air with shouts and curses.

The general layout of the mill was not very different from what was used in the production of coarse brown sugar. But instead of tables containing rectangular molds for the thick syrup, there were two long bamboo benches, one on each side of the fireplace and parallel to it. Resting on them, in neat rows, were molds of another kind. These were conical receptacles made of cane stalks with the pointed end cut short and facing down. The open ends made them into funnels which were in turn secured by strips of cane tied with fiber. Fitted inside each mold was a kind of cone-shamed lining made of fresh plantain leaves which served to seal any cracks and to prevent possible filtration.

And now, in order to boil the juice and later the syrup, Matías Puglla employed, for the first time in the history of Yangana, not the primitive single boilers which required a tediously slow process of successive operations, but instead a large metal container holding three evaporators at once. They boiled in turn the juice, the first syrup, and finally the syrup at the point of crystallization, ready for cooling in the molds.

What was more, to facilitate the purifying of the juice and unstrained syrup he used, again for the first time in Yangana, not the traditional lye according to age old custom, but bicarbonate of soda. When thrown by handfuls into the boiling liquid, this powder instantly produced a yellowish foam which caught and separated out all the impurities in the juice. This task of collecting the scum with the big skimmer from all the corners and angles of the evaporator may have been the only time when Puglla's foolish face showed some flash of intelligence. With malicious fury he attacked all the crannies where the scum—sticky and striped with dark blotches—tried to cling to the boiling syrup. After an hour's struggle the liquor became free of impurities and turned clear. When the concentration of sugar had reached the right point, the syrup was vigorously agitated in a cold container and was ready for pouring into the big molds.

What would eventually be a loaf of sugar was now packed in the soft wrapping of the mold. The bottom of the funnel was pierced clean through by a long sharp sliver of cane which served as a plug. Once the beaten up syrup had solidified, the man handling it pulled out the dagger—so to speak—leaving a deep wound in the center of the cone through which the coarse dark sugar bled, thick drop by thick drop, clarifying and purifying itself in a slow intermittent hemorrhage.

To make this purging operation easier, Matías Pulla did as he had seen done and had himself done in Chaguarpamba, he placed a cake of damp clay mixed with ash over the mouth of the mold. This helped the syrup or rather molasses to percolate by gravity through the mass of sugar and drain into another receptacle. The molasses was unpalatable at first, with a dark color and strong smell. After a week, the cake of clay was changed and the molasses came out clearer, sweeter and more palatable. With the third cake of clay, a week later, the purging process ended and it was time to lift out the solid loaf of sugar from the mold which had shaped it. The product was as dazzlingly white as quartz; nevertheless a trace of humidity still remained. In order to give the heavy sugar loaves the rock-like hardness they would later acquire, they were exposed to many days of sun and dew. The hot dry air by day and cool dampness of the dew by night set them like concrete. All that remained to do was to wrap them in dry cane-straw, load them two at a time—pointed ends down—on the backs of mules and transport them to the city to compete with the granulated sugar brought by the local merchants from the big sugar mills of the coast.

How could people not be grateful to foolish Puglla when on the road to the city all they had to do to restore their energy and quench their thirst was to suck bits of sugar dipped in fresh water, their hands moving steadily from container to mouth and mouth to container?

But those who observed him noticed that his forehead was narrower than ever.

(39)

Next came Rosita Sandoya, illicit distiller and smuggler of rum and other spirits.

She owned a little grocery store and in the regular course of business, she bought great quantities of coarse brown sugar in blocks; quantities that were clearly greater than what she could sell in her retail store or send wholesale to the city. This was the first thing that aroused the suspicions of the excise inspectors from the Government Monopoly of Alcohol and Tobacco, when sent on duty to Yangana.

Secondly, although she had been granted a license to sell rum at retail, her wholesale purchases of rum from the official warehouse were quite obviously much less than what she sold. Thirdly, the rum that she served to her steady customers tasted better and was purer and stronger than what came in barrels from the Monopoly. Fourthly, her regular customers bought it for less than the price established by the Monopoly for sale over the counter. Fifthly, the anisette that Rosita Sandoya sold in her little liquor store was incomparably superior to the Monopoly's anisette. Sixthly, the same thing was true of the well-aged rum from Rosita's cellars: there was just no competing with it either in price or quality.

With all this background, it was little wonder that any inspector who arrived in those parts naturally had a special assignment to check on Rosita Sandoya who was the undoubted cause of the poor business done by the Government Monopoly in Yangana. Each new inspector, ever mindful of the strict instructions from the district manager in person, thought to himself while on the road that with his rifle and his iron fist, he was on the way to root out wrong doing in that remote region. Thinking these thoughts, he straightened himself up in his stirrups.

But when he reached Yangana, stiff and sore after three tiring days' journey, he had barely dismounted in front of the wretched poorly furnished house that the Monopoly provided for its agent, than a handsome, well-scrubbed, nicely combed serving girl appeared on the scene, with an outsize lunch box in one hand and a big overflowing basket in the other. The basket held everything that might appeal to someone just arrived all travel-stained from the road: a water jug and basin, clean smelling towels, fresh water and soap. While the girl was arranging what she had brought, a boy showed up literally covered with an assortment of furniture and furnishings. This second emissary brought a folding cot, a rolled up mattress, ironed sheets, fine blankets, a little table, two chairs and a hammock. There was even mosquito netting, complete with its cords and ready to hang up. To say nothing of the chamber pot.

A cloth was quickly spread on the table and as quickly covered with steaming dishes. The bed was made up in a moment, the wash basin placed in its metal stand, the towel hung up and the hammock slung between the corners of the wretched little room. While the pretty servant girl was stretching out the hammock and the mosquito netting, she took care to display her sturdy legs to the newcomer, who now that he saw all these unexpected comforts, found his head full of exciting ideas. He decided that, with a little bit of luck and skill, his time of exile in these solitary regions might not turn out so badly after all.

And when the two servants, the handsome country girl and the serving boy, were ready to leave, they recited with one voice the following singsong message to the hollow cheeked traveler: "Miss Rosita has sent us to welcome you and to ask how you are after the journey, and that here is a bowl of soup for you and a little drink to make you forget the hardships of the road."

"And what about this bed?" asked the inspector.

Again the two voices in unison, "It, too, is from Miss Rosita for your use while staying in this town."

"And how much will bed and board cost me?"

Again the two voices in unison, "They will cost you nothing and don't hesitate to let her know what else you would like."

A day or two later, the inspector was already pinching the bottom of the pretty country girl and he reflected that all this was a thousand times better than setting himself against Rosita Sandoya, making an enemy of a likable and influential woman, and having to spend eighty percent of his salary on food, laundry and an occasional woman to calm his senses.

There were cases, of course, when an inspector's compliance was not so easily obtained. Sometimes this was preceded by a period of steady barrage by the inspector and a gradual withdrawal of the furniture and other effects loaned by the lady. The poor man soon found himself eating badly, sleeping on the bare ground, bitten by mosquitoes at night, without a chair to sit on, obliged to take his laundry to a washerwoman, without a shaving mirror or a wash basin.

He would finally decide to give up the useless struggle, to shut his eyes to Rosita Sandoya's fraudulent tricks and to enjoy the prospect of an easy life instead of faithfully serving a stingy government which had no feelings of gratitude for its most loyal servants.

As a result, in this remote corner of the country, the Ecuadorian Treasury continued to be deprived of the revenues which she was neatly and happily pocketing.

Rosita Sandoya who was still young, plump and attractive with endearing eyes, made no effort to disguise either her activities as a smuggler or her methods of corrupting the government inspectors. On the contrary, when anybody asked her how she had thought of a system that gave her such excellent results, she would say:

"I learned from the gringos in the foreign companies. That's what they do with our Government and they get whatever they want. It costs a little, but you gain more."

People who heard her say this and who knew what she was referring to because they had read about it in the opposition newspapers—which reached Yangana two months late—said that she was quite right.

"As Montalvo used to say," Don Vicente Muñoz would begin......

If matters began to look threatening for her, such as a shakeup of Provincial Authorities and the transfer or dismissal of negligent inspectors, Rosita Sandoya would make a trip to the city taking with her an imposing caravan of gifts which finally overcame the firmest resolutions of the new administrator. This gentleman also understood that in the last resort he could enjoy her favors as the price of official lenience.

The makeup of this mule train of gifts for such exceptional cases followed a regular pattern.

The first item was a mule from the Quille brothers' pastures, broken and trained by one of the Mendietas, its shiny silver-studded saddle and bridle made in the Japas' saddle shop.

Next on the list were two hundred pounds of hand-hulled long grain rice, clean and white, harvested in the bottom land below Yangana.

Fifty pounds of the best dried meat, glistening with fat, selected from the strings hanging in the patio of José M. Medina, the butcher.

Two hundred pounds of loaf sugar from Matías Puglla's mill, so hard, so dry, so flinty that when broken into pieces it seemed to glow in the dark.

Fifty pounds of smoked cheese from the cheese-loft at Presentación Pullaguari's who owned the best herd of dairy cows in all the countryside.

A large jar of guaya jelly, smelling of myrtle, heavy, hard and concentrated and made by Rosita with her own hands.

A well-fattened capon.

Fat birds of all kinds: huge turkeys, long-legged chickens, corpulent ducks.

One hundred pounds of lard.

And as a change of pace:

A hat woven of the very finest palm fiber.

A special traveling bag for journeys in the Province, beautifully embroidered in different colors, with the owner's initials and the year it was given.

When Rosita Sandoya returned with her drove of unloaded mules and, sometimes, a quiet look of animal relaxation and released senses, Don Vicente Muñoz, whose head was full of historical references, would say to her, without her understanding the full significance of his remarks, "Here is our Queen of Sheba back home. As Montalvo said..." and he'd start a new commentary.

(40)

Next came Don Baltazar Zárate, merchant.

He was the principal economic tie between the distant (and hard-to-reach) city and Yangana along with its surrounding countryside. The businessmen in the provincial capital knew him well and used to talk among themselves about the taciturn but at the same time ingenuous way he had of proposing a transaction. He had never bought anything on credit. He didn't owe a cent to anyone and his system of paying on the spot to wholesalers in need of cash enabled him to obtain very considerable discounts.

His shop and warehouses were in his own spacious and well-situated house. A large storeroom which opened onto the inside patio was reserved for raw hides, coffee, grains and lard. This line of Yangana products would be traded for goods from Peru: drill, sheeting, corduroy, linen cloth, white soap, dried fish, wheat flour and rock salt.

At regular intervals Zárate loaded the Yangana articles on long trains of donkeys, thus making room for new stock in his overflowing storehouses. He drove the train to the Peruvian frontier and there exchanged these local products for Peruvian goods. The greatest difficulty he had to overcome on the return trip was to get the rock salt through the customs since its importation was prohibited. But he always succeeded somehow since this particular article enjoyed a sure market in the Province; people wanted it not only for household use, but also to feed their cattle once a week.

In his youth, Zárate had been a poor carrier and mule driver so that he knew all the province and a good part of Northern Peru. The fact that he now owned a good grocery and hardware business had by no means made him sedentary in his habits, however. In fact, he himself always took personal charge of his convoy of pack animals on their long trip to the distant southern frontier.

It was on these occasions that the man showed real animation, his eyes lit up with unwonted sparkle and he dressed with great elegance—quite a contrast to his behavior at home—a sore point with his, family. They, especially his daughters, found it intolerable that a man of his position, one of the mainstays of Yangana should, for example, go barefoot. Furthermore, that he still ate his meals squatting down at the fireplace just as he had when he was a wretched drover paid by the day. They had furnished a dining room in his big house where he could or rather should sit down with them at a table. But it was quite another story when he had to make a trip.

When on the road he wore a fine white shirt with starched collar and cuffs. His necktie had to be of black silk with the ends tucked under the buttons of a well-cut serge waistcoat. His trousers; too, were of serge. Instead of boots, he preferred Russian leather shoes—dating from his youth—with silver spurs. His legs were protected by dark red leggings.

A wide belt held his money, a pistol of the best German make and an ample supply of shells. Over his fine waistcoat he wore a top quality striped Peruvian poncho of vicuña wool in the latest style. He liked to throw the front fold over his right shoulder with a resolute, gallant and almost defiant air, quite a contrast to his obsequious manner behind the counter. Since he always covered his head, day and night, he wore a freshly blocked palm fiber hat on these trips, complete with a perfectly fitted cover of rubber cloth.

If he paid great attention to his personal appearance when traveling, his mount was decked out in a similar ostentatious style. Ever since the previous evening, his assistant would have been busy cleaning and polishing the harness and trappings. The great strong Peruvian saddle-mule which Zárate the merchant rode on his trips shone with silver. A little traveling bag, half empty, had been placed on the saddle, and over it a Peruvian vicuña wool traveling blanket to keep the seat soft and dry.

Zárate gave orders to the drivers to set out at daybreak and go on ahead with their loads. He himself left at eleven o'clock after lunch, lightly spurring his mule so that it started off at a smart clicking pace in front of the people who had come to see him off.

The light machete hanging from his saddle-bow jangled against a carbide lantern for use when traveling on dark nights.

Don Baltazar Zárate had his own ideas about merchandising and merchants for whom he expressed nothing but contempt. "They are all thieves and fools as well," he would say. It seemed odd, but at the same time significant to all the people in Yangana, that a businessman should speak in this way about his competitors. Yet people preferred to buy from him because—apart from other obvious advantages—they liked to hear him declaim against businessmen.

"I treat the city merchants as they deserve," he would explain to his circle of friends and customers in Yangana.

"They try to wear me down with all their talk, but it doesn't work with me. I know that all of them owe money to the big wholesalers in Guayaquil and that the day those Guayaquil wholesalers cut off their credit, good-bye talk. I, who owe nothing to anybody do not pretend to be more than I am, nor would I exchange my bare feet for their feet wearing shoes that they cannot pay for."

A little later, after selling a quart of kerosene or ten cents worth of needles, or buying a dozen rawhides, he would take up the thread again. "And the Guayaquil wholesalers sing the same song to our city merchants as our merchants sing to me. But our merchants take them seriously and are impressed. That's why I think that they're fools. Why don't they know what I know, that those same big Guayaquil importers are in debt to the even bigger foreign importers and that if the foreign importers stopped giving credit the Guayaquil men would be ruined."

He would go on, "The only reason I have this store is to avoid being robbed. The merchants steal like highwaymen. This enraged me so much that I became a merchant myself so as to break them by underselling."

Another reason he gave for thinking that merchants were stupid—"real fools"—was their abject surrender to banks and bankers. "The banks are to blame for the bad state of business," he would say.

"Then why have anything to do with the enemy? Look what I do! I've built up my little capital without any help from those crooks. They know when you're in trouble and they put a rope around your neck. I don't know who are worse, the bandits I knew when I was a drover in the Piura desert, or the bankers. The bandits at least run some risk. So you see, sir, these imbeciles of merchants get involved with bankers in the belief that an alligator won't devour another alligator. That's how they get trapped."

Finally, Baltazar Zárate was a Germanophile, also in his own way. He believed in the innate good quality and superiority of German products.

He considered Solingen cutlery to be the best in the world, and whenever he was offered an article manufactured in a foreign country and strongly recommended to him, he would ask, "Is it German then?"

He also had it firmly in his head that all Germans were tremendous eaters who could eat more than any six of his countrymen put together. He had got this idea when as a young man he happened to cross the Piura desert in the company of a German who ate enormous rations while on the road and cooked huge quantities at every stop.

This terrible defect offset their great virtues as manufacturers.

Like his bare feet and his eating habits, Zárate's daughters also disapproved of his tendency to remind people all the time that in his youth he had been a mule driver.

In recent months Baltazar Zárate had begun to behave like a budding philanthropist. His over-generous contribution toward the cost of the new bell had flabbergasted the organizers. Furthermore, he had promised to provide a town band and was planning to order the instruments directly from Germany so as to eliminate voracious intermediaries—"those scoundrelly merchants," as he called them. He was expecting the catalogues!

It had not been hard to persuade him to join the exodus from Yangana, a town which he loved as dearly as he loved German manufacturers.

But the urgent nature of departure had not allowed him time to put on the fancy garb he traditionally wore on his business trips.

(41)

Next came José Angel Maridueña, the prince of liars.

He was about forty-five, married, but with only a few children. Everyone agreed that his reputation was deserved and unquestioned.

To look at, he was tall and stout with big flapping hands and very long arms. He spent his life exaggerating, exalting and declaiming. Starting with the customary "good morning," to the most solemn declaration under oath, he harangued and waved his arms frantically. In his mouth the dullest daily gossip became a sensational bulletin. He collected scraps of news from his neighbors to concoct the most extraordinary lies. He liked to talk about savory food and when he did so, he expressed his enthusiasm with so much dramatic effect that he positively drooled and slobbered. People said that he had a passion for food and that to hear him was to believe it.

Apart from this he boasted a variety of skills. He had beautiful handwriting and considered that this gave him the right to be a freelance correspondent for the newspapers in the capital. Every two weeks he managed to send in long reports of the Yangana neighborhood giving sensational news, sometimes true and sometimes imaginary. These unsolicited contributions from Maridueña were often honored by publication since there were times when they provided a news story with every imaginable detail, written, furthermore, in perfect Spenserian script.

His written versions of events, however, lacked the lively and engaging style of his viva voce accounts. When he was speaking, his large and extraordinarily expressive hands gave the impression of actually molding, as it were, the tale he was telling. Although this effect was lost when written down, the material interest of the story was somehow preserved in the beautiful handwriting. As a result, Yangana had more than once attracted the attention of the Government and also been taken into account by foreign news agencies.

The first of his fabrications to cross the boundaries of his native land and run through all America was an account of an armed clash supposed to have taken place between a group of Ecuadorian peasants and members of the Peruvian Civil Guard stationed on the southeast frontier of Ecuador. Casualties were reported—by the Ecuadorians of course—to have been four Peruvians and one Ecuadorian killed and two on each side wounded.

An opposition newspaper in the capital raised the alarm by printing the following news item from Yangana, beneath block headlines:

"The encounter took place on Ecuadorian territory and was caused by a dispute over some small plantings and tobacco fields owned and worked for generations by Ecuadorian peasant farmers. The invaders set fire to one of the houses and wounded the owner with machetes. While the peaceful farmers were defending, inch by inch, the land which they had enriched by their labor, the armed Civil Guards who had violated our territory lost four, killed, and left two more wounded on the field of battle. Two of our men were wounded, including the owner of the burned house who, as already reported, had been slashed with machetes."

"Events of this kind," continued the article are a daily occurrence in these remote regions of our country. They show all too clearly that the Government and the Army do nothing either to defend the integrity of the hearths and homes left by our forebears, or to recover the territory which the audacious usurpers from the south snatch from us day after day."

The very same day the story appeared, it was picked up by international news services and transmitted as follows:

"Six soldiers were killed and one wounded in armed clashes between soldiers of the Peruvian and Ecuadorian garrisons on the southeast frontier of Ecuador."

The press account went on to say, apparently quoting reliable sources, that "The Ecuadorian State Department, acting through the Ecuadorian ambassador in Lima, has demanded an explanation from the Peruvian Government."

Two days later, one of the great Argentinean newspapers published an editorial condemning such incidents and calling for harmony in the family of American nations. Then the Ecuadorian State Department, in the face of so much agitation, ordered a commission of inquiry.

Now, the actual truth was simply that Don Baltazar Zárate had returned from one of his business trips to Peru and happened to be telling for the nth time an old story of his about bandits in the desert, in which he himself at that time a young drover, was the chief figure. This dusty old tale of long ago had been overheard by Maridueña: that was all.

The most curious thing about Maridueña's fabrications was that once he had told them, he began to believe every word of them. In the present case he was completely convinced that the bloody encounter had actually taken place just as he described it, and he was boiling with rage at the negligence of the Government for not keeping a garrison on the southern frontier. He almost wept with grief at the thought of the martyred defenders of the fatherland and their tragic deaths in the border skirmish.

Another lying story which grew and spread with extraordinary speed described the discovery of fabulous gold-bearing deposits in a mountain range overhanging the river valley below Yangana.

According to Maridueña, a man had gone down to the river to look for some stray cattle. When he reached the left bank he was told that the speckled cow and the little bay-colored white faced bull with twisted horns that he was seeking had crossed the river and climbed the hill on the other side. The man did the same. He followed the road on the opposite bank but his inquiries of the scattered farmers who lived on the hillside were fruitless.

Finally, one afternoon while he rested sitting on a rock, he noticed that the quartz at his feet was sparkling with gold in the sunlight. He broke off a piece of rock, realized how heavy it was, and contrived to grind it up. When he blew hard on the ground quartz, there was the gold, like fish scales. But a few days later several fierce-looking characters appeared and mounted guard over the site of his find. They lived on the hillside and from all signs, were determined to prevent any intruder from exploiting the deposit. The poor fellow who had actually made the discovery could not set foot again on the place nor even continue the search for his lost animals.

In the case of this particular story Maridueña seemed stricter and more careful than usual. He said he would wait until it was confirmed from reliable sources. The first time he told it he seemed to remember overhearing it being told to somebody else, or perhaps he had dreamed it and could not remember when. To plant the fiction better and give substance to the spell of his eloquent hands, he hurried out one Sunday to tell it in the barber shop. The fascinated crowd listened to him with open mouths and greedy eyes.

Less than a week later, one of the men who worked for the Pullaguari brothers and had come into town with some cattle for the slaughterhouse told him—José Angel Mariadueña—that he'd just heard from one of the Pullaguaris that a man from the neighborhood of Yangana had found a gold mine on the other side of the river. He added that Pullaguari had learned it from several people in town. As soon as Mariadueña was sure that others now believed the story on their own account, he put on a show of innocent curiosity and persuaded this man of Pullaguari's to repeat it all to a crowd of bystanders.

"Didn't I tell you?" he scolded them looking hurt and reproachful. "The news is true. The Pullaguaris have reported it."

The Pullaguaris were serious men and if they said it was so, it probably was so. After this, at least five more people repeated the story, always to Mariadueña's astonishment at such sensational news. The counterfeit currency was now in circulation and since it had come full circle it was almost impossible to tell who had started things.

Now that this version of the story had been certified by such dependable sources, Mariadueña felt that he could safely repeat it in his beautiful script on two pieces of ruled paper and send it off to a newspaper in the capital and also to one of the Guayaquil papers.

Nobody knew what happened to the news after that, but it was never published. On the other hand, a month later a mining engineer from the American Company in Curipamba got the strange idea in his head to take a month's vacation hunting mountain lions in the densest jungles of the range across from Yangana. This meant a difficult journey by muleback during the worst of the rainy season. And a little later still, an Ecuadorian Government Commission, as if following the footsteps of the fretful gringo, proceeded to expropriate several tracts of uncultivated land located in the same area.

Those who knew most about the whole affair understood that the gringo had returned from his adventure bearing a bitter grudge against Yangana. His report to the management at Curipamba dripped with fury and sarcastic scorn for "those half-breed clowns who don't know what they're talking about nor what they have."

The same sources added that the government geologist had split his sides laughing at the samples of rock sent to him for assay by the official commission who went to take over those favored lands "where the Yankee was already smelling out plunder."

José Angel Maridueña had another talent—he was a good cook. His specialty was a stupendous rice a la Valenciana which Father Navarro had taught him how to make. This Father Navarro was a famous Spanish priest who used to go about trying to induce countryfolk to worship the embalmed body of his mistress, telling them it was the relic of a saint.

The priest had adored his beautiful woman while she was alive—she really was a little Spanish beauty—and after midday mass on Sundays he used to prepare rice a la Valenciana for her. He cooked it with the best imported peppers, together with two fat hens, and served it to her on his knees. When this woman of Father Navarro's died, he went mad with horror and passion and abandoned his parish, carrying the corpse in a glass-covered coffin from village to village. Before he left, he bequeathed Maridueña a cookbook the size of a missal. José Angelo swore that Father Navarro sang mass from this book "and from this book I've learned to prepare such delicious food."

He also knew how to put splints on bruised or broken arms and legs. Those huge hands of his were perfectly adapted for such work. A few tugs, a little feeling and rubbing of sprained bones and pulled tendons was often enough: a treatment that was simple, cheap and not too painful.

Finally, he had an exceptional gift for friendship and his greatest pleasure was to ask a favor for somebody else. This, too, could be included in the list of his' skills. But he was incapable of asking so much as a needle or pin for himself. On the other hand, if he saw a friend in trouble he would run out into the street waving his arms like a scarecrow flapping in the wind. His heavy but kindly hands grasped the shoulders of the first person he met. Face to face, pressing his great stomach against the man's chest, he made him listen to his appeal. For example, "You won't leave this spot without giving me something for the widow so-and-so. She has to bury her son tomorrow."

If the contribution was at first refused, he used physical force to detain the reluctant donor. "You're not moving a step. D'you hear?" He followed this up, if given a chance, with the whole story of the unhappy woman's crushing privations with her orphaned child. In the end it was not unusual for the subject of this requisition to find himself pressing his contribution in Maridueña's warm hand with tears in his eyes.

Since Mariduena was both a big eater and a poor man— something that unfortunately did not indicate his usual skill—there were times when his great belly was not filled. This did not prevent him from positively exuding joy when he invited the first person he met in the street to share a meal, even though it meant going hungry himself.

While his guest was stuffing himself at his table with his food, this invincible fraud would keep rubbing his hands and swallowing saliva—for he was truly a glutton. On these occasions, he was often so spurred on by hunger that he would put his elbows on the table and begin forthwith to tell his latest lie.

Here he was, on the march, shouting and talking and walking all at the same time, since he could neither think nor talk in any other way.

He promised himself that he would send a sensational report to the newspapers, just as soon as possible, describing in detail the terrible event which had driven the people of Yangana out into the untamed jungle.

What a story that would be, if he managed to tell all that he had seen, all that he had heard or believed he had heard, all that he had done or believed he had done!

(42)

Next came Agustín Carrasco, tobacco grower and a fastidious, exacting smoker.

He was the best grower in the whole region, no doubt about that. He cultivated his own little patches so as to enjoy the luxury of smoking tobacco that he himself had planted and processed. He was, in consequence, the bitterest enemy of the official tobacco monopoly from the first day it was established by the Treasury.

His whole life—including the youthful years which are usually so full of romantic distractions—had been devoted to perfecting the art of tobacco culture. His object was to savor the delight of smoking it himself and to satisfy his professional vanity when he listened to the fulsome praise of knowledgeable smokers.

As a result, he was the ideal grower, since he handled the tobacco from seed to smoking. Connoisseurs said that anybody who paid close attention to what Carrasco did would wind up an expert in the whole science of tobaccology. But owing to the last few years of monopoly by the state and of apprehensive clandestine cultivation on his part, his plantings were no longer extensive. On the contrary, he grew only what he needed for his own use, nothing more except four or five rows to give his friends an occasional whiff of aromatic smoke.

When it was time to plant his patch—his little hidden patch—he looked for a quiet hollow, sheltered from the wind. The soil had to be light and sandy with a good proportion of humus. It needed spading and turning several times to loosen it up properly.

The carefully selected seed was started in a seed bed. As soon as the sprouts were big enough he transplanted them with a touch as delicate as a watchmaker's and tended them with almost passionate care as they slowly grew. He walked round and round the little plot many times each day, examining the plants one by one. He spoke to them as he counted the new shoots. One of his proudest moments would come when he could show some of his close friends a piece of land where, eight days after transplanting, not a single little plant had wilted.

How well he understood these things!

He knew how to manage so that the leaves should grow neither too long nor too broad. "Nothing longer than forty centimeters or broader than twenty-five—that's the formula," he would assert.

He knew how to prepare and regulate the application of fertilizers, avoiding those with too much nitrate since they would produce leaves with thick ribs and veins.

He knew how to hill up the plants after first forking them all round.

He knew that the lower leaves, the ones touching the ground, were of bad quality and should be pulled off.

He knew the right time to nip off the tops of the plants, at the delicate stage when the buds appear. For this he preferred the quiet hours of early morning or late afternoon.

He knew when the changing color of the leaf was telling him that harvest time had come.

He knew how to select the mature leaves as he cut them, choosing only the best.

He knew how to arrange the mature leaves on their way from field to drying place.

He knew how to hang the leaves on a cord stretched between two poles, so that they caught every breeze.

He knew how long the turbulent orgy of fermentation should last with the microorganisms reveling in the company of chlorophyll, carbohydrates and starch.

He knew how to regulate the chemistry of fermentation so as not to exceed the proper temperature.

He knew when it was time to take the tight bundles of fermented leaves, spray them with an aromatic mist flavored with wild honey, and give them the final "waxing."

And last of all, he knew how to wrap up these tobacco leaves—leaves so sweet smelling, almost intoxicating with their tarry flavor, so supple and so pungent. He made them up into big cylindrical rolls of tobacco firmly compressed and bound with cords of *pasalla* bark.

Then came the moment of real delight, and how well it had been earned!

The famous *huanlla*—the roll—with its long slender body and the two round black heads was to be decapitated and cut up into little pieces. The chopping block and the sharp heavy knife were waiting for it, first to slice it into thin rounds and then to fine-cut it.

Before long all the toil and trouble, the sweat, the anxious hopes, the slashing work of the knife were converted into a cloud of smoke which enveloped the dogged head of 'Don Agustín Carrasco.'

He drew deep breaths as if resting from a long day's work. He was relaxed after all his efforts. His eyes were half shut, he spat freely and gave himself up to daydreams.

That was the moment when, with a touch of appropriate elaboration, he summed up his own character.

"My friends," he would say to the guests invited to sample the first fruits of the crop, "I am nothing but a man who smokes—really, that's all I am. I was married between cigarettes. While lighting a cigarette, I became a widower. The worst things in my life have happened to me in the pause between one cigarette and another. That's why I know I shall die when I stop smoking. And I shall stop smoking when I die."

His friends had often heard this self-interpretation and said nothing to contradict it. Some among them, in fact, shared his opinion that for many people life is nothing but a comfortable place where you can smoke delicious cigarettes, a spot well supplied with tobacco where you can spend your time dreaming, with half-shut eyes, in a haze of smoke.

(43)

Next came Doña Justa Carrero—Señorita Justa—considered a living saint.

She did not look like a saint. Don Vicente Muñoz could not pardon her for looking so healthy, so worldly, so bourgeois.

"A saint," he affirmed, "should be thin, slight, anemic and feeble. Her hands should be pale and cold. She should speak in a low, sepulchral voice. She should walk with her eyes on the ground. She should have a rosary between her fingers. She should eat little and poorly. She should think of her body as the unclean prison of her immortal soul, not to be adorned but rather to be looked on with infinite scorn and loathing. Day and night she should think only of God and of life beyond the grave. She should frequent the church and the confessional. Her knees should be calloused. She should be chaste, absurdly chaste, even in thought. She should wear a hair shirt under dirty old clothes. She should be devoid of any sexual attraction. She should be incapable of offending anyone's ears with a lie or a rude word. Finally, either her intellectual faculties must be almost non-existent or she must be definitely unbalanced to have entered a profession neither hygienic nor graceful!"

"But here we have a person," he would say, summing up her case, "who meets none of these requirements that I consider indispensable. She is plump robust, ruddy, thickset. She married young and has had several handsome children who are proof of the pleasure she took in reproduction. When she amuses herself—for she does amuse herself when she feels like it—she does it openly, body and soul with wholehearted merriment. She looks you in the eye, doesn't mind a joke, and is not shocked by the frailties of others. Nor does she spend all her time kneeling on the bricks of the church floor or in the confessional. She dresses neatly and looks as if she washed and bathed regularly. And in spite of all this, my friends, we consider her a saint!"

"All that she really is," he would continue, "is a very correct and proper person. An excellent woman, worthy of the highest praise. Let's try to define and analyze what makes her a saint."

"Can it be because she puts up with her husband's drinking bouts? No, other women suffer the same thing. Can it be because she has never quarreled with her mother-in-law? No, she's never had a mother-in-law, since her husband was an orphan. Can it be because she has always said to a person's face what she would also say behind that person's back? No, some of us are as frank as she is without enjoying the same reputation. Can it be because she has known how to bring up her children properly? No, since that means nothing more than being a good mother or a good father. Can it be because she has never been jealous of her husband? Hombre! Perhaps that's why! Or because she has never told a lie? Perhaps for that. Or because she's not inquisitive, nor interested in other people's affairs? Ah! That may be it! That may be what makes her a saint."

"Now, my friends," he would conclude, "We must sum it all up. Who of us, poor sinners that we are, can claim such a total? Granted that between all of us we can combine our individual virtues to reach the same level of morality. But she...she has them all and at the same time. What's more, she withstood for years the blandishments and assaults of Shameless Carlos who at the time was in the prime of life. Who of you, my friends, could have withstood such a thing and come out the winner?"

"At this point the guffaws of Don Vicente's audience made him pause. When they had quieted down he gave his final observations in a different tone of voice.

"She dignifies her surroundings wherever she may be. The moment she appears, the conversation shifts and begins to treat of higher, purer and, more serious matters. Language improves, there are no more off-color jokes and the company is to a certain extent refined just by her presence. Big Mouth Camilo, for example, doesn't open his lips, he sits up properly and almost seems to be in a trance. When drunks catch sight of her, they stop drinking and talking nonsense. People attending a wake remember where they are and behave accordingly."

"Wherever she goes, she brings with her sanity, direction and moderation no matter what disorder or confusion she finds there. If there's a brawl or quarrel, she stops it on the spot. When you see her, you want to do a kindness or to be useful to somebody. My friends, when you've been at some meeting that was getting out of hand, have you heard a shout, 'She's coming! She's coming!?' Everyone feels small, very small, as if caught by a stern father in some despicable act such as robbing a beggar. In an instant composure is restored and people look at each other, perhaps ashamed of what they have been saying and doing. And this, my friends, all this is something that can be achieved only by saintliness. Montalvo used to say about this, apropos of the parish priest of Santa Engracia......" and so saying he would embark on a new commentary on Montalvo, in order to make it clear that he himself was enchanted by the stout figure of the saint and that by no possible means could he be suspected of laughing at her.

(44)

Next came Big Mouth Camilo Isidro, the man with the most offensive vocabulary in Yangana.

He was a tall spindly character with a weak frame and a certain natural delicacy of movement. When greeting people, he took off his hat with a ceremonious air, a gesture which seemed to mark him as somebody with perfect manners.

But it was another matter to hear him talk.

If you answer his courteous salutation with a similar one of your own, you will really hear something. He will reply thus, "........."

If you are exasperated and neglect to answer his morning greeting the next day, he will vilify you saying, "........."

If you try to win him over by inviting him to share a glass of Rosita Sandoya's best anisette, he will accept, thanking you like this, "........."

If you agree to do him a favor which he has begged of you, he will thank you in these terms "........."

If you refuse to be of service to him on the grounds that a man who uses such language does not deserve to receive the slightest consideration from you, he will repay you with, "........."

Here he comes now with his face tied up in an immense dirty handkerchief. He is suffering from an agonizing toothache which he interprets as a sign that one of his mistresses must be pregnant.

Dare to ask him how he feels and he'll employ the most select words and phrases in his repertory to answer, "………"

(45)

The last ten travelers were disabled in various ways.

Asunción Medina, first cousin of the butcher with the innumerable offspring. He was paralyzed, the result of an unbridled honeymoon. Policarpo Alvarado, crippled years before when a beam from a bridge under construction had fallen and cut off both his legs. In spite of this frightful calamity he remained undaunted, acknowledged by everybody to be a vigorous day laborer who was not afraid of pick or shovel, and he was also a good horseman. Antonio Masa, a pure Indian from the mountains who had learned to cut his hair short and wear long trousers and had lost his right hand in a sugar mill. Doña Mercedes Guabán who walked almost on all fours owing to an injured spine. Doña Teresa Tenemasa whose coffee-colored goitrous throat was covered with lumps as big as *chirimoyas*. Agustín Fierro, one of Don Lisandro's progeny who had once been a strong man but was now quite disabled. Two huge hernias in his groin gave him a horrible colic every month. Nicanor Bazarán, blinded by smallpox while still an infant.

Three more were invalids too ill to walk or to ride who were carried along on stretchers made of thin poles and shaded by sheets like a tent. One of these sick people was a woman only recently risen from childbirth and who since the first day of the journey had been burning with fever.

A fourth stretcher had been burned with all its covers at the fifth stopping place, since it was no longer needed. The patient who occupied it had died, nobody quite knew from what cause, and he had been buried on the spot, near one of the campfires which had been lit on the newly cut path. A rough cross of green wood had been shaped with a machete and on it José Angel Maridueña, using a piece of charcoal and in his beautiful lettering, had traced the initials M.O. since Matías Ortega was the name of the first victim since leaving Yangana.

To sum it all up, what was coming on the move was perhaps a true cross section of humanity; a compressed and abbreviated world in which vices and virtues, good or bad temperaments and aptitudes, the grandeurs and miseries of man; conduct, thought, and action; hunger, reluctance to die, fear, hate and love—all were represented.

All ages were there. The old and the young, adults, children, nursing babes. Men and women; beauty and ugliness; Whites, Indians and Mestizos; Mulattos, Zambos and Blacks; thin people and fat people; tall and short; thieves and devout women, illiterates and musicians, house builders and gravediggers; handsome girls and deformed bodies; drunkards and braggarts; quacks and inks lingers; the unbalanced and the blockheads; optimists and skeptics. Broad brows and narrow brows; black eyes, brown, blue, green and steel colored eyes; gay and sparkling eyes; somber eyes, eyes yellowed by jaundice; bloodshot eyes. Soft skins and wrinkled skins; hairy skins and smooth skins; cool skins and hot skins; sweaty skins, delicate skins, rough skins. Mouths without teeth, thick lips, thin lips, harelips, lips that were rosy or pale or dry...

The odor from this mass of human bodies, sweating, dirty, soaking wet—was dominated by the sometimes exciting, sometimes pungent, sometimes repugnant smell of armpits. Mingled with it on the line of march was the smell of fresh cut branches, rotting leaf mold, the hides of pack animals and of earth trampled by hundreds of hooves and soiled by dung from the jostling herds.

A nascent society was slowly slipping and struggling along as the machetes opened a path through the jungle. It was a society driven forward by an explosive will to conquer or die.

(46)

Joaquín Reinoso's senses had not deceived him after all.

Night had almost fallen before he was within gunshot of the traveler's camp. A whole community was coming.

No sooner did they catch a glimpse of Reinoso's campfire in the shadows of the ravine, and hear the distant sound of the river, than they gave a great cry of wild joy, shouting the words, "Palanda! Palanda! Palanda!" over and over again in an impassioned chant.

For a good while longer, the more emotional ones kept on with their hoarse refrain, "Palanda! Palanda! Palanda!"

Joaquín Reinoso crept slowly forward, crouched down, hidden by darkness and the thick tree trunks. He tried desperately to recognize the first groups which he could hardly see. But it was no use. He would have to wait until the first fires were lighted; the order to do so had only just been given.

A little later he could make out that Curly Ocampo seemed to be the man in charge. He could easily recognize Curly Ocampo, his boyhood friend, his companion in scrapes and escapades back there in Yangana, who later on and up to a few years ago had worked with him in the gold mines at Curipamba. And Curly Ocampo was evidently obeyed by the others, who also were from Yangana.

For he was the one who sent off a gang of men to cut enough firewood to last all night.

For he was the one who ordered another group to feed the hungry herds of animals.

For he was the one who gave orders to prepare food.

For he was the one who forbade the drinking of a swig of rum or strong chicha to celebrate the joyous fact that they were only half a day's march from their journey's end at Palanda.

For he was the one who like a commander-in-chief of an army began to make the rounds of all these groups to ensure that his orders had been carried out.

It was Joaquín Reinoso's town, people whom he considered his own, who were coming!

The frightful tension of the past two days, the fear of an unknown danger, had given way to a state of bewildered rejoicing.

It was enough to strike him dead from pure amazement. The whole thing seemed so ridiculous, so unlikely, that he kept thinking he was dreaming. Had all the inhabitants of Yangana gone mad? What fly had stung them all, everyone of them, and driven them in a body to this isolated spot? Should he present himself to this band of crazy people, tell them who he was, and offer to take them to the river where he had his house, his little farm and his garden? And what sort of food supply would they have with them? Weren't they about to fall on him like a plague of locusts and devour the fruits of his labor?

And his wife who was waiting for him alone in the night, what might she be thinking when he had neither returned nor given the signal they had agreed upon? Could he manage to find his way back through the pitch dark forest and reach home at daybreak, give her a reassuring whistle and tell her the extraordinary but encouraging news that he had just seen all the people that you would see in the square at Yangana on a holiday? Could he say that they were headed toward the little house that the two of them had there in Palanda, just to pay them a friendly visit and at the same time sweep up all that the young couple had planted in their forest clearing?

Was it a reason to rejoice?

Was it a threat of starvation?

Was it a deadly peril?

INTERLUDE

The Drunken Hymn to the Seeds

Gordillo, the dropout agronomist, was watching over the huge load of seeds that Don Eliseo Aliaga had brought with him. The thought struck him that in view of all that might happen, something should be done to maintain the indescribable joy felt by the travelers of the exodus at the sight of the promised land. The flickering light from Joaquín Reinoso's campfire down in the hollow seemed to be calling Gordillo and to inspire him with an irresistible craving to "find myself next to a jug" as he liked to say. But Curly Ocampo, that stern commander of the expedition, had forbidden drinking in camp.

Don Eliseo Aliaga had brought with him a large gourd of the very best and strongest chicha, which he used—oh cruel fate!—to rub on the nostrils, ears and feet of the animals to prevent exhaustion. If only he, Gordillo, could manage to slither toward the coveted vessel without being seen!

"The God of the Drinkers is on my side; he too is traveling with us," he exclaimed to himself when Don Eliseo Aliaga told him to keep good watch while he left the camp site for a moment. In five seconds Gordillo had filled his own bottle-gourd and carefully put it against the root of a big tree. Then he put his lips to the mouth of the gourd, tipped it up toward the dense treetops and took a long long pull.

When Don Eliseo returned, stumbling over the roots and opening his eyes as wide as he could to see where he was going, he noticed an unmistakable smell of spilled liquor in the cool damp air of the forest night.

"It looks as if my gourd has tipped over and is spilling," he said to himself and went to straighten it up. He found it well corked but on shaking it, he may have noticed that it was lighter since he exclaimed as if he meant to be heard, "Hum!"

And thought no more about it.

Joaquín Reinoso was hiding close by, right behind the sacks of seeds covered by saddle blankets and sweat cloths from the pack animals. He had witnessed the whole scene and felt like laughing and knocking over Gordillo's bottle. But he had seen this young man's face before and might be recognized if he came out. It was better to lie low.

As for Gordillo, he soon reached the stage when he could no longer contain his joy. He looked around in all directions in search of someone he could trust not only to share his jubilation, but to share it with the same uproarious feelings. He had to bite his tongue to keep from talking, from shouting, from declaiming even before the whole world. He felt a rush of warmth all through his arms. To his blurred vision, Curly Ocampo and his high moral standards had slipped a notch.

The level of liquor in his bottle had also gone down.

All of a sudden Gordillo seemed to have made up his mind. Without hesitation he approached the austere Don Eliseo.

"Listen, Papá Eliseo," he said "For God's sake, do me a favor."

"Speak up, boy, and not so close to my face or you'll make me drunk."

"What I want to ask of you, Papá Eliseo, is that you listen to me."

"I'd sooner listen to you than smell you," he answered.

"The fact is, Papá Eliseo, that I want you to hear my song of the seeds."

Don Eliseo shrugged his shoulders.

"Than I can sing it, Papá Eliseo? Yes, I'll sing it. Because if I don't sing it this very moment I'll die. I'll die as sure as God's in his heaven. Here goes!"

So began the tipsy song of the seeds, chanted by Gordillo, the half-crazy bohemian dropout from the School of Agronomy—a song which Joaquín Reinoso had to listen to whether he wanted to or not, and which ran thus:

"First of all this crazy man must sing to you, oh seed of mirth, the mellow chicha made of sprouted seeds and which have made a crazy man more crazy, more talkative and more of a nuisance."

"Understand it well, this crazy fellow no longer cares if Curly Ocampo, the tyrant of the camp, punishes him severely, nor does he care if he wakes up poisoned by alcohol and with a tongue dry as cotton. He'll surely find a new supply of nourishment. For the moment the crazy man is squandering that fictitious merriment that is ready to his hand, the spendthrift is wasting tomorrow's harvest. He knows this but hardly gives it a thought! The seeds are here in the sacks and the saddlebags and it's easy to hear them germinating in this warm climate."

"Crazy Gordillo has been reflecting on the road that this precious load which has been entrusted to Papá Eliseo Aliaga is bringing an unknown seed to the new land, the virgin land. Have you heard the sound of the seeds jingling along in their saddlebags? Haven't you heard the music of dry grains rattling against the lining of the bags as the animals go trotting by?"

"For some days now the crazy man has been your friend. He too is an unlucky lonely man who is part of the future that awaits you. For you are also the beginning of life itself! And the crazy man should bless the cause of eloquent mirth which makes him run the risk of punishment and talk out loud from this pile of seeds that Papá Eliseo Aliaga is guarding. And now let's see if the crazy man truly understands how the power and potency of this sacred chicha is born into the world. Would you like to know?"

"So be it! So be it!"

"Each grain of corn contains the germ of a hundred foolish words uttered by a drunken mouth. In a moist atmosphere, one hundred percent humid, the grain of corn, white, glassy, polished hard as an ivory tooth, feels dark forces stirring in its entrails. A sharp pain stabs it—you remember what it's like to lose a tooth?—and it tries to scratch itself, kicking and struggling like an animal stuck in the mud. It breaks open its shell and puts out a little arm, a little white arm which wriggles to calm the itch. The arm grows and if it can find something to hold on to, it changes into a stalk. It reaches an immense size, like a lance standing straight up with its plumes and ribbons waving stiffly. Seven months later, the tooth that has fallen on the ground has produced an ear of corn full of new teeth."

"I beg you, black Vilela, don't allow the little white arm to grow too big! What the crazy man likes is to drink the seeds! You are the one who controls their destiny while they are still sprouting. Corn ready for brewing! Oh corn now split in half with your entrails spilling out, you are committing a crime against nature, far from the deep earth! The vat where you are fermenting is hot to the touch. It is clear that you are indignant at being deprived of the earth where you should be taking root. Next they submerge you in great pots of water with a little sugar where you continue to suffer, and they make you give up all that you have in body and soul."

"In big-bellied earthenware pots as big as wine skins, some fellows are waiting, little fellows, very little chaps. They are waiting for the liquor to cool and while they wait they are incubating the mirth of man. Blessed art thou, Mother of all fermentation!"

"After three days the chicha begins to make a bubbling sound. It is belching merriment! That's how the crazy man finds it where it is hidden. The corks are popping out. It sparkles, it has a tang, it is spiritous and spiritual, heavy, tasty and kindly. Those invisible little insects, those little people, have given us ready made joy!"

Fires were being lit at the campsite nearby and the stinging smoke from partly burned green branches drifted through the trees. The drunken orator's eyes began to water. He looked all round, coughed a little, assumed that a rapt audience of farmers was listening to him behind the smoke, and went on with his theme:

"And now that the crazy man is merry thanks to the work and kindness of the corn chicha which he has been drinking in a private place, he will also praise barley, his unpretentious companion when he is hungry. Yellowing fields that seem at first like a sea of gold! He has sowed barley, too, his feet sinking to the ankles in the furrow behind the lumbering oxen. He has broadcast handfuls of seed high in the air, throwing them against the wind and into the future. He has done this in September when the corn has been harvested and piled in shocks or stored in cribs, where only dry and brittle stalks remain in the fields. You grow, oh little rough barley, in the cold of the high slopes of Yangana, up on the mountain ramp that leads to the sky. You don't need burning air and hot water like your cousin rice.

"The crazy man has known you since you were a little girl, barley kin! You begin as a feeble sprout, a shoot like a hair pushing up its little thread out of the ground. A little later, you can be touched with the fingers, my little delicate friend, half-opened, swollen, unbound, already turning to malt. Thin rough leaves appear on you. Soon you are pubescent and the ear begins to form its knot of little bristles to protect the nascent grains like a wire fence. Whoever squeezes one of those soft grains between his fingers will see a stream of milky juice burst out—milk not yet clotted into albumen. The crazy man loves to pull off the full grown spikes and slip them upside down under a girl's skirts. The ear immediately starts to climb up, helped by its rough coat, and goes on climbing and caressing with each movement of the girl's body."

"After the harvest comes the great yellow shock of sheaves. Next the sheaves are untied and the stalks are spread out on the threshing floors. The crazy man grows more impudent among the treading horses on the bare threshing floors. That's where he has made love to the girls, tumbling them on heaps of chaff. The only witness was the impassive pile of grain which had been swept by rough brooms into the middle of the floor. The straw, too, lends itself to serve as a mattress for nocturnal trysts—straw beaten up like foam by the horses—brittle, trodden down and voluptuous straw."

"Now comes the great moment. The women toast you, little barley corn that you are, in the midst of a black smoke like the smoke made by these worthless cooks who now surround the crazy man. He who takes a handful of the grain while it is still hot can smell the wild wholesome aroma of your toasted little belly. As soon as you are cold, you are loaded in great bags and taken on the road to the mill."

"Then the roasted barley is again heated by the bite of two grindstones and smells marvelously. Behind the old mill with its walls all shot through and perforated by wasps and wild bees, you can hear the rush of foaming water pouring on to the mill wheel."

"Then you leave this noisy place full of sweet smelling white dust and, surrounded by men, women and pack animals, go on to the screening house. Hands rub over the flour, still warm from the mill, scraping the horsehair sieve like a silent but fragrant tambourine."

"The delicious everlasting powder falls through the screen. The crazy man loves this toasted meal even though a handful of the dry dust is enough to shut his mouth for a while. That would stop him from talking about the seeds in the sacks, the sacks where he has just flung himself down."

"And that would be a betrayal of the most sonorous seeds in all creation, the ones which love noise above all else, oh you beans worthy of all praise!"

"Beans! Beans which fill dozens of these sacks, beans to be sown in the land of Canaan. They are merry because they are firework makers. They enjoy the pomp and detonations and salvos in honor of digestion. They inflate the stomach as full as a bladder. Hours later, the bladder, instead of bursting, prefers to vent air loudly. Cover your ears and noses, oh ex-neighbors of Yangana!"

"Beloved beans, tasty, nourishing and scandalous, how-much gunpowder you expend in salvos. But in exchange, how little do you demand of the farmer. You grow in the shade of the corn, you embrace the cornstalks, twisting and turning like love's memory in the heart of a sad widower. You are planted together with corn about October. The crazy man has witnessed your birth, when the rascally linnets with their twittering song and their bibs on their chests swoop down on the furrows and brazenly dig you up with their beaks. You were such a poor little thing then. Buried in the ground like a torn-off testicle, you finally split into two fleshy little wings between which a little neck comes up which later on turns into a leaf. There are times when you are abandoned with nowhere to stretch out your twisting tendrils. That is when you have to crawl on all fours and curl and twine wherever you can, scared and raging like a bitch with pups."

"But there are times, oh Papá Eliseo! oh my friends! When common string beans take it into their heads to compete with broad beans and grow big and flat like a big toe. When one of them assumes this imposing look, he changes his name to horse-bean. He seems to be the bully of the family, with the imbecile and menacing look of a born braggart. He is the Primo Carnera of string beans. There is no doubt that he suffers from a glandular deficiency. The small variety of string bean, the little pretty kind, is preferable, or the *Zarandaja* which has a crest on its back and which—listen well! does not inflate the stomach. That is why no nighttime salvos of heavy artillery are heard in a house where the sleepers have been eating *Zarandajas*!"

"But if you want to harm a young married couple, feed them common beans and cabbage. And cook with onion, plenty of onion. The crazy man knows how to describe it all."

"Cabbage, how he understands her! She's a lazy, evil-minded woman with wide skirts who has come from the cliffs at the edge of the sea to settle in the gardens of America. She's a fat big-bottomed lady with starched and rustling petticoats. She smells of sulphur and provides this same sulphur for the accursed cannon shots that the crazy man talks about."

"And the onion! You have made the crazy man cry as if in pain. He has wept from that pain just as he has wept for his woman and the untimely end of his career. Come hither to the crazy man who knows where you come from and how you behave underground!"

"It's like a mole, Papá Eliseo and friends all! A mole which is shaping a pear below the ground. On the surface it is a nobody: a greenish tube crowned with a little white plummet swaying like a bell in the sunshine! But inside the ground! There the pear is swelling as if with toothache. The bulb is made up of a series of delicate concentric skins growing fleshier near the heart, sometimes red and sometimes white. It looks like a great botanical tadpole spiked through its head, with a few hairs on the outside skull. It smells bad but tastes good! And how bad it smells on your neighbor's or your fiancée's breath! That's why the crazy man always says that the cure for marriage is onions, beans and cabbage."

"Papá Eliseo and friends all, what do you think of that prescription?"

"Now, friends, the botanists have discovered the most unexpected relatives of the onion. First, the sharp toothed little cousin garlic whose aromatic smell is not unpleasing and who is also one of the crazy man's favorites. Then, close to garlic comes the languid lily, the noble in the house, the aristocrat of the family who exhales a marvelous perfume like an elegant lady's handkerchief. And for heaven's sake, what has the smell of garlic to do with the fragrance of a lily? The crazy man is equally happy with the leek, known by its wide trousers shaped like drumsticks, and with the eye-watering onion itself—both of whom are said by those who know to have come from faraway Afghanistan a long, long time ago."

The moment had come when the orator should fix his eyes on his audience and complete the spell. Gordillo straightened up with some difficulty on the pile of sacks and gazed all around with a questioning look before ending his masterpiece.

But Papá Eliseo and a few curious listeners who had originally been laughing at what Gordillo was saying, had by now completely forgotten all the rollicking eloquence and were roasting meat by the light of the fires.

"Please listen, my friends," he cried out to them when he saw he was abandoned, "listen, because the song of the seeds isn't finished yet. The crazy man still has to talk about fruit: about avocados, those green packets of butter which, by the way, I would gladly squash against some noses that are present and absent at the same time. He has to talk about plantains with their thighs swollen by erysipelas and their big golden-gloved hands; about pineapples, oranges and peanuts; about all this Noah's Ark of seeds that we are leading into the future and a new life."

But nobody wanted to go on listening to his song, except Joaquín Reinoso, who was afraid of being discovered if he so much as moved while the stream of eloquence poured out over an audience "with their noses present and absent at the same time."

PART TWO

YANGANA IN ITS AGE OF INNOCENCE

Foreword by The Author

A year before the great exodus, a young gringo had arrived in Yangana. He said he was a North American and that his name was plain Mr. Spark. He remained in Yangana for many months studying the flora of the neighboring hills and forests.

From reliable sources it was learned that what interested him more than anything else was the varieties of *Cinchona* tree. So he had naturally chosen that particular province out of all the provinces of Ecuador, and in that province he had chosen the mountains around Yangana where the best *Cinchona* in the world, the famous *Cinchona Succirubra*, grows freely in its wild state.

He made the town of Yangana his headquarters for exploration, and after roaming and exploring tirelessly through the surrounding woodlands, declared that he had finished his work in the region. One day he told Don Vicente Muñoz, in his by now acceptable Spanish, that he had decided to go eastward to the Amazon and thence downstream to the Atlantic. His idea was to follow the footsteps of the great historical explorers, especially the path taken in the last century by a scholarly and consumptive Englishman whom he greatly admired called Richard Spruce. Spark had added—again according to Muñoz—that this predecessor had left him hardly anything new to say or to study about *cinchona* trees. We shall see later that Spark may have talked about his plans to somebody besides Muñoz.

Some days after making this announcement—something which those in the know said was very painful to him—he set off with a sizeable party of machete-armed bush choppers, guides and a few pack animals. His first point of reference was the course of one of the small tributaries running southeast to the Amazon. The people of Yangana saw the campfire lit by the travelers on the pass of Colambo where they were about to cross the eastern range. Then, the subsequent course of his adventures became a legend in the town where he had stayed for so many days—a legend with ten different versions. For, in fact, nothing definite about him and his travels could ever be found out.

He left behind in Yangana a surveyor's level and some tripods which he considered too cumbersome to take with him, and a number of blank notebooks.

Six blank notebooks and one other......

The following is the text of what the traveler had written in that forgotten notebook. It was found, together with the others, on a table in the Convent at Yangana, his point of departure for the perils of the east. It finally wound up in the files of the Provincial Police headquarters, following an official inquiry by a punitive military force dispatched to what had been—to quote Spark—"The unique and flourishing town of Yangana."

He wrote these words in his careful fountain pen script, with a kind of reticent admiration. Nobody knows for sure the present whereabouts of the Gringo Spark of the

American Museum, although in Yangana people were convinced that he had met a tragic end.

The Author

THE GRINGO SPARK'S FORGOTTEN NOTEBOOK

(1)

A Town of 1500 Inhabitants and a History of over 300 Years

This picturesque little town is already old, but in spite of this, there is no trustworthy account or chronicle of it. It can be deduced from the Parish Baptismal Register of Santa Rosa that Yangana was already a dependent benefice in the 18th Century, at the height of the Colonial Epoch.

It is apparently established that Spaniards from the city of Loja built the first houses and laid out the public square in the customary way in the center of an open space. It was not far from an Indian settlement from which it took the Quechua name it was known by from then on.

In the square they built a massive church of adobe blocks whose solidity enabled it to defy the assaults of time. Before long, the growing little town became a milestone on the road which the Spaniards followed in their search for gold. They were looking for gold-bearing deposits in the regions to the east of Yangana, so the little town served as a convenient operational and supply base. But when the Indians annihilated the most advanced reconnoitering parties, Yangana soon found itself cut off from the world, far from the point of penetration on the frontier and even further from the city.

Even now it takes almost six days march on a rough road to get from here to the city, and that is only when the weather is favorable. If the rivers that you have to cross happen to be in flood, or if the road is muddier than usual, the journey can take twice as long.

A few years ago, the Republic raised the town to the status of a Parish in recognition of its antiquity. An executive decree placed it under the jurisdiction of the Department of Territorial Division, something that would have escaped the notice of the inhabitants had it not coincided with the arrival of an unwelcome intruder—the first Government Commissioner for the Parish.

This first representative of Civil Authority inaugurated an administrative service of the worst kind, which as time went on grew even worse. Those who succeeded him continued the tradition of being totally alien to and uncomprehending of the ways of the community. For, as I have had the opportunity to observe for myself, there is one custom which the authorities of this country never fail to observe: they take great care to pick their subordinates and collaborators from the very people who can do most harm to the society they are called upon to govern.

With such a system it is not surprising that a community which up to then had lacked civil authority should consider the coming of a resident representative of the Central Government a clear disaster. They looked back nostalgically to the time when the national administration, although neglecting the theoretical duties of a guardian, allowed them to live in peace.

The feelings of sympathy which this little town and its people aroused in me have more than once made me feel sorry for them and to some extent consider them as justified in their continuing struggle against those who enforce the law.

(2)

Topographical Description

Yangana lies in the center of an extensive inclined plane shaped like a rough trapezoid. The upper end terminates on the ridge of a mountain range and the two sloping sides are bounded by deep ravines which empty their streams into a river at the foot of the hill. One of these streams, in particular, cascades down in a series of waterfalls which from a distance provide a spectacular sight. Its periodic winter floods have left a truly gigantic cone of debris and have scoured out a great part of the arable bottom land, making it worthless. The other stream, called Fox Creek, although it carries a greater volume, runs slower. This makes it possible to divert a good part of its water for irrigation on the farmlands and pastures surrounding the town. As for springs of drinking water for both man and beast, there are just two in this little town. One wells up behind the church right in the center of Yangana and the other has its source up on the hillside. This one supplies the very best and purest water.

The more turbulent of the two streams, the one which does so much harm to the bottom lands along the river, has been given an expressive name. It is called "Destruction Creek." With this name the good people of Yangana show their opinion of its treacherous ways.

The barometric altitude of Yangana is 1,298 meters or 4,257 feet, according to readings that I took in the square and carefully rechecked four times. As will be seen, the zone is subtropical. Grains can be grown on the side of the mountains, while the land from Yangana down to the river is suitable for tropical crops. The lower you go, the hotter it gets, the soil is damper, the woods denser and the fruits of the earth grow better and larger. But this bottom land of the valley is unhealthy. The people who live along the river have a pale, sickly color and shiver with chronic malaria.

When the townspeople wish to distinguish between the different areas of the surrounding country, they refer to their relative altitudes. They call the part lying between the town and the river, "The Hot Land." It follows that "to go down to the Hot Land," means to go looking for the best crops of sugar cane or plantains and the best tasting and biggest cassava. "To go up the Hill" means to walk over the country where grain is grown, where there are pastures and cattle pens. The town itself and its common lands lie in the middle, at the junction of two distinct climatic systems.

There is a revealing detail concerning the distribution of workable and irrigated lots. The best pieces belong to three landowners from the city, who as a rule manage their property through an overseer while they themselves seldom put in an appearance and then only for a few days.

All the time I have been living in this region, I have only once seen the doors of one of the manor houses open. But this is not all. The inhabitants are unanimous in painting a sinister picture of how these landowners originally obtained their property. They affirm that these men have no legal title, but have arbitrarily occupied town land which since Colonial times was classified as common land. One of the reasons why the landlords so seldom visit their holdings is no doubt that they are aware of the stifled hostility which the townspeople feel for those whom they consider the usurpers of their inalienable rights to the common lands of Yangana.

The river which flows in the background is not what a river might be. Perhaps it should blame itself for paying no attention to the fate of its basin. All of the left bank is parched and sterile. For this reason the inhabitants of Yangana, who have always considered the river as belonging to them, complain that it has thought only about conquering the Andes. They accuse it of forgetting that it should also have worked at building up broad banks of good land with the same materials that it was stripping from its sullen victim, the mountain. And this, without taking into account that its tributary streams, on their way down to join it, covered great tracts of good workable land with rocks torn up by the floods.

In other words, the river below and the landlords above had between them, or so said the townspeople, prevented Yangana from being what it might and should be.

(4)

Appearance of The Town

It has hardly any streets. The houses surrounding the only square are not lined up in wholly symmetrical order. The church, as already noted, is in the square. And behind the church the hillside.

Most of the houses have only one story. Their walls are of compacted mud, lath-and-mud, or adobe blocks. The pounded mud floor is almost always well leveled. There is one medium size, single panel wood door. The roof is generally tiled. As for the few thatched houses, some are roofed with straw thatch brought down from the hills and some with sugar cane leaves.

Under the roof there is a loft or attic accessible from the floor inside. It is constructed of poles of wild cane secured to the hewn beam rafters of the roof. The loft itself is dark and serves as a corn crib. It is reached by a ladder made either of palm poles or wild cane.

The way these houses are built is another illustration of the fertile duality of the climate. Not only in the choice of roofing material—sometimes straw from high up on the mountain and sometimes dry leaves from the cane fields—but also in the varying thicknesses of wall, methods of ventilation and use of construction material. So that in the same place you find buildings typical of both temperate and tropical climates.

The houses usually have two rooms. One serves as common sleeping quarters and living room, and the other, the most important and most used, is the kitchen. In fact, you can say that in these parts the house is really reduced to the kitchen. While the first room is opened only twice a day—once to go to bed and once to get up and go to work—the kitchen is closed only at night.

In most of the houses guinea pigs are raised and kept—a custom adopted from the aboriginal Indians. It is a strange and interesting sight to see them running between people's feet like huge rats. The characteristic, nauseating stench of urine from these herbivorous animals fills the whole house. The little creatures squeal with delight when they hear their owner come in with a bundle of grass and weeds under his arm. They swarm around him tearing and gnawing the leaves, clicking and grinding their teeth. What is more, this troublesome, disgusting rodent does not eat just grass; it eats everything that it finds on the floor of its "pigsty."

The fireplace is at ground level. Three or four big stones called *tulpas* support the earthenware cooking pots. The middle pot contains boiled grain of one kind or another. The other pot, or two pots, contains soup with plantains and more grain or a meat stew.

In the evening, the people of the house sit around these great black stones eating and talking until bedtime. Only a few houses have dining tables. The cook passes platefuls of food straight to the diners who eat with the plates balanced in their hands or resting on their laps. The diners remain squatted on the floor or sitting on low clay seats which jut out from the wall.

That is how most of the people live. Naturally there are exceptions. Next to a tiny two-room house there may be a large Spanish-style mansion with rectangular patio and a large paved entrance hall. In houses like this you will find plenty of spacious rooms, their wood floors carefully dovetailed and polished, with windows looking out to the street on both sides of the front door. As for the patio, if it does not have a garden with an ornamental pond in the middle, it will boast a pavement carefully and artistically designed. Sometimes they are also decorated with sculptured arabesques carved out of cattle bones.

The furniture in these houses is generally made of cedarwood. A lithograph of the Sacred Heart of Jesus or of Our Lord of Good Fortune usually occupies the place of honor on the drawing room wall. In spite of much elegance, however, there is no plumbing.

But the houses that the people here consider to be the most desirable of all have, in addition to what has just been described, broad brick passageways and a vacant lot behind the back wall. This lot is closed in by an extra high mud wall and provides space for a fruit and vegetable garden, a pig pen and a hen house. All kinds of household tools and cleaning materials are also stored there. It is sometimes a shame to see how the barnyard fowls have converted beautiful fruit trees into a filthy roosting place with their nightly droppings. Sanitation is not the strong point of this community that has been so kind to me.

(5)

Diet

The daily fare usually consists of two dishes—one based on meat and the other on cheese. The first is a kind of stew made of fresh or salted meat, cracked bones, red annato seeds for color, lard, salt and spices. Add pieces of green plantains and slices of cassava. Sometimes a handful of rice and, more often, some cabbage leaves. Just before taking the pot off the fire, throw in some freshly picked oregano. This dish is the mainstay of the local diet.

The second is a soup of various grains and legumes called *moteporoto*. It is very thick, based on cheese, beans, boiled corn, peas, small pieces of green bananas, rough-ground parched barley, plenty of milk and lard and, on occasion, watery rice cooked with smoked cheese curds.

The unfailing accompaniment of these two dishes is "The Boil," which could perhaps be figuratively described as a real institution. A great earthenware dish or pot is smoking in the center of the table—in those houses which have a dining room—or where there is no dining room, then in the center of the circle of diners squatting on the floor. This pot contains boiled corn, great swollen yellow grains like bursting acorns; or else slices of cassava root split from end to end along the tough central core, boiled with a little salt and sprinkled with crumbs of fresh cheese which soon melt into rubbery strings.

Or there might be a bowl of roasted barley ground into sweet smelling yellow meal to be dropped by handfuls into the broth of the second dish. This produces a thick *chapo* or mush with the grains imbedded in it like candied berries. Or there might be half a sack of avocados waiting to be opened by the hands and knives of the diners, the seeds tossed into the patio or to the guinea pigs.

Again, half-ripe plantains roasted on the hearthstones or scorched skin and all, in hot ashes. Or again, the *molloco* of green plantains cooked in the skin and ground up with roasted peanuts on the big millstone by the bench at the door.

There are times, too, when these "boils" are enriched with great strips of sun dried meat or pork crackling. As for bread—the wheat bread which for us is a basic food—there is not a sign of it. In these parts it is an article of luxury. Yet for us the very word means food. "Our daily bread" is for us what fills our stomachs and wards off hunger.

After March, when new crops begin to come in, the daily fare is more varied. The second of the main dishes is seasoned with coriander and garden stuff. Steaming green corn bares its little teeth from the bottom of the pot; you can enjoy the most tender of new beans, green peas peep out temptingly from their beds of white rice; while *achogchas*—split open zucchinis—float in the broth looking like bits of dead rats.

This is the time of year when juicy summer squashes and cucumbers hang on every fence; when the hillside pumpkins, big-bellied as cows, swell up like balloons under rain and sun. The striped valley pumpkins bring their rosy meat to perfection in the shade of century plants, and the *zambo* gourds, sweet and juicy as watermelons, grow large inside their glassy shells. The men who live here lay hands on all these members of the *cucurbitaceae* family and cut open their stomachs as if slaughtering sheep.

After the two main dishes and the "boil" there is always a little dessert. This final sweet is sometimes rice pudding with milk and syrup; or it may be barley mush fried in lard and brown sugar; or cream cheese and syrup; or squash cooked in milk with all its delicious seeds; or marvelously sweet slices of just cooked valley pumpkin; or, simplest of all, half a loaf of coarse brown sugar by itself or with roasted peanuts.

And on holidays, or when there are guests, nothing is easier than to grab some of the barnyard hens by the neck, or look for eggs in their nests, or catch one or two of the guinea pigs squeaking or scurrying about in the kitchen, or the young goat that is trying to get out of its pen. Then there is the fattening pig who eats all the garbage behind the house; the young bullock grazing in the stubble. In short, these good folk have a whole great larder at their disposal.

But they also say that for them the poorest of meals is compensated for by coffee at the end, just as the other side of the coin is that there can be no good meal without coffee. Their method of preparing coffee is not identical with the Arab practice, although it is very like it. They call it here "frightened coffee," no doubt because the grounds are boiled directly in the water until about to boil over, when cold water is brutally added. This almost immediately shoots the grounds to the bottom and stops the furious bubbling up. Brown sugar is added when the boiling point is first reached and the resulting brew is black, very strong and bitter, and unbelievably fragrant. They really enjoy their "frightened coffee," savoring it in great swallows.

(6)

Clothing

What is worn every day must be considered apart from what is worn on Sundays. The first of these two categories shows—as does everything in Yangana—the simultaneous influence of cool highland and hot lowland. These differences of climate interact to such an extent that it is difficult to describe.

The people in better circumstances wear cotton clothes at work: canvas or Peruvian drill trousers, a poplin or linen shirt next to the skin, and underdrawers of the same material. At dusk, when the air turns cool and the day's work in the field is over, they wrap themselves in the ample folds of a poncho, woven either of cotton or of heavy wool with colored stripes. Some people just put on a jacket over their work shirts. Everybody wears a hat either of ordinary palm leaf or of barley straw woven into decorative fringes and curlicues. As for their feet, most of them wear *Ozhotas* or rough rawhide sandals they have made themselves.

A few of them wear shoes every day while others go completely barefoot except when they have to cut their way through all kinds of thorny trees, bushes, briars and thistles in the woodland.

Sundays are a really colorful occasion. The townspeople can often be seen sporting trousers of good English woolen cloth, patent leather shoes and starched shirts with butterfly collars. Some of them enjoy showing off a vest since vests are unbelievably popular. For anybody with city tastes, it seems downright ridiculous to see the vainglorious men of Yangana in their vests and freshly blocked hats with ponchos instead of jackets draped over their top quality cloth waistcoats.

To be sure, you can also find men who dress in a style that could be called quiet and unobjectionable. They wear a three-piece worsted suit. The shoulders of the jacket are neatly ironed and the cuffs of their perfectly creased trousers fall on a superb pair of Russian leather shoes. They wear a felt hat and it is not unusual for them to flourish a silver mounted cane of carved hardwood.

Well-dressed riders can also be seen parading the streets on a Sunday, showing off their mules with their silver trappings. Riding breeches and boots are indispensable. Decked out this way, they attend sporting events or cockfights riding spirited mounts. Their horses or mules are left tied at the door of the cockpit, just as they are tied in front of a fiancée's house, or at the saloon, or at the colonnades of the central square. These gentlemen also take care to display their handguns in richly ornamented holsters with a belt full of shells.

As for the women, it's cotton for daily wear and silk or fine cloth for parties or holidays. The length of the dress varies according to age. Those who are over thirty wear ankle length skirts. Younger girls show more or less of their legs depending on their parents' rules. No criticism about clothes can be leveled at the girls who have just finished their education in the city, except that as the years go by they wear the same Sunday clothes they brought with them on their return home. So that as far as city tastes go, these ladies are a living anachronism with clothes long out of style. But in Yangana, of course, they are still the latest word and will long remain so.

Young women who could be called nice middle class girls always wear shoes with cotton stockings up to their knee. When they "go out of the house" they cover their heads and shoulders with a black shawl of silk or fine wool and often put on a good cloth dress. They don't use face powder or rouge or lipstick and never pluck their eyebrows. The only cosmetic they use is soap and water.

If they're just visiting a neighbor, or on some routine errand such as going to the mill or placing an order with the carriers to the city, they throw a soft, brightly striped woolen shawl over their white or colored cotton house dress. Some of these shawls are heavily embroidered with really beautiful patterns. They don't cover their heads or bother to change anything except perhaps to put on high heeled shoes in order to look taller.

Middle aged or elderly women wear the most heterogeneous garb in the village. It is influenced not only by economic inequality, but even more by social status and background. A barefooted woman may pass you in the street wearing a *centro* or short flannel dress of some solid color, tied at the waist and adorned with a wide hem or "sweeper" which trails on the ground.

Next you see a *follona*, meaning a woman with flannel petticoats. She wears a wide skirt of smooth, soft imported flannel, a linen blouse with red embroidery at wrist and shoulders, and a fine kerchief spun and woven in the province of Azuay. Further on, you may see a very dressy lady walking by in expensive spike heeled shoes, her starched petticoats and bodice rustling and squeaking like great cabbage leaves.

Here I must mention in passing a piece of information which may sound frivolous, but which can be easily verified. When the women of Yangana reach the age of forty, they no longer wear underdrawers. Let the sociologists find the answer to this perhaps not so innocent riddle.

And another item which is perhaps unimportant, but is certainly fact: the women of Yangana—all of them—seem to take very great pleasure in heavy gold rings and gold necklaces studded with pearls. It is not unusual to come across really valuable precious stones set in pieces of jewelry made with excellent taste by the silversmiths of Yangana. After all, however, the women of Yangana are not exceptional in their love of jewelry.

(7)

Hospitality is the Rule Here

I have just finished writing the above chapter heading and it sounds as though I am about to describe a Utopia. Nevertheless, if I use the word Utopia in this particular respect, I am not exaggerating. The people of Yangana are amazingly hospitable. They have no conception of such a thing as an inn or a hotel. A stranger must lodge in somebody's house, not as a boarder, but as a guest. Neither bed nor board will cost him a cent. The same applies, naturally, to his mount.

If you are a foreigner and start to look for lodging for travelers, you will be wasting your time. On approaching the town, your porter or guide will ask you where you are going to "dismount." The only place where a stranger can "dismount" is at somebody's house—somebody who will receive him not as a customer but as a friend. And when you leave, don't be so stupid or rude as to ask what you owe for the meals and lodging provided for you. These good people would truly resent it. That would suggest that the hosts were mercenary, when on the contrary they really enjoyed helping their fellow human beings in this way.

By the same token, they will some day expect you to do as much for them. It is a fact that they take it for granted that this kind of hospitality is reciprocal. You are obliged to receive the homeowner in your house, if the occasion arises, just as you were received in his. For example, if my good friends from Yangana were to visit the East Side of New York City, they would not dream of looking for a hotel. No Sir! They would go straight to my apartment. They would "dismount" at my doorstep. Just think what New York or London would be like if this were a universal custom.

Another point in their mores is this. If the transient lodger repeats his visit, he incurs an unspoken obligation to take a gift to the householder. A consequence of this is that when people go on a trip to the city, they take special care to fill a saddlebag with suitable presents. These include such things as loaves of brown sugar wrapped in plantain bark; little gourds full of guava jelly; avocados when in season; the best oranges they can find, and top quality sun dried meat. However demanding the recipient may be, you can be sure that he or she will be more than satisfied with these varied but carefully chosen gifts.

I have been assured that the concept of hospitality is so warm and all embracing that it includes a guarantee of safety and protection in case of assault for both the person and the property of a guest. I admit, however, that up to now the circumstances of my life here have not given me a chance to test the truth of this assertion. And I do believe that given the extraordinarily high moral character of these good people, it would be rare indeed for them to be so blinded by feelings of violence as to forget a duty which they have always spontaneously recognized.

(8)

Means of Communication

What this region suffers from more than anything else is the total lack of roads. The whole province is affected by the resulting inevitable isolation.

The town is about sixty miles from the provincial capital and it takes four, five, or six days to cover this distance over a wretched trail which was originally roughly paved with stone. More often than not, as I have said before, it takes the full six days. There is only one bridge in the whole stretch of this so-called road. In winter, both riders and mounts risk their lives fording a series of torrential rivers in full flood.

So, when the people of Yangana go to the city, or on a business trip to the neighboring republic to the south, they have to make daily forced marches in order to reach a *tambo* or post house where they can spend the night. Once there, they can sleep under a roof, sheltered from the almost certain nightly rain, not to mention other discomforts too numerous to catalog.

The *tambo* is a holdover from an excellent pre-colonial Inca system. The building consists of a miserable shack, almost always uninhabited, standing at the side of the road near a stream. Livestock can be tethered in a little open space furnished with stout hitching posts. Behind the little shack there is usually an abandoned field of sugarcane and an overgrown patch of grass where the traveler can find free fodder for his beasts. And in the combined kitchen and sleeping quarters he has to cook his evening meal from rations he has brought with him.

For this reason, anybody who plans a trip in these parts will do well to learn how to cook unless he is prepared to hire a guide-carrier to keep him company, since these carriers all have to know how to cook as part of their work.

In the case of inhabited *tambos* the novice has no great problem since he finds there a welcoming and understanding innkeeper who is a competent *tambero*. But experienced travelers have also worked out among themselves a tacit arrangement to make up for the tremendous deficiencies in uninhabited *tambos*. Each one or each party on quitting the *tambo* leaves behind whatever might be useful to the next wayfarer. A box of matches, tallow candles, dry kindling near the fireplace, cut fodder for the animals—all this will often be found under the roof.

To sum it all up, it is really a shock to discover that the only link between Yangana and the city is a dreadful cobbled trail. It is no exaggeration to say that no repair work of any kind has been done since it was first opened by the Spanish conquerors several hundred years ago. Furthermore, there is no postal service and no telegraph!

As a matter of fact, a good friend of mine of whom I shall speak later on, Don Vicente Muñoz, is the founder and president of an Improvement Committee. This group continually petitions the government for a weekly postal service to and from the city and a telegraph line to put the deserving and productive little town in contact with the rest of the world. Up to now, the only response has been vague promises couched in pompous bureaucratic verbosity.

There is a practice here, however, which does to some extent compensate for the lack of mail service and which is followed with truly religious faith. I refer to the scrupulous and conscientious way in which travelers—and this includes the most humble and stupid-looking carriers—execute "commissions" and collect and deliver letters.

If you give a five-page shopping list and ten or twenty letters to one of these people, you can be quite sure that even if it means delaying his return by a day or two, he will bring back everything that was ordered. It will be in excellent condition and will have been purchased at the lowest possible price. Nor will he charge a cent for all this. He will also bring answers to your letters even if the recipient happened to be out of town at first.

Amazing though it may appear, you must never offer him a fee for his services. But wait a minute! He will even things up later by asking you in turn to do some errands for him. It is a fact that I, myself, have seen carriers clothed in tattered rags deliver a letter to its recipient together with a very considerable sum of money. I have never heard of a case where remittances of this kind have gone astray or been misappropriated, even though they have been handed over without hesitation and without witnesses to people to whom I, as a matter of principle, would never have entrusted a penny.

These carriers have an astonishing ability to remember every detail of a verbal commission. Ten, twelve or fifteen different people may give separate sums of money to a carrier to make purchases for them in the city. When he returns, a week later, they all receive what they ordered without the slightest mistake in amount, quality or description.

But all these virtues do not fill the unforgivable gap resulting from the lack of a postal service in this little town. It is a real penance for me to be obliged to live in these solitudes far away from my own people. Letters from home take fifty or sixty days to reach me. The postmarks show that they reached the, port city of Guayaquil in twenty-four days, more or less. The remaining delay is between Guayaquil and Yangana. From Guayaquil they get as far as the provincial capital and there they stay in the mailbag until such time as a carrier or other traveler asks for them in my name.

The same thing happens with my newspapers and my bulletins from the Foundation. They take as long to come from Guayaquil to Yangana as from the United States to Guayaquil. In an entirely different way, it seems to be as unbelievable as the traditional, admirable hospitality of Yangana. Perhaps I should have brought a short-wave battery radio with me, so as to know, day by day, what is happening in the world. But I did not, and truly regret it......up to a point.

(9)

A Paternal Government

These good people feel an abiding resentment against the national government. They have asked for a state supported mixed school. It has been denied. They have offered to bear the cost of a school once it is authorized and a site designated. It has been denied. They have begged for a weekly mail service. It has been denied. They have begged for a highway to the city. It has been denied. They have begged the Department of Public Works to do something to repair the dreadful old cobbled trail. Denied. They have begged for a telegraph line. Denied. They have begged that two scholarships at the city high school be allotted to students from Yangana. Denied.

The only contribution made by the government was to send them a Commissioner who invariably oppresses them. The excise inspector for the state monopoly of alcohol, tobacco, matches and salt is no better. He is guilty of all kinds of corruption and extortion. He confiscates the shipments of salt smuggled in from Peru and all the home-brewed beer he can find. Add to all this, the unannounced visits of rural property assessors. They look into every corner, take into account the most insignificant articles of personal property, and write everything down in their notebooks.

Soon after the assessors have left, the tax collectors make their appearance shaking demand notices in the householders' faces and insisting on immediate payment because "the taxpayer should help to defray, through both direct and indirect taxation, the expenses of the government which provides so many services."

It is obvious that a government that only collects taxes from Yangana and in return systematically disregards all the complaints of the inhabitants, can justly be described as "delightfully paternal," to quote my good friend Don Vicente.

As for the actual behavior of the Commissioner and its disastrous consequences for the community, it is worth describing in a separate section. It cannot be overemphasized.

(10)

The Commissioner

Although the personal ethical standards of the people of this region are far higher than is usually the case now-a-days, the reverse is true of the administration of justice. Here it is a revolting caricature and a profoundly demoralizing one. I believe that in the end it could corrupt the most honorable society.

I myself have lost no opportunity of speaking to this effect to anybody in this little town who would listen to me, including, of course, the civil authorities. The instinct of these patriarchal communities is very rarely at fault. In this case public opinion is unanimous in declaring that times were better for the parish before the advent of this grotesque masquerade of political and judicial administration. It brought with it innumerable and farcical corruptions, connivances and prevarications.

The people of Yangana had at first hoped that the Commissioner nominated for their town would be one of them, and with this in mind they had submitted a list of the most notable residents to the provincial governor. As a result, the arrival of a total stranger was greeted with looks and feelings of profound dismay.

The new Commissioner found that the so-called "office" designated for his use was totally devoid of official furniture. It consisted then, and still does, of a single rented room in a house overlooking the square. The owner of the building has not received a penny of rent from the government since the office was first opened. The table belongs to one of the neighbors and so does the chair which serves as the seat of civil authority. The rest of the furniture is made up of a slatted bench where people in search of justice, or called before the court, can sit and wait.

Add to this a screen of cotton cloth and a bed where the government functionary can sleep, since he sleeps in the same room where he "administers justice in the name of the Republic and by the authority of the Law." There is no lack of writing materials, however. A rural Commissioner, it seems, can barely sign his name. This void is filled by his secretary, a stranger like himself, who is versed in the art of giving an appearance of legality to every kind of corruption, and who is hated just as much as his superior.

When these two gentlemen need money for their personal needs, they have recourse to an infallible method. They seize the first two or three head of cattle that wander into the square, tie them in front of the Commissioner's office, and keep them there in stocks, so to speak, until the owner appears. Cattle and hogs have always run loose in this town, since it is a community of ranchers and farmers where there is no urban life. As a result it is almost unheard of to invoke the letter of the law and apply police regulations to the owners of these animals, even though it can always be said that laws were made to be observed and that lawbreakers should be punished.

We would say that it depends on how and when. Because it makes one's blood boil to witness judicial rulings shamelessly influenced by every kind of preference, according to the influence and financial position of the litigants. For example, the great neighboring landowners have never been fined for any infraction of the law, just because they are rich and powerful. On the other hand, a poor farmer or laborer whose cow has been impounded by the police has to pay up on the spot, the fine being, of course, divided between the Commissioner and his secretary.

On Saturdays and Sundays it is the drunks who are taken into custody. This produces even more money, since freedom has to be bought for man as well as beast. It is truly disgusting to see how these drunken fellows are sentenced. There they are, piled up asleep on the porch of the Commissioner's office until they are shaken, dragged to their feet, brought more or less to their senses and summarily fined for breaking police regulations—the fine to be paid on the spot. If they pay up then and there, they can go free. If not, they stay there until some relative or friend rescues them.

Something else worth describing is the part played by these authorities in the so-called "electoral process." Since they live in a democracy, elections for local representatives, for national congressmen and senators, and for the Chief Executive must all be by free and secret ballot. The commissioners in rural parishes—including, of course, Yangana—play their part in the procedure. They seem to be bound by a sacred pact with the governor of the province, to ensure the victory of the candidates of the party in power.

The formula is simple. I personally saw how it operated in Yangana. Every day during the legal period set aside for registration, the neighbor's table which we have already heard about is brought out to the portico of the

Commissioner's office together with a number of large hard cover books. The governor had sent these books days ago by means of an express messenger who, we assume, to make better time, came on foot carrying them on his back. The table and the books are taken indoors at the end of the day and produced again the next morning, repeating the process every day until registrations are closed.

The Commissioner is in charge of the whole business in the capacity of registrar, town clerk, and poll watcher. He sits there all day with his elbows on the pile of books. This stage setting and props then disappear for a while to rise again at election time. Strange to say, however, not a soul approaches the table all this time, either first to register his full name and signature or later to cast his ballot during the several days that elections last. Nobody. Nobody would be so foolish.

Why should they? Nevertheless.........every day during elections, a great number of votes are counted and verified. The final count gives a most comforting result. All the candidates endorsed by the provincial governor, on orders from the administration, are elected unopposed and by overwhelming majorities.

The Register of voters is loaded with fictitious names and signatures. As for the ballot slips which the Commissioner as town clerk and poll watcher has been taking out of the ballot box every evening, to be sealed until elections are over, they have been cast by his own hand, packets at a time. This has been done, no doubt, in the name of all the shadows who came to put their non-existent signatures in the Register.

It can be inferred from all this background how much the people of Yangana respect the authority of the law and the protection of the state. Also what they think of the political and administrative morality of those who represent it.

I remember reading, some years ago, an English translation of a satirical book by an Ecuadorian who used a well-known English pseudonym, "Jack the Ripper." Somewhere in the story there was a scathing description of how the rural commissioners in Ecuador conduct political elections. Well now, that account would seem a farcical misrepresentation to anybody unacquainted with the reality. The fact is that the distinguished Ecuadorian writer whose Spanish name I do not remember at the moment, was not lying. He was not even exaggerating.

I have gone to some length to relate these disagreeable details. They stand out in odious contrast to a still unspoiled community which does not deserve the cruel authority imposed upon it. I have done this because these details must be taken into account in order to understand why these people did what they did a little over a year ago to the Commissioner who preceded the present intruder. Perhaps it was indeed an act of savagery. Nevertheless, few rebellious actions could be more easily justified than that of these poor people.

What happened was that one night they assaulted the Commissioner's quarters, dragged him from his bed in his underclothes and beat him unmercifully. They then took him barefoot, prodding him with a stick all the way, to a little hillock outside the town. There the ringleader of this angry mob, a man called Joaquín Reinoso who had been victimized by the Commissioner two days before, inserted three six inch tallow candles in the official's rectum, leaving him for dead.

The provincial administration heard what had happened and immediately dispatched a magistrate accompanied by a detachment of armed police to conduct an inquiry and establish responsibility. The affair was growing complicated. The man Reinoso, alarmed and convinced that his victim had died on the night of the assault, escaped— probably into the virgin forest to the southeast of the town.

The depositions taken by the magistrate threw no light on the matter. In fact, to quote my friend Don Vicente Muñoz, they reminded him of a famous couplet from an old Spanish play:

> "Who killed the Overlord?
> Fuenteovejuna, my lord!
> And who is Fuentaovejuna?
> All of us."

The quartering of armed police and soldiers in the town left a trail of terror, abuses and exactions. The inhabitants cursed the very memory of it.

"What a town full of idiots!" was the governor's comment, according to Don Vicente, "they cried and clamored to be made a parish, and now that the government has granted what they wanted, they rebel against the representative of civil authority and ram fifty cents worth of tallow candles up his ass. We must flog the whole lot of them."

The order was carried out to the letter by the police and soldiers.

This unjustifiable official retaliation was called "pacification," and a semi-official newspaper referred to the provincial governor as "The Pacifier." There was no hint of irony in the title.

(11)

A Self-Sufficient Primitive Economy

The economy of this little town is to an extraordinary degree almost completely independent of the outside world. While the all-embracing ties of commerce are unifying our whole planet with a vast interchange of raw materials and manufactured products, the exact opposite is true in this tiny community. Its economic self-sufficiency increases all the time. Although it may be an advantage to depend so little on outside markets, it also leads to a kind of material backwardness. Yangana lives in a closed circle, economically speaking, and one that is—why not say it—inadequate and foolishly bucolic.

They want to owe as little as possible to the world of foreign manufacturers. They in fact consume hardly anything produced outside their own economy. A good part of the inhabitants, the poorest and humblest, make their own clothes. They spin and weave the cloth from the wool of their own sheep and the colors come from using vegetable dyes which they know how to extract and handle. All the materials for building are produced locally except nails, hinges, saws, bolts and locks. They make most of their own furniture with machetes and axes. If it is a matter of finely finished pieces, there are skilled joiners and cabinet makers among them.

The blankets on their beds have been woven on their own hand looms and are certainly of excellent quality. The greater part of their tableware—plates, dishes, bowls and cups—is made of baked clay which the local potters fashion into truly beautiful pieces. And the people who live outside the town make nicely shaped wooden trays, platters and spoons.

Very few iron tools are used for farm work. The only piece of iron in the plows is the plowshare. The rest is constructed of wood by hand. Machetes which serve as both tools and weapons are of necessity bought more frequently than other tools. These limited purchases of iron or steel articles obviously do have to be imported from overseas.

I have seen them consume only one imported food product, and that only once a year. I mean canned sardines for Good Friday. Otherwise they can afford to ignore the immense production of canned, bottled or packaged foods sold allover the world.

They carry on an elementary kind of trade with the northern part of Peru, based on barter. They need cotton cloth, perhaps a piece or two of imported silk, on rare occasions a few lengths of English broadcloth. Add to this, dried fish, hard soap and always rock salt. In exchange, Yangana has plenty of cow hides and goat skins, fat steers and leaf tobacco. The Peruvians who come to the frontier go back home thinking they have made an excellent bargain with this barter. And the good people of Yangana, back too from the frontier, feel exactly the same way, that they have driven an excellent bargain at the expense of their neighbors to the south. Each party considers themselves to be smart businessmen who have got the better of the other side; they congratulate themselves while on their respective roads home, and there is no bad blood.

Their needs are not expensive, nor do they feel a driving urge to maintain any particular standard of creature comfort. Most of them, in fact, do not understand what we mean by the expression. It has never crossed their minds that their town might need plumbing or a sewer system. For their needs in this matter, they do as Moses suggested to the Israelites in the wilderness: they go to some nearby open space and dig a hole in the ground with a paddle-shaped stick.

It is a significant fact that although they understand the use of the wheel—how could it be otherwise!—they never use it for purposes of transport, and not much for other purposes. There is not a wheel in Yangana except the potter's wheel, those in the five bronze and two wooden cane mills, or in the old grist mill, or those belonging to the wheelbarrows which take the clay to the brick and tile works, or those used in tobacco rollers. There are also wheels, of course, on the three or four sewing machines in the town.

Yet, craftsmanship in the town is excellent. Some of the pieces of machinery just listed, for instance, were made wholly in the town. There are foundrymen who can complete a set of bronze grinders for a sugar cane mill in less than a week. Others know how to make and set up the whole apparatus for distilling rum, including the boiler, the coil, and wooden barrels properly fitted with iron hoops. And the water-powered grist mill was built with no outside help of any kind.

It was also local artisans and laborers unaided who built a really sizable bridge spanning the river on the southern approach to the town.

The grist mill and the bridge are their most outstanding accomplishments. They look on the bridge with special pride, since they built it with their own strength, their own supervision and their own money.

These people were expressing a feeling of pride in their self-sufficiency when they said that everything in the town was their very own.

(12)

A Local Hero

Of course Yangana, too, has its famous son. It was not going to lag behind any other Ecuadorian town. Their celebrated figure is still alive although far from home. He had to leave a place that would have been too confining for one of his overpowering personality. He is living now in the capital of the country where, in the belief of his erstwhile neighbors, he is loved and admired by all. He plays an active part in national politics. He has traveled abroad and spent years in the diplomatic service in Europe and the United States.

It is many years now since Doctor José Antonio Abril left his birthplace. So the young men of Yangana are not acquainted with him personally and this they truly regret. They spend hours listening to Don Vicente Muñoz, who was a classmate of his, telling of the boy's intellectual achievements when he was in college. No doubt that from the start he had been an infant prodigy which by itself was a great honor for Yangana.

The distinguished lawyer Abril, however, seems to pay very little attention to his native town. More than forty years have passed since he left. As soon as he became influential and well known, he dropped all correspondence with his distant friends and relatives. He never answered their letters. From time to time a resident of the provincial capital would visit Quito and manage to obtain an interview with the famous native son. On his return home he never failed to report this event to his friends. Some time later the people of Yangana would hear about it, too.

They firmly believed that he had great influence in all political affairs, since for so many years he had represented his province in Congress, first as a representative and then as a senator. They had hoped and trusted that through this man's powerful influence Yangana would benefit from government grants and subsidies for a school, a highway and a telegraph line. Alas, the local hero remained deaf to all of the petitions of his fellow townsmen.

Not long ago the town was faced with the urgent need to reaffirm and reestablish its inalienable right to the ancient common lands of Yangana. They had been illegally enclosed by the neighboring landlords. Once again the townspeople appealed to the town's own famous man in the hope that he would put all to rights by obtaining an Act of Restitution from the government. Incredible as it may seem, the all-powerful personage did not even have the courtesy to acknowledge the repeated petitions addressed to him.

But listen! These people are so infatuated by blind trust and affection that nothing can alter the admiration and respect they feel for their illustrious compatriot. If you want to make enemies in this village, all you have to do is speak slightingly of Doctor José Antonio Abril, the lawyer who is accustomed to plead before the highest courts of the Republic, and who is practically a permanent senator for his native province. This prescription never fails and for that reason I don't recommend it.

(13)

Beliefs and Superstitions

Babies are christened when the priest makes one of his profitable visits to the neighborhood, once or twice a year. This is the time for these little beings to join the Roman Catholic congregation. It is also the occasion when couples who have been married only by the Civil Authority can sanctify their union with the sacrament of ecclesiastical matrimony.

The patron saint of the town is Our Lord of Good Fortune, represented by an image of Christ, scourged, sorrowful and bleeding. It rests in a red chair covered with stains and seems to have fainted. This mournful figure holds the crown of thorns on his knees. No doubt the sculptor had intended to give a picture of the utter exhaustion resulting from the mockery and ill treatment to which Christ had been subjected before he was brought before Pontius Pilate. But an almost bloodthirsty fascination with suffering had prompted these people of Yangana to tear off the head of the image and enclose it in a glass case.

The severed head could then be carried around from house to house on the eve of the annual fiesta as an object of adoration for the faithful. Those who were honored by this sacred visit put the head on an ordinary table. It was a macabre sight to a stranger looking at it from a distance, all blood-stained on a tray, atrociously and cruelly lifelike. Its astonishing realism brought to mind the story in the Bible' of the beheading of John the Baptist. There was Herod's gift lying forgotten on a table, covered with blood and with its sorrowful weeping eyes like that of a slaughtered lamb.

The parish priest of Santa Rosa is also responsible for this remote parish of Yangana and always comes for the Fiesta. The townspeople of course do their best to make it a splendid occasion and the priest takes the opportunity to spend ten or fifteen days there.

On the spiritual side, he administers the appropriate sacraments to such of the faithful who present themselves. Apart from this, he receives innumerable requests for memorial masses, either sung or recited. The charge is ten sucres when sung and five when recited. There is a short sermon in the morning after gospel reading and another in the evening in honor of the Patron Saint. Every day he exhorts all present to think of their souls and to repent their most recent sins.

He gently reminds them of the passage in Holy Writ that enjoins the "payment of tithes and first fruits to the House of the Lord." He advises them to settle accounts promptly at harvest time with the collector who has contracted for the year's first fruits.

For the temporal part, he pays a great deal of attention to the proper upkeep of the priest's residence and of the church. The belfry is empty and cries out for a good-sized bell with silvery tones. He finds it unforgivable that he cannot count on a harmonium to accompany a sung mass. He complains of the lack of sacred ornaments and vessels and that there is not one good painting or statue of a saint in the church.

The good priest does what he can to remedy this situation by soliciting contributions from the faithful. But bad luck pursues him. He never manages to collect half the cost of whatever it is that he's trying to get. So the ancient church remains as dilapidated as before.

There are times when the acts of worship and devotion last-longer than the stipulated nine days. This can happen, for example, when there has been a good harvest and the souls of the faithful are more likely to feel love and gratitude toward the good Lord. Those members of the congregation called upon to bear the cost of each particular day's ceremonial do so with real good will, directed straight up to Heaven. What is more, they must be well prepared since it is no light responsibility to underwrite the cost of a day's fiesta. Each solid citizen in turn has to answer for the whole expense of his designated day, starting with mass at sunrise. The program includes songs, a band of musicians and a fireworks display in the square at night complete with the loudest rockets and blazing torches. It also includes a long sermon with the priest in full vestments and regalia and the church illuminated by candles of all sizes, clouds of incense, a huge bonfire of brushwood in the middle of the square and finally the enormous supper.

The Yanganans have some curious preferences. They have more faith in San Vicente de Ferrer than in God. While the annual fiesta is in progress all hopes are pinned on our Lord of Good Fortune. The rest of the year the value of this particular devotion drops alarmingly, but there are other favorites. When properly blessed water is available, people with stomach ailments drink it in great quantities, convinced it will cure them. Similarly, patients suffering from backache or kidney trouble are bathed in holy water. All this allows the priest to sell it by the barrel.

They firmly believe in sorcerers and witchcraft. They are convinced that skilled first class wizards know how to change into animals and as easily regain their human form. Many tales are told with firm conviction to confirm the truth of this. They consider the elements of nature as conscious beings endowed with, human desires and intentions. Ponds and streams in neighborhoods frequented by sorcerers have been known to rise and swirl for no apparent reason. There are lakes that seem peaceful and innocent, their surface calm as can be, but when anyone approaches them, they rise up as if trying to swallow the visitor. The wind, too, is given to fits of rage up on the hillsides and often lustfully pursues the farm girls through the barley fields and threshing floors.

The washerwomen down at the river call to the sun to come out from behind the clouds and dry their washing. They entreat him with all the strength of their lungs. They repeat, "Ruddy Face! Ruddy Face!" until he shines out again and sends his rays down over the wet clothes spread out on the bank.

The Lord of Hosts is also for them the God of vengeance. Someone who has a mortal enemy is often reluctant in this peace-loving land to avenge himself with his own hand. He prefers to take advantage of the Almighty's hand. He lights a little kerosene lamp dedicated to the Holy Sacrament in the belief that as the oil is consumed, so will his enemy waste away. And what a wonderful thing is faith! If the enemy remains unharmed, the devotee is not dismayed. "It just wasn't convenient." That was all.

The calamities that routinely strike their houses and farmlands are also resisted with religious prayers and exorcisms. The owners await the arrival of the priest to handle the situation. Whether it's a matter of spoiled seed, of crops plagued by insects or damaged by blight, or if a house is infected by disease, the minister of God is glad to come.

He recites his exorcisms, sprinkles holy water with a brush held in his right hand, while a finger of his left hand marks the place in his book where he can read the appropriate words of the ceremony. The good father risks nothing since he knows how the suppliant's mind works. If the affliction is cured in the course of nature, it is because of the prayers. If the affliction persists, it is because God wills it. Faith in the efficacy of exorcisms, prayers and incantations remains undiminished. Of course, even in Yangana there are skeptics. I have met at least one.

(14)

The Day's Work

The tasks of cultivating the earth and of making such articles as can be made at home are performed in ways that belong to a bygone age. You could in fact call them medieval, combined with some noteworthy holdovers copied and adapted by the first Spanish settlers from the indigenous Inca social system.

Farmers here have a powerful friend—the good earth. Both the climate and an abundant water supply make the whole region exceedingly fertile. There is no need for the never-ending labor of the Old World. The soil is so easy to cultivate and so fruitful that you feel that a farmer ought to sing at his work. The best proof of this is the almost unbelievable fact that some fields are planted without ever being plowed.

Here is a description of how land in Yangana is prepared and cultivated. If planting is to be done in the woodland, the first thing is to fell the trees. Machetes and axes are the tools for this. The fallen trees are then usually cut into firewood or made into charcoal. The remaining branches, brush and debris lying where the trees once stood are allowed to dry out a little and then burned to clear the ground completely. The fire sometimes lasts for weeks and when the flames have finally died out and the ashes are cold, it is time for the first planting.

The planter uses what is called a *tola*, a long sharp stick or stake. He thrusts this into the ground, opens a hole or crack, leans over, and drops in the seeds—that is, if he is planting corn or beans or some other grain. Then he carefully covers the hole and its seeds with topsoil and ashes, using the same stick. This is all he has to do. Everything else is taken care of by the rain and the dew and the dampness of a subsoil which has lain for ages in the shade of the forest.

A field of corn or beans growing on recently burned land is a startling sight. Blackened tree stumps are still standing everywhere. Death seems to have passed over the land like an invading army, leaving heaps of charred corpses on the battlefield. While on the same spot life is beginning to flower again under the hand of the planter. All that is needed to repeat the process is to plow the same field with a yoke of oxen year after year until the earth is finally exhausted by, say, its tenth crop.

The ratio between what is sowed and what is harvested is truly amazing. Abundant is hardly a word for it. It illustrates the difference between this soil and the arable land of Europe and even the best land in the United States.

To fence in their fields and pastures these people have no need whatever for barbed wire. In most cases they plant quickset hedges. On the high pastures the *agave* or century plant is used. The method is this: first they dig a long shallow trench, taking care to cut big clean sods with the edge of their spades. They then use these sods to build a low wall parallel to the trench, and on top of this wall they set out mature *agaves*. The vitality of this plant insures its taking root immediately. Planted as they are in a thick interwoven line along this ridge of freshly turned earth, they soon form an impenetrable barrier bristling with innumerable sharp black thorns.

Fences in the bottom lands near the river below Yangana are constructed of a choice of two trees which the people of the region call *pinllus* and *porotillos* respectively. Slips or cuttings of uniform height are planted so closely that by the time they are fair-sized trees you can hardly see between the trunks.

In the town itself house lots are shut in by mud or adobe walls more than six feet high, so that nobody can look over them. It is easy to understand the reason for this when you consider that these back yards are used by members of the family for many personal purposes. There is no danger, however, of thieves climbing a wall since robbery is practically unknown here.

The only other kind of fence which can compare with the quickset hedge or the mud wall is post-and-rail made from cut and split wood. This is generally used for corrals and cattle pens, and the wood preferred is from the *faique* tree, a species of acacia or locust.

First a double row of stout posts is driven or buried deep into the ground, each pair being equidistant from the next pair. Split or hewn rails are then slipped between the posts so that each end of each rail is firmly held between two uprights. Rails are added until they are high enough to prevent livestock from getting out. It is also not unusual, where stone is available, to find corrals made of stone mortared in mud.

As the fields rise higher on the hillsides, the soil needs more intensive cultivation. If you look upwards from the town at plowing time you can see dozens of yokes of oxen laboring at their task. The same number of plowmen there are at work on a given farm anyone day, will be seen on another farm the next day, and in this way they cover in due course the whole extent of arable land. This fact is easily explained by the system of communal labor known as the *minga*.

Minga is a Quechua word used nowadays to signify a gathering of all the neighbors, on a previously set day, to work on the farm of one of them. The work is free except that the owner of the land must provide plenty of fodder for the oxen and plenty of good food for the plowmen. He is also bound in turn to do his share of work, together with his oxen, when called upon to help a neighbor.

Exactly the same system is followed for weeding, grubbing, harvesting, threshing, thatching a house or rounding up cattle. In short, the *minga* is the favorite work pattern in these parts.

This is the way a day's work goes during a *minga*. The *mingueros*, as they are called, are ready to start work very early, often by six o'clock, since they have answered the call before daybreak. They have already breakfasted and swallowed a mug of rum to make up for the early rising. This first libation of the day is called "having an eye-opener."

Fortified by breakfast and the eye-opener they set to work, each one eager to outdo his neighbors. By noontime they are ready for dinner and between them—if they are a large gang—often consume a whole cow, washed down with great drafts of strong home-brew or fermented cane juice or swigs of rum. The second half of the day's work is accompanied by singing and shouting. They knock off at five or six and then comes the tremendous evening meal. By this method the whole task is completed cheerfully, quickly and economically.

It is hard for these people to grasp the idea of a farm laborer working for wages and paid once a week. Nor will you find here the kind of laborer who has no little piece of land—either his or someone else's—which he can cultivate for himself.

The parcels of land that drop down to the river do not need as much labor as the upland. The soil in this bottomland is richer and less exacting. In spite of the relative indolence of those who work there, the crops are better. The fact is that over and above the excellent climactic conditions already referred to, every year the winter rains strip the uplands of their best and most fertile top soil to deposit it on the lowlands.

As for the artisans and craftsmen in the little town, almost all of them are also, to a greater or lesser degree, farmers or ranchers. They divide their time between working the land, caring for their animals, and practicing their trade. And when they do practice their craft, they do so as if conferring a favor on a friend.

The relation between an artisan and his customer resembles more than anything else the relation between someone who asks a favor and the person who grants it. For instance, suppose that a screw or nut on my theodolite needs fixing and that I know someone who is a skilled mechanic. Well, I have to go and see him in person and beg him—as a very special favor—to take care of my problem. And he will

183

do it because, as he will assure me when he finishes the job, it is a real pleasure to him to be of service to me.

I have to follow the same procedure with the cobbler who mends my shoes, or with the tailor who cleans and presses my clothes. I confess that there are times when this pretentious nonsense is almost more than I can take. I find it exceedingly irritating to be obliged to beg these people to do something which they should feel bound to do by their profession and for which they will be properly paid. One is not asking them for charity; they will be paid on the spot and they know it.

Actually, I have been astonished to observe that the people of Yangana show an incredible lack of interest in money. An authentic illustration of this, which I found hard to believe at the time, happened to me during my first week in the village.

I was eager to lose no time in starting out on my first exploration into the *cinchona* forests of the mountain range and I set out to hire six men to go with me as workers and guides. I tried to negotiate the matter myself, showing them money and offering them double the usual local rate of pay. But my prospective helpers took umbrage at this and roundly declared that they found it offensive that anyone should presume to ask hard-working folk to go wherever some stranger wishes, just because he offered them money.

They turned their backs on me and began to mistrust me. They were convinced that anyone who tried to pay more than the customary rate was hatching some sinister plan and setting a trap for them with these tempting offers. They went away one by one in spite of my offering even more money. This first lesson and others like it finally opened my eyes.

When I learned to treat the men as friends, I found that I could then obtain all the laborers or guides that I wanted. But they never stopped reminding me that if they went with me, it was as friends. And a word or phrase that one of them may have thought out of place or in the slightest degree disparaging was enough to wound his touchy feelings. If that happened, it never failed to result in his walking off the job without waiting to collect the wages due him.

I am not ashamed to confess that I have profited immensely from being among the people of this place, whether in the village or in the field. It may sound naive to say that when I first arrived I never imagined that I could learn anything from them. But it turned out that they have taught me many valuable lessons. I have already said it and I say it again, I consider them to be of exceptionally high moral character. In this totally isolated region, a fragment of humanity has remained unspoiled. Perhaps my sympathetic feelings for them cause me to exaggerate, but I do see a resemblance between them and our puritanical forbears in Pennsylvania who lived in similar isolation. But some defect in our culture has led us North Americans to believe that a great gulf separates the two worlds.

(15)

Education

These people like their children to go to school. They pay private teachers and insure that the system used is exactly the same as when they themselves were in school. In other words, the teaching methods employed in Yangana are the most outdated and stereotyped that can be imagined. In fact, this must have been how old Don Lisandro was taught all those many years ago. Considered in the light of modern educational theory and practice, the system in use here is both rigid and tyrannical.

The schoolmasters or mistresses are content with very little pay. They receive weekly contributions of food of various kinds, and every month a few small coins from each pupil. Since it is the parents who directly bear the cost of the school, they think that they have every right to criticize the teaching, draw up the curriculum and choose the textbooks. It follows that the Christian catechism is obligatory. Friday, apart from being the day for the weekly collection, is devoted in both morning and afternoon sessions to learning by heart and reciting the doctrines of the Church. The school week is from Monday through Friday, leaving Saturday and Sunday free.

The parents' interest can be judged by the fact that some of the children have to walk three miles each way to attend school, which means leaving home very early in the morning if they are to get there on time.

The appearance of the pupils is as diverse as their ages. The greater part of them are little barefooted children. You hardly ever see one wearing shoes. To make up for this, they wear hats all day except when actually in class. They carry their few textbooks—purchased in the local stores at the beginning of the school year—in a cloth bag or a basket of cane strips. The pupils who do not live in the town and have to come from the outskirts or even further, bring cold lunches with them in their bags or baskets. They have time to eat this at noon since classes are from eight in the morning to twelve and then from two to five in the afternoon.

Some of the pupils are only just learning to read but are already in love or engaged, but there are others who started very young and by the time they are thirteen have nothing more to study. They have got through all the textbooks and don't know what to do with all their wonderful knowledge.

When the school year ends, two weeks before the fiesta of Our Lord of Good Fortune, a committee of prominent citizens visits the various schoolhouses to preside over the public examinations. The whole town is there. There are speeches and awarding of prizes. The pupils recite patriotic poems learned by heart and sometimes there is a comic skit. The public shows the greatest interest and listens with fascination. These good folk are not very critical of a spectacle or a performance. However artless or foolish it may be, they are genuinely entertained. When it comes to theater, they have a weakness for the drama that at times verges on the ridiculous.

What little furniture the schoolhouse has is of very poor quality since it has been purchased by private contributions.

The sum total consists of a few long benches, long enough for ten pupils in a row with desks attached, a little writing table, a rough, wooden cabinet, a blackboard in a corner and a chair for the teacher.

One classroom must serve for all grades and there is only one teacher. The lowest grades and the dullest pupils are in the front row, the upper grades sit at the back, and there are always some who have to sit on the floor for lack of desks.

There is no sign of a map. Maps are unknown. Primary education lasts from three to four years. For girls it's a year less, which is considered more than enough for a woman. After all, people say, a woman needs less education—much less. In exceptional cases pupils who have gone as far as they can here, go on to the city to finish the elementary grades and go on to High School. The few who succeed in graduating from High School seldom return to a home town which now seems primitive and confining.

The good people of Yangana are distressed by this tendency of their brightest children not to come back after once experiencing, the freer and more cultivated life of the city. This is no doubt one of the chief reasons why so many parents who could afford to give their sons a better education do nothing for them beyond the rudimentary instruction of the local school. I know several cases of this sort and have heard the same fear expressed many times. These anxious parents look on the city as a fatal source of attraction which will end by stealing their sons. There are rare exceptions such as my friend, Don Vicente Muñoz, who after graduating from the city college had returned to his birthplace loving it even more than before.

The same thing happens to the girls. If their parents send them to finish their education at the Catholic College in the city, they come back disagreeing with everything, they find life boring and old-fashioned and they never cease to mourn the city. They consider the little town too horrible for words.

Things that never used to upset them now seem coarse and contemptible. Under these circumstances, the parents are the first victims. It is they who love Yangana and who see in the city a fatal lure for anyone who stays there more than a short time, a trap to be avoided at all costs.

What if life in Yangana means nights without radios, no sound of an automobile, no evening entertainment at the movies. What if there is nothing to do but talk and play parlor games by the kitchen fire or tell stories round the dining table until it's time to say goodnight and go to bed! Worst of all they no longer love the countryside. They no longer feel any of that communion with nature which means so much to some of us.

So nothing will change matters so long as the school system lacks a properly qualified and constituted faculty capable of following a recognized curriculum. It will continue to be stereotyped and inadequate, ruled by blind tradition and the teacher's caprice. With no obedience to set principles or to a unified program, perfect chaos reigns within the rigidity of the routine. Corporal punishment will remain the disciplinary cornerstone, with protracted kneeling down, the punishment for minor offenses and whipping on the hands or buttocks for graver misconduct.

(16)

Entertainment

The people of Yangana are exceedingly fond of shows of all kinds. Their participation in fiestas is truly delirious. They let themselves go body and soul whenever they have an opportunity of that kind.

There are four basic occasions for mirth and merriment: birthdays or personal saint's days; picnics; agricultural celebrations like harvest time; and religious celebrations. It also goes without saying that Sunday is never allowed to pass unnoticed. The standard Sunday amusements consist of such things as cockfights, throwing tiles at a mark and wrist-and-finger wrestling. Some of the men play old Spanish card games such as twenty-one or *caida y limpia*, or *briscón*. And they shoot dice. The men can also be found drinking in the rum and *chicha* shops. Meanwhile, the younger women go visiting since they are obliged to be quieter and more discreet than the men.

Family parties and celebrations such as a saint's day or birthday or wedding are marked here—as they are everywhere else—by dancing and drinking. In the silences between dances, the ladies sing traditional folk songs which begin sweetly and rather sadly, but gradually end with a spirited and lively *fuga*. After a few rounds of drinks and a few songs, things begin to warm up. Now is the time for dancing the *chilena* or the *sanjuanito* both accented by nimble steps and waving handkerchiefs. The delighted onlookers clap their hands to the beat of the guitars.

If the night is cold, the hostess herself serves everybody half a cup of steaming hot *draque* to "warm them up." Every family has its own secret recipe for this drink. Starting with the standard base of white rum, the lady of the house does her best to impart the most appetizing flavors by adding unsuspected ingredients. Making a really good *draque* which satisfies the exacting palates of the assembled experts is an achievement to be celebrated all night.

When everything and everybody has reached the right temperature, it is time for cooling drinks. There is a choice. Great jugs of *cocada* are brought in first. It is a sweet freshly made concoction of rice and ground coconut, redolent of spices. Next is peanut *chicha*, cold and full-bodied, smelling of roasted peanuts and sprouted corn. Or fermented sugar cane juice, watered down and slightly soured with bitter orange juice. Or "Chilean water," an explosive mixture of milk, sugar arid rum with real zest to it.

Coffee is served at midnight with an incredible assortment of pies, cookies and desserts. The mistress of the house will take no excuses and insists that all her guests eat as much as possible of these delicacies. As for the coffee itself, this time it's not "frightened coffee" but double-dripped concentrated essence. Down the center of the table are bowls of the whitest and hardest loaf sugar. I must add another interesting detail related to the service. Wherever the guests may be entertained, they will always find the same china, glass and silver. And this is explained by the fact that no house in Yangana has a complete set of anything, whereas between a good many of them they can furnish all that is needed for any kind of celebration. Actually, the better-off families do have a bare minimum of common quality tableware for their own daily use, but there are few of such families in the town.

Outings in the country and fiestas at the end of one of the *mingas* already described, are the happiest occasions imaginable. Suppose, for example, that a group of friends decide to spend the day on a farm cooking and eating the first tender ears of new corn. They all set out early in the morning with plenty of food and drink, prepared to spend the whole day under the trees. Each person or family brings suitable contributions. This time, naturally, the indispensable fare consists of green corn, boiled on the cob and eaten steaming hot with freshly made cream cheese. Chicken broth has already been served. After the corn come guinea pigs roasted whole on long hardwood spits. All this is washed down with any amount of chicha and hard liquor for those who want it.

After the meal, everyone plays games out in the open field: blind-man's-bluff, forfeits, three-legged races, hen-and-chickens, and so forth. After that, comes a little music and singing until it's time to go home. It is all very pastoral and artless, pervaded by a delightful air of innocence.

Another favorite excursion is when a whole cavalcade rides out to the river to fish. This means taking along sticks of dynamite as well as the usual provisions since the fish are to be caught by setting off dynamite in the deeper water holes. It is a rather brutal system, but produces plenty of fish and it also gives the swimmers and divers a chance to show their daring.

The women are not expected to be very venturesome in these expeditions since it is well known that the river banks are full of poisonous snakes. The final example of an enjoyable outdoor pastime is provided by the butchering of a fat hog, a barbarous event which is an excuse for a big fiesta and a tremendous meal. There is a kind of culinary ritual for this business which is scrupulously observed by the participants and which takes all day.

Here is an account of how these good people proceed with the job.

The day before the hog is to be slaughtered, the owner goes up into the hills to look for *llazhipa*, a wild fern which burns with an unusually quick hot flame. He returns with a great load of leaves on his back or on his mule's back. The dry leaves of this fern are stiff and rough but can be bound up into a light bushy brush.

The next day, when all is ready, the butcher gently and skillfully scratches the hog's belly until the animal stretches out on the ground, happy and half asleep. This quiet dream is rudely interrupted by a knife thrust under the shoulder, straight to the heart. After the last death shudder the warm body is completely covered with a layer of dry fern leaves. A stone is quickly put between the victim's jaws, the wound is plugged with corn husks, and all is ready for scorching the hide.

Everybody invited is expected to be there in time for the skin roasting. The scorched hide is scraped with a sharp knife blade and water, the singed bristles and rough hair are torn off to reveal the richly browned skin. Great bowls of boiled corn and fine salt are standing ready and no time is lost. Pieces of roast skin, cut off the meat and eaten on the spot are considered the most delicious morsels imaginable.

After an hour or two, it is time to enjoy the crackling. Strips of skin, with all the underlying fat, have been cut up into handy sizes and fried in a large crockery pot with much popping and hissing. As the hot lard is rendered from the skin, it is dipped out with a ladle and poured into another vessel to cool off and set firm. After two hours the pieces of skin have given up all their fat and turned into the most mouth-watering crackling.

A plate of crackling with freshly boiled corn is considered a sumptuous dish in Yangana. Nobody dreams of refusing it.

Great care is always taken to prevent the hog from "kicking" the guest. Since everybody has eaten a great deal of fat, heavy and indigestible food, it is considered necessary to "cook" all this grease. So the next thing proffered to the guests is plenty of very strong aniseed brandy, enough to make one weep with joy. The aniseed content is supposed to have a beneficial effect on the intestines. It enables them to fulfill the hard task of handling a banquet of pure pork.

To go back to the *mingas*, those collective working parties that I have already described, and to the celebrations they have afterwards, the food and, the way it is served follows the same general system as the others. The difference is that the feast is not purely for pleasure or amusement. The prime and all-absorbing purpose of a *minga* is the work to be done. Only when the day's task is finished and night has fallen, can the workers relax and enjoy the rustic pleasure of abundant food and drink and lively revelry to the tune of flutes, guitars, rum and fermented cane juice.

I was very surprised to find that there is no bull-fighting in this little town which, in so many other ways, seems to have preserved the traditions of Old Spain. I have asked a number of people about this and find that there has never been a bull fight here at any time. Nobody thinks that a fierce bull is a beautiful and admirable sight, but rather an unruly beast to be rounded up and caught as quickly as possible. There is no wish to have him provide a spectacular entertainment. Fed plenty of salt and with a ring in his nose, he soon becomes one of the household and as gentle as a lamb.

One thing that the inhabitants do seem to have inherited from their Spanish ancestors is a passionate love for the theater. Although I have to admit that I have never been present at a performance, I have observed their enthusiastic preparation for a fiesta which is to be enlivened with *comedias*. The whole town is in a bustle of anticipation. I am told that on the night of the show, the audience fills every seat and every corner, looking and listening with rapt attention.

There are times when not one, but two or three performances follow each other on the same night, starting at nine o'clock and not ending until three or four in the morning. The idea that anybody would think of leaving before the final curtain is considered absurd. The spectators await the unfolding of the plot or the conclusion of the story with breathless interest, regardless of time and fatigue. And when it is allover and day is about to break, they go home reluctantly, still commenting and remembering. For weeks after a theatrical performance, it is a topic of conversation in every house. It is an event not easily forgotten.

(17)

The Dead

As we have seen, the life of these people is tranquil and quiet. It would be hard to find a more peaceful place than this little town. When Death comes to collect his due, the feelings of those called upon to pay it and the feelings of their families are governed for the most part by the proportion of Indian blood in their veins.

The whites face the final moment of trial in their own traditional way, with subdued dignity. The Indian, on the other hand, has different ideas and sentiments. He is more of a pagan and observes rituals which make a fiesta out of a funeral. A stranger here finds nothing of unusual interest about the mourning of the whites. But the indigenous population, or people who have been brought up among them and share their feelings, express their grief in a more interesting style.

There are two particular customs that I found very moving. The first is the *velorio*, or wake, complete with its funeral oration. The second has, I believe, been mentioned by a previous traveler. It is the bizarre way people from outlying parts of the parish take the body to town for burial in the cemetery. The deceased, fully dressed including a hat, is mounted on the back of a horse or mule, just as if he were alive, and thus he rides into town.

Once I happened to be present at a wake in a little house well outside the town. The head of the family had just died and his widow and children were watching over the body, already placed in its simple coffin. There was none of the mournful silence usually associated with these occasions. The immediate family were wearing broad black bands of cheap cotton cloth wound round their hats right up to the top of the crown. But the whole gathering—all those who had been invited verbally by the bereaved relatives and the family members as well—were talking and laughing as if it were the most natural thing in the world.

When an Indian or half-Indian has died, the mourners first take the body to the nearest creek where it is washed very carefully and at great length. The women also wash all the clothing worn by the deceased. This ceremony takes up the better part of a day and is called *pizcha* or *Pichica*. Food and drink is provided by the family, the food being cooked over makeshift fires on the bank of the stream.

The body is then taken back to the house of mourning where it is put into a wooden coffin painted black. A few hours later it is taken to the town cemetery. A special litter or bier is used. Four men at a time take turns carrying it on their shoulders.

But before this, when the corpse is still in the house, the principal female mourner begins the funeral lament. In a high-pitched wailing voice she extols the virtues of the deceased, weeping and crying that henceforth there will be nobody to carry out the household tasks as he did. There are times when the sentiments and eloquence of the celebrant are so moving that the company weeps unreservedly. I found nothing ridiculous, not for a moment, in the whole ceremony. The primordial feelings which make these people howl like wounded animals and give free expression to their grief have nothing laughable about them. There is a touch of grandeur about it all that aroused my sympathy and even reverence.

The open expression of grief, however, lasts only a very short time. As soon as this psalm or responsorial for the dead is over, the whole group sets off busily for the cemetery, taking along a good supply of liquor and the tools needed to dig a grave. Once in the cemetery, the men set to work opening up a tremendous deep trench. It's a task that takes hours and is really a kind of minga. The men take turns and eat and drink abundantly between working spells. When they have reached a depth of about twelve feet and thrown out all the loose earth, they carefully lower the coffin to the bottom and shovel back the displaced earth.

By this time, all present beginning with the family of the deceased, are completely drunk. They return in a bunch to the house of grief, singing and howling as they go. Night has generally fallen when they get there. If the deceased happens to be a child, the whole ceremony is extraordinarily lively and cheerful. Both going and coming, there is spirited music all the way and the fiesta lasts for another day.

Again, I repeat that this series of ceremonies is observed only by the Indian families outside the town. The whites and the mestizos who make up the greater part of the population follow, with slight variations, the old Spanish customs which have nothing remarkable about them.

What really distresses most of these people is that very sick neighbors often die without having a chance to confess their sins, because the nearest priest lives so far away. The people of Yangana, most of whom are devout Christians, are deeply grieved by the calamity that so often befalls one of them who is so unfortunate as to die without confession to a Catholic priest and without receiving the sacrament of absolution.

As mentioned before, there are groups of Indians who live furthest away from the town who practice another method of taking a corpse to the burying ground. They mount the corpse on a mule, which seems to them to be and actually is the simplest way to do it. The dead person is carefully bathed, dressed in Sunday clothes including a hat set tightly on the head. Then the jaws are tightly tied up with a bandana. In this garb the dead person is lifted up, put on the animal's back and tied to the saddle with feet placed in the stirrups.

To prevent the body from losing its balance from the movement of the mule, the mourners secure it with a stake running up the back, from the saddle to the shoulders, and another stake in front pressing on the chest. Supported in this way, the corpse has no trouble traveling long distances at a fair pace. On reaching the town, the coffin is obtained, the traditional ritual observed in the cemetery and the burial is completed in due course.

Everyone of the few travelers who have happened to visit these remote corners of the world has remarked on this weird and curious custom of the posthumous ride on muleback.

(18)

The Story-telling Tradition

A community which has so little contact with the rest of the world, where life is peaceful and work leisurely, is a community which must find its entertainment with conversation, street corner gossip, critical comment, fables, fairy tales and stories of all kinds. By long tradition, the people here have developed and cultivated a surprising aptitude for telling stories. Even the stupidest and most ignorant member of this society possesses this effortless and untaught facility. Anyone of them can entertain you the whole night through with story telling.

You will be astonished to meet the narrator next day When he is not weaving fiction or relating anecdotes. You may find him to be a dull fellow, often shy and timid, a slow thinker. But set him down by the hearth, give him time to listen to one or two tales, wait until you're sure that the atmosphere is favorable, and you will witness an extraordinary change in this boorish fellow. The spirit of story telling seems to have descended on his sluggish brain and transformed him into a captivating and interesting narrator. You may even feel ashamed that you had come prepared to scoff at tales told by such rustic simpletons.

If the conversation happens to turn to fables about animals, for example, his explanation of why dogs have the habit of smelling one another will go something like this:

"In the far-off times when animals could speak, a dog once found a ten centavo piece lying in the road. A committee of dogs was formed to decide what was to be done with the money. Since the sum was not enough to buy anything useful or profitable, they agreed to buy two ounces of incense and perfume themselves. The committee, in the name of the king, summoned all the dogs to take part in the ceremony."

"The law-abiding dogs presented themselves as ordered and were duly perfumed. The king then decreed that those who had not obeyed the summons would be punished. And that is why the dogs who obeyed are known by their good smell, are respected for it and allowed to pass freely. By the same token, when the disobedient dogs are smelled they are detected as unperfumed and are fined accordingly."

Stories of this kind could be told a hundred times without boring the listeners. They love to hear them over and over again with a truly childish delight. The teller of the tale is immediately subjected to a barrage of questions so that his audience can listen once again to the familiar tale. Some of his audience may be interested in comparing or contrasting different styles or details used on different occasions.

Suppose, for example, that they want to know why cats always shake a piece of meat before eating it. The narrator explains it thus:

"During the same epoch when animals still knew how to speak, the mice were always complaining that the cats hunted them unmercifully. So they stole a coin to buy some pins. In those days, the cats used to eat meat—their favorite food—without taking any precautions. So the mice hid the pins in a piece of meat and left it in the head cat's larder."

"Along came the head cat and swallowed it in one bite, pins and all. An hour later, the cat was at death's door. So he called his friends around him and told them that his last wish was to advise them never to forget to shake their meat before eating it, in order to be sure that there were no pins hidden inside it."

Another favorite story was the fable of the little mice who allowed themselves to be caught unaware by the duplicity of their enemy.

"Mother Mouse was an experienced and cautious person. Every time she went out to get food for her children, she warned them not to leave the nest because the enemy would catch and eat them. 'We mice have an enemy,' she used to tell them. But once, when the mother had left the nest, the children ventured out warily from their hiding place and they saw a spirited horse in a stall."

"The horse was stamping his hooves, neighing, tossing his head and treading down the straw as if he were furious. When they saw such a fearful and terrible monster, the little ones turned tail and scampered away and hid at the very end of the nest with their hearts fluttering. When Mother Mouse came back home they told her that they now knew who the enemy was and they described what the horse looked like. Mother Mouse told them to be more careful and to be sure not to disobey her again, but that what they had seen was not the enemy. The next day she went out again, and again told them to be very careful. And once again the little mice paid no attention and went outside."

"This time they had barely left the door of the nest when they saw a rooster flapping his wings, strutting up and down, crowing as loud as he could and scratching the ground with his claws. The little things were so scared that they scurried off and when Mother Mouse returned they told her that this time they really did know the enemy. She said that was not so, that the creature they had seen that morning, that proud and angry gentleman, was not the enemy. Once again she had to go out, and once again begged them especially to be very careful not to let the enemy catch them. But they disobeyed her just as they had before and ventured out for the third time."

"They crept out a little way, very quietly, and this time they found a cat with his eyes shut, dozing and purring by the hearth. 'What a kind good gentleman,' they thought, 'How piously he is saying his prayers, why—he doesn't even look up at anybody.' And while they were admiring this devout cat who had actually been watching them all the time out of the corner of his eye, he caught them in one jump and ate them all."

During Holy Week, which was a time of soul-searching and meditation, people would listen to pious moral tales and histories until they were drowsy with sleep. The following is an example of the kind of thing they preferred:

"This is the story of a cobbler who went straight to Heaven when he became a lay-brother in a monastery."

"This cobbler was a foolish ignorant fellow, which made his salvation much easier. He once went to church and heard that to go to Heaven one should perform good works and follow the straight and narrow path."

"He was a very painstaking craftsman and made every pair of shoes with scrupulous care. As a result, he soon lost everything he owned and found himself penniless. He then decided to leave his native town. Since he had been told that he should follow the straight and narrow path, he started out straight ahead and followed his nose, wading through swamps, climbing fences and walls and crossing precipices."

"On the way he happened upon a gentleman lying in the road, badly beaten and covered with blood and wounds. Our man picked him up, carried him to the nearest creek and washed his wounds. Then he shared his meager ration of boiled corn with him and continued his march. Further along he met another man in the same straits and took care of him in the same way."

"He finally reached a Franciscan monastery where he was given a good meal. As he was about to lie down and rest, he noticed a little chapel and there he saw the same gentleman he had found lying in the road, but this time he was nailed to a cross."

"When the cobbler saw this, he began to scold the crucified man. 'You must be a bad character,' said he, 'and that's why people set upon you and beat you wherever you go. But don't take it to heart since I am going to lift you down from up there and give you a bite to eat.'"

"So he went to the kitchen and begged the cook, who was a lay-brother, for an extra serving of food. The lay-brother gave it to him and, out of curiosity, followed him to see what he was up to. He found him sitting down talking kindly to the crucified man who had been taken down from the cross and was eating the food the cobbler put in his mouth."

"The lay-brother ran and told the Prior who, when he saw what was happening, asked the lay-brother to pray to God on behalf of the monastery."

"Then God, since it had really been the crucified Lord himself who had been conversing with the foolish cobbler, promised to make arrangements in Heaven so that food would never be lacking in the kitchen of any Franciscan monastery."

When, however, the demands of the, priest who visited Yangana at harvest or fiesta time seemed more excessive than usual, the parishioners' taste in stories took on a slightly Voltairian twist. This led them to relish such tales as this:

"The priest who figures in this story was called Miguel and he lived for many years in the neighboring town of X. Don Lisandro knew him. He was a stingy priest and a great runner after women. One day he set out for a farm in the country outside the town, on the pretext of hearing a confession. But his real object was to visit a pretty little wench who lived there."

"He ordered his best mule to be saddled, packed up a good lunch, and off he went accompanied by his servant. This servant was a young lad who was always hungry since the priest never gave him enough to eat. They had to travel a fair distance and the priest was in a very good humor, so before starting out he gave the boy a handful of corn and told him to roast it and take it along in a gourd to eat on the road."

"On and on they traveled and the serving boy got hungrier and hungrier. The worst of it was that every time he took out a little corn from the gourd, the priest got angry and scolded him, asking when he was going to stop stuffing himself."

"And so it went until late in the day when the poor boy was half-dead from hunger. It was only natural, therefore, that when the priest asked him who owned a fine farm house that they happened to be passing, the servant replied, 'I don't know, father,' although he knew the answer quite well."

"Further along, they came to a great tree with a huge trunk and luxuriant foliage whereupon the priest asked the servant what kind of a tree it was and the boy answered that he did not know. Still further along the road, when they were not far short of the girl's house, they came in sight of a corral full of fine cattle. Once again, the boy said that he had no idea whom the cattle belonged to, although he knew perfectly well."

"By this time the servant was so enraged at the priest for making him suffer such hunger that he decided to square the account for good and, all. And so it turned out, as we shall see."

"What happened was that the holy priest got up in the night and started to carry out the plan he had made with the girl during the day. When he was sure that everybody in the house was asleep, he began to crawl along on all fours toward the wench's bed. Just then the servant boy who was lying awake because he was so hungry, called out, 'Sir priest! Sir priest!'"

"The blessed man had to scramble back quickly so as to be able to answer from his own bed. 'What do you want, boy, at this time of night?' 'Do you remember, Father,' said the boy, 'that on the way here you asked me who owned the big farm house we passed on the road? Now I recall who it is: it belongs to Don Joaquín Villa of Guachanama.' 'And you wake me up just to tell me that? You insolent brat.'"

"An hour went by and the boy pretended to snore so as to put the priest off guard. Once again the holy priest thought that everybody was asleep and began again to crawl along the floor, feeling for the bed of the charmer who was ready and waiting. Her mother was snoring gently. The priest had almost reached his goal this time, when he heard the boy callout to him as loud as he could, 'Sir priest! Sir priest!'"

"The holy priest had to scurry back posthaste to answer the little rascal from his own bed. He was boiling with rage lest the girl's old mother should find out what was going on. 'What do you want now? You dolt!' asked the priest, diving into bed."

"Do you remember, Father, asking me the name of that tree with such luxuriant foliage standing by the roadside? I've just recollected that that tree is called a '*Cazhco*.' 'And so you've woken me up just to tell me that, you little thief?'"

"The hours passed, there was a deep silence in the house and the priest's servant and the old woman were both snoring. The priest realized that it would soon be daybreak, so he made another attempt. Just as he reached the girl's bed, the servant who had only been pretending to be asleep, fetched him back with the same cry, 'Sir priest! Sir priest!' The holy priest was now beside himself with fury, but had to get back into bed before answering, 'What else do you want now? It's almost daybreak, you bastard!'"

"'Do you remember, Father, that when we were near the creek at Uriguanga, we came to a corral full of fine cattle and you asked me who owned them? It's just come to my mind that the corral belongs to the heirs of the deceased Anastasio Valverde of Celica.'"

"So with one thing and another, before the holy priest knew it, the roosters were crowing and the first rays of dawn were showing in the sky. He had spent the whole night crawling on all fours between his bed and the girl's without getting what he came for. And he was puffing and snorting with rage."

"The holy priest did not wait for the full light of day. He refused to accept breakfast, saddled his mule with his own hands and left the house as if shot out of a gun or as if the Devil were carrying him off. He drove the scoundrel boy ahead of him, only to have him take to his heels, with his master's saddlebags, and disappear on a lonely stretch of road before he was punished."

These people also have rather confused ideas about human destiny. Generally speaking they believe in Fate. They express this with great conviction in such favorite phrases as "It's not the bullet that kills, it's Fate," "Nobody dies the day before," "The days were numbered." The phrase or the proverb is then illustrated with a fable.

If somebody doubts the inevitability of his destiny, a listener will quote the story of the poor man who was born to be poor and always urged on his donkey with the words: "Get up, jackass! Get up! Don't you know that he who is born poor will never be rich!" Or the tale of the man born under a lucky star who became the most skilful and successful thief in the world thanks to the fickle light provided for him by his own star.

They are so passionately given to telling and listening to such stories that the most insignificant happenings in their own past are endowed before long with a more or less fictitious character. An example of this is the history of the origin of the vast estates which enclose Yangana like a ring of iron. The description has in the course of time become a narrative which could be entitled something like this: 'The

Sad Story of the Lazy Fellow.' It is a long circumstantial story about real people some of whom are still living.

This story made such an impression on me that I decided to put it in writing as faithfully as I could, just as I heard it for the first time, sitting by the fireplace.

Many years ago, —Don Lisandro Fierro remembers it very well—a character by the name of Emilio Gurumendi came from the city on a visit to Yangana. He had a compadre there, an Indian called Trinidad Quizhpe, who whenever he had occasion to go to the city where Gurumendi lived was always telling him to name a day and make up his mind to pay him a visit. He always invited him with the same words, "I've got a little pig for you. We'll eat it together, my dear compadre, come on, you'll feel at home with us!"

Compadre Gurumendi was very poor and had a hard time of it. He was supported by a woman who owned and operated a little eating-house where he owed a considerable bill. This bill was eventually paid off in kind. He slept with her, and she fed him.

Compadre Gurumendi was in a way a handsome man— tall, white, robust and bearded, though his skin was unhealthily pallid. He was famous for being the laziest man on earth. He passed the time happily, and could have passed his whole life doing absolutely nothing, hands stuck deep in his belt, only showing his huge thumbs with their enormous nails. He lived down by the river in a wretched shack that he owned. It was the only thing that he did own. He did not drink, but he smoked and slept a good deal. Nobody ever knew how he had become friendly with the man who later on became his compadre.

Compadre Gurumendi followed a daily routine marked by the most deadly monotony. At half-past seven in the morning his one-panel door opened a little. The solitary man had got out of bed. He pitched out the contents of his chamber pot into the middle of the dirty street. An hour later, he went down to the river bank carrying an old jug. On his return he made a fire to boil the water he had brought back.

His breakfast consisted of strong coffee, sugar and bread, all brought home the evening before from the eating-house. He never washed or trimmed his luxuriant auburn beard. About ten o'clock he clapped a greasy old black hat on his disheveled head and sallied forth in the direction of one of the squares in the center of the city, where he could sit in the sun on a bench and furtively collect thrown-away cigarette butts.

At eleven o'clock the guard at the municipal jail was changed. The brisk marching step of the relief squad was heard as they rounded the corner of the square. For Gurumendi, this meant that it was time to go to his woman's eating-house for dinner. He entered the place scratching himself and without greeting her.

"Here comes Don Emilio" announced the cook.

"Then go ahead and put a piece of steak in the skillet for the lazy good-for-nothing," grumbled her mistress.

The man set to greedily. The owner had to limit the food served, and of course take away the vinegar cruet and sugar bowl in time, for voracity like his had never been seen. The one thing that was freely provided to him was boiled corn. This always hit the mark, since if there was one thing that this character was fond of it was hot *mote* with grated cheese.

His meal finished, he would get up and leave the place, "like a dog," without even saying thank you. Then he strolled leisurely through "his" park, stopping to chat with an ex-cigarette maker and watch him making saddle-cruppers. Soon after this, he retired to take a siesta until six o'clock in the evening. When the street lights were lit, he knew it was time to go back to the eating-house. He ate his supper and stayed seated for a long time with his elbows on the table until all the other diners had left.

The lazy rascal was waiting in case the owner told him to stay and spend the night with her.

"Well, I'll be going," that was his way of saying good night. He took a page of newspaper out of his pocket and the cook, who was about to go home herself, put into it a roll of bread, some sugar and a handful of ground coffee. Holding his twisted paper parcel, all sweet-smelling of roasted coffee, he repeated his eloquent leave-taking, "Well, I'll be going."

"All right, stay then," the woman would sometimes reply without looking up at him and with the same sour face with which she had greeted him.

At this, the lazy fellow's eyes sparkled and he did not wait for the invitation to be repeated. He never, however, spent the entire night with her and nobody knew what time he left her.

This man was so fundamentally indolent that he never would have accepted any of the many invitations from his compadre Quizhpe, if it had not been for a rather serious quarrel that arose between him and the owner of the eating-house. It was all because he had eaten, behind her back, a whole big bowl of roasted peanuts which she was going to use next day to make one of her best-known dishes, her corn stew with cow's feet and peanuts.

Thereupon the stout woman blew up and told him to his face that it was a shameful thing that he had done, no less shameful than to allow himself to be kept by a woman. That she sweated and toiled from morning to night to make a living while he did nothing but fill his stomach at no cost. That she had made up her mind to put an end to such a state of affairs with a mean-spirited character who could not even see to it that she was treated with the respect due to her.

As for the man himself, the center of this storm, he decided to take a trip to Yangana and visit his compadre until the horizon cleared up.

A few weeks later, compadre Trinidad Quizhpe went to the city on errands and was the bearer of the first gift that Don Emilio had ever given anybody in his life—a crock of eggs which of course had come from Trinidad's hens. The recipient, naturally, was the irascible eating-house keeper.

Relations immediately began to improve. She sent him a gift in return and also a letter with a piece of sensational news. At forty years of age she was pregnant. And he was the father of this being who was stirring in her womb!

For the first time in his life the lazy fellow suddenly looked at the earth with a real desire to work it and produce something worth while.

He excitedly folded the letter and told Compadre Quizhpe he would like to go with him when he made his morning rounds of the little farm.

"Compadre, I'm going to have a son," he told him, taking him by the arm, "Now I'm really going to work. You'll give me a tiny little strip of land, won't you, compadre? You have more than you know what to do with."

His mind was already full of imaginary farm projects.

Soon afterward he happened to be on his way to a watering-hole in the woods and found himself standing on a little hill crowned with acacia trees in full foliage. From this high spot he could see stretching below him the limitless sweep of the Common Lands of Yangana. The cinchona forest stretched away right up to the Cordillera.

Up to now he had always looked on this land without interest or affection; but this time it seemed to him like a mother, a kindly, fruitful life-sustaining mother. He could see the open places in the forest where the hand of man had cleared the ground for cultivation. It was in these bare patches that the commoners of Yangana—his compadre Quizhpe among them—planted their corn, their cassava, their beans......

Emilio, the lazy man, the inexperienced father-to-be, decided to scratch the ground.

Thanks to the letter he carried in his pocket he had begun to have a worthwhile objective in his life. He had someone to work for, a reason for working. It was his son, as yet unborn, whom he must support, bring up, educate and to whom he must leave an inheritance. Come on, Don Emilio, to work!

The fertile soil was waiting for him. Although geologically old, it was fresh and new. All that was needed was to tickle the surface and make sure that the seed

213

dropped on it was protected from pests. The earth was ready and willing, like a poor man's good cow.

The lazy man was transported by enthusiasm. He sat down on the ground, there on the acacia-covered hillside, in front of his Indian compadre, who could not really understand what it was all about, and began to pat the earth, stroking it as if it were a little child's cheek, exclaiming, "You, dear earth, must give of your abundance for my son."

And the lazy man, flat on the ground, watered it with tears of long-delayed joy at being a father while his friend the Indian stood waiting for him, motionless as an idol with impassive little eyes and a face of stone.

And a few days later, "Compadre, take what you want and fence it in," said the Indian to the lazy man. That was how a clearing was started, a fence made to close in the little field, a parcel of land planted with corn.

Nothing strange or unusual about it. At that time anybody could do the same.

The only duty or obligation which the beneficiary could not avoid was that of opening up the fences after the crops were harvested, so that any of the farm animals in the town could graze freely in the stubble. At the same time, each farmer was never allowed to forget that the watering-holes for the same animals had to be properly protected by a palisade of stout posts to prevent the beasts from muddying the water.

Five years later a little curly-headed boy could be seen running about the patio followed by a flock of hens, with the crown of his hat full of grains of corn, and calling out at the top of his voice, "Chuck, chuck, chuck......"

The child scattered the corn on the ground, the whole flock of hens scrambled for it, the house dogs greedily joined in, the frightened hens squawked and fluttered in all directions.

And the stern voice of the ex-eating-house keeper could be heard swearing at the dogs with the threatening words they well understood, "Whip! whip!"

At noon a horse and rider stopped at the door. The dogs came out from the shade, fawning and wagging their tails, and sniffed at the stirrups.

The master dismounted and made his way to the kitchen followed by all the dogs gamboling and jumping for joy.

The little child ran and threw himself on his father as the man waited for him, squatting on the floor with outstretched arms. The field planted that first year had spread, and now reached right around the acacia-crowned hill. One side of the rough rectangle marked by the fence of acacia rails, now ran right up to the forest. The wood of the fence was freshly cut and the whole length of the clearing on both sides could easily be made out. And what huge shocks of corn! and what an enormous corn-crib!

The corn served to fatten hogs.

A start had also been made on a herd of cows.

These were signs that although prosperity could not be said to have arrived, it was surely coming. Prosperity, that is to say, by the standards of these remote areas. The house was well stocked. There was enough to eat and to spare. Water and firewood were a few steps away from the little house.

When his son Javier Gurumendi was seven years old, his father went back on a visit to the city, a journey calculated to clear up the image of his painful past. And it did.

The way he succeeded in presenting himself had a tremendous effect. Seven years had made a dramatic change.

The mules that both he and his son were riding were caparisoned with style. Closely following them came his compadre Trinidad Quizhpe's eldest son driving a string of pack animals.

The lazy man, himself, appeared rejuvenated. He now had a sunburned healthy look that he had never had before. He still kept his full beard and there wasn't a gray hair in it although he was over fifty. He was well dressed.

His idea was to leave little Javier in a parochial boarding school in the city. After primary grades, he would go on to secondary education, and finally college. His son would study for a profession. He had made up his mind about that, and for that he would work, for that he had been working body and soul in the fields. Yes, sir, he had a son and he was scrupulously carrying out the obligations of a father.

Years passed and Javier grew to manhood. But he hated his studies and never managed to graduate from secondary school.

He had become a great hulking fellow over six feet tall and weighing almost 180 pounds. His feet were huge, he was strong as an ox and his deep bass voice earned him a humorous notoriety. His schoolmates used to amuse themselves by imitating the great oaf, hunching up their shoulders to their necks and making their voices as coarse and gruff as they could. This burlesque never failed to convulse the girl students.

The young man spent his school holidays with his parents, at home in the country. Each time he returned there, he could not fail to notice how the farm that his father had begun in the Yangana Common Land had grown.

At first it was called an *estancia*, which in those parts is a word only used to describe a comparatively small parcel of land. After a while it was called a *fundo*, and finally was considered an *hacienda*, a designation commonly accepted as implying a considerable landed property belonging exclusively to one owner.

Nevertheless, in the eyes of his neighbors in Yangana, this outsider whose presence they had tolerated so kindly, this untiring worker who up to a short time before had labored personally in his fields helped by the fellow-workers of a *minga*, was still thought of as a "commoner," however well-off he may have become.

The two compadres, the white man and the Indian, had grown old together. They used to visit one another on alternate Sundays and share their thoughts and memories with real warmth and affection. The erstwhile vagabond, now all wrapped up in his son, and the Indian, now all wrinkled and worn but still standing straight with his lean body, his tobacco-colored skin and his numerous children who treated Javier with a certain respect when he came home on vacation. The two old friends loved to talk of their long relationship and how each had begun to work the land.

Don Emilio had grown garrulous. His recurring theme— after his adoration for his son and his memories of the ex-eating-house keeper now long dead—was the inexpressible gratitude he felt toward his Indian compadre. He told all the world that it was thanks to the encouragement and support of his compadre that he owned what he did and had become what he was.

The city held no attraction for him. Besides, his Javier objected to his father's going there and was frankly annoyed whenever he did. So why contradict his son? Better to visit with his Indian compadre who was so dear to him.

"One of those rare cases of genuine gratitude," was how the people of Yangana explained it.

The old lazy man had always scrupulously obeyed the age-old laws and customs of the community. He really behaved as a joint owner of Common Land. His neighbors, his good neighbors, bore him no ill will as a stranger. When harvest was over, he paid his tithes and first fruits to the priest of the neighboring parish—there was no year-round resident priest in Yangana—and duly opened up his fences and allowed the Yangana livestock to graze freely on the stubble. He regularly sent a man to work in his place on the *mingas*, since his own strength was failing.

Great tracts of land still remained absolutely free and unoccupied. Anybody could go there with a yoke of oxen and return dragging a hardwood beam for his house. Anybody could take a donkey in there and bring back a load of good firewood cut in woods that belonged to everyone and none. On the drier hillsides the thick-trunked cotton-trees offered every year the gift of their heavy pods, bursting with fluffy white kapok fiber to be gathered up by the first comer. The groves of cinchona trees, already thinned out by the local bark-cutters, still gave freely to all who needed quinine. Let he who wants to harvest, harvest. This was the natural order of things. Who could ever want to interfere with such a generally beneficent order of things?

Yet there was one among the people of Yangana who was destined to be such an evil man.

Javier showed only too clearly his contempt for the unspoken tenderness of his father. He had become ashamed of his parents, ever since he had learned in the city, in the most brutal and vulgar way, that his mother was a dirty slatternly eating-house keeper and that his father lived for years at her expense.

This did not prevent him, however, from never losing an opportunity to extract everything he could from the old man. He was an accomplished exploiter of his father. The older he got, the more practiced those time-honored tricks which produce sure results when money and affection are involved. Before long he had become a perfect example of a bad son. It seemed as if fate had shaped him for the express purpose of tormenting his father.

What made things worse was that the man who had once been so lazy felt completely unable to gainsay his son. The stern countenance that he assumed in Javier's presence was nothing but a shield to cover his weakness, a way of controlling the impulse to throw himself into the arms of this sturdy offshoot who was carrying on his name and his now enfeebled personality. He saw himself in this miraculous late flowering of his life. But a better self, more handsome, overflowing with youth and strength! He knew in his heart that if this other self demanded it, he would give him all that he possessed or might possess, mortgaging his life if he had to.

But there came a day when Javier, for the first time, came up against an unequivocal NO! from his father.

He had arrived in Yangana unexpectedly after an absence of more than two years, and had gone straight to the "manor house." Without wasting time he told Don Emilio that he had something very important to discuss with him.

"Let's talk clearly," he said. "You have some money, don't you, father?"

The old man scratched his head and was silent for a while before he answered.

"My boy, I might have about seven hundred sucres."

The young man received this reply with a contemptuous gesture.

"And what would all this land of yours be worth?"

"What! Javier! This land is not mine, it belongs to the Community of Yangana."

"Yes, yes." They said something about that. That's why I'm here. I've been looking into it and I've found out that there's a legal way to acquire private property rights to that land. Do you understand me?"

At this, the old man forgot the respect that he felt for his son. He raised his hands over his head and exclaimed:

"That land belongs to the Community. To take any part of it from the Community would be stealing. That is something I will never do, never. No......No."

After a moment of vindictive silence on the part of Javier, his father thought it proper to add:

"Don't you know, my son, how it was that I was able to use this land? I owe a debt of gratitude that I am not going to repay in such a way. You must understand, my dearest son......"

"I'm not interested in hearing that old story," Javier broke in angrily, "All I want to know is what provision you've made for the future, apart from those seven hundred sucres. What are you leaving to me? You yourself have no legal right to what you are working on. You can't even sell it."

Both men fell silent for a long time, the younger like a wild beast watching lest its prey should escape.

The strapping fellow stood there choking with rage. He looked at his father's shoulders. He could not take his eyes from the skinny neck that could so easily be strangled in revenge for the crime of moving left to right and from right to left in refusal. In an effort to control the violence of his feelings, he stepped out into the open courtyard where he could see among the clumps of bamboo the whole sweep of bottom lands, so carefully tended by the man who had once been so lazy.

But the contemplation of this green and peaceful landscape stretching into the distance did nothing to allay the covetous malevolence of his thoughts.

He was incapable of understanding or sharing the satisfaction of a farmer gazing at a well worked field. "The only effect it had on him was that" he kept asking himself, "How much can I get out of this?"

But for all his rage, Javier gained nothing in this first encounter. Although he considered his father a fool, and treated him as such, he was forced to recognize that he had lost his first round. The old man firmly refused to change his mind.

On Javier's return to Quito after his fruitless expedition, he got in touch with the well-known lawyer Zapata and asked his advice, telling him how discouraged he was by the failure of all his efforts.

"No matter that your old man has denied your request," replied the lawyer. "Any district judge will grant me a power of attorney from your father to you. Then all that has to be done is for you, as representing your father, to petition the legal distribution of this land. What an idiot he is! We'll make him a landowner in spite of himself! I'm determined to get the better of this character and force him to become the sole owner of half a parish. However much he may resist, I'll rout him and make him a rich man."

So saying, he rubbed his hands and smiled with almost astonished self-satisfaction. "The truth is," he added, "that I, too, my dear Javier, want to be a landowner. You'll give me a slice and I'll be your neighbor, your near neighbor. It won't be a bad deal for either of us.

The hulking young fellow was not fully convinced. He still believed he would never overcome his father's stubborn objection.

But the lawyer who for years had practiced in all the courtrooms of the Republic, walked to a bookshelf, took out a black bound volume, opened it, licked his fingers and began to turn the pages. Having found what he wanted, he motioned to Javier to sit down with him, and slowly read the following passage:

"The law of the 24th of October of 1863," he quoted, "defined reverted lands in these terms" 'Article 2. Reserved or reverted lands are those that are not private property and are included in the sites set aside for Indian towns and villages, being destined for common or individual use by the indigenous inhabitants.'"

"Such is the case of Yangana." And he went on reading. "Further on, Article 15 states, 'Reverted lands which the indigenous inhabitants have been using as a community shall continue to be used in common, and those lands which have been distributed for the individual use of each indigenous inhabitant, and which are still so possessed, shall remain freehold property of those same persons, whatever the extension of said lands. Such grantees shall have the right as legitimate owners freely to dispose of said lands, and the Governor of the Province is authorized to confirm and confer the respective title-deeds.'"

When Javier heard the wording about indigenous inhabitants, he scowled and swung around sharply in his chair.

"So that when I appear in court as representing my father, I'll have to affirm that he is an Indian? My father is no Indian, and I'll never present myself as the son of an Indian."

The famous jurist burst out laughing and explained that in the first place the word indigenous did not have exactly the same meaning as the word Indian. In the second place, he went on, even if it was understood in that sense, injurious though it might sound to somebody who considered himself American, he, the lawyer, must be allowed to finish his reading of the legal articles bearing on the matter which he and Javier were considering.

With that, he launched forth on what he fancied was a brilliant dissertation which would serve to open the eyes of his client and old school-fellow. He wound up reading him excerpts from what he described as "The Amendment of November 5, 1867," confirming proprietary rights to occupiers of land who had filled certain requirements, with no need to take into account their race or social or economic condition.

In this way all obstacles were easily removed.

A month later, on instructions from the highest political authority in the province, the name of Don Emilio Gurumendi was entered in the Register of Property as owner of the estate known as "Sevilla del Oro," with boundary lines conforming to those described in the petition presented by the son of the interested party, authorized to act for his father. All legal formalities had been complied with. The law had been scrupulously observed. From the judicial point of view, the newly adjudged title was incontrovertible.

This was the first annotated entry of this kind ever made in the Property Register of the canton to which Yangana belonged. The concept of legal private ownership of land, of exclusive title-deeds was born that day in the parish.

The erstwhile lazy man, Javier's father, with his ragged clothes, the idle vagabond who had with one jump become a father and an industrious worker, was transformed without his knowledge into the proprietor of half Yangana.

Ten years later Don Emilio Gurumendi began to pay the penalty for the crime weighing on the head of his unfeeling son.

Javier had mortgaged "Sevilla del Oro" to a brother-in-law, and the mortgage had been foreclosed.

The poor old man was now quite deaf and nearly blind. Since he could hardly see anything, he was unable to rid himself of the chiggers which burrowed into both of his bare feet. He would stick a few needles in the lapel of his threadbare jacket and feel his way, so to speak, to the house where his compadre Quizhpe's sons were living. He would knock on the door with his cane and implore them piteously, "For charity's sake, please dig out a few of my chiggers. I cannot stand their itching any longer."

His feet were now a disgusting sight. Under his toenails and skin, between the oozing sores caused by the scratching and digging of the day before, the yellow chiggers were growing deep down.

But nobody paid any attention to his plight. He had done them enough wrong, even though it was his son who had been the real criminal in his father's name. So the old beggar was obliged to push in the needle with his own hands, feeling and pricking where the itch was worst. His heels too, and the soles of his feet, were ringed in yellow where the chiggers were working under the skin.

To be able to sleep, he kept a stock of corn husks to scratch with, since the unbearable pain caused by the parasites burrowing under the skin and laying their egg-sacs like fat white pearls, was even worse at night. And those corn husks came from the same fields that he himself had once worked with his own hands.

So he lived on for a few more years, tottering about Yangana, a bent, loathsome and almost tragic figure. In their innermost hearts people were sorry for him, but did nothing for him. They felt that they had no right to protect that bowed head from its ordained fate.

The general opinion was that the father was paying for the sins of the son. And since the agony of anyone human being is an absolutely personal matter, this grotesque and revolting pilgrimage made by a man through streets that had in other days witnessed his prosperity, obeyed an inexorable decree which had to be fulfilled.

The town of Yangana was now surrounded by three great estates. Javier, who still owned half of the first one, was living in Quito where he had married and had three children. His hobbling, blind and forgotten father adored him as much as ever.

Patiently waiting the day when sooner or later fate would demand payment from Javier too, Yangana calmly watched. True, he was far away. Nevertheless the town trusted blindly that one day he was bound to come back, driven by an irresistible force. And since he had been blessed with children......if he himself did not pay, there would still remain, in the last resort, his innocent offspring. Somebody of his blood had to settle the heavy account. While he lived and while his sons lived, the tremendous and unavoidable obligation was safely underwritten.

Perhaps this was the most terrible of all the reflections of the people of Yangana concerning the story of the lazy man. They were firmly convinced that somebody had to pay the debt owed by Javier Gurumendi for what he had done to a town that had treated his father so generously. They believed that the poor old man's penance had not satisfied the thirst of the Gods.

Comforted by their faith that sooner or later the last act of the drama would be played out, the people of Yangana watched from afar while Javier Gurumendi grew old without any calamity befalling him in his empty existence. They began to be surer than ever that after Javier's death, his surviving sons would infallibly be called upon to settle the dreadful account. So that when Javier's eldest son arrived in the town, only a few years ago, to take possession of

"Sevilla del Oro," they were ready and waiting for something decisive to happen.

"He who sins must pay for it," was the serenely complacent remark of everybody who saw him return to fulfill his destiny.

In this story the oral tradition in Yangana has preserved the account of how the original owners' of the land were plundered and despoiled of their rights and how they look upon those who profited from the despoiling of their rights and how they look upon those who profited from the despoiling as intruders and oppressors. And further, that the disinherited are only bidding their time until by fair means or foul they can regain their lost lands. In this tale I see, the germ of innumerable future disorders. If this germ is allowed to develop, it will seriously threaten the town. Even now it often clouds the clear sky of that community where crime is almost unknown and where life is tranquil and innocent.

The truth is that from the start these aggrieved people have endeavored to obtain the return of their stolen lands. They wanted to expropriate these neighboring estates in a way that is perfectly in accordance with accepted rules of peaceful and law-abiding procedure. They have petitioned the Legislature year after year with exemplary and unwavering patience. But in the end, even though their cries remain unanswered and unheard, the townspeople seem to be unanimously resolved to obtain justice for themselves, one way or another.

I foresee great danger ahead if this should happen. When I think about the situation it makes me wish with all my heart that I were a person of influence, in a position to help these people persuade their "paternal government" to find a solution for this increasingly serious problem. And I say that it is increasingly serious because, as I have already described earlier, the provincial government has its own ideas about the Yangana people. It considers them, it will be remembered, to be a dangerous mob inspired by criminal instincts and deserving, if not to be hanged, at least to be repressed with an iron hand.

In spite of the dark clouds which, looked at from this point of view, are gathering over the truly wonderful peace and serenity of Yangana, I have faith in the more sensible and the cooler-headed of the citizens. I believe that they will be able to calm the more excitable elements. They still cannot believe that sooner or later the Republic will not do them justice and decree the return of these common lands to those whose forefathers owned and cultivated them from time immemorial.

(19)

Au Revoir Yangana

I have given a rough sketch of the material and spiritual characteristics of the community of Yangana. It is a place that I happened to visit and where I spent more time than I had intended when I planned my botanical expedition to the Ecuadorian Andes. I look on it as a place which is still wholly pastoral.

The people here manage to provide for their needs and to desire only what they can easily come by.

Good clay for making their pots and pans can be found anywhere, with also plenty of kindling and firewood to bake them. The tiles made here are first class. Lumber for roof beams and rafters is cut only a few hours away, even if some of the nearby woods have been fenced in. A man can leave home at daybreak with a yoke of oxen and be back by nightfall with all the posts, crossbeams, rafters and blocks needed to fashion doors, window frames, furniture and floor boards.

They spend little or nothing on clothing since they make almost all of it themselves—shoes, ponchos, hats. They spend hardly anything for light. There is no problem about paying the rent, since practically all of them own their own houses.

Their cattle can graze freely over the countryside outside the town the moment they get beyond the property of the big landowners. In every corral, you will find milk, cheese, whey and cottage cheese. Syrup and molasses are produced in the cane mills, bubbling in big sweet-smelling pots. Fermented cane juice, barley beer (chicha) or white rum are sources of the greatest if transitory merriment.

Pigs by the dozen are fattening in shady pens behind the houses. The greater part of the soil is fertile and easily worked. The grass in the upland pastures is rich and nutritious.

The peas that grow on the hillsides may be a little hard. To make them tender a small cloth bag containing a handful of ashes is put in the pot where they are boiling. And it is great fun to pick them over before putting them in the pot. They are placed on a big wooden tray which is tilted up and down while your hand slides them from one end to the other.

Ears of corn grow big and white and juicy. They are first enjoyed when still tender, when the tassel on the husk is beginning to turn dry, when you can press your fingernail on the grains and squeeze out drops of thick milk. Later on, the sun dried husk protects its shining, brightly colored ear, soon to be ground into meal or to be roasted so that it opens like a rose, like our popcorn.

Orange trees bear all year round and so far no disease has ever struck them. On the hills above Yangana ripe *chirimoyas* fall to the ground from their own weight and serve to fatten the herds of pigs roaming the fields.

Higher up the mountain, the wild cherries, the *zapotes*, the *chamburos*, the *babacos*, the *toronches*, the *quiques*, the *joyapas* are slowly ripening.

In the bottom lands below the town the medlars, papayas, pineapples, avocados and mangos offer their first fruits to the first traveler who passes on his way down to the river.

And since the more the land drops down, the more malaria there is, it is a blessing that the cinchona tree can be found under the very eaves of the town. Its bitter bark is, the best remedy for tertian malaria.

The bottom land never stops producing.

While long stories are being told by the fireside and the most extraordinary lies are listened to without protest, kernels of new corn are popping in the embers like gunshots. Cassava roots and half-ripe plantains are baking in the coals. There is a wonderful smell of broiled sun dried meat. All this comes from the loaded shelves and lofts, the teeming corrals, the, overflowing granaries and corncribs.

And there is not one beggar in the town.

There have been times when wind storms have lashed and battered this tranquil way of life. Crops and fruit trees have been destroyed and stripped. A human life has been cruelly snuffed out. And passions have on occasion also taken their toll, just as lightning strikes a century-old cedar tree.

But the storm has always passed. The skies have cleared. The victims have been counted and the survivors comforted. Those who have shared the threat of impending disaster have embraced one another, and for many a year have told and retold, embellished and woven fantasies about how Destiny drains the honey from their lives only to replenish them again. "How long will this kind of life last?" I ask myself.

Long years will pass, decades, perhaps centuries. This age old community which has no history, which lives on tales and memories told and retold, on innocent fables and homespun legends, will survive. Will it win its fight with the big landowners? Or will it lose? Whichever side prevails— the spirit of the people or the power of money, serious disorders may be the outcome. But come what may, I believe that peace will return, and with it those interminable discussions and conversations that will add another chapter to "The Story of the Lazy Fellow."

Perhaps my countrymen will not take it as just a piece of ridiculous sentimentalism on my part if I tell them that at times I feel a longing to come back here many years from now and end my days in this place.

If only I could! I would be borne to the cemetery on the same kind of bier that is still used to carry the dead. If death happened to surprise me at some distance from town, perhaps they would see to it that my body rode in on horseback. And these good folk of Yangana, with alternating spells of grief and merriment, would dig a grave fifteen feet deep to bury my bones for all eternity. And as the years went by, the tellers and forgers of tales by the fireside would elaborate a fantastic story around that rather strange person they knew as "the gringo": a story that I would never have dreamed of personifying.

If I could return!

INTERLUDE

The Ballad of Sad Euphoria

There was one omission in Spark's written recollections of his stay in Yangana. He made no mention of what the Yangana people later referred to as "the tragic flirtation of Mr. Spark and Juanita Villalba." That is why the actual story, which might have been an interesting one and was in any case one of the latest in the Yangana repertory will now never be told with all its wealth of detail. This applies especially to the psychic events and questions which made up the greater part of it.

The fact is that it is hard to believe some of the episodes related by the sensationalistic and cruelty-loving storytellers at the Yangana firesides. One of their versions told how Mr. Spark had died at the hands of the headhunters of the Amazon. Another dealt with the coming to light of the macabre trophy itself, the head of the unlucky explorer-shrunk into a miniature by the devilish art of the savages. Now converted to a *tzanza* it ended up, in the possession of Juanita, to be cherished in memory of the stranger who had been madly in love with her...Tales like this seemed to be altogether too melodramatic and cheap to be true.

Finally, it seems that this version about Mr. Spark having been lost on his daring attempt to cross the Amazon forest, passing by and beyond the villages of warring tribes, was not supported by clear evidence. And so there were those who still thought it perfectly possible that the young scientist might appear any day in the pages of some North American magazine as a hero of these most dangerous scientific exploits.

These are the reasons why the love story of Mr. Spark and Juanita Villalba can never be properly told. It oscillates between the explorer's notes and the suppositions of acquaintances. It seems a pity that the chance was lost of learning about another trait of the Yangana character and a new chapter of local legend.

And this, too, is why nothing concrete can be said about the Ballad of Sad Euphoria except that it tells of how two very different lives were joined for a moment, as if at a crossing of two roads, which then separated into parallel lines never to touch again.

Never to touch again?

We cannot form any definite opinion about this, one way or the other. No doubt it would be very effective to give a melodramatic ending to, a barely suggested story if it were not quite likely that the story is not yet ended.

Juanita and the gringo met for the first time at Don Vicente Muñoz' house, where the girl had gone to look for some books she wanted, to read again and for something to talk to him about. It was the day after the explorer's arrival and the meeting was purely by chance.

From the very start, they disliked one another. Even Don Vicente was acutely aware of it. Later, they each frankly admitted it to their common friend. Curiously enough, what most irritated both of them was the other one's laugh. Juanita could not stand the gringo's guffaws. "How the self-satisfied imbecile brays like a jackass!" she had exclaimed in horror. As for Mr. Spark, "Your friend, Don Vicente, has a most exasperating way of smiling and a very annoying and monotonous way of talking," said the gringo.

Nevertheless, by the third day Mr. Spark began to be interested in Juanita because she was so eager to take the opposite side in a discussion and clearly took pleasure in stretching it out interminably. It never failed to impress him that one day she would maintain a firm opinion on a subject under debate, and the very next day would argue for the exact opposite with astonishing versatility, seriousness and effrontery.

But what really upset him was that she, so young and beautiful, should have such a hard and hostile attitude toward life and should gratuitously make herself unbearable by always ending the most provocative arguments with the same stabbing and senseless refrain. To say nothing of the look in her eyes, so insolent and mocking under their finely arched eyebrows.

As for Juanita, she noticed that the gringo, the bad tempered gringo, as she began to call him, spoke with a kind of shy, bantering tone and had an intriguing way of looking deep into her eyes. He had about him an air of amused and impertinent complicity which seemed totally out of place. Naturally this appearance of crafty diffidence only served to make Juanita even more merciless and virulent in their discussions and debates, where she felt on firm ground.

She also found a minor source of amusement in the way the young conversationalist spoke Spanish, which at times made her burst out into uncontrollable laughter. Finally, she found herself faced by a stranger, and a foreigner at that, who seemed to know more, very much more, than Don Vicente and herself put together. He had a kind of naive sense of humor that agreeably surprised her. All these impressions so excited Juanita Villalba that the nostrils of her beautiful straight nose positively quivered with anticipation.

Don Vicente had often had long discussions with her about everything under the sun, divine or human, and they were both well acquainted with each other's point of view. But here was something new. What, for example, would this Mr. Spark think about friendship, something in which she barely believed? What about love? Nobody attacked it more sarcastically. What about having children, a problem she regarded with horror? What about marriage? She hated it with all her soul and always criticized it unmercifully. And what about sentiment? What would this foreigner think about sentiment? Something which seemed to her unbearably silly.

To gringo Spark the girl appeared to make a comedy out of everything, which he felt was pure pose. But interesting in spite of it. At times he found her to be a cynic. He had never liked cynical women, and the systematic skepticism day in and day out of this waspish South American village girl rather distressed him. It did not in any way seem to fit in with the ambience of this serene village.

At other times she struck him as a voluntary exile, a young and handsome Diogenes in skirts who had chosen to live not in the staves of a rotten old barrel, but in the sylvan tranquility of a faraway little town. There was no doubt that he felt a kind of sentimental revulsion. That was it— revulsion. He reflected that he himself was also a skeptic at heart. And that a skeptical man and a skeptical woman could not possibly be good company. In the give and take of friendship and love it was a source of grief to him that both parties should recognize the respective deceits employed by the other in the course of their daily relations.

This led him to the conclusion that a skeptical man should look for an open-hearted woman who would not persist in destroying his illusions, but would allow him to live a few moments of forgetfulness and make-believe before each harsh awakening. A man and a woman who have discovered each other's sentiments by a kind of merciless x-ray, and have managed to keep their minds clear even at times of supreme intoxication, make up an explosive and very dangerous combination.

Consequently it was not a pleasant matter to be on intimate terms with this dreadful and horrible country girl. He had enough to do struggling with his own treacherous cynicism.

On one occasion Juanita and the gringo were overcome by a kind of lightheaded frivolity in the heat of an argument, and took it into their heads to see if they could undermine Don Vicente's peace of mind, which was already not as secure as it had been. They seemed to have joined forces to scandalize him by throwing in his face a whole series of outrageous opinions on matters which for Don Vicente should have been treated with the greatest respect. The good man had always believed that there were certain subjects— or at least there still remained a few subjects—so sacred that nobody could throw mud at them or treat them with scorn or sarcasm.

But Juanita saw no obstacle. She was unrelenting in her iconoclasm. The gringo played his part in the game while stealthily watching the movements of the enemy. He found her unbearably arrogant and was confirmed in his original impression. Juanita was only posing when she adopted a totally false position.

This was the beginning of a kind of unceasing struggle between the two, both holding tenaciously to their respective points of view. She had to prove to him that her thinking, was nothing but the result of her attitude toward life, and vice versa, that her attitude toward life was the result of long and matured thought. Under no circumstances would she allow herself to be accused of a deliberately perverted attitude or of an intolerably insincere and pedantic "pose." She maintained that when she was reacting according to her embittered thoughts; she was faithful to her beliefs, and that action was following concept in an ironclad formula, closed and definitive.

As for the man, he liked to think of himself as possessing acute intelligence and a precise sense of human values. He was a naturalist, accustomed to classify neatly and to make definitions based on generic affinity and specific differentiation. Among the ingredients of the girl's spiritual makeup which aroused his curiosity, he searched for a treacherous purpose, a hidden intention, a skilful pretense and the urge to hide an excessively sentimental heart beneath a mask of a sort she considered elegant. But anybody who became involved in the dark complexities of such a spirit, unless from purely intellectual curiosity, as muted and as objective as possible, would find himself in a sea of trouble.

The dialogues between these two characters, so watchful and on their guard, sometimes took on a strange and extraordinary tone. You could almost say that they were curing a sickness while they talked. They seemed to be jealously punishing their own emotions. And it was curious, truly curious, to listen to some of their polite formalities.

For example, when they were first introduced: "It is a great pleasure to know you, Señorita. I put myself at your orders."

"I have neither the pleasure of knowing you, nor do I put myself at your orders. I hate lying and I do not wish that the first word I say to you, whom I neither hate nor love, should be a lie."

And once, when he tried to tell her that he found her exceedingly interesting, "Don't think I'm trying to bring water to my mill, as you people say. I haven't the slightest interest in pleasing you or in arousing your gratitude. But I confess that you are a marvelous person. You have a beautiful sarcastic smile which in your case, wounds without offending. Too bad that I feel bound to confess—quite objectively, of course—that in truth there's a great deal of somber charm about you."

"I'm in a mood to accept the compliment, since it comes from the mouth of such a learned young man. And since I cannot avoid making you a present in return, I have to tell you that you're a gringo with only one defect, which is that you haven't completely stopped being a gringo."

There were times, too, when he dropped his guard. Like a mischievous boy he would amuse himself by slipping in a few phrases of English which she managed to understand and answer immediately. Mr. Spark felt flattered at being comprehended, but when he complimented her by saying, "Why! You understand every word of English that I speak to you. It's extraordinary!" She answered, "To me it's more extraordinary that I can understand what you say to me in Spanish." No, there was no truce between them.

"You are a beautiful savage," he remarked, wishing perhaps to fight a rearguard action. But she always provoked him to continue the duel.

"You are right, Mr. Spark, when you return to your own country, which I hope will be before very long, I shall take great pleasure in sending you your head reduced to a miniature as a souvenir. It will be all shriveled and shrunk. Don't be ashamed to carry it on your shoulders."

On one occasion, Doña Patrocinio was at a party and observed in a loud voice, her eyes sparkling with mischief, "Juanita is acting like a gringa." The girl turned red at the sally and was obviously upset—something very unusual for someone who was always so sure of herself.

And one clear night the young explorer took his theodolite out into the middle of the town square to observe the stars and make pertinent notes. A short time afterward, by the light from Don Vicente Muñoz' oil lamp, he tore into shreds all the sheets of paper he had used for his mathematical calculations.

"This cannot possibly be the azimuthal coordinate," he exclaimed sharply. "I've never made such a stupid mistake."

"The 'mister' must be in love," was the considered conclusion of Don Vicente, who had witnessed the outburst.

When Mr. Spark set out again on his second plant-hunting expedition in the forest, saying that he would be away for a month, Juanita completely gave up her visits to Don Vicente's house, whereas while the gringo was in Yangana she stopped by almost every day.

And as for Mr. Spark's calculation that his trip would take him at least thirty days, he came back a week earlier on the pretext that he had to write and send off a report to his Institute. But the men who were with him in the bush reported that he had written up-his report in his tent, that it was finished before he returned, and that as for mailing it, all he had done was to send it by express by one of his own men at the camp who had delivered it directly to the post office in the provincial capital.

While in the bush, the men who were with him had heard him humming a tune all the time. They recognized it as one of the songs which Don Vicente had asked Juanita to sing at the send-off party in Yangana the day before the expedition left town.

It is a known fact that Juanita had secretly embroidered three silk handkerchiefs with the initials A.S., which were certainly not her own. And it is equally certain that she did not mean to give them to anybody. No, that would have been too pretentious and her hatred of pretension was well known. She herself had declared it emphatically to A.S. and she was very true to her convictions, such as "Never to make oneself ridiculous by sickly expressions of sentiment." Like all skeptics, Juanita was dogmatic and this was one of her dogmas.

Four months after Mr. Spark arrived in Yangana, Juanita was carefully darning his socks. This was known personally to the Señora Patrocinio, to Doña Pascuala, and to Froilán Zapata, the local inventor and mechanic. Nevertheless the dialogues between the two continued to be as abrasive as ever.

"The place you darned in the heel of my sock has blistered my foot, but anyway I can do nothing about it. It's impossible to find acceptable socks in this town. And you at least are not wholly useless when it comes to helping me to take care of my old ones..."

"If I mend them badly, it's on purpose just to see if it will make your stay here and in the surrounding forests not quite so pleasant. You might feel too much at home, and we have every reason to fear that in time you might forget the way out."

There obviously existed a strong mutual attraction. In spite of this, they were perhaps afraid that the moment they could talk together without offense, they would come face to face with the fatal truth. And so they continued to exchange sardonic impertinences, malicious looks and sneering smiles.

For example, the gringo had received a letter from the Institute reminding him that he was expected to return. His hand shook slightly when he showed it to Juanita, who passed a horribly sleepless night and got up next morning with dark lines under her eyes.

"What's the matter with you, Juanita? Can it be that your loving friends have played a trick on you with piñon seeds?"

What he was referring to was the trick of giving someone a drink flavored so as to disguise the taste of the piñon seeds in it—medicinal seeds—which produced a tremendous cathartic effect on the unwary patient. This was an accepted diversion in Yangana. But in the case of Juanita, the gringo knew perfectly well what was the real cause of the black circles under her eyes. The two were fated to torture each other continually, refusing to admit what was obvious, since both of them had strong characters and solid self-esteem.

And another time, when they were walking back together from a wake and he was apparently a little tipsy, he suggested that in the future they address one another with the familiar "thee" and "thou." No doubt that she liked the idea, but true to form, she answered roughly, "And what would we gain by that?"

Under ordinary circumstances the gringo would have smiled at the girl's ferocity; but this time he made up his mind never again to ask her for anything. He would cloak himself in a studied coldness and not emerge for anything in the world. He said to himself that he too abhorred ridicule with all his soul, and that he had not come to the farthest corner of the earth to tremble, sigh and implore at the feet of an absolute savage. Asking for the use of "thee" and "thou" was a very innocent request and it did not deserve such rough treatment.

The final days were days of implacable duel and sarcasm. Words snapped like whip-lashes and the antagonists watched each other like two fencers looking for a vulnerable spot in the enemy's guard. Their eyes sparkled with feverish brilliance.

People who heard and saw them at this time whispered to one another, "The gringo and Juanita are madly in love."

There were now only three days left before the gringo was to leave for the Amazon. For a moment they were alone. The man's voice, vibrant and strong, seemed to break and fail in an emotional pitch, which made Juanita's eyes shine with an eager questioning look.

"In spite of these months of merciless strife......" he began to say, when a loud voice was heard in the corridor outside. And the confession, yes probably the confession, remained unspoken just as the girl was beginning to yield a little.

Soon after, Juanita's eyes had regained their usual expression and the traveler immediately knew that the one favorable moment had been lost forever.

There were now only two days left before the gringo was to leave for the Amazon. Juanita Villalba, the skeptic, purchased and lit a votive candle for the figure of Christ crucified, demanding a miracle as the price of her humiliation. She begged for it out loud and on her knees. The gringo must not go. With her everything was exacting, imperious, tyrannical. This was a case where God should prove to her that He really existed. If the gringo stayed, it would be because there was a God who cared for the happiness of His creatures. If this failed, she would once again believe in absolutely nothing. Once again she would systematically doubt all feelings of any kind, including the purest. Once again...

The day came for the gringo to leave for the Amazon. Spark had been up since daybreak, personally supervising the loads of man and beast. He was more talkative and jocular than ever before. There were moments when he seemed to have been drinking. No, he had not been drinking. Doubtless he was only trying to distract his thoughts by talking.

His helpers and porters had-already gone on ahead, guided by Curly Ocampo. They had contracted to take him as far as the first navigable river, at a place where there was a government outpost and where he could find experienced boatmen to go downstream as far as the ford at Manserriche.

As for now, he meant to set out about noontime, and the mule he would ride as far as the divide at Colambo, where he expected to stay two days taking observations, was waiting for him under the portico of the parish house.

The very hour had come for the gringo to leave for the Amazon! He suddenly went into the parish house and there he found Juanita furiously trampling the sacred painting in front of which she had knelt almost continuously for the two preceding days. The stub of the unfinished candle was still smoking.

It was too late to put herself on guard. Juanita realized almost joyously that she had been caught red-handed. There was no point in pretending any longer.

"Yes, my gringo," she said, "it is useless to deny it. I love you."

And only an hour earlier, when he had gone to say good-bye to her, she had been cold and correct, her delicate eyebrows still arched in ironic insolence. Now she was defeated, and the man who for so many months had loved her as few men ever can love stretched out his arms to her and heard her sobbing against his rough traveling clothes.

It was now four in the afternoon. By this time, the saddled mule was in the sun and some considerate man had loosened the cinch strap tied to one of the columns, the mule remained quietly dozing. From time to time it flicked and swished its tail at the flies. When the sun sets, the animal was still there.

Nobody knew for sure at what hour of the night the rider had come at last for his forgotten mount.

...

For the next two nights a bonfire could be seen burning brightly on the mountain top at Colambo. That was the only

245

clear message ever received after his departure. It must be added, however,—and this was the origin of a whole series of more or less fanciful legends—that people said that about the same time that Mr. Spark was supposed to have perished, the bonfire up on the peak of Colambo started to burn again, and went on burning for several stormy nights, fed and stirred up by the dead lover's hands.

What is actually known is that the man crossed the range, and that he reached the outpost at X where he hired boatmen and bought a canoe. The men who had accompanied him from Yangana were paid off with generous bonuses. The only one he kept on for a short time was Curly Ocampo. And here again we run up against a whole mixture of versions.

According to some, Curly managed by a miracle to escape the gringo's miserable fate. It was even added that Curly had contrived to bring with him the shrunken head of the unfortunate explorer and give it to Juanita. The thread of the story gets lost and hopelessly tangled after that in flights of speculation. Ocampo, who was in a position to talk, flatly denied any knowledge of the young scientist's reportedly horrible death. Juanita refused to say a word and, according to the more suspicious gossipers, she also swore Curly to silence.

Knowing as we do the ever fanciful story-telling habits of the people of Yangana, it would be an act of bad faith to report any more of the loose and contradictory information available up to now. Some of the most important sources of reference are lacking. It would be impossible to give a credible account.

The whole affair was a bitter one, but it was also joyful. She had reason to be happy, wildly happy, and to be unlucky, hopelessly unlucky. The impassive scientist had felt very much the same thing, perhaps even more poignantly than the girl. It was a matter of painful emotion, but also, no doubt about it, when they finally spoke the truth to each other they both felt a kind of sad euphoria.

And when the bonfire up on the heights of Colambo had finally died out, Juanita's eyes never lit up again.

Nevertheless she had to recover. What she did was to revert to the monotonously repeated refrain she had formerly used to express her concentrated scorn for life: —"well and what do we get from this?"

But now this sounded false to her. She was angry at the idea that she could console herself with such a stupid expedient and cried out, "What a hypocritical impostor I am! I'm merely trying to deceive myself!"

Is Mr. Spark still living? Did he really die in the wilds? This ballad of the Sad Euphoria cannot give the answer. The ballad does not even explain why it has such a title.

Better to leave it as it is: an unwritten tale.

PART THREE

The Last Merrymaking in Yangana

(1)

Now we go back to the scene at Palanda where the marchers from Yangana have made camp near Joaquín Reinoso's house and where Curly Ocampo is telling Reinoso and his wife what had brought them there.

Curly Ocampo gave another push with his feet so that his heavy body could continue to rock gently in his hammock while he went on with his story. As for Joaquín Reinoso and his wife, they were all eyes and ears, consumed with curiosity.

All around Reinoso's cramped little house, high up on its posts, cooking fires were being lit in the open spaces he had recently cleared for planting. Clouds of smoke reached the two men and the woman, making them cough and their eyes water.

The Fiesta promised to be better this year than in any previous year, began the narrator in his deep warm voice. Everything seemed to favor it. There was tremendous enthusiasm. We had always wanted to have a good bell for the Church and now we were about to have it. Just to think of the forthcoming celebration for christening the bell and raising it to the belfry made us jump for joy. We young folk had never seen anything of that kind. The existing little bell, cracked and out of tune, had been hung long ago when Don Lisandro was a boy.

The old fellow is still sturdy? interrupted Reinoso. What good clay he's made of! It might be bronze.

Don José Toro undertook to cast the new bell, continued Curly Ocampo, You know what "the Bull" is like when he takes on a job. When he puts his head somewhere, his whole body has to follow, however tight a squeeze. So one fine day he turned up at Roque Vásquez' brick and tile kiln, and we all know what Roque is like—a mean, sly, prickly character—but this time he couldn't wriggle out of doing his share. He had to let his own workmen bear a hand digging out clay from the puddling-pits. And with this first class well beaten material Toro shaped the mold. Between you and me, the big-bellied fellow made a most beautiful mold. Round the rim he imprinted his name in the wet clay.

Everyone in town was curious to see the mold. Roque puffed and snorted with anger at the crowds which flocked to the shed where the mold was kept, to gape at it with their mouths open. And he could have wept with rage when he caught rascally boys taking advantage of times when a batch of fresh tiles, still soft and unbaked was left unguarded. The young scoundrels would run all over them, leaving the marks of their feet—their 'hooves' as he called them between clenched teeth—and ruining the whole batch.

On instructions from the parish priest, Papa Toro had also put on the mold the name with which the bell would be consecrated, "The Immaculate Conception."

My friends, you should have seen how we cut acacia for firewood, and how Carob trees fell like cornstalks. Another group took charge of hauling out the wood and delivering it at Roque's yard. Roque did get some profit after all from using our abundant firewood, reimbursing himself for some of the damage done by those mischievous boys. What beautiful firewood it was that we had stacked up next to Roque's sheds! It was so thick and heavy that the strongest oxen could drag only a few logs at a time. Only the best would do, since the bronze had to be heated to the point where the molten metal would run like water.

The stack of logs reached to the roof and it did one good to smell the fresh cut wood. We had more than enough firewood. At least, at the very least, sixteen loads. That was how much, sixteen good loads.

On the day set for the casting, the whole town was on edge. To tell the truth we weren't altogether happy. In fact we were more than a little scared. Scared that the job would turn out badly and that in the end we would be cheated in our hopes. Because, my friends, you know as well as I do that it's no easy matter to cast a bell properly. There are times when the mold is too big and the bell has no ears. Other times the mold is too small so that some metal spills over and is lost. At other times there is a shortage of firewood just at the critical moment, the metal does not melt completely and cannot be cast.

At still other times, the bell turns out with a crooked rim; sometimes the mold itself cracks when the molten metal is poured in. And then there are times when the bell comes out looking beautifully perfect with everything complete, but the proportion of the metal ingredients has been calculated wrong, producing a dreadfully harsh tone. Finally, owing to a similar error, it may end up too fragile, like somebody who is sickly from birth, so that when least expected it will crack in the middle of a peal.

That's why Papá Ox always said that making a bell is not as easy as making a son. We put ourselves to no trouble at all to make the child, yet he comes out perfect and with what a voice! But with bells it's no joke. Molten bronze is neither a friend nor a woman, it's a wild beast. It must be handled with caution, with skill and with courage.

We began early in the morning, very early. Into Papa Taro's crucible went a stream of kettles, spurs, bronze sugar cane grinders, old bronze stirrups and what he called the 'noble soul' of it all. This noble soul consisted of some silver spoons, a splendid old much-mended copper pot and a handful of gold coins. Little gold coins, so bright and ringing.

Three men helped the fat fellow feed wood to the furnace. The blazing flames were a fearful sight. Imagine, my friends, there were red hot coals as thick as the rafter of the house. The heat made you sweat no matter how far you were from the fire. The coals turned white, pure white from the heat, while the flames roared all around the crucible. Inquisitive onlookers were kept at a distance, outside the furnace room. The boys, above all, were not allowed anywhere near since by nature boys are never satisfied until they have touched everything they set eyes on. Six men were guarding all possible entrances.

Papá Toro had sole charge of the crucible. Ah! What a devil of a man! He had taken off his shirt and there he was up on top, going round the crucible with a great iron bar in his hand, streaming with sweat and all covered with soot, his jaunty ribboned hat on his head and a fierce scowl on his face. What a bull neck! What a barrel of a chest, what huge arms! The flames lit up his broad face. His hairy chest was covered with sweat and dust. The veins on his arms stood out like rubber bands. Every so often he shouted orders to his helpers down below.

We had already consumed a good many loads of wood when we saw that the whole crucible was beginning to turn red like a pepper. I swear to you, my friends, I never would have thought it possible that such rough thick clay walls could be heated to such a degree. The only crucibles I had ever seen turn red were the little ones used by silversmiths. And when I was in Curipamba I never had time to see the foundry because I was always down in the mine.

But as for seeing a crucible of this size (and here the narrator stretched out his arms as if trying to embrace a huge tree trunk) looking like red hot iron, I thought it impossible. The molten metal inside had changed color, too. It also was red, but a red that was beginning to turn white. All the objects that had been thrown into the crucible still kept their shape, but you could see that some of them were beginning to soften like wax in the sun. You could also notice that some of the metals, just like people, resisted more than others. Now that I remember, there was a huge bronze stirrup that had been contributed by Don Pablito Mosquera the tapir hunter, and this stirrup went on swimming in the molten mass almost up to the end.

There was a slight pause. The creaking of the hammock ropes and stretcher could be clearly heard as it swung gently back and forth. The narrator passed his right hand over his thick beard, resumed his steady swing and went on with his story.

The bell came out so well that we could not believe it... We just could not believe it. The mold had been so beautifully shaped and the lines of the bell itself were so exciting that you wanted to eat it. It was like a fifteen year old girl. When we moved it to the square, we wanted to caress it. But we still didn't know how it would sound. Would it have a rough harsh tone? Would it have good volume? Would it chime sweetly? Sure it had a pretty face but would it perform as well as it looked?

The hussy was heavy, he added, and she had a lovely figure. Ocampo's enthusiasm seemed to grow by the minute.

The narrator got to his feet to emphasize the next few sentences, and the hammock stopped swinging.

She was as high as this, he said, extending his forearm and open hand as if feeling the first drops of a shower. She was as high as this and we all loved her.

We had put something of ourselves in her—our metals, our work, our anxiety—for all of us she was like a favorite daughter. Nobody paid any attention to the women. I tell you that even the young men hardly turned to look when they passed by the little street where the 'Virgin of the Wild Fig Tree' lived. The bell was everybody's sweetheart.

She was everybody's darling, he repeated, getting back into the hammock which he had left for a moment to stretch himself. We felt like embracing her and carrying her off. If she had not been so heavy, goodness knows where she would have ended up. Do you remember the story of Juan Garin, how he stole the monstrance from the church and took it into the woods so that he could cherish and adore it all by himself? But that mischief of a bell stood fast on the ground as if she'd been planted there. She flirted with everyone but went off with no one!

What with the new bell, the preparations for the Fiesta proceeded as never before. The priest was doing business in all directions and didn't miss a trick. Since we were all in such good spirits, it was the easiest thing for him to get money from us and to recruit help to neaten up the church and the parish house, inside and out. We all bore a hand. Something that anybody could see, my friends, was that we all seemed to be in harmony and that we were working as if moved by a single will. Between you and me, I'll tell you that the town had never appeared so united.

For example, when it was a matter of giving three coats of whitewash to the walls, some went to fetch lime, others to burn it; these went for pots and pans; those went for brushes, buckets and ladders. It was like a *minga* where the whole town was working. Just like that, the whole town.

When some of the beams in the parish house had to be replaced, and the tiled roof on the corner next to the sacristy had to be repaired, why some went to cut logs up on the hillside, others contributed tiles, those who lived further away beat up clay for plastering. Nails came from I don't know where, as did axes and every kind of necessary tool. And nobody charged a cent. Who were they going to charge?

Something else that had to be done was to clean up the church tower and dress it properly, so that it would not be ashamed to receive the new bell. For you must remember that the hussy was there at the foot of the church waiting for us to lift her up to her place and make her sing. Soon the belfry too was as elegant as a bride. No sooner did we see it with its face clean and scrubbed than we realized that our little tower was not so bad after all—she'd only had a dirty face.

And so—here Curly's voice took on a touch of sorrow—we left a tower that did not look so bad alongside the bell which we had given.

Doña Patrocinio had already been rehearsing the theatrical presentations, for about a month. This year she was planning a comedy which had been very successful a good many years before, and also a pantomime which Don Vicente Muñoz had written himself, satirizing and making fun of the landlords. As usual, there would be songs, speeches and dancing. And, naturally, the prettiest girls in town would have parts in the play.

Two days before the Fiesta began, strangers began to arrive. Some of them were from remote parts of the countryside, uncouth, rustic people whom we had never seen till then. They were really a ludicrous sight. They looked like wild cattle. As soon as they reached town they formed long lines in single file. Wherever the leader went, all the others followed like a string of ants, as if they were afraid of being attacked. They stood looking with their mouths open at any foolish thing they saw in the street. When they found the bell, they began to walk round and round it with their eyes like saucers, as if it were a strange animal. But it was they who were the strange animals! The local boys would sneak up behind one of these wild cattle, snatch the hat off the clown's head and run off with it across the square.

In fact, all the neighboring countryside was pouring into Yangana. There had never been such a famous Fiesta as this one. The last one, my friends, the very last.

These boors, some of whom were setting foot in the town for the first time in their lives, went straight to the parish house with mule-loads of food for the priest. His larder was overflowing by this time and what he really wanted was cash. He had enough provisions and to spare. That was why for some time he had been celebrating one novena after another with a sung mass and a sermon every morning, distribution of blessings afternoon and evening, and a procession every Sunday.

He appointed a number of lay majordomos to assist in organizing all this and, of course, to bear the expense. That crafty priest had brought a portable harmonium with him and also a singer of sacred chants and hymns. It was beautiful to hear the harmonium and the lovely voices of the choir girls singing to its accompaniment. Especially when they were intoning the litany, you felt as if you were in love and overcome by an urge to drink or ride off with a girl at full gallop.

There were traveling merchants, too. The Peruvians had brought good salt fish. There was kerosene for sale, linen cloth, drill, shirting and sheets. There was great coming and going of buyers and sellers, loaded mules, and porters with sacks and bundles. Tents and booths were set up in the square to feed so many people. Money flowed. And chicha flowed, too. The best corn chicha. It flowed by mule-loads, my friends. The government rum shops were bursting. We had drunks in the street from the very first day to the last. How those people drank!

Ocampo was silent for a moment, thoughtfully cracking his fingers one after the other. Then he smacked his tongue as if savoring something sweet and repeated, How that good chicha flowed!

At that, Joaquín made as if to get up and interrupted him eagerly. "Now that we're on the subject, Curly, wouldn't you like a mug of that good chicha to wet your whistle?"

Curly's only answer was to look up at him incredulously. "Won't you accept a mug of my chicha?" repeated Joaquín. "I have some back there in the kitchen which isn't yet full strength, but which isn't bad either."

Before Ocampo could recover from his astonishment, Joaquín stepped quickly into the kitchen and dipped out a gourd of chicha from the big pot, where it was quietly fermenting. He handed the still dripping gourd to his guest who took it with both hands and put it greedily to his lips. He took two drinks. The first was a short swallow followed by a smack of the tongue on the palate and a grunt of approval; the second, a long draft sustained until with a gasp, a grateful smile and a nod of the head, all was gone.

"But won't you join me?" he said to Reinoso, giving him back the gourd and wiping his mouth on his shirt sleeve.

"And why not?" answered Joaquín, and he moved to serve himself.

"Your chicha is excellent, Joaquín. And you, Rosa Elvira, you've done yourself proud. It's incredible to me to find liquor like this in this solitary place. I confess, Joaquín, I haven't touched a drop since the day we left Yangana. There were times when I could hardly bear it!"

To return to the Fiesta. The day before the great day turned out to be really entertaining. After a sung mass with farewell peals and chimes from the old cracked bell, about 10 o'clock in the morning the rascal Don Pablito Mosquera arrived from El Toronche leading a live tapir on a rope. It was a startling novelty since most of the people there had only seen tapirs when they were already dead and butchered. There were those who stopped looking at the new bell and ran to stare at the tapir. The animal was tethered in the parish house yard and the curious could see it from the doorway. The boys threw stone and lumps of clay at it from a safe distance. Some said it looked like a pig, others that it was more like a donkey, while still others said it reminded them of pictures of an elephant. All agreed that it was very repugnant and very unusual—a phenomenon, something that had been born by mistake.

But the best part of the story is that Don Pablito Mosquera, that joker, then turned loose a fine specimen of a 'Colambo' snake, about six feet long, in the midst of the curious crowd standing round the corral. You never saw such a scared lot. Most of them thought that such an enormous snake must be poisonous. In their haste to escape, they pushed and jostled one another so frantically that some were badly bruised, while the lucky ones got away with their ponchos or shirts torn to pieces. Those of us who were looking on from a distance nearly died of laughter. We nearly died of laughter, my friends.

About eleven o'clock, the best thing of all happened, or rather it was the worst thing. The squires showed up at the parish house. That silly dude Ignacio Gurumendi was riding a handsome piebald mare bought in the city. She had tiny ears and moved like a shower of rain. She was such a high-stepper that her hooves seemed to touch the stirrups as she trotted by. As I said, her master had bought her in the city—he had always had a fondness for good animals.

That young Indian Zapata, with his neck like an avocado, was riding a very good-looking bay mule. She was a young animal of the best breed. She paced as gracefully as the mare, and it was worth seeing how she responded to the spur. The barrel of her body was slim and shapely, her hooves so small that the rider felt not the slightest jar when she was trotting. All that, when you consider that her master was a dirty Indian. What could he know about riding? Imagine, Joaquín, the beastly fellow whose only skill lay in crime and wickedness left the reins loose on the little mule's neck, but even then, with no hand to guide her, she went along beautifully. It made one want to train such a fine animal as she should be trained.

Last of all came Don Pancho Villaviciosa, since the worthless old fellow had been provided with the worst mount. It was the miserable little horse that belonged to his peon, Isaias Armijos. It looked more like a donkey than a horse and its saddle and bridle were in wretched condition. The poor beast showed no sign of wanting to gallop, not even when coming to town.

The priest came out to the middle of the square to receive the squires, fawning and making himself ridiculous with attentions. He himself led the mare by the bridle and conducted them to the parish house.

Some of us were so angry at seeing the three men all together that we bit our lips. The fact was that for a week past, the priest had been preaching to us that this Fiesta was a chance to forget old grudges and hatreds. He said that he would do all he could to bring about a reconciliation between them and us so that we could live in peace. But one thing is certain. When you have been hurt, the wound is not healed with a handful of ashes. It's not removed as easily as that.

The narrator stood up again, his legs wide apart and a fierce look on his face. Standing there by the empty hammock, he put his hand on his heart and struck his chest.

I had a foreboding, my friends. I had misgivings. "Something evil is going to happen here!" I thought to myself. Everything that happed later flashed clearly in my mind's eye! What ever got into these imbeciles that they should put their heads in the tiger's mouth? The feeling I had was terrible, I tell you it was terrible.

As Ocampo repeated the words, "It was terrible…it was terrible," he raised his arms and clenched fists high over his chest. Something evil was about to happen there…

(2)

The whole thing began, my friends, he went on after a pause, some time ago, with the death of old Javier Gurumendi in the Capital and the arrival of his son to take possession of the estate 'Sevilla Del Oro'.

He got back into the hammock and asked for a cup of water. "Water?" asked Rosa Elvira in a reproachfully teasing tone. "Water, my dear girl," repeated Curly Ocampo.

Nevertheless, she came back from the kitchen with the same gourd as before and as full as the first time. It was received with a broad smile.

Up to that time, he continued, the people of the town had never known what it was to suffer want. Just think for a moment because you yourselves remember how things were before you left to come here. When did we ever have to buy straw or used cane sugar stalks from the estate? When did anybody stop us from cutting firewood in the forest, free to all? When did we ever have to ask somebody's permission for our boys to play ball in the pastures behind the parish house? When were we ever denied a pan of cane juice for our pigs? When was there ever lacking a cup of fermented juice for us when they were grinding cane at the big house?

When did our cattle ever find themselves up against a fence on their way to the nearest watering place? When, my friends, did our cattle ever go hungry and at the same time see green pastures the other side of a barbed wire fence? When were we ever denied water from the irrigation ditch, the only condition being that we clean out the headgate and the intake at the beginning of the irrigation season?

So it was that the people of Yangana had never known what it was to suffer until the coming of that insolent dandified Ignacio Gurumendi. Nor had they realized the full infamy of his father Javier. But it seems that even Javier had never fully exploited the rights he had acquired so treacherously. While he lived, the lands of his estate remained unfenced and we still looked on them as belonging to the community.

At first Ignacio was welcomed. He even appeared to be a congenial fellow, affable and good natured. People were prepared to forget, the stigma of his name. Why should he be blamed, said the more kindly among us, for what his father had done, any more than his grandfather could be blamed—that poor old Emilio who had died blind and eaten by chiggers? Although, to tell the truth, when we first heard that he was coming we were very uneasy. But Yangana was very generous and open-hearted to him and at the beginning all was forgotten.

As it turned out, we were mistaken. Between you and me, I don't think Ignacio Gurumendi was very strong in the head. He allowed himself to be deceived and led by old Zapata, the lawyer, who is more cunning and evil minded than the Devil himself, and the two of them began to stir up a peck of trouble. Just think of it, my friends, they proposed to fence in the estates. Before we realized what was happening, the town was surrounded by a circle of barbed wire. If you took this road—a fence. If you went that way— a fence. You went to cut a donkey load of firewood—a fence. You went down to the gully—a fence. You went to take your yoke of oxen to water—a fence.

And to say that all this was legal, my dear friend! "I am within my rights," asserted Ignacio Gurumendi. It's not I, it's the law. What recourse was left to us?

What we did then was to cut the wire on the fences since if he had law on his side, we had justice on ours and these lands had been ours for all our lives and we hadn't sold them to anybody...But the District Commissioner—the same one whom you dealt with, Joaquín, brought a criminal suit against us with the idea of delivering a knockout blow once and for all.

When Joaquín and his wife heard this they were obviously startled. "But...but...didn't the accursed man die that time?"

His hour had not yet come, answered Ocampo in a grave voice full of meaning, it was being reserved for this last time...On the occasion you refer to, Joaquín, the vicious rogue hovered between life and death for fifteen days. In the end his body recovered. But only his body. As for his soul—there was no cure for his soul, it was past saving.

Joaquín was astounded. So, after all, his voluntary exile in this wilderness, his flight from justice and the law, his abandonment of his birthplace—none of this had been really justified! Had he linked his wife to his own fugitive existence and all for nothing?

He asked some more questions. But Ocampo was eager to go on with his story and only turned the palms of his hands to his audience, as if telling them to wait for the sensational part. He stood up again and in the most serious way asked for a light.

Joaquín's wife ran to the fire, moved the burning wood to one side, and picked out a hot coal of almost smokeless hardwood. While the woman held the lighted stick in her hand, Ocampo carefully prepared a cigarette from dried cornhusk and some tobacco he had managed to bring with him. When the cigarette was properly rolled, he took the light and put it to the tobacco, his broad face squinted and wrinkled from the smoke.

"And so the bastard didn't die that time?" Joaquín muttered still trembling with amazement.

"Better for him if he had died then," answered Curly Ocampo who had just taken a long luxurious drag on his cigarette. He blew smoke from his nostrils and mouth and went on with his story.

The lawyer Zapata acted for and supported the Commissioner in the city. In turn, the Commissioner protected the interests of Zapata, that dude Gurumendi and old Villaviciosa. So that the cards were stacked against us, my friends. There was nowhere we could turn. The lawsuit was going very badly for us. Add to this that the Governor of the province was prejudiced against us. Ever since the business of the tallow candles and the Commissioner (with a sly grin at Joaquín) he had his eye on us and considered us a town full of savages...

The people of Yangana had already asked Don Vicente Muñoz what he thought should be done in this situation. Unfortunately, the old man was a believer in peaceful settlements and "gentlemen's agreements." But what I say is how was any peaceful settlement possible with those people who were stealing our lands? What sort of settlement, tell me, could you possibly expect from those vermin who if they had been gentlemen would never have robbed us in the first place? And seeing that the lawyer Zapata had a personal interest in the whole affair, how could we hope for a favorable judgment?

Acting on Don Vicente's advice, we did not take a firm stand at the very start, which was what I thought we should do. Once we had accepted the abuse, it was hard to stop in the middle of the road. These thieves thought it was cowardice on our part and that they could do what they wanted without our saying a word.

Again, at Don Vicente's suggestion, we started a campaign to obtain from the government a supreme decree ordering the return of these lands which were really ours but which now made up the estates of the three squires. Don Vicente sent letters and petitions and a power of attorney to Doctor José Antonio Abril who, as you know, was not only a well known lawyer but our fellow townsman whom we had blindly trusted up till then.

It seemed to us that the Government would itself benefit by acceding to our request since we were prepared to pay much more than the cost of the reversion process, provided that the lands that had always belonged to the town of Yangana were returned to us.

In the end, spend what we might, it was all in vain. Too much intrigue in Quito, too much influence. And the famous Doctor Abril gave us not the slightest support. By the way, I'm telling you this in confidence. The others don't believe it. They think that Doctor Abril did all he could for us...But I myself am sure that if he did anything at all it was to accept a bribe from the other side.

(3)

The beginning of real trouble, continued Curly Ocampo, or rather the first spark that touched it off, was because of a cow.

Yes, because of a cow, he repeated in that way of his, for he loved to pause a moment and repeat certain phrases. He kept swinging in the hammock and looked at his hands as if he were afraid that they had disappeared in the semi-darkness of the night, since now the only light in the little house came from the flickering fire. For the third time, and this time even more seriously, he used the words that he considered the strongest and most expressive, it was because of a cow, my friends...

"And how did that happen?" Joaquín felt obliged to ask, "could it have been one of Papá Gustán's cows?"

That's just what it was, my friend. You figured it out perfectly, answered Ocampo, delighted at such perception.

In fact it was not such a wild guess. When Joaquín himself had still been a neighbor of Papá Gustán's in Yangana, the old man's animals already enjoyed a well-earned reputation for trespassing and stealing.

Joaquín clearly remembered one of them—a very old she-donkey. This animal would enter people's houses when nobody was looking, go into the kitchen and put her muzzle into the pots of steaming corn. However often she burned her mouth, it made no difference. She had learned a number of tricks for lifting bars and opening doors and gates, and could withstand any amount of beating without letting go of her booty. She would fill her belly with barley, bread and molasses and chase off the house dogs by kicking and biting in all directions. Her ears were all doubled over from tick bites and hung down over her eyes, giving her an absolutely grotesque appearance.

She had the strangest partner and accomplice in the world, an old ox with a lame leg and only one horn who served her to some extent as a bodyguard and shared the beatings given her by the victims of her depredations. And Reinoso; being well acquainted with the polygamous old Gustán, immediately thought that soon after his flight from Yangana, a new set of domestic animals dedicated to street larceny must have replaced the aged pair.

Ocampo cleared up this point immediately.

The successors to the mutilated she-donkey and the hulking great ox, were the dog known as "Guard-your-master," and a red cow. It was this cow that started the fight. It was soon after the arrival of that little squire Ignacio Gurumendi. He and that scoundrel Zapata were engaged in some business or other connected with surveying their boundary lines. This time Gurumendi had brought peons from the city to work on the estate. There were about twenty of them, with all the barbed wire they needed. With the help of these men, a good part of what was our land was soon fenced in, as I was telling you just now.

They closed in the pastures known as "The Cactus Field," "The Dead Acacia," "Deer Pond" and "Fox Creek," putting a padlock on all the corral gates. It seemed to us that we were not only locked out, but locked in. That was when we began to cut the fences at night which was the reason for the criminal lawsuit which caused such an uproar. And nobody said a word to those who were shamelessly stealing our common lands!

From now on matters took an ugly turn. Very ugly. It appears that that villain of a Commissioner, seeing that he could not harass us as much or as soon as he wanted to by means of the lawsuit, began to give bad advice to the little squire. And he went about it in the most underhanded way.

He was said to have asked him with a rather mocking and distrustful smile, "It is true, isn't it, Sir, that you are a brave man?" The young man did not wish to appear lacking in spirit and answered, "Of course I am."

The Commissioner, who had an account to settle with the town and was determined to get rid of this thorn in his flesh some way or the other, then asked him, "In that case why are you letting them destroy your fences? I've been thinking, and the lawyer Zapata agrees with me that with a court ruling properly petitioned and duly handed down, I can ruin these bullies and pass judgment on them. It would do them good to rot in jail for a year."

"And do you think that they'll just bow their heads meekly and let you put them in jail?"

"I have already, through lawyer Zapata, requested the Governor of the province to give me the necessary support."

"And do you believe that the Governor of the province can really insure your safety at the moment you'll need it? In the time it takes a posse to get here from the city, these outlaws will have done whatever they want to."

"Lawyer Zapata has already written to me that two well-armed state troopers are on their way here to be billeted in the manor house where I shall supply all their needs."

"And do you really believe that the Governor can dispose of enough armed police to send two men to every manor house, to live there at government expense just to provide bodyguards for the owners?"

So by dint of argument and persuasion, the Commissioner got Squire Gurumendi into a corner. He convinced him that what he ought to do was to send the best men that he had brought from the city to patrol the fence that ran near the square and to fire at any suspicious object that moved.

That silly dude from Quito, to avoid being called a coward, followed this bad advice. After all, to sum up, my friends, somebody had to pay that old unsettled account. My own opinion is that his father was really and directly the one to be blamed. But the father had died without canceling the debt. Between you and me, my friends, don't you agree that everything was bound to end up as it did?

What happened was that one of those nights two gunshots were heard near the manor house, which was located, as you remember, about three blocks out of town, followed immediately afterwards by the most dismal howling and groaning. I got up with my rifle and looked from the window. I could see nothing. I could tell by the sky that it would soon be daybreak. Some drunk who shot a dog was my first thought. But there had been two shots and that pitiful groaning, too. I went back to sleep, however.

I got up very early, put on my clothes and went out to see what had really happened. I soon reached a spot where I found Ulpiano Arévalo, Don José Toro, that disheveled wife of the Chino, and Papá Gustán. Papá Gustán was weeping bitterly. Four fence posts had been knocked over and a few feet beyond them, but outside the fence, the dog "Guard-your-master" and the red cow were lying close together on the ground, both shot. The dog was stretched out in a pool of blood. The red cow, the thieving cow, had her muzzle stuck in the ground and she couldn't move. I can remember the scene as if I were still there. The mud under her head was all churned up by her stertorous breathing. And there was blood everywhere.

To put an end to the poor animal's sufferings, I myself cut her throat. When we skinned her, we found that she had been shot with a load of birdshot and rock salt. Papá Gustán took the skin off his dog, too, weeping all the time.

Ocampo managed with great skill to get one last puff of smoke from the minute cigarette-end between his fingers, contriving goodness knows how, to avoid burning his lips. He threw the butt on the floor and ground it out with his broad bare foot. He spat copiously on the floor, wiped that out, too, with the sole of his foot and changing his tone, gently suggested, "What do you say, Joaquín, shall we have another bowl of that famous *chicha* of yours? It's good enough to wake up the dead," he added, as Rosa Elvira responded with a smile and a nod of the head.

About seven o'clock, continued Ocampo, Don Vicente Muñoz appeared on the scene. "What do you think of what they have done to us, Don Vicente?" I asked him fiercely, looking him full in the face. Nor did I at all like the answer he gave me on the spot. He said that we must put up with it a little longer! Put up with it! We'd already put up with it more than enough! "True," he said, "but let's wait until the government decree comes, it can't be long now." He recommended moderation.

You know, my friends, how he is always counseling moderation. His argument this time was that if we acted violently now, the Governor's report would lay all the blame on us and we would lose our case. He quoted the old saying about the bread being burned in the oven door. In the end he won us over with that eloquent voice of his and the smooth way he presents everything. But we hadn't foreseen what happened at noontime. What happened at noontime! he said softly to himself.

You could easily imagine that in his mind's eye he was looking on at the whole scene. No doubt he was searching for the proper words with which to describe it. But first he had to live it over again and put together the details.

"Well, what happened at noontime?" asked Joaquín with a tinge of impatience in his voice.

The animals' bodies had been removed, but there was still blood all over the ground and it was right in the middle of the path to the watering place. Now, as you well know, by noontime the cattle get thirsty and start coming down toward the water from the acacia patch on the hillside—the only pasture which had remained unfenced. They began to crowd together at the spot where "Guard-your-master" had been killed and where the cow had lain dying.

You know, my friends, how cattle behave when they smell blood. First they put their muzzles to the ground, sniffing and tossing their heads, moaning as though they were sick with glanders. As soon as they are sure that it is really blood, they start pawing and scraping the ground with their forefeet, and finally take to bellowing in the most terrible way.

When the first beast bellows like this, all the others nearby come running as if chased by a fierce dog. Their flanks are heaving and trembling with fear. They all do the same as the first one. So that, believe me, in a short time about sixty head of cattle had gathered there, pawing the ground, sniffing the blood, all the while bawling and bellowing horribly.

Well! I came to see what was happening and all the others came, too. I've never forgotten it. There's a strange thing about cattle. Some of them express feelings more than others. This time they resembled nothing so much as human beings. Just as with suffering people there are some who show their grief more than others, while there are some who keep their sorrow to themselves and give no sign of emotion—so it is with cattle.

On this occasion I remember noticing a skinny little cow belonging to that disheveled wife of the Chino José Vallejo, the carpenter. It looked as if the animal was about to die of grief. She was stamping the ground and moaning in the most mournful way imaginable. She kept looking at the other beasts individually, turning round and round as if calling them to come and see and mourn with her. And after she had looked at the cattle, she came and gazed at us.

She seemed to be wanting to say something to us. If animals could talk! What wouldn't she have wanted to say to us? Her eyes were so sad that I thought she was going to cry, but animals don't know how to cry. I'm not lying. She looked us in the face, all of us who were there, as if reproaching us. How could I make her understand that it was not our fault? She looked more intently at me than at the others and I do believe that if that skinny little cow could have spoken, it would have been to me. In that case, if I had been able to answer and explain everything to all the animals, it was to that cow that I would have addressed myself. She would have understood better than any of them.

I'm not exaggerating when I tell you that Don Vicente, who had come with the rest of us to see what was happening, burst into tears when he heard the chorus of bellowing and lamentation, headed by the skinny little cow who kept walking round and round us. As for me, it made my hair stand on end. I felt like going after the men who were really guilty, kicking and dragging them to the spot, cost what it might, and denouncing them in front of the cattle, saying "These are the ones!"

We finally decided to drive all the animals down to the watering hole, and afterwards we stayed there a long time talking it over among ourselves. We were all wrought up and even Don Vicente spoke much more emotionally than he had earlier in the morning. You could see that the scene had deeply moved him. I liked it when he said, "God grant that this may be the last blood shed because of this miserable lawsuit with the squires."

He then made one of those eloquent little speeches of his, a kind of defense of Papá Gustán's poor dead animals that had been such thieves. "That red cow," he began, "and that dog had a right to live. They were part of the personal life of Yangana." He went on to say that it was true that we were often justifiably furious with them, but we had no right to kill them. The worst punishment they had deserved was a good beating, to make them let go of their booty when they had been so stupid as to allow themselves to be caught in the act. In fact there were times when they were smarter than we were and managed to collect their percentages, so to speak, or almost to take the food out of our mouths so that we couldn't help laughing.

He reflected that pests such as these animals of Papá Gustán's are perhaps a necessary part of life. They oblige us to practice patience, to use our wits and to understand the intelligence and craftiness of animals. They did not deserve such a death. He wound up, as is his way, with I don't know what quotation from Montalvo.

Between you and me, I believe that that chorus of bellowing lamentations from all those cows had more effect on Don Vicente than anything we could have said to him. And from that time on, I noticed that Don Vicente put himself wholeheartedly on our side. He was with us body and soul. He was on our side.

Ocampo was not a man who could remain very long without moving. He had emphasized these last words as if to dramatize the silence which followed, and now once again he got to his feet.

This time he went as far as the balcony at the end of the cramped little corridor and from this height looked down in the direction of the clearing. He surveyed the smoking fires and the people camped around them, and tried to make out through the confused murmur of the crowd, whose voices were the loudest. Some of the fires were already slowly dying out.

In fact there was a noticeable contrast between the brightness of some fires and the feeble flickering of others. It was also apparent that where there was more flame, there was generally more sound of talk and movement of people.

It seemed as if the human presence itself gave life to the fires. The animals could be heard pawing and stamping and gnawing the bark on the trees, accompanied from time to time by a, soft mooing, a quick whinny, or the bark of a dog.

A few steps from Joaquín's little house a sentinel, his rifle slung on his shoulder, was pacing back and forth in front of his dying fire. He moved four steps forward and four steps back again, and each time he emerged from darkness to cross in front of the fire and return to darkness, it was like the opening and closing of a shutter. At each end of the patrol, the darkness swallowed up and then returned the armed man.

Ocampo, with his back to his listeners, stood for a long time watching the sentinel closely, his hands clasped behind him.

"And what happened then?" asked the Reinosos after waiting politely. The woman's voice seemed to betray a touch of disappointment, since what she really wanted to hear about was the Fiesta, and not a word had been said about it for a long time.

(4)

Two days later, one of Sebastián Mayta's breeding cows came staggering up to the door of his house as if drunk, and fell dead. At first glance there seemed to be nothing wrong with her, except that she was passing blood. On opening her up, her intestines were found all torn to pieces. Those villains, those abominable villains, had adopted the practice of seizing any of their neighbor's animals found in their pastures, inserting the barrel of a gun in the rectal orifice, and firing a load of buckshot.

To even the score, we people of the town grievously wounded two of that dude Gurumendi's cows. When he least expected it, he found the poor animals beaten to death in his own corral at the manor house. After this he seemed to pull in his horns, so to speak, as if he realized that things weren't going so well for him.

But once again we were mistaken. Between you and me, my friends, when anybody strays from the highway, it's hard to get back on the road again. We should have remembered this and been warned in time. What we did next was to send word to him through Don Vicente Muñoz, who seemed to most of us to be the best person for the job.

From that moment on, I was convinced that the little squire was really stupid. When Don Vicente called on him, he was so offensively arrogant as to be ridiculous.

"How do you do?" Don Vicente had greeted him. To which the other replied in these terms, "And how do you think I'm doing, living among these savages, your fellow townsmen?"

"It is precisely on their behalf that I have come," said Don Vicente with that blessed patience of his, and disregarding the references to savages.

"Then you could have spared yourself the trouble," replied the fellow. "I want to have nothing to do with them." "But you, Don Ignacio," said Don Vicente in his turn, "ought to know what their proposals and suggestions are before you reject them."

He appeared to hesitate a little at this, changing his tone of voice and asking Don Vicente to sit down.

"What is it that you have to say to me, Don Vicente?" "It is not much, Don Ignacio. Merely that if things go on as they are going now, they give every sign of ending badly. Badly for you and badly for us. It would be better to pause and reflect a little before going any further."

"Then why didn't you say so to those people before they made me lose my two best cows?" retorted Gurumendi.

"There is still time to call a halt, Don Ignacio. For the moment we are even. They cut your fence, you brought a criminal suit. Then you sent men to kill two of the town's animals, and yesterday the town killed two of yours. So far we are even, Don Ignacio. The matter can rest there. You will keep the pastures fenced in until the courts and the Government decide. The town will say nothing to you and do nothing to you. But you cannot fence in the water place for the cattle. That is one thing that you cannot do. The people of the town will never agree to that."

From what Don Vicente reported to us afterwards, up to this point little Squire Ignacio had been listening to him, making an effort to control himself. But when he heard this last prohibition, he could stand it no longer and burst out. At

277

that moment he made himself perfectly ridiculous, showed himself to be a braggart and a swaggering bully, and spewed out his innermost thoughts.

"Know and understand, you miserable make believe lawyer, that since my father's death I take orders from nobody. Know and understand, and go and tell it to those boors, that I have every right to do as I am doing because I am a landowner with title-deeds legally acquired and registered by my father. I have my lawyer and I know what I am doing. I need no advice from ignorant people. I won't be ordered about. I intend to do here, within the limits of what is mine, exactly what I feel like doing. And as for that absurd threat about expropriating my estate—I laugh at it. My family lives in Quito and I have influence there. That suit of yours will get nowhere. Nor will I allow access to The Donkey's Waterhole."

"If you want to, you can make another water hole further downstream by the big Ceibo tree. But I won't stand for a public watering place on my land. If I did, your cattle would break through into my pastures and destroy the fence on that side and that is something I will never allow. And if they threaten me in other ways, such as saying they will stir up the whole town against me, I scoff at that too. I have guns and the law is on my side. Apart from that, I'm a man, a real man. Something else—I've asked for help from the government and it won't be long coming. When it does, we'll see who rules in these parts—the instincts of these savage brutes or the law and order of the authorities."

"Let them just remember the last time a squad of police came to suppress this gang of criminals. And now they want to rebel a second time. It looks as if the only time they keep quiet is when they're being flogged. That's what they need now—flogging and more flogging. Just let them wait and see. And as for me, I won't give them the slightest help."

"Everybody comes to the end of his road," answered Don Vicente, as calm as could be, "take care, Don Ignacio, you are still very young and too impulsive. Think twice. Do not follow the road to violence. Both you and we have too much to lose."

My own opinion is that Don Vicente was not the best person to try to negotiate with a man of Gurumendi's character. I said so at the time. Don Vicente is first rate when dealing with people who want to understand and are capable of understanding. But to approach this so-called gentleman calmly and courteously merely made things worse as far as I could see. No doubt at all but that he imagined we were afraid of him. The result was that instead of gaining something, things merely got worse. Added to it was the rage we felt at his gross treatment of the emissary chosen to speak for the whole town. It was one more insult received from this imbecile.

And then the worst thing of all happened when the three landowners agreed among themselves to oppose us in everything. In everything, my friends. We could go nowhere without coming across some treachery they had been plotting. They were reported as repeatedly saying that they were determined to defend themselves. But their real intention was to stir things up until we were boiling with rage. We took good care not to fall into the trap that they and their ally, the Commissioner had set for us. They spied on us continually in hopes of breaking us for good. Tempers were still at this high pitch on both sides when summer came and with summer came the Fiesta.

The business of the bell, however, made us forget everything else. What was more, the parish priest arrived at the same time and he decided to take a hand in the dispute. Between you and me, my friends, and speaking frankly, he did all he could to negotiate a settlement. He preached to us about peace and nothing else. And he talked long and seriously with the squires on the same theme. If you believed what the priest said, they completely changed their way of thinking during that time. He trusted, too, in what some of us were saying—that the Fiesta provided the best possible opportunity for a reconciliation.

I ought to mention another point, my friends. The more experienced among us did not want the squires to be present at the Fiesta. I sent word to them to that effect. In the first place, we wanted to have fun and enjoy ourselves in peace. Secondly, there would be heavy drinking at the Fiesta and if the best of friends sometimes fight each other when drinking, how much more likely would we be to quarrel with the squires if they showed up.

And I must make it clear that their answer to this was not at all uncivil. They said that they would attend Mass the morning of the Fiesta. That they would return later for the Fiesta itself and go home to their respective manor houses that same night.

When we received this answer there were two different opinions in the town. Some of us thought that the simple act of their coming to the Fiesta at all was a provocation; others maintained that on the contrary it was a sign of good feeling toward the Fiesta. It was argued in their favor that they had made generous gifts to the church, undertaking among other things to bear the cost of christening the bell. And finally Don Vicente who knew before hand that they would be attending the Fiesta, thought it would be a good idea if they stayed for the theatrical performances, where they might hear something that they ought to hear.

So he had written the little satirical sketch or pantomime which I told you about, and was ready to produce it in order to give them what he called a little instruction in discretion. Poor Don Vicente! He didn't know what he was getting into! Scholar and man of books that he was, what did he know of the fury of a populace deprived of its rights! He didn't know what he was getting into.

(5)

This is the story of the fight, my friends. As I was saying earlier, the preliminaries turned out, in spite of those spoilsports, to be as merry and lively as could be. About eleven o'clock when Mass was over and the congregation had scattered over the square, the squires came and made some fatuous speeches to us. It was then that the priest came out as far as the middle of the square to receive them and invite them to the parish house. They had lunch with him there, eating and enjoying the gifts of food that the parishioners had given him. By the time they had finished, it was three in the afternoon and the sun was very hot.

At the stroke of three the post boy showed up riding a donkey and strangely enough, wearing a waterproof poncho in that frightfully hot sun. He rode through the square exchanging jokes with everybody he met and when he reached the parish house, he shook out a big bag he was carrying. The rascal had filled it with those red hornets. The whole angry swarm flew into the square stinging and raising welts in all directions. I tell you, not even the landowners could escape them. One of the little creatures gave Don Pancho Villaviciosa what he deserved and after a few minutes his mouth looked like a ripe mango squashed on his face. The thought struck me that the three of them had come with evil intentions and when a man is full of evil intentions, they are bound to come out.

It was obvious to everybody that that scoundrel of a post boy had done it on purpose. As for old Villaviciosa, it was useless to put a tobacco-and-rum poultice on the swelling.

He was a most ridiculous sight with that ghastly purple lip. Like the other squires, he was full of evil, that was all.

Ocampo paused after these words, rubbing his eyes with his fists as children do when they want to cry. Then he stretched out his hands and passed them over his broad fleshy face, the right hand on the right cheek and the left hand on the left cheek, stroking his thick bushy beard. Finally he clasped them again, rubbing them together enthusiastically.

"Doesn't it seem so to you, Joaquín? Doesn't it seem so to you, Rosa Elvira?" he asked after a moment, as if collecting his thoughts or as if by rubbing his eyes he had come face to face with reality.

Reinosa and his wife's thoughts were no doubt far away, imagining for themselves the scenes which their guest had just been evoking. They seemed to jump at so sudden and unexpected a question. "Why, yes, Curly, that was it," they both answered, "sure, that was it." Then Joaquín asked, "And what about the riding contests? Spearing the ring at full gallop? Races and challenges?"

Reinoso was referring to the traditional afternoon sports on Fiesta day itself—horse racing in the square; riding full tilt at a hoop dangled from a pole and then carrying it off on the point of one's lance; wrestling on horseback.

That was just how it went, Joaquín. There was riding at the hoop. More than forty contestants took part in it. More than forty there were. Maybe sixty. And some fine horses, too. The Mendieta brothers, the horse trainers, performed on some really handsome colts. No doubt about it, in the last days of Yangana there were some really good horses and mules in the town.

Old man Baltazar Zárate had bought two most beautiful colts at the Ayavaca horse fair on one of his trips to Peru and had brought them back with him. It appeared later that they had been stolen by the man who sold them to Baltazar. The price had been suspiciously low and furthermore he had insisted on delivering them outside Ayavaca in the middle of the night on condition that Baltazar would never bring them back into the neighborhood. "I couldn't bear to see them in some one else's possession," the man had said to Baltazar, "I have been a horse breeder all my life and have never liked to sell a colt since I love my livestock as I love my family. I'm only selling now because necessity drives me to it." Words, just words...but I'll say this, between ourselves, the brands had been counter-branded very carelessly and certainly looked suspicious.

So much for that...but we are talking of tilting at the hoop. Ramón Plaza, who has always been rather a slippery character (you remember how when he gallops he twists sideways in the saddle as if he had a boil on his left buttock?)—fell from his mount and almost killed himself. It pretty well split his head and gave him the fright of his life. You should have seen the panic he was in when he found himself on the ground and heard all those horses thundering behind him. The whole square seemed to be shaking. Have you ever noticed how short tempered and violent you feel when you're riding in company with other horsemen? As for me, my hands itched to strike a blow at somebody, anybody. That's what happens when you're riding along in a whole group.

That's why, when the sport at the hoop was over and the tourneys and free-for-alls were about to begin in the square,

I ran as fast as I could to the parish house and asked Squire Ignacio point blank to lend me his fine piebald mare to ride in the contests. And he agreed. I'm sure I didn't look very friendly. He handed her over to me all saddled and bridled! You should have seen how I made her sweat in the races. When I went to return the animal she was frothing at the mouth and looked as if her back was covered with soapsuds under the saddle blankets. She was trembling like a jelly. Don Ignacio didn't say a word. He looked away. He knew that if he'd refused me the mare it would have started something more than he could handle.

On the other hand, that busybody, the Commissioner put his nose in where nobody wanted him. "Your mother sure raised an impudent son when she raised you," he said to me. To which I answered, "Not even the ten cents' worth of tallow candles that they shoved up you that time seem to have done you any good, you cringing toady. Who asked you to carry a taper in this funeral?" And I felt like knocking his hat off. But I controlled myself since at least the little squire had behaved like a gentleman that afternoon.

The script for the competitions was written in part by Don Vicente and in part by Shameless Carlos. Don Vicente's verses were a bit difficult, but we all understood Shameless who is neither scholar nor writer. Perhaps that's why I don't swallow everything that Don Vicente says. In any case I still remember perfectly all of the verses written by Shameless.

We pranced and curveted across the square in squadrons of sixteen horsemen each, in two lines of eight. At the corner of old man Baltazar's house we reined in our horses and Shameless began:—

"Open your heart, beloved town,
For the Fiesta in Yangana,
Began five days ago
And will end tomorrow.

Open your heart, beloved town,
For you must know what is
Tomorrow's program,
Which is our duty to perform.

We have a captive
In front of the parish church
Who will be living with us
Locked up in her prison.

It will be early tomorrow morning
That she will look out from her balcony,
And gaze over the green valley
Of Yangana all about her.

We know that high up on the tower,
She will forget her grief
And sing with her sweet voice
A song to salute the valley.

Tomorrow will be a day of great festivity,
A bell has to be raised on high,
Tomorrow the work must begin
Punctually at the stroke of eight.

Open your heart, beloved town,
All Yangana moving as one
Tomorrow we must raise the bell
Punctually at the stroke of eight."

As soon as Shameless had finished these verses, he curveted his horse around and shook the pennon on his lance. Then he took his place behind the last squadron, which galloped across to the opposite corner of the square.

Damasio Sánchez, who has such a fine singing voice, had already ridden ahead of the troop. Taking off his plumed hat, he sang:—

"Tomorrow at the stroke of eight,
You will have to sweat, beloved town,
For a beautiful captive
Is waiting for us.

Tomorrow at the stroke of eight,
Young and old together,
Must bear a hand
Resolved to do their utmost.

The wise King Solomon
Has sent word to us
That the bell is the sweetheart
Of all our young men.

That as brothers we must not quarrel,
Nor show spite or jealousy,
That we must take care to avoid
Any possible misfortune.

And that therefore it is better
That the little shining bell
Should be christened by the priest
And remain untouched on high.

The young men and boys of Yangana
Who fear and respect King Solomon
Must all be present tomorrow
In solemn procession.

For the sweetheart belongs to no one,
And also belongs to everyone,
And to prevent strife or jealousy
She has taken a solemn vow.

She has sworn that in homage to Yangana
She will remain unwedded,
And sighing up on her balcony,
Must pass her life as a virgin.

In homage to Yangana
She will weep when we are weeping,
And will be as merry as a little girl
Whenever we rejoice.

For the same reason, our young women
Will not envy or hate her,
But rather will ask her prayers
That she will send them a lover.

Open your heart, beloved town,
Yangana the noble town
Prepare to rejoice when we
Ring out the bell's first peal."

After this, the Clown sprang out from the last row. The part was played by José Angel Maridueña who surely was a most comic figure. Instead of a cape, he was wearing an old poncho and under the poncho a long frock coat. His trousers, too, were suitable for the occasion—one leg sky blue and the other one yellow. He was riding a very tame and very lame young ox. His hat had so many feathers on it that they almost completely covered his head. He jabbed the poor ox with his lance and began one of his crazy doggerels:—

"Open your heart, beloved bull
My poor town is lame.
So that is why I have climbed up
On my partner's back.

In the time of the apostles,
Men were barbarians
Who killed the birds
That were up in the trees.

Up there, on that hillside,
I saw two bulls fighting,
One was black and white,
and the other ran away.

Throw shame out of the window,
You snub-nosed creature,
And come with a new husband
To the Fiesta in Yangana.

People call me crazy
Because I am lacking sense.
As for you, you are lacking something
Which I have just eaten.

Since I am only a clown,
I have to keep my secret
Since I don't want people to know
That I have not shown you respect.

Open your heart, beloved cow,
My poor town which is lame
Has had the forbearance
To listen to a poor madman.

Little clown, big clown,
Stop your clowning,
Finish your show with grace
And talk no more nonsense."

Once more Shameless Carlos who has a gift for these
things, took the lead at the corner by the parish house. He
made his horse rear up on its hind legs to clear a space in the
crowd, and recited his second piece:

"Attention! my fine fellows,
Attention! Be as sharp-eyed as hawks,
For you are about to hear
How to raise up the bell.

Let Don Baltica provide
Two yoke of strong oxen,
Eighty yards of rope.
And eleven men to help.

Let José Taro stay sober
To steady both eye and hand,
And prevent the beautiful captive
From loosing her bonds.

Let Chinito the carpenter
Prepare a strong capstan,
And ten ropes strong enough
To bear the strain.

We hereby give orders to Curly,
Who knows all about machinery
To take charge of the operation,
Employing his mechanical skill.

We order Don Ulpiano
To leave his rifle at home,
And to hang on to those ropes,
Having first spat on his hands.

As for Don Víctor Zaruma,
He must forget his hides for a while,
Following the good example
Of the author of these verses.

And Serafín Armijos
Must let his hands be quiet,
And not hold or wave
Those San Ciprian's wands of his.

And you, blacksmith Agustín Labanda,
First cousin of the forge,
The bell is of metal,
And you understand her soul.

Don't be jealous of Papá Toro
For taking over your work,
Be a good companion to him,
And help to raise the bell on high.

Let the brothers Japa, the harness makers,
Shut up shop for a day,
And share with Yangana
Their well-earned joyfulness.

Attention! My brave fellows,
Attention! Be sharp-eyed as hawks,
I'm going to let you know
What a treat is in store for you.

Those in charge have prepared
The most delicious chicha,
And a good supply of rum
To be served by the girls.

For those who prefer cane-juice,
There will be plenty of that too,
So whoever wants to make merry
Will have no difficulty.

Medina has prepared
The most tasty dried meat,
Which his thirty daughters will serve
With great bowls of cassava.

Puglla will play his part
High up on the bell tower,
With four blocks of sugar,
His well-refined sugar.

The Virgin of the Wild Fig Tree,
She who is Queen of Yangana,
Must come, bringing with her
Juanita Villalba.

For they too must help
To distribute among the crowd,
Water to the thirsty
And dainties to the hungry.

And if they don't want to come
I will be obliged to believe
What I have heard tell,
But not wanted to understand.

Which is that the Virgin of the Fig Tree
Has a serious rival,
And, consumed by jealousy,
Has sworn revenge.

Little Yangana bell,
That is something you must prevent,
For if your life has been spared,
You must give away your freedom.

Come all you handsome girls,
And with your glances,
Fire all your lovers' hearts
With will to work.

Open your heart, beloved town,
All Yangana moving as one
Although the oppressors want to humble you,
They can do nothing to you.

Tyrants will never triumph
Over this our town, Yangana,
For whatever we may be lacking
Our resolution will prevail."

At the fourth corner of the square, Damasio Sánchez and the Clown again came forward. When a space had been cleared and the crowd was quiet, they spurred their mounts lightly and began to sing by turns.

Sanchez:

>   Open your heart, beloved town,
>   All Yangana moving as one,
>   We belong to the finest earth
>   In all the land of Ecuador.

Clown:

>   Who can bear more children
>   Than Medina's wife?
>   And who can win a lawsuit
>   Against the contentious Jiménez?

Sanchez:

>   Who knows more about books
>   Than the Yangana Spaniard?
>   Who can argue better
>   Than Juanita Villalba?

Clown:

>   Who is more of a widow than Pancha,
>   Who has devoured three husbands
>   And routed Shameless Carlos
>   Just by looking at him?

Sanchez:

> Who can win against Maridueña
> When it's a matter of lying?
> Who can outlast Don Lisandro
> In avoiding the Grim Reaper?

Clown:

> Who can ride like Mendieta
> The champion horse-tamer,
> Except for his own loved one
> Who still denies him her favors?

Sanchez:

> Who can better set fire to a house
> When his fate commands it,
> Than Fermín the Match,
> The faithful slave to the flame.

Clown:

> My name is Happy-go-Lucky,
> Nephew to Willy-Nilly,
> And that's the reason why
> I am the Prince of Yangana.

> Little clown, big clown,
> I don't want people to tell me

To abandon the field
And leave them in peace.

Little clown, little clown,
Your store of wit is exhausted,
Leave the field to honest folk,
Not a single joke remains.

Prepare a better repertory
For next year,
And return your borrowed trousers
To their rightful owner.

Farewell, my beloved cow,
I mean my native town,
If my fun and joking fell flat
It was not your fault."

With hoots and shouts the crowd dragged the clown from his mount and tore his borrowed trousers to shreds, leaving him in his underclothes. When calm was restored, Damasio Sánchez ended the performance with these verses:—

"Open your heart, beloved town,
Be alert, boys, and hawk-eyed,
For tomorrow is the last day
Of the great Fiesta in Yangana.

Tomorrow at the stroke of eight
We expect you without fail,
To raise our beloved bell
High on the church tower.

Since we are good people
And we love our land,
We have made a bell
Which will stay with us forever.

From the top of the tower
She will be watching over Yangana,
Looking out from her balcony
Like a true sentinel.

We shall place a bell on the tower,
On her great day,
She will weep for our sorrows
And laugh when we are merry.

Open your heart, beloved town,
Be alert, boys, and hawk-eyed
Tomorrow at the stroke of eight
We will raise the bell."

(6)

The next day, my friends, we actually had to raise the bell up to the tower. It was a great day for Yangana. We've never had a *minga* like it. There was more rope than we needed. Every man brought a length strung over his shoulder. What made it harder was the problem of dividing up the work among so many willing hands. We used more than one yoke of oxen, and a winch. The winch belonged to Don Baltazar Zárate and had been overhauled and put in good order by the Chino Vallejo. Even then we were afraid that it might be too old to stand the strain. For many years it had served as a hen roost in a corner behind Don Baltazar's kitchen and was all stained with dirt and grease.

The blocks and tackle that we tried first were not strong enough, and came apart like tinder. We were getting scared. Don José Toro nearly fell to his death off the tower when a poorly made rope pulled out. We all shouted ourselves hoarse when it happened.

Little by little, inch by inch, the bell moved up toward the belfry, hoisted by pure muscle. The ropes began to smoke, my friends. Yes, they were smoking. They had to pass over and chafe on the squared beams of the tower. The cords were stretched like guitar strings. We didn't altogether trust the winch, so we handled the ropes in such a way as to take some of the strain off the shafts. We were actually hanging from the ropes like a swarm of wasps on a block of sugar.

At one stage, the men who were holding down the winch left it and jumped as high as they could so as to grab the rope as far up as possible. They hung there, struggling and writhing like snakes, until the rope moved a little and they could touch ground. Then they did the same thing over again. There were plenty of blistered and bleeding hands. What we really should have had was a pair of iron tackle blocks. There's nothing like them for lifting heavy loads. You agree, don't you Joaquín? Down at the mine in Curipamba one man by himself, using those tackles, could lift a dynamo from its base like a rotten tooth.

While the narrator was giving this description of the scene at the church tower, he was standing in front of his hammock and in his enthusiasm had rolled up his shirt sleeves. There were moments when he acted the part of one of the workers, wildly grasping the hammock rope, his whole body bent like a spring. It looked as if he were trying to tear the hammock off its posts. So much so, in fact, that Rosa Elvira protested teasingly, "Listen, Curly, here where we live it's not easy to make new ropes..."

We were sweating there for almost two hours, continued Curly, but I'll tell you something, my friends, those who were pulling and hauling, weren't the only ones who were sweating. The onlookers were sweating, too, from pure nerves. Perhaps even more than the workers. The priest himself, who has such a red face, was as white as a bone and sweating like the others. He rolled up the sleeves of his cassock and was waving his arms like a scarecrow.

Some of us were so hoarse that we could only talk in whispers. Then there was almost a tremendous row about who was to ring the first peal on the bell. "I'm the one who should, because I lost two ropes broken on the job and nobody's going to pay me for them." "I shall be the first to ring because I gave three loads of firewood for the casting."

"It should be I because I gave twelve pounds of bronze and a pair of antique stirrups." "I should be the one because I am one of the chief sponsors and have contributed a fat cow." And the bell was still a virgin. We still had to hear her sing. How would she turn out? How would she behave? We were afraid that our bell, so beautiful with such a handsome figure, might have a croaking voice after all. But it wasn't so...

We were all outsmarted by Juan Vásquez, the potter who makes himself out to be so dopey. He had sneaked up into the belfry and hidden there. While all the others were arguing at the church door, and almost coming to blows, he had safely locked himself in. Then he caught hold of the bell-rope and set to work pulling on it like a madman. Next he struck his head out from on top and tossed down his old hat. He was as happy as could be. What chimes that bell had, my friends. We wouldn't have thought it possible. She sounded as if she were made of gold and silver. We wouldn't have thought it possible.

Now we were more in love with our bell than ever. She had all the virtues. And while Vásquez was up there ringing, the rest of us down below were jumping for joy, embracing one another and throwing up our hats. Even the coolest-headed seemed to be out of their minds. The square wasn't big enough to hold all the sight-seers. Even those who didn't have a penny in their pockets were counted as taking part in the christening of the bell. Everyone -tried to be more generous and better mannered than his neighbors. It followed that there was food and drink everywhere in the square. There was a cooking fire in this place a fire in that place. Anybody could get a good piece of salt meat on a skewer and roast it in the embers.

There were tubs heaped with boiled corn cassava and plantains. There were jars and crocks of strong chicha, kegs of cane-juice set on the ground, piles of all kinds of fruit. There were fresh cheeses smoked cheeses wrapped in leaves stacks of sugar in cakes and blocks roasted peanuts. With all this there was enough to feed everybody in the whole town and quench their thirst as well—plenty to eat and plenty to drink.

What was more the handsomest and the best dressed girls were the ones who waited on us scurrying around from one side to the other carrying baskets of food. You should have seen, my friends, what a sight we presented by the time it was two in the afternoon. Enough to say that hardly any of them showed up for Mass and the peddlers and hawkers were in the same condition. All signs indicated that before long every man present would be drunk.

The squires had passed the night before with the priest in the parish house and they must all have fared well at lunch since they were as flushed as could be when they appeared about three o'clock. Villaciosa's stung mouth didn't look much better and it made you want to laugh to see him all swollen and only half awake.

Joaquín's wife, Rosa Elvira, had noticed that by now the glow from the kitchen fire barely served to illuminate the scene. She got up and disappeared into the darkness, picking up and dragging along a knotty piece of firewood which left little splinters on the floor behind her. The two men heard someone puffing and blowing repeatedly and forcefully, obviously directed at the fire, for a moment later it responded first with a crackling sparkle, followed by the soft rustling of an updraft. Then it flamed up brightly again, shone on the walls of the little house, and clearly showed the woman coming back through the doorway. The men had been silently waiting for her.

"And what then?" asked Joaquín.

The funniest sight of all was to see Doña Patrocinio's alarm. She was beside herself for fear that the theatrical performance—her show—would be overlooked and never put on. She kept sending messages to this person and that person, begging them to stop the actors from drinking. "How can they keep on drinking under such circumstances. Tell them not to be so gross, so stupid. They can drink any time in all their lives, but they only have tonight for the play, for our comedy. If they must drink, they can start again after the final curtain…"

It looked as if the unheeding tipplers would get the better of her, for by this time the reveling was widespread. But, as you know, Doña Patrocinio isn't one to be easily defeated. She herself set out to scour the square and the colonnades recruiting people to get, to work on the platform and flooring for the stage. According to what she told us afterwards, when she had calmed down—for she never stays angry—it got to be six o'clock and still nothing done about the stage. But she kept after it so energetically that by nine in the evening everything was ready and in place.

You can be sure of one thing. When Doña Patrocinio puts in her hand, she always brings something out. She brings something out. "Yes, Doña Patrocinio gets results…she gets results," repeated Curly with a wide sweep of his right hand. He said it again, stretching out his hand with the fingers spread like a fan. He closed his fist, as if clutching something, drew his arm back, and held it close to his side.

"The Reinoso" couple thought this a really expressive gesture. They could easily imagine Doña Patrocinio's determined behavior, her vigorous movements when faced by an obstacle, her expression so smiling and at the same time so resolute.

(7)

At that moment a little child could be heard crying in the next room and Reinoso and his wife both turned and got up as if to run in the same direction. But since Rosa Elvira was ahead of him, Reinoso decided to stay with the story-teller, who had interrupted his tale.

"A girl?" asked Curly.

Reinoso looked almost offended by the question and answered in a tone of hurt dignity, "A boy, naturally."

"And what is he called?"

"The same as his father. His name is Joaquín."

"How old is he?"

"The little rascal is already ten months." The "little rascal" was known in Joaquin's house as Joaquinillo.

"In that case," responded Curly Ocampo, "he makes a pair with my Adriana, because I have to admit that my latest one turned out to be a girl. But what a charming little creature she is, a real darling."

"I don't know what would have become of us in this wilderness of a forest without this blessing," continued Joaquín. "The rascal is our comfort and consolation. And how bright he is."

"Well, my little Adriana is exceptionally bright, too. She's almost too clever. I'm crazy about her. Of course, little girls are as bright as can be, almost from birth. They're far ahead of little boys. But mine is a real sparkler."

"That's fine, and yours is at least growing up where she sees other people. But ours is out of luck, he's all alone except for us, but in spite of that he's full of grace. To realize how intelligent he is, you ought to see how he crawls after his mother. He follows her as far as the top of the ladder, but not a step further. He stops there, looking down, and even if the gate on the ladder is open, he doesn't go further."

"You mean to say that as little as he is, he doesn't try to go down the ladder for fear of tumbling down?"

"Unbelievable, isn't it? But the little scamp knows that there's nobody who'll watch over him all the time, so he takes care of himself. Just think, the other day he was sitting by himself down there on the ground while his mother was getting water from the river, and he noticed a snake curled up asleep only a few feet away. He had evidently crawled a little further off, very quietly, and when his mother came back he pointed like this (and here Reinoso moved his hand in the vague uncertain way very little children do) to show her the snake, saying at the same time 'ta-ta-tata.' His mother looked where his hand was pointing and there was the snake asleep near the cloth where the little fellow had been sitting."

"Frightened as she was, she killed the snake on the spot. And do you know what, Curly, as soon as the snake was dead, the child pointed at it again with that cute little finger of his and repeated, 'ta-ta-ta-ta,' as if he was telling us that he's not afraid of snakes. You see?"

"Good enough," said Ocampo a little testily. He ventured to add, "As for mine, my little Adriana obviously has never been in such danger, but I do believe that if she had been, she would have known, too, how to behave under the circumstances." He went on after a moment, "But you don't know, Joaquín, what she did only three weeks after she was born when her mother had to leave her at home all day with a neighbor to take care of her. Believe it or not, she already knew who her mother was. The neighbor was also nursing her baby, and we supposed that our snot-nosed little darling would clamp on to the woman's breast. Well, she did not. Our neighbor put her nipple in the baby's little mouth and the knowing creature held it in her mouth but didn't suck. The woman had to feed her boiled liquids with a spoon until her mother came back."

"Is that really so?"

"That's not all, Joaquín," he went on with growing enthusiasm. "When her mother returned she naturally expected the child to throw herself on the breast after practically fasting all day and being wild with hunger. But no, she rejected the breast. That little bit of a person was so resentful of her own mother. The little sniveler had to be paid attention to, loved, caressed and coddled before she could be persuaded to take nourishment."

Things were now more or less even between the two fathers and they were silent for a few moments. They looked happily at each other. They were delighted at having related the accomplishments of their own children. Now the time had come to praise the friend's child.

"And what sort of appetite does little Joaquín have?" asked Ocampo.

"The bandit is a real glutton. His mother has plenty of milk and she gives it to him...Just listen how many times she nurses him. By five in the morning, he's already awake and starting to gesticulate and call out. He knows where to look and drinks his fill. Then he stays a while playing in bed, while I go outside and attend to my chores until my wife calls me for breakfast. When I come back in, he's already in the kitchen, following close behind his mother wherever she goes."

"So we give him a gruel made of plantains with wild honey which is the only sweet we have here. He drinks this until his little belly is round as can be. About eleven o'clock the scamp is begging his mother to nurse him again and he sucks until he's out of breath. Then he sleeps until well into the afternoon. About three or four o'clock he wakes up. He's not fretful or bothersome when he wakes. He stays quite a long time in bed, talking to himself. Later on, when he is cooler, his mother takes him down to the river, bathes him and nurses him again. An hour later, we give him another serving of gruel or some strained drink of whatever is at hand—such as ripe bananas. He likes papaya, too. Oh, if he could have oranges here! I'm sure he'd really love oranges."

"And how many teeth does he have now?"

Joaquín hesitated a little at this question. He did not like having to tell his friend that Joaquinillo was rather backward in the matter of teeth although he was already ten months old. All that Joaquinillo could still boast of was a mouth—his father would have called it a little muzzle—with rosy gums and nothing more.

"He doesn't have any as yet. He's been lazy about it," he answered. "But Rosa Elvira says that it's better that way, because when they do come they'll be harder and last longer. She says that when teeth come early, they also get cavities early."

But Ocampo, whose little daughter already had three or four little teeth, although she was the same age as Joaquinillo, could not accept such a theory.

"Don't you believe it," he retorted, "when teeth come out at the proper time, it's a sign of strength. My little girl is a really sturdy child." He said nothing more than that, "My little girl is a really sturdy child," by which he meant sturdier than Joaquinillo.

Reinoso, however, was not one to give way on this point. "I'll accept it in your case," he agreed. "Nothing strange about that. Little girls develop more quickly than little boys. When little boys are still cracking their eggshells, the girls are already strutting about the barnyard and flirting with the roosters."

It was now up to Curly Ocampo to play his little daughter's next card in this competition. He chose to enlarge on her remarkable natural neatness, her innate refinement and generally excellent character.

"Tell me," he asked Reinoso, "does your little boy let you know when he wants to pee-pee?"

"Hombre, to be frank with you, he still hasn't learned to let us know. I like to tell the truth."

"Well," said Ocampo with a triumphant air. "Adriana certainly lets us know, and I, too, am a man who tells the truth and nothing but the truth. Even when she was younger, she was always extraordinarily cleanly. When she's in her mother's arms and feels the urge, she wriggles herself free and gets down on the floor. This way her mother doesn't have to wash many diapers since the child hardly dirties her clothes."

He realized too late that these last words could have been considered tactless. It was rather discourteous to refer to clothes—either abundance or lack of them—when he was in Joaquín's house where there was hardly enough to cover the nakedness of the two grown-ups so long out of contact with the world. But Joaquin burst out laughing at Curly's words.

"My boy shits when and where he feels like it, why should I deny it? But neither does he give his mother extra work by dirtying his clothes. For the simple reason that he has none."

Curly was a little annoyed at himself for his indelicacy and decided to stop singing the praises of his little girl, at least for a while. He would make amends by giving his friend a chance to tell more about his wonderful little son.

So he asked, in the kindest way, "How does he greet you when you come home from-work?"

Reinoso began to feel a rosy glow coming over him. He had just been given the opportunity he wanted more than anything else now that after so long a time he could finally talk. It was only since yesterday that he could talk with somebody other than his wife. If he could only tell it right, what a marvelous story it was!

"You should see it! When I'm still a hundred yards off, I begin to whistle, but really loud like this," and he bent his little finger, put it in his mouth, curled the end of his tongue round it and gave a shrill whistle.

"The little sniveler, from what his mother tells me, is wild with joy as soon as he hears it and tries to get off the bed any way he can. When he gets on the floor he makes his way by himself to the head of the ladder and sits there waiting for me like a kitten, with his little hands raised and calling out, 'papá, papá, papá, papá.' Then his mother asks him, 'is your father coming? Is that your father?' And the little scamp nods his head and repeats, 'Papá, papá, papá…'"

"As soon as he can see me, I give another whistle, and he answers. You should see it, he answers me. Naturally not by whistling (Ocampo's face was about to break into a bantering smile), but by lifting up his hands, waving them excitedly and shrieking out loud as if he wanted to cry or laugh, but he's really laughing like crazy. He then stretches out his little arms and when he can reach me, he throws himself at my feet and embraces my knees. He holds on to me like this while I'm putting my tools away in a corner, squeaking and gurgling as if I were the one who had to nurse him."

"He keeps on pleading and coaxing in this way until I take him up by his arms and lift him high up. When he's up there, I toss him still higher and then catch him under his little armpits and begin to let him down. When his head is on a level with mine and he can see my face getting nearer and nearer, he almost dies of laughter. Then I prop him on my waist and the rascal amuses himself by pulling my beard. He grabs hold of my whiskers with both hands, without any consideration for me and tugs them to right and left."

"The next step is when I lie down in the hammock, face upwards, and he straddles my stomach. He stays there a good while, talking to himself and giggling. As like as not, he'll wet my stomach while he's there. What a prankster he is! He knows what he's doing and wets the few clothes I have left. Finally he falls asleep in my arms."

Joaquín said the words, "He falls asleep in my arms," in a surprisingly soft and tender tone. He turned his eyes to gaze sweetly at his arms, the arms where in his mind's eye his son was lying cradled, gently rocking.

The two fathers remained silent, looking at each other. All of a sudden Ocampo exclaimed, "I'd like to see the little fellow."

It was what Joaquín wanted with all his heart. He wanted to show off his boy, while Ocampo wanted to see the child in order mentally to compare him with Adrianita, to see how they measured up in face and figure and which was really the better. For, according to Ocampo's way of thinking, his little darling was the most exquisitely beautiful child in the world. If only she could have been there at that moment to dazzle Joaquin and his wife!

Joaquín Reinoso was thinking, "Why miss this opportunity to temper Curly's fatherly pride? In the first place I shall show him that my child is a boy, which gives me a head start. Secondly, I demonstrate that he is handsome, since from what I know of Curly Ocampo's older children and considering how ugly his wife is, it's likely that his vaunted Adrianita is actually a common little Indian. This will allow me to carry on at length and embarrass him, deeply embarrass him so that he'll be consumed with envy however well he may disguise it. What's more, as far as health goes…why there's no child healthier than my rascal."

Joaquín's reflections produced an immediate result. Disregarding the protests of his wife who had gone to hush the child by lying down beside him and lulling him to sleep, he brought out his son wrapped up in old pieces of cloth. The creature looked like a little bear that had gone to sleep determined not to worry about a thing until the next day.

And the two fathers, the one who was showing off his possession and the one who was examining it, thought to themselves with deep inner satisfaction that their own child was the better. They were proud of themselves and wonderfully at peace.

(8)

In the middle of the square, began the narrator as he resumed his story, there were three lighted gasoline lanterns. And there were three more in front of Doña Manuela Cuenca's portico where the stage was always set up as far back as I can remember. The program was to be more or less the same as usual. Except that this time, as I told you just now, my friends, Don Vicente had written a pantomime satirizing the landlords and this pantomime was to be performed before the comedy. It was entitled, "Beware of Still Waters."

"My idea is this," Don Vicente had said during the last rehearsals—"to make the squires understand the risk they are running if they persist in harassing the town as they are doing now." But this only shows, thought I, that you don't know them. I kept quiet, however, because I did not want people to say that I was always against Don Vicente with whom I happened at the time to be on very good terms. But I never believed that the squires would change their ways just on account of this. You don't tame a rampaging bull by slapping him with your hand. That's not how you quiet a rampaging bull.

From very early, the square was packed. The truth is that the greater part of the men were half-drunk, or at least still feeling the effects of the afternoon's drinking. The smartest ones came carrying stools or chairs on their heads so as to be sure of a seat. Right up front, next to the stage, were two unoccupied benches made of slats. These were reserved for the reigning Madrinas of the Fiesta, for the priest, the squires and local officials. I was peering out from the stage through a hole in the curtain and had already noticed that although it was nine o'clock, those benches were still empty.

As for me, I was by now completely cool and collected again. But it has just struck me, my friends, that I haven't said anything about the curtain itself which was the cause of so much trouble later on. The old curtain, the one that you knew with the national flag on it, was unserviceable. Doña Patrocinio always took charge of it after each Fiesta and the last time had apparently wrapped it up by mistake in some paper that had been spattered with molasses. The result of course was that the ants and cockroaches had eaten it to pieces. So that when the furnishings for the stage were unpacked, the curtain was found in tatters.

Since a good heavy cloth suitable for that purpose was not stocked in any quantity in the town, and there was no time to order it from the city, the only solution to the problem was to make a new curtain out of some very heavy red flannel that Don Baltasar Zárate had had in his store since goodness knows when. So we had our new curtain but not with the tricolor. This was another piece of bad luck, as you'll see later on. It was another piece of bad luck.

At this point one of my friends came up and said to me, "Do you think the squires will come? I think not." To which I answered, "On the other hand, I think they will come. Yes, under the priest's protection they'll come. Seeing that they've been drinking, they'll feel brave."

"It would be, too bad if they missed the show."

"How d'you suppose they'll take it?"

"Let's see how they behave, the villainous crooks."

And while we were speculating whether they would show up or not, there they were at the corner of the parish house. First came the priest and they followed him. Last of all came the Commissioner. They all sat down on the front benches. At almost the same time, the Madrinas made their appearance and took the remaining seats. The show was about to begin.

BEWARE OF STILL WATERS

A Farce in One Act and Three Scenes

There are No Personal Allusions

Scene One

The action takes place in one of the parks on the north side of the big city. The time is afternoon.

Characters: Señor Desvalijado, a gentleman who is robbed in the street, two smooth city sharpies, a young student and a clown. Señor Desvalijado is very fat and very elegantly dressed. He is wearing a heavy topcoat, a tall hat and spats and carries a cane.

As the curtain rises, he is alone on the stage. He takes a large cigar from his coat pocket and lights it, seats himself on one of the park benches, leans back and smokes his cigar with visible pleasure. The first city sharpie appears on the right, wearing a mask and a cap pulled low on his head. The second sharpie comes out on the left, dressed like the first. They move cautiously toward the gentleman. At the same time the young student appears at the back of the stage, sees the two sharpies and stops warily, hiding behind a tree where none of the other three can see him.

Sharpie Number 1, advancing with a large shiny knife against his lips as a sign to be quiet, "Don't move, Fatty!"

Sharpie Number 2, coming close up with a revolver in his left hand, holding it by the barrel as if not wishing to scare the gentleman to death, "Be so kind as to let me have the

317

exquisite cigar." Señor Desvalijado relinquishes it without hesitation.

Sharpie Number 1, "Would you be so kind as to hand over your wallet?" Desvalijado looks this way and that, sees nobody but the two sharpies, and reluctantly gives up his wallet. While doing so, he can't help revealing the sparkling rings on his fingers.

Sharpie Number 2, "Don't you find those rings on your fingers rather bothersome? Why should a heavy person like you add so much more to your weight? Allow me, my good friend, to lighten those fat hands of yours," stripping off the rings.

Sharpie Number 1, "Distinguished Sir, could you tell me what time it is by your watch?" Señor Desvalijado now has the anguished look of a drowning man who can see no life saver anywhere. He reaches in his vest pocket and pulls out a large gold watch on a heavy gold chain. "It's beautiful, isn't it?" observed the sharpie, "Let's see what make it is. Why! Does it have a little chain too?" So saying, he next removes the wretched man's scarf and takes two pins out of his cravat.

After this, a kind of thieves' frenzy seems to seize the two scoundrels so that they almost dance round Señor Desvalijado, alternately snatching at and plundering the poor man. (Much action here.)

Sharpie Number 2, "will you give me your silk hat?" (Takes it off his head.)

Sharpie Number 1, "Will you allow me your cane?" (Takes it from his hand.)

Sharpie Number 2, "Your topcoat is made of the best cloth, isn't it?" (Takes it off his back.)

Sharpie Number 1, "My! My! What a lovely jacket you have!" (Takes it off him.)

Sharpie Number 2, "I really admire this vest of yours! We already have the watch chain, let's have the vest to go with it." (Takes it.)

Sharpie Number 1, "But what's the good of a vest without trousers? That's how a Jívaro Indian dresses. We must have the trousers, too." (takes them away). Señor Desvalijado is now left in sad shape, although at least his shirt is a very long one. His underdrawers reach to his socks. The two sharpies take to their heels, no longer brandishing their weapons.

Señor Desvalijado shouts and calls out in an unintelligible gibberish. A policeman promptly appears on the scene. He is dressed as a clown, but you can see he is a law-enforcement officer by his metal badge, his club and his army style cap. His face is powdered white. Four blown-up bulls' bladders are dangling from the end of his club. On reaching the spot he halts at the strange spectacle presented by Señor Desvalijado. He looks at himself and his own appearance, turns to study the gentleman's appearance, and is enraged when he realized that the gentleman's clothes are even more ridiculous than his own. His indignation is apparently quite genuine.

Clown, "Sir, my good sir, what is this I see? How can a man of your age be so brazen as to appear in public in such an indecent condition?" (He walks up and down, twirling his club and smacking Señor Desvalijado's buttocks with the bladders.) "Be advised, sir, that this is a park much frequented by children and respectable people. The public deserves more consideration and respect from you."

Señor Desvalijado tries to speak, to explain what has happened. But the clown is more furious than ever and loses his temper.

"And to make things worse, you want to argue with me. Don't you even respect the authorities? Instead of helping to raise the moral tone of the city by good example, are you trying to corrupt established manners and customs? What a horror!" (Blows his police whistle. Marches across the stage, driving poor Señor Desvalijado who hasn't had a chance to say a single word in front of him. The policeman keeps smacking the man's buttocks with the bladders. When they reach the wings on the left side he pushes him off-stage calling out to an unseen fellow-policeman, "Take him to the police station."

Señor Desvalijado, who is still trying to say something, only has time to cry out, his voice hoarse with fury, "Carajo!"

Now that he has got rid of the gentleman, the clown returns to the scene. "Has such a thing ever been seen before? Has anybody ever seen a person worse dressed than a state employee? This is something that can never be permitted."

The young student, who has remained hidden while all this has been going on, cautiously reappears and approaches the clown.

Student, "Good-day officer."

Clown, "What's the matter, boy?"

Student, "It's that this gentleman whom you arrested had just been robbed and stripped by two thieves."

Clown, "Say that again, will you?"

Student, "I'm saying that some thieves robbed that gentleman of everything that he was wearing. And that it's not right that the victim should be sent to the police station when the guilty ones are the criminals who left him naked."

Clown, "Did you say robbers?"

Student, "Yes, officer, robbers. I saw them."

Clown, "And which way did they go?"

Student, "Over this way, in the direction of the church."

Clown, "Ha, in that case, it's my duty to pursue them immediately. I won't stop until I've run them down. It's my duty."

Student, enthusiastically, "That's how it looks to me, officer. This crime cannot be allowed to remain unpunished. It's really fine to do your duty as you are doing it."

Clown, "I'm after them! Those crooks won't get away with it so easily. What thieves! I swear I won't leave them in peace for a moment! Robbers! Robbers!" (Runs off stage blowing his police whistle again.)

Student, after a moment's hesitation, "What conclusion should I draw from all this? What is the formula for living correctly?" (He seems suddenly to change his mind and throws a book he has been carrying under his arm, to the ground.) "I've found the answer. I won't study another line. The road is clear to me, also the best and quickest way to face up to any situation. The proceedings are perfectly simple. And it should be even easier in those far away regions barely touched by civilization. No more of this slow path I've been following step by step. The other is the best, the quicker, the most effective and the most direct! Long live modern civilization! Long live the magic formula!"

Curtain

Scene Two

The scene is set in the patio of a well-to-do gentleman's country house. On the left is the sugar mill. On the right, the entry to the stables. In the background there is a reception room opening off wide double doors. A hammock is slung between the columns of the portico. There are broad window sills suitable for sitting.

Characters: "The young student; Don Todo-Aguanta; Dr. Pica-Pleitos, an attorney; Commissioner Señor Vela Autoridad; and the Clown."

The young student looks older now. He has a little budding mustache. He has changed his student's garb for riding clothes. He is wearing riding boots and keeps slapping them with a smart riding crop. Don Todo-Aguanta

****

Todo-Aguanta, "Yes, Sir, it would be robbery. Barefaced robbery."

Student, after draining the mug held out to him by Todo-Aguanta, "Justice, justice! Here is an infamous fellow, a vile slanderer, the destroyer of his neighbor's honor, a man who tries to ruin an honorable reputation, a man who would drag a gentleman's honor in the mud! Help, Doctor Pica-Pleitos!"

Pica-Pleitos, (hurrying in from the direction of the stables with a large book under his arm, a great pair of spectacles on the end of his long skinny nose and wearing a battered old tall hat) "How can I be of service to you, my honorable friends?"

Todo-Aguanta, "This rash young man, carried away by the impetuousness of youth and his lack of experience, wants to take away my estate on the pretext that it belongs to him."

Student, winking at Doctor Pica-Pleitos, "This crazy old idiot has just shouted out that I'm a thief."

Todo-Aguanta, "What I said to him, Doctor, was something else. I did not say that he was a thief. I said that anybody who really tried to take from me what is mine was a thief. But I said it jokingly since I believe that this young gentleman too can only be joking with me."

Student, "I spoke and am speaking seriously. I say and affirm that this place is mine, and just because I've said it, this insolent character has called me a thief."

Pica-Pleitos, "Looked at legally, nothing could be simpler. To hand down a judicial ruling when two litigants both believe they are in the right, the approved procedure is to consult the Civil or Criminal Code. (Opening his book.) Here it is: Ownership of real estate is acquired when title deeds are entered in the District Land Registry. My friend, let me see your duly registered title deeds."

Todo-Aguanta, "I neither have nor need to have a title of any kind. Nor did my father have or need one. My grandfather needed it even less. All this was acquired and has been held in good faith. It belongs to me because I have inherited it from my forefathers. Because I have covered it with my own plantings. Because it will in time belong to my children. This is mine. And whoever tries to take it from me is a thief. Nothing but a plain thief."

Pica-Pleitos, "And as for you, my young friend, on what do you base your claim?"

Student, (taking a bundle of yellowing papers from his breast pocket), "I have my argument here in my hand. Here are my documents. These papers Doctor, state that I am the legal owner of all this. It follows that, it is mine. The law supports me. I obey the law and this man, too, must obey it. I have already told him so. Otherwise it would merely have been wasting my time to come here and argue with such a hard-headed ignoramus."

Pica-Pleitos, avidly examining the papers, "Oh! August and sacred majesty of law! Your divine rule reaches even here, to these remote limits! What would become of the world without you? War of all against all, as an English writer has said. You protect the weak from the brutal privileges of the strong; you reestablish the balance threatened by the dark forces of evil. Thanks to your all-wise renown and the vigor of your decrees, the world lives in peace and harmony and progress is possible for all humanity. Hail to the written law, the salutary guide and pattern which guarantees universal concord and the peaceful coexistence of all peoples."

"Here, too, you are about to fulfill your sacred ministry, dispensing the sacrament of justice, rendering unto Caesar that which is Caesar's. All that surrounds you, my young friend, is yours. I congratulate you for this. The fruit of your labors, testifying to your noble efforts to improve the land, your constant struggle and sacrifice triumphing over wild nature, all this is of inestimable value. You have every right to it. And I, man of law that I am, put myself at your orders. My duty is to uphold the law, and the law is on your side.

Hail to the noble law! Hail to your health, kind beneficiary of the law and to the person who enjoys your favor! At your service!"

Todo-Aguanta, "I don't quite understand the learned doctor's gibberish, but it sounds to me as if he said that my estate does not belong to me."

Pica-Pleitos, "I was not addressing you, you country boor. My salute to law was couched in the highest literary terms, representing an inspiring flight of fancy which you were incapable of following. But you have indeed perfectly understood the conclusion which dealt with the land that does not belong to you. In effect, the estate belongs to your young master. You are nothing more than his laborer. Do you understand? His servant."

Todo-Aguanta, "I cannot allow myself to be robbed of what is mine and mine alone. I believe that justice will guarantee and defend my rights, however much you may assert the contrary. Since I do not wish to start a quarrel with gentlemen, I prefer to inform the proper authority of the facts. I shall lose no time in presenting my case, since I have other matters to attend to on my estate."

Student, "But haven't you heard what a learned lawyer has just said about my rights? The authority you mention will tell you the same thing that the lawyer has told you because the authorities have to obey the law and you have heard what the law says about my rights. The lawyer has told us the truth and you should be grateful to him, for now you finally know the real truth of the matter. The whole truth and nothing but the truth. Not what we had only thought to be the truth. So here we have the truth, which is that you own nothing at all."

Todo-Aguanta, (rubbing his forehead with his big hands and paying no attention to what he had just heard), "Well now, young man, I believe that I shall end up being really angry with you. And if the authorities think what you say they will think, I'm beginning to believe that I shall have to be angry with them too. And as for those laws that the lawyer has under his arm, if they say what he has been kind enough to try to make me understand, then I shall be obliged to quarrel with that big volume too. But what you all really must want is to make fun of a poor country fellow so as to see what a hillbilly looks like when he's in a rage. Isn't that your intention?"

Student, "And do you think, my good man, that I would have come all the way I have come, leaving all my own affairs, just to make fun of somebody I've never seen before? I am from far away, but my claim is clear and sure. And that is why I am here, to claim my rights. The first thing I do, I said to myself, is to speak personally with the individual who has willfully occupied my land. And then, if he resists, to have him evicted by the authorities."

Todo-Aguanta, "As I still see it, either you people are joking or I shall have to call on the authorities to make you leave me in peace."

Pica-Pleitos, (loudly clapping his hands, at which Commissioner Vela makes his appearance as if responding to an agreed signal), "There's no need to call for the authorities since the authorities have come to us. My dear Vela, good day to you."

Señor Vela, "Good day, gentlemen. Shall we have a drink, since more then three friends are meeting here?"

Todo-Aguanta, "I'll fetch it, sir," goes out in search of rum. Pica-Pleitos, "Everything is ready. All that we lack is your confirmatory."

Señor Vela, "What was that little word you threw at me?" Pica-Pleitos, "What I mean to say is that all we lack is your support for the argument that we have expounded."

"Señor Vela, "What was it you said that I should support?"

Pica-Pleitas, "That you should say the same thing that we have been saying."

Señor Vela, "I will do what I can, always of course provided that you people do what you, can for me."

Pica-Pleitos, "Naturally! We will all benefit from this. An honorarium is an honorarium and the word itself is derived from the word honor."

Todo-Aguanta, returning with brimming glasses which he serves to those present, "You have come at the right time, your honor. I want you to clear up for us a matter that is of great importance to me. You must protect me from this young stranger who declares to my face that my estate belongs to him and that he intends to take it from me. Since you represent the highest local authority and you know me perfectly well because I have always served you when you needed it and since you are well acquainted with the source and history of my property, you can explain to this young gentleman and his lawyer that they are mistaken, that the property I possess is my own because I have acquired it honestly. You must also tell them that in these parts we all live together in peace, enjoying the fruits of our labor."

Señor Vela, "I see that it's a matter of administering justice. So let's hear the other side in order to understand the respective points of view."

Pica-Pleitos, "By your leave, Sir, as a lawyer I represent the interests of this gallant young man and in that capacity I can assure you that my client's petition could not be more just and more strictly according to law. Although I could deliver a discourse expounding the legal principles which support my client's claim, I prefer to quote from the documents which I have here in my hands and which speak more clearly than any lengthy forensic exposition. These documents are the title-deeds that justify my young client's claim. Here they are," he takes the roll of yellowing papers from the student and hands them to the Commissioner.

(Señor Vela, examines them, scratches his head, takes a few steps, obviously uneasy), "This...and this...we have some papers..."

Pica-Pleitos, "Do you see, you brazen swindler? This gentleman, acting in his official capacity, has just ruled against you. You are nothing but a shameless usurper of other people's land. That is what the appropriate local authority has stated emphatically."

Señor Vela, "I see that in the case before us...there are...some papers...this...and this..."

Pica-Pleitos, "Are you convinced? An official ruling on this case has now been handed down. What is more, this ruling will be enforced immediately in order to insure the right of my client, the defendant, to the estate which you so infamously pretend to be yours. We shall now drink a toast to the young owner and to his well-deserved victory over spurious interests which endeavored to block his path and deny him the benefits of what is rightfully his. And so I drink to the future prosperity of this privileged spot," (raises his cup and drinks. The young student and the official drink likewise.)

(Todo-Aguanta throws the contents of his cup on the floor and the lawyer sees it.) "And if you persist in not believing what is clearly evident and in refusing to surrender the property, I tell you that in the eyes of the law which supports and protects us you are...at the very least an arrogant rascal and in any case, unless you retreat, a thief. That's the proper word, a thief. Isn't that so, worshipful authority?"

Señor Vela, completely confused by the yellowing papers and the barrage of questions, "Well now...speaking frankly...I think..."

Pica-Pleitos, "It is decided. Not another word. His worship is right. And if you continue to make a nuisance of yourself, I shall demand that you be sentenced to prison as being an unruly character, a robber, a slanderer and vilifier of honorable citizens, an impudent cynic, a tale bearer and gossip, a disrespectful and irresponsible person, illiterate, ignorant, mentally retarded, insolent, an unbeliever, fraudulent, insubordinate, a rebel and a conspirator. And what is more, I shall obtain judgment against you and have you locked up in jail for fifty years."

Todo-Aguanta (bursting with rage), "And so you intend not only to strip me of my property, but to imprison me as well? And all this under the very nose of the authorities? In what country are we living? Infamous wretches! After a barefaced robbery comes a prison sentence! Oh, what thieves you all are, you ought to give me back this instant even the rum that you drank from my bottle! Thieves! Villainous thieves."

Pica-Pleitos (with an air of highly offended dignity), "May it please your Honor, by virtue of express and appropriate legal requirements, with which you are well acquainted, I hereby accuse the citizen Todo-Aguanta of being the author of innumerable infractions of the Penal Code—among others, lack of respect for the authorities by calling them infamous, and slandering my client by calling him a thief. And I hereby request, since he has been caught in the very act of transgression, that you make use of the powers with which you are invested to order the immediate imprisonment of this audacious and disorderly offender."

Señor Vela (overcome by the flood of legalistic eloquence and by the visible prospect of a bribe, takes a whistle from his pocket and calls the police. He stands glaring at Todo-Aguanta.) Enter the Clown of the first scene, that is to say the policeman. "Take this criminal in charge and accompany him to jail." (Exit the three winners in this affair. As they cross the stage, the young student openly gives Señor Vela a handful of coins which the official pockets with a self-satisfied smile.)

Todo-Aguanta (voluntarily giving himself up to the Clown-Policeman and addressing himself to the others on the way out), "I inherited something else from my father beside this estate of mine—an old proverb which says, 'Beware of still water!' I believe that this is one time when I shall really have to get angry."

Clown, "And what has happened? Although both as policeman and as clown it is my duty to know everything, I find that in this case I know nothing."

Todo-Aguanta, "What has happened is that they want to steal my estate and to do a better job of it they are putting me in jail."

Clown, "Don't worry yourself, at least not yet. Don't be in such a hurry, leave the pain for later on, you'll have plenty to choose from."

Todo-Aguanta, "Could anything be worse than this?"

Clown, "There certainly could, old man. You're only just starting. The worst is to come—what will hurt most. Isn't it true that your wife is still young and still handsome? Don't you have pretty daughters?"

Todo-Aguanta (smiling at the thought of his beloved family), "I should say so. A most handsome wife and very beautiful daughters."

Clown, "In that case the Clown was well advised to warn you to save the pleasure of weeping until later. Until the time when you are safe in the cell where I am about to take you, unless you resist, and where you will notice growing on your forehead. Pica-Pleitos is skillful and has a seductive voice with married women, and as for your pretty daughters, they will soon be pregnant by the young student. You'd better save your tears until all this happens. Don't start so soon, old man. All things in their proper season there is time and to spare."

Todo-Aguanta, "Ah, that would mean the shedding of blood, much blood. I would kill all the guilty ones. The still water would turn into a raging torrent of blood."

Clown, "Don't get into such a state, old chap. It is time for me, to take you to your cell and you must come with me because, for good or for bad, I represent order and authority. And something else, since I have treated you well and given you good advice and have not laughed at your sufferings, you should give me a tip of one sucre because this poor clown is feeling rather sad and wants a drink of rum."

Todo-Aguanta, (effusively), "Here it is, my good friend. You are the only person who has shown me any kindness all day. You will help me to bear my loneliness."

Clown, "Now that I am leaving you in jail, I shall hasten to the young student and ask him for two sucres, telling him he owes it to me for having securely locked up one of the most dangerous enemies of law and order and social justice. I am a servant of the State which is your guardian. The state is one guardian and I am another guardian. The only difference is that my unhappy destiny is to be a jailer to someone who should not be in jail and to protect those who should be in jail. I am the State, as my captain said. And both of us are a real calamity. Now I'll go for my two sucres for the Clown is sad and clowns should not be sad. Order and security. Obedience and respect. Here's to merriment, ha, ha! Farewell my poor friend. To your health! Ha, ha!"

Curtain

Scene Three

(The office of the local authority, a most farcical place. In the corner to the left is a desk and on the desk a machete in its sheath. There are two wooden benches made of slats. In the right hand corner is a wall diagonally across from the other walls and enclosing a door of iron bars leading to the jail. Outside this door is a projection made of adobe, forming a kind of bench for the guard to sit on. As the curtain rises, fifteen townspeople enter on the left in a noisy group, and stop in front of the official's desk. Señor Vela jumps to his feet when he sees them rush in. The clown-jailer, who has been pacing back and forth in front of the bars, stops with a puzzled look and stares at the mob. Loud cries are heard from the back of the cell. It is the voice of Todo-Aguanta imploring his people to help him. All speak in chorus, carefully choosing their words so as to be clearly understood.)

Chorus:

> "We have come, Sir Judge, because
> We wish you to grant liberty to Todo-Aguanta,
> And to put the robbers in his place,
> And free us forever from their clutches.

Señor Vela:

> "In the name of the law I cannot grant
> That which you request.
> Todo-Aguanta is in prison for his crimes,
> And the law punishes the guilty.
> Be gone from here my friends, I urge you,
> Respect the orders of the courts,
> Go back to work on your land,
> And count on my regard for all of you.

Chorus:

> "We cannot depart from here
> Leaving Todo-Aguanta a prisoner,
> Because for us he represents
> John Citizen unjustly jailed.

Señor Vela:
> "The law protects the masters
> And I am bound to uphold that law,
> I do not wish to avail myself of force
> Or disturb the peacefulness of our town.
> Once again I wish to remind you
> That I am the authority which represents
> The Supreme will of the Government
> Before the citizens of this village.
> And whoever refuses to obey my orders
> Shall be denounced as a public enemy,
> And will have to suffer the consequences
> For refusing to listen to me.

Chorus:
> "For the last time, Sir Judge,
> Will you set Todo-Aguanta at liberty,
> Will you open the barred cell
> And imprison the robbers?"

Señor Vela (indignantly):
> "I owe obedience only
> To the orders of the Government.
> You are not a government
> But only people of a town.
> And the people should obey
> Orders proceeding from
> The authorities and the laws
> Which maintain security.

Chorus:
> "Come on lads,
> We have no other recourse,
> We will arrest the Judge,
> And open up the jail."

(Two of the townsmen step forward and take Señor Vela by the arms, dragging him out of his seat at the desk and grasping him firmly by the wrists.)

Voice:
> "Now, Todo-Aguanta, prisoner that you are,
> We give you leave
> To break down the door
> And join the people.

Another Voice:
> "Todo-Aguanta, from this moment you are free.
> Such is the will of the people.
> We must see that justice is done
> Since the hour we have waited for has come."

Clown: (Seeing the turn that events are taking, faces the crowd and looks very kindly at them.)

> "From now on
> I shall speak only in verse,
> So as not to be put in the shade
> By my new prisoner.
> As an authority
> He was most ignorant and evil-minded,

And such a coward that from very fear
He would blow the flute.
I want to be with all of you
Because I represent order
And order goes with force,
Which always has its way.

(He turns and speaks to the deposed official)

And don't you be annoyed at me,
Since you were so stupid
As to forget to ask me
For my strong help.
And as soon as you can
Regain your position,
I shall obey your orders
Without fear or hesitation.

Another Voice:
"And now I demand that we go
And fetch the robbers
Who put Todo-Aguanta
Unjustly in jail,
So that the people may judge them
In a court of last appeal,
And that the trial be presided over
By our friend Todo-Aguanta."

(Six of the group hasten out. Don Todo-Aguanta, as soon as the Clown has unlocked the door to his cell, is welcomed by his friends with warm embraces all around. The cell is locked again, this time with the ex-judge inside.)

Clown:
>"While we are waiting for the transgressors
>To be arrested and brought in,
>We should designate
>Who is to speak in this trial.
>I offer myself as a witness
>For the prosecution
>Giving evidence of unbelievable iniquities
>Committed by the deposed official.
>I can even give evidence in verse
>If the court allows it,
>Since one thing I have always liked
>Is to disregard the rules of rhyme and grammar."

(The men return, bringing the young student and Attorney Pica-Pleitos under arrest. The two are startled to see Todo-Aguanta sitting in the seat of authority, and surrounded by people of the town, giving all the appearance of an impromptu court of law. Meanwhile, one of the slat benches has been placed in front of the desk and Attorney Pica-Pleitos and the young student have been made to sit on it. The Clown, his face all grimaces, goes to fetch Señor Vela. When Vela has taken his seat beside the other two, the Prosecutor, who is standing near the barred door of the cell, bows and begs leave to speak.)

Prosecutor: "We are a community which lives by its labor and harms nobody. We have what we need to support ourselves and we defend and will defend what is ours, loving our peace and our liberty above all else. From our forefathers we have inherited a legacy of experience, toleration and hard work which we wish to preserve and defend for our children. Broad are the common lands which belong to all the people of the town, but at the same time belong to no one individual. They are like air that is breathed and water that flows. If some one comes here with evil arts learned elsewhere and tries to take away from us what is ours, we are obliged to strike back in self-defense.

"If somebody tries to snatch from us the air we breathe, we have to strike back in self-defense. If somebody tries by subterfuge to seize what has never been his, we have to strike back in self-defense. If the local authorities serve the interests of somebody who has bribed and corrupted them, instead of protecting those who have right on their side, then we must defend ourselves against the authorities also, although in theory they represent the established government.

"In the present case an attempt has been made, by means of a judicial trick, to deprive our fellow commoner and joint landowner Todo-Aguanta of what rightfully belongs to him. This is equivalent to an attack on the rights of a whole community. What is more, he has been unjustly imprisoned because he tried to defend what was being taken from him. Falsified title-deeds have been produced and used against him, and he has been falsely accused of insulting and disobeying the authorities. I therefore hereby move that we resolve to protect this commoner and joint owner, making his cause our cause and thereby setting an exemplary precedent.

"Furthermore, I request that this people's court, which is familiar with all the circumstances of the case under consideration, forthwith restore and reaffirm all his rights to the commoner and joint owner Todo-Aguanta, declaring at the same time that we are ready to defend them as if they belonged to the whole town. Furthermore, I request that the corrupt and venal representative of the government be dismissed from his position and punished as the people may decide and themselves effect. Furthermore, I request that the real and undoubted usurpers who have come here only to disturb and alarm the peace and security of the whole neighborhood be summarily expelled forever from these parts, under pain of the severest penalties if they return."

Todo-Aguanta: "My friends! I do not wish to preside over this trial because I harbor personal rancor against those who have offended me, and I wish to see them punished. I therefore beg that some other person be appointed to take my place in this People's Court. I cannot be impartial; I want with all my heart to see them receive their desserts, but I do not wish to be an evil and unjust judge like, for example, Señor Vela."

Voice: "Let's name somebody else, since no guilty person should go unpunished."

The New Judge: "The accused may speak."

Pica-Pleitos: "Should I speak in prose or in verse, in legal language or in common terms?"

Judge: "Speak as you ought to speak here, that is, so that everybody understands you."

Voice from the back: "Give them two hundred lashes!"

A Similar Voice: "Ride them out of town on jackasses!"

Another Voice: "Rub soot on their faces, the brazen scoundrels!"

Another Voice: "Let Reinoso come and take care of the official!"

Chorus of Voices: "Call Reinoso! Call Reinoso! Call Reinoso!"

Another Chorus: "Down with the Squires!"

Another Voice: "Expel the enemy! Expel the enemy!"

Another Chorus: "Expel the enemies! Expel the enemies! Expel the enemies!!"

Chorus: "Beware of still water!"

Another Chorus: "Out with the squires!"

Another Chorus: "We should summon Reinoso! We should summon Reinoso!"

Another Shout: "Let's mount them all on jackasses!"

Curtain Ahead of Time

(10)

"You must not think," continued Curly, picking up his story at this point, that the last part of the play had been performed according to the original script. No, my friends. From the moment the squires were seen all sitting together on their slat bench, unwittingly reminding us of everything that they stood for, the dialogue changed. Don Vicente Muñoz, lover that he is of soft words, never imagined that this would happen. The result was soon evident. Each phrase was harsher than the preceding one. Beginning with the second scene, the prompter was saying one thing and the actors another. Poor Don Vicente was in agony.

Zaruma, the tanner, as you know is, a rough character when he's in his cups and he has a voice like thunder. It was he who gave those first shouts from the crowd. He was standing near the curtain and from time to time—out of pure good will and without being asked—he had been helping to raise or lower it with those great hands of his, shouting at and scolding the stage hands and scene shifters whose job it was. The voices of the chorus had finally cleared his head and roused him to join in what the actors were saying. Then the people down in front immediately followed suit. Some of them did it just to imitate his raucous voice, but most of them because they felt a real urge to cry out against the squires since, at least in my opinion, the play could not have been more provocative.

And when one of the chorus, up there on the stage, shouted out, "Down with the squires!" the words became a refrain repeated from a hundred throats. It wasn't just

Zaruma and his crowd. It was a resounding voice that echoed with a rhythmic beat allover the square. Next they took up that other phrase, "Beware of still water," which they repeated over and over again, stamping and keeping time with their feet.

You know, my friends, that wherever Zaruma may be, you'll also find Agustín Labanda, the blacksmith. To tell the truth, Labanda himself was almost sober but he too was in a bad temper because the Commissioner, at the start of the fracas, had stood up and called out, "get that drunk out of there," referring to his bosom friend. At this, Labanda placed himself next to, Zaruma, threw out his chest and answered at the top of his voice: "Then come and throw him out yourself, you cringing toady!"

Now perhaps, my friends, you may ask me how the squires and the Commissioner himself could possibly put up as they did with all those outright allusions to them in the play. You would have thought that the most sensible thing for them to do would have been to leave as soon as it was obvious they were not welcome. But it's my belief that they were afraid of openly affronting the public; or else they were scared to make their way out through all the crowd surrounding them; or else they thought it better to pretend they had seen and heard nothing. Or for all these reasons put together.

In any case, the fact is that they endured it until the uproar broke out and the Fiesta became a rout and an assault aimed directly at them. By that time, when they finally tried to leave, the mob would not let them go...and there was the very devil to pay. It was truly lamentable, the misfortune, the terrible evil which then fell upon us like a stroke of fate.

When the public intruded on the stage and began to chant the refrain which had started in the chorus, the squires, preceded by the priest tried to retreat, but they couldn't advance one step through the crowd. The mob was determined not to let them go, forming a ring around them and shouting that refrain, "Down with the squires" in their faces. The worst thing that happened was that that humbug Joaquín Torres who is half sorcerer and half herb doctor, sneaked up to Zaruma and slipped him a little glass vial about the size of an ampule of quinine, whispering to him, "break it as close as you can to the squires!" The tanner took the vial and tossed it up in the air quite openly so that it fell at the very feet of the squires.

Seconds later there was the most disgusting and unbearable stink of rotten eggs where they are standing. The bosses were even more enraged and began to swear and curse in the efforts to escape. But nobody heeded them since at that moment Zacarías Fierro forced his way up to them through the ring of men and shouted out: "You arrogant braggarts, you don't leave here until you've promised never to return. This is the town of Todo-Aguanta, the long-suffering one, but we all have suffered enough. The man who tries to leave without our permission dies on the spot!" And there he stood in front of them, glaring at them with that fearful look he has when he's furious.

All this took place almost at the very foot of the stage, just where the squires had been sitting as the guests of honor. Then at this point, while they and the priest himself were practically imprisoned in a ring of men who wouldn't give an inch, Doña Liberata Jiménez, drunk as usual and virago by nature, clambered up on to the stage, tore down one of the drop curtains that was in the way, and threw out her arms asking for silence. At first the crowd took it as a joke and whistled at her; although every head was turned toward her. Doña Liberata took no notice and just went on motioning to them to be quiet. When they were tired of laughing at her, that great burly woman began to speak.

"It's now or never, boys! You've got to take the advice of a woman who has spent her life in law courts fighting for justice. I am that woman, and let me tell you from my own experience that you've got yourselves into a legal mess that shows no sign of ever coming to an end. You may say to me that you trust that the government will recognize the justice of your claim and will order the restitution of the properties which had always belonged to the town of Yangana as public lands. You may say that you hope this will happen because you have received offers of help and you have representatives in Quito authorized to plead your case. You may say to me that the proposition you have made to Congress is an excellent one because its terms provide for Congress to pay the landowners only half or perhaps less than half of what Congress will receive from the commoners of Yangana.

"You may say to me that Congress will rule in favor of the majority since in a conflict where three people are on one side and a thousand on the other side, it is the duty of Congress to support the many even if the few have to suffer.

"This might be the case only if we were living in another world. But since we are living in this world, things won't go the way you think they will. If the members of Congress once began to do what you are asking them to do, they would have to vomit everything that they have swallowed over the years. They are bound to defend the bosses because they too are bosses. They are all the same lot and have to help one another.

"When has a shirtless worker ever gone to the Government to defend the rights of other shirtless workers? When the bosses allow it. And the bosses are not so stupid as to allow it—never. This is something that has to be fought for.

"I see very clearly, friends, that here we have only two choices, either we leave the town, abandoning everything that is there and go far away into the forests to the east in search of virgin land that we can claim, or we take by force the land that we know belongs to us.

"I am convinced and I shout it out loud, that if at this moment when we have the masters in our hands we don't seize this opportunity, we'll never have another chance. I believe that if here and now we forbid them ever to set foot in Yangana on pain of death, and that if we then take them over to the other side of the bridge and make them understand what will happen to them if they ever come back, they will finally realize that it is useless for them to fight against a town, against a whole community, against a population that is resolute and united, because they are the pitcher and the town is the rock.

"I have been and still am a disputatious and litigious person, and as such I repeat what I have always said, that we must stop believing that all will be neatly arranged for us in Quito. This is a matter we must settle ourselves. However badly it may turn out, it will be better than what the bosses in Quito will do for the bosses we have here. Don't you remember my lawsuit about that mare? Sure you remember it. Bear that in mind and don't let the same thing happen again.

"Tell me which you prefer, boys, to recover our lost land, come what may, or go far away from here, abandon our town and look for new land?"

"Stay with what is ours!" shouted some.

"Let them get out of here!"

"Beware of still water!"

"Toss them in a blanket for a send-off!"

"Make them eat shit!"

"Let's hear Don Froilán Zapata, shouted others because, as you know, my friends, Don Froilán loves the sound of his own voice, especially when he's been drinking and at that particular moment he was still drunk.

"I drink to the harmony and concord of these joyful moments," he said. "I drink to the solidarity and brotherhood which unite Yangana the unredeemed! I drink finally to the brotherhood of Man. There should be among us neither resentful people nor injured people! Why spoil our merriment at this time? Weren't we enjoying and celebrating our famous Fiesta as we have done since time immemorial? Long live the harmony of all the world!"

"Why doesn't that drunken idiot keep his mouth shut?" called out several of the crowd, while others caught hold of the man and dragged him down from the stage.

"He's a relation of Attorney Zapata of Quito," remarked several people. No wonder he was said to be against us and for them.

"But don't they see that he's just as drunk as can be?"

"He may understand his tools and his nuts and bolts, but what does he know of this problem?...The last thing we want is harmony and concord; he's a fool!"

So the argument started up again. The next thing we knew, and without so much as by your leave, another drunk scrambled up on the stage. He was a fellow who had only arrived in Yangana two days before the Fiesta began and he hadn't drawn a sober breath since. He was the boozer who carried on so about the seeds, your namesake by the way, Joaquín. His last name is Gordillo if I remember right. This character has stuck close to us ever since the Fiesta and won't leave us for anything in the world—or in the next world, either, as far as I can see. He fancies himself as an orator and in any case, was so drunk that he hardly knew what he was saying and cared less. This is the gist of his contribution:

"You can consider me an outsider and a stranger, and refuse to listen to me saying that I am an outsider whom nobody has invited to the party. You can refuse me permission to speak on the grounds that you are gathered here to discuss matters that are of concern only to you and that a stranger has no business talking about problems of which he knows nothing. All that he does then is to prevent those who really understand the matter from giving their opinions.

"But you cannot doubt the sincerity of what I am saying since I declare here and now that in this struggle between the interests of a few individuals and the sacred interests of an overwhelming majority, I am unconditionally on your side—you who represent the majority. It would have been much easier for me to have remained a mere spectator who

347

listens to both sides and takes the part of neither. I'll tell you something very frankly and I assure you it's not just to move your feelings and gain your approval—though I don't deny that your approval means a great deal to me.

"What I refer to is the fact that you have completely won me over by your behavior toward people who seek your hospitality, even if they have come here by chance and for only a short time. It is only three days since I arrived, no more. But in those three days in Yangana I have learned to love and respect the town. What do I own? What is my exclusive possession? What can I offer? Unfortunately, nothing at all. Or rather, I have only one thing. I have my destiny, which I am sorry to say isn't worth much. No matter, I give to the people of Yangana this one thing that I can give. From this moment the destiny of this town, which I am convinced hangs or is about to hang in the balance, is my destiny. Let me take this opportunity publicly to offer myself. Oh Yangana! Your fate is my fate! From now on I belong to Yangana. I share its fortunes!"

"What a grateful throat!" shouted out some of those people who make jokes about everything. And they handed him up a glass of rum which the tipsy fellow swallowed without putting it down. He was unable to say another word and had to be helped down from the stage. That name of 'Grateful Throat' has stuck with him and he'll never shake it off until the day of his death.

"Get to the point, get to the point!" shouted some others. With this, Zacarías Fierro returned to the charge. He could not contain himself.

"You're going to spend all night talking and making speeches!" he said in a rage. "We have something more important to attend to here. Let me..." and he moved forward a few steps until he was face to face with the squires. You could see from a mile off that they were in a panic. Gurumendi was white as a sheet of paper and he's usually red-faced. Attorney Zapata was ashen and his lips trembled. As for Villaviciosa, his hair was on end. Just like that, my friends, his hair on end and his mustache bristling. The priest was the only real man of the whole lot.

He seemed perfectly cool even though one eye kept twitching in an odd way. That happens sometimes to people when they are agitated. You know Juancito Vásquez, the one who wets his bed? When he's frightened, his right shoulder begins to jerk and he grimaces with the right side of his face too. Well, one of the priest's eyes kept twitching and he half-smiled and covered the eyelid with his fingertips. He asked the crowd to grant him permission to leave and to take the squires with him since they were his guests. At that Zacarías told him straight, "We have no account to settle with you, my dear Father, our business is with these criminals!" And he began to bargain, so to speak, and I couldn't help laughing. The bargaining went like this:

Zacarías: "Let me have them for a moment, dear Father, one at a time."

Priest: "No, Zacarías, these persons and their lives should be neither injured nor threatened by the town."

Zacarías: "It's only for a moment, dear father. I'll just give each of them a couple of slaps and then I'll be quiet. We'll go home to our houses and they to their estates."

Priest: "No, Zacarías, restrain yourself, what craziness are you contemplating?"

Zacarías: "Look, Father dear, you can lend them to me just for a little minute, that's all. You'll say a Paternoster and I'll punch them. Just as soon as their noses are bleeding and they've lost some of that bad blood of theirs, I'll let you have them back, Father, safe and sound!"

Priest: "For the last time, Zacarías, control yourself."

Whereupon, Zacarías acted as if possessed. He gave the priest a great shove and pushed him to one side while the crowd gave way enough to leave an open space as if for a cockfight. Gurumendi, who had barely managed to control himself all this time, stepped back a step and drew his revolver. As soon as he had drawn it he fired, and kept firing until he'd emptied it. He was so scared that he just aimed wildly at the mass of people. You could hear groans and somewhere over in the shadows a woman was seen tottering away, all bent over and covering her face with both hands.

"Only one slap, dear Father," Zacarías kept on repeating as if he were out of his mind, and while still talking he made a lunge at Ignacio Gurumendi and seized his hand. More than ten men followed and all fell upon Gurumendi…We could distinctly hear a dog howling, probably hit by one of Gurumendi's shots. From that moment all the people surrounding the bosses seemed to have gone mad. Everybody wanted to beat Gurumendi with something or other as he lay on the ground. Zacarías Fierro was the most implacable. "Let me have a little moment, too," he kept shouting like a lunatic. "Let me have a little moment too," while he was beating on Gurumendi's still warm body.

Ever since then I have been asking myself and wondering how it was that I didn't interfere energetically at the time, and try to stop the dreadful things that happened. To this day

I can't figure it out. What I do remember is that I felt a kind of paralysis of the will, a reluctance to prevent others from doing what they wanted to do. This had never happened to me before. My friends, it was exactly like when you are napping under a tree after a good meal and can feel the flies on your feet. You want to shake your legs, but at the same time there's a kind of titillation on your skin and a most marvelous laziness and unwillingness to stop the flies from enjoying themselves on your body.

In the end...and I'll be frank with you, not only was I reluctant to go against the tide, but I allowed myself for a moment to be carried away by the intoxication of the mob. Just a little moment, as Zacarías would say. The result was that without knowing how or when it happened, I found that my hands were sticky. There was no sign of a cut or wound on them. To this hour I'm not positive where that blood came from. It may have been Gurumendi's blood. As soon as I saw it I came to my senses and controlled myself. I wanted to climb up on the stage and shout out to everybody to contain themselves, not to commit such stupidities, that the dispute could be settled without bloodshed.

But as soon as I stood up I felt that same pleasurable tickling I've mentioned, just like when you're enjoying your siesta and the flies are buzzing round you. It was a feeling of inertia, no doubt the result of drinking all day and of the tremendous uproar from all the people. At the same time, my friends, I felt an urge to respond to all that shouting. If they want to tear down the curtain to make a banner for a demonstration, well then let them tear it down. If they want to take down the gasoline lanterns to light the parade, well let them go ahead and take them down. If we need torches of cane-stalks, well let them send and get armloads of dry stalks from the nearest sugar mills.

Long afterwards, when it was all over, the priest reproached me, "You could have stopped it." When he said that, I felt that he was right and I was sorry...Between ourselves, the whole thing weighs on me as if I had been as guilty as anybody there. Why should I deny it? Why should I hide it from you, Joaquín, who have been my best friend and shared the adventures of my life? Why should I hide it from you, Rosa Elvira, you whom I have known since you were growing up in the same block? At this point Ocampo's clear voice, that voice which had been so deep and sonorous, so warm, turned hoarse and low and seemed to strangle in his throat. He kept passing his right hand over his chin and seemed at times to tug at his curly beard. He had abandoned the hammock some time before and it looked like a fishing net half gathered up and folded. While he was talking he had moved back close to the wall and had spoken with his head hanging as if he were an accused man being cross-examined by a stern prosecutor.

He finally straightened up, took a deep breath and cleared his throat so that his voice was once again strong and clear. Meantime, the flames of the fire flickered with a deep purplish red, tinting the storyteller's dejected face a rich copper bronze. What good would it do me to hide it, my friends? My hands were stained with blood. I didn't know when or how. Gurumendi had been killed in a cowardly way. It was unmanly. It was unworthy of us. The truth is that everything about the assault on Gurumendi was so violent, so unexpected, so completely out of control that there was no time for second thoughts. Ah! if only I had had time to reflect for a moment!

(11)

"Your wound is still fresh, Curly," remarked Reinoso, "it still hurts. Time will pass and ill ease your bitterness I, too, when couldn't sleep at night, used to see the commissioner writhing on the ground and thought that had killed him. After a while that memory was still sharp, but it was by then a familiar—you might call it a friendly memory."

After a short pause, he changed his tone and said to Ocampo, "Can you spare Rosa Elvira and me for a moment while we go to the kitchen and prepare something that is lacking?"

Ocampo once more stretched himself out comfortably in Joaquín's hammock, smiling happily at what seemed to him such kind understanding on the part of his listeners. He let out a deep breath as he settled into the hammock, crossed one foot of his fully stretched legs over the other, put his hands and interlocked fingers between his head and the web of the hammock, contemplated the toes of his wide bare feet and suddenly felt an urge to whistle. And whistle he did, a tune part merry and part sad, part lively and part mournful, which reminded him of the time when he was boxing champion of the mining camp at Curipamba.

At the same time he carefully studied his feet in the semi-darkness, the same feet which he had referred to a short time before when he was comparing the reluctance to shake off the flies at siesta time to his unwillingness to oppose the brutal vengeance of a mob. So he quietly waited.

There seemed to be something mysterious about what the two Reinosos were doing in the kitchen. They were obviously preparing something. One fact was clear—the plot, whatever it was, was being hatched in the ramshackle kitchen and nowhere else, since the firelight was slowly getting brighter. Yes, the fire was definitely brighter than when Ocampo had last spoken. And his firelit figure lying there took on the appearance of a bronze statue gently swinging in the hammock.

He couldn't help being intrigued by the way the husband and wife kept looking at each other every time they came out of the kitchen, with an air of partnership or collusion. But it seemed to be a merry kind of collusion, soothing, understanding and trusting. They did not look at him as a wrongdoer, but as the old friend that he was who needed their help to drive away so many sad thoughts. There had been a time when they too had suffered from the same thoughts and had to overcome them in the most despairing solitude. They were planning something behind their guest's back. He would have to wait.

After a little while, a wickedly enticing aroma began to seep in from the kitchen. Curly had already had to move his lips and tongue and cheek when he was whistling, but this smell positively made his whole mouth water. The pot on the fire was exuding a hot rich, greasy cloud of steam which reminded him of his favorite home-cooked food. Perhaps it was chicken soup? Or meat and vegetable stew? The smell was simple and straightforward, devoid of any suggestion of not easily identifiable ingredients and it seemed familiar.

He didn't have to wait much longer before he saw two calabash bowls coming from the kitchen, full of the stew that had been announcing its presence from afar. Curly Ocampo took his bowl in his left hand, carefully balancing the scalding liquid, and stirred it with the wooden spoon in his right hand. He looked around for some firm place to sit down and found it on a low tree stump set against the wall opposite the kitchen door. He took his place and looked as if he were squatting, since his chest was almost on a level with his bent knees.

At the bottom of his bowl he could touch chunks of meat and they felt as if they were heavy and juicy. He began to blow on the piping hot broth, carefully taking the first sips. He decided to leave the chunks until later, until the broth was low enough in the bowl for him to see them, and they were cool enough to be handled easily without spilling broth over his knees.

What happened next was that when enough of the broth had been drunk, two little hands looking like human hands, undeniably human, emerged like islands floating on a sea of grease. Ocampo stared at the bowl as if he could not believe his eyes, then he tilted the bowl to one side the better to see the solid part of the meal and went over to the partition by the kitchen where there was more light. Yes! no doubt about it, they were a little child's hands. About seven years old, he judged. One of them was stretched out straight from the wrist, with the palm up in the classic and pitiful gesture of a poor beggar. The other looked like a clenched fist pressing against the side of the bowl, thumb uppermost and edge down as if about to strike a slashing blow.

That open palm! The lines used by fortune-telling hand-readers were clearly traced on those boiled palms. Even in death the thumb was in its proper position relative to the fingers. The fore and middle fingers were half bent upward. The little finger was slightly crooked..."They could well have been the hands of my Juanito," he thought with a horrified shudder.

When at least he spoke, his voice was so sepulchral and charged with emotion that the Reinosos turned serious and looked ashamed. They had been silently watching the disconcerting expressions on Ocampo's face which in turn betrayed feelings of fear, ferocity, disgust, hate and tenderness. Now came the question in a horribly altered voice, "What the hell is the meaning of this?"

The couple realized that they could not go on with the joke and that it had been played at a time of extreme nervous excitement not at all suitable for games. They immediately and candidly confessed what it was all about.

"It's monkey meat, Curly. It's the easiest meat for us to get here. You'll soon learn to eat it..." "And I'll tell you," added Reinoso's wife, "that the monkey's hands are the tastiest morsel, especially with salt—that salt that you people have brought with you and that we haven't had with our food for so long..."

Ocampo, who felt in a ridiculous position and that he had childishly allowed himself to be made a fool of, thought that the least he could do under the circumstances was to demonstrate to his hosts that he was a determined fellow and, as he had always described himself, "ready for anything." So, although not exactly making a brave show of it, he stifled his revulsion, took the two monkey hands, put the palms together as if they were praying or applauding, and began to eat them by turns, starting at the backs.

(12)

The priest really turned out to be quite a man, continued Ocampo in a casual tone, still sitting hunched up, with his head on his knees, on the little stool made of a tree trunk where he had eaten the unexpected dinner. A real man, my friends, he repeated loosening his belt, since he kept his presence of mind while at the same time remembering that he was a priest. When he saw Gurumendi fall, he gave a great shout, opened his arms wide to show his chest and cried out, "Aim here, shoot here!!..." To which the crowd answered, "We have no quarrel with you, Father." "Then, for my sake respect my guests, you stupid dolts," he shouted.

The priest came out of it safely, and with the help of some of us managed to rescue Villaviciosa and Doctor Zapata, though the latter had a good slice taken off his ear. "They are my guests," he kept repeating to us. Then he courageously offered to take the sacrament to the wounded lying in the square, and to go wherever he was needed. "Water for the wounded!" was heard on all sides, and also "Death to the bosses!"

Doctor Zapata and Senor Villaviciosa remained lodged in the parish house and the priest, after leaving them there, begged the mob to respect the right and custom of hospitality which the people of Yangana since time immemorial had always recognized. Having said this, he locked the doors of the parish house and immediately set forth to minister to the wounded and provide them with suitable religious consolation.

A little boy, one of the Indian Benito Alulima's sons, went ahead of him carrying a gasoline lantern. The men who went with him followed along like tame sheep, in no way resembling the same people who a few moments before had been capable of devouring the bosses and swallowing them whole.

The sight of the pious congregation filing across the square, and the priest in his gold embroidered vestments, made us wish that the terrible thing that had just happened had been a bad dream and that there would be nothing to lament, nor any terrible consequence for us later on.

The stage which had been the scene of the half-finished play, where the actors had improvised all those insulting lines and allusions to the squires, was now dark and its red curtain half torn down. You will see later, my friends, what trouble that red curtain caused for us and what lies and calumnies it gave rise to.

You know, my friends, how people are in Yangana. Between ourselves, and I know you'll agree, they get all excited by any new thing and run after it as if they had nothing better to do. Well, they were now all in a state of agitation and gathered in great groups allover the square. The saloons and liquor stores were all closed for the time being, no doubt because their owners feared that the rioting might break out again. Wherever there was a cooking fire or a bonfire, you could see a circle of people, all talking and commenting on what had just happened. Some of the kinder-hearted ones had already hastened to pick up Gurumendi's corpse which was still lying in the square, (for I must remind you, however long it's taken me to tell it, that everything had actually happened in less time than it takes to say the Lord's Prayer).

At the same time, two other things happened in the square which, now that I've thought carefully and calmly about them afterwards, I do believe helped to make matters worse. The first was a rumor which ran through the crowd to the effect that the servants and employees of the late Ignacio Gurumendi had gone to get weapons and were on their way to attack the town. The second, was a similar rumor, this time that among those killed or wounded by Gurumendi when he was shooting blindly at the crowd, was Panchita Amancay, López the Match's niece, and that she was dying.

At this point Joaquín interrupted him brusquely, looking him full in the face. "But, friend Ocampo, you haven't told me a thing about that villain of a Commissioner. And I'm interested in knowing what became of the accursed fellow."

Ocampo satisfied him immediately, although in rather vague terms. "There were sharp machetes around that night, Joaquín, and the criminal's hour had struck at that very moment…"

And with a gesture that conveyed his meaning more expressively than any words, he dispatched to the next world that man so hated by Reinoso in particular and by Yangana in general. After a pause, he added in a kind of commentary: "You should have seen the cut, old boy. It looked like when you've slashed open a ripe pumpkin…"

But, my friends, as I was saying, a rumor had started to the effect that a band of armed workers from Gurumendi's estate were on their way to sack the town, and Angelote Maridueña happened to hear it.

Once again the crowd gathered in front of the stage to listen to Maridueña and, what was worse, to believe what he was saying. The fat fellow still had in his hand the clown's stick with its bladders. He held forth in his usual way with sweeping gestures, raising his voice to a shout, alternately stooping down, stepping forward, falling back, spreading out his legs, standing on tiptoe, jumping around as if stung by wasps and slamming down the bladders against the floor every few moments.

He said that it was quite true, that the men from the estate were well armed, that there were at least fifty of them headed by the majordomo who was himself one of those bad Indians from Ibarra, that he had given them rum mixed with gunpowder. And yes, they had already been heard coming at a gallop through the lane by the Virgin of the Figtree's house, positively foaming at the mouth with rage. That this was confirmed by one of the Cholo Mayta's sons who had seen them with his own eyes, rearing up and reining back their horses in that very lane, down by the side of the little square on the road to Don Eliseo Aliaga's farm.

And what was more a young nephew of that crazy Matías Pitarque had been almost ridden down by the squadron of armed men and had seen them receiving orders to storm the town through the four sides of the square. And to crown it all, that they had cans of kerosene on their saddle-bows and meant to burn down the whole town.

At this point Shameless Carlos who has always said that Angelote Maridueña is nothing but a bundle of lies, asked leave to make a proposal. This was what he said: "don't set much store by what Maridueña is telling us since although he is my good friend, he is more a friend of exaggerated stories. I don't believe we are in any danger since we have Zapata and Villaviciosa locked up in the parish house and the workers know that if they try to attack us, we'll take it out on their masters. They know, too, that there are many more of us than them. It seems to me that the best thing for us to do is to guard the bosses as strictly as we can, since otherwise they might quite easily escape and then really rally their workers to carry out reprisals against us."

When Maridueña heard this speech, he swelled up as if out of his mind. He wrung his hands with the most alarming conviction, and swore by God and the memory of his dead mother that he had personally seen the squires and the priest take off through the orchards and pastures behind the parish house, climb over a mud wall, and make a bee line through the farm lands in the direction of their respective manor houses. He calculated that since the fugitives had headed straight out across the pastures and orchards, they had had time to be already on their way back at the head of their men, including the local revenue collector and the two policemen who had slipped away when the riot started.

Shameless Carlos, who likes to be sure of his facts, remained unconvinced and proposed sending a delegation to the parish house to see what had really happened to the squires. After leaving some men there, they would return to report. This was done and the delegation came back almost immediately, visibly alarmed. They had found all quiet in the parish house—not a soul there. "You see!" shouted Angelote Maridueña, now that he was supported by the facts, "Didn't I tell you that we were surrounded?"

Then the crowd, filled with a combination of fear and fury and believing that the priest had quite likely betrayed them, set to work searching every house in the town, one by one. They were looking for the priest and the bosses, as carefully as if they were needles, swearing they would strangle them all. And they were after the police and the revenue collector as well whom they suspected of having stayed in the town to give information to the workers preparing the assault in the little square where the cholito Mayta had seen them. And people began drinking again in order to be prepared, as was said by many that night, to face whatever might be ahead.

Afterwards there was a lot of talk against me, criticizing and blaming my behavior at the time. People have said to my face that I did nothing to control the excesses of the mob when they could perfectly well have been checked in time. They could have said the same of Don Vicente, but not a word about Don Vicente...The truth is that in the first place I had been drinking steadily for some days. That's nothing. You, my dear friends, between ourselves, know that there are times when I suddenly realize that a novena is coming up and, devout person that I am, I happened to be celebrating one...

Then, in the second place, I was angry, very angry in every sense and with reason. Just think, there were actually some despicable loudmouthed characters who went around saying that just because I had helped the priest rescue the other two squires after the mob had murdered Gurumendi, had sold myself to them and was secretly on their side. And, last of all, nobody asked my opinion about anything that night. Of course not. A drunkard who has been boozing for seven or eight days in a row doesn't deserve to be consulted or considered in any way.

"But, my dear Curly," said Reinoso with a smile, "can see here and now that people didn't hold such a poor opinion of you very long." Reinoso meant that it had been obvious to him when he had been watching the last day's march and when camp was being pitched, that Ocampo was in charge of everything. But even now Reinoso noticed the almost angry tone in which Ocampo was proudly describing his part in the whole affair of the Fiesta. It was clear that Ocampo was still bitter because from the first moment the conflict started, he had not been empowered to guide the fortunes and the future of the community.

"And what happened next?" asked Reinoso, anxious to hear the rest of the story.

As for López the Match, this was how he got involved. He walked up to where a group was standing around one of the wounded who had not yet been taken from the square. He looked as he always does, half serious, half smiling, his face all covered with scars. He was carrying a torch of cane straw in his hand and in fact seemed perfectly happy. With the other hand he was holding a great bundle of straw to replenish his torch. He had just heard that among those wounded by Gurumendi's revolver shots was his niece Panchita to whom he was very much attached and whom he had helped to bring up.

He appeared with his torch in his hand a few moments after she died. "Panchita has just breathed her last," he was told. The Match knelt down on the ground by the girl's body, dipped his hand in his water gourd and moistened her lips with his fingers. At first he couldn't see any wound. Then, putting his torch close to the dead girl's face, he noticed a slight swelling on the edge of her upper lip. That was all. The bullet had gone clean through her mouth.

The Match got up very slowly, first on one foot and after a pause, the other. He begged one of the bystanders to take care of his water gourd, to make sure that dust didn't get into it, and especially to trickle some drops of water from time to time on the dead girl's mouth. "The poor child may still be thirsty," he ventured. With that, he left his niece and walked off, still carrying his torch and with a ghastly look on his face, in the direction of the canefield on Gurumendi's land, just outside the town.

Several others followed him out of curiosity. He went straight ahead and in full view of everyone set his torch to two of Gurumendi's canefields down by the irrigation ditch. Next, he moved up along the ditch, following it upstream until he reached the late owner's house where he threw the torch up on the roof.

Since Squire Gurumendi's manor house was the one nearest to the town, it was not long before we could see from the square a great fire over in that direction. We learned later that the Match had made another torch and moved on accompanied by a whole band of men howling like wild beasts and shouting, "Long Live Yangana the Free. Down with the Squires!" They reached Dr. Zapata's house and then Villaviciosa's; set fire to them both and on their way back burned the cane fields too. They escaped the heat of the flames by walking down through the irrigation ditch, getting back to town covered with ashes and soot, soaking wet and still in a rage.

It couldn't have happened otherwise. The Match, as you know, has been pursued by flames all his life, and he had just passed that way. From the square, you could hear the roar of the fire. The cane fields burned for about two hours and the only reason the whole town didn't catch fire was that the irrigation ditch ran behind the parish house. Otherwise Yangana would have been reduced to ashes that very night. To ashes. Just as it was reduced afterwards, before we left That was when I began to take charge of things.

As for the armed employees from the landowners' estates, they never showed up. No such thing! The priest and the squires who had escaped from the parish house, thinking only of their own safety, had taken the road to the city the same night. And the four corpses that Gurumendi left before he died, together with his own body were taken to the church where the wake lasted until next day. Mamá Justa directed the matter helped by some pious and obliging neighbors. They spent the whole night in the church, praying and chanting and asking God's pardon for the sins committed by the people of Yangana at the Fiesta of Our Lord of Good Fortune.

And so ended good Don Vicente's little play with blood, bullets, tears and flames. Something else that I forgot to tell you, my friends, was that as long as the fire lasted, that brand new bell of ours never stopped ringing for one moment, lamenting like a crazy orphan. It had rung for the first time that morning, announcing a fiesta. We had been happy, very happy. But it was to be the last merrymaking in Yangana, my friends.

We could hear the prayers in the church, although it was still deep night with hours to go before dawn. The squires' cane fields over by the irrigation ditch had been burning for hours and it was not yet day. What a long night it seemed to us! And what a sad night! Between the morning and the coming of night, just like that, between morning and night, fate or whatever you want to call it, had left us ruined and disgraced. Our hands had been clean that morning and by nightfall they were stained. Four dead bodies and Gurumendi's and the Commissioner's. And this had happened in Yangana where there had always been peace and we had loved one another.

Ocampo bowed his head like a man in torment, rubbing his bearded cheeks in despair. "It seemed as if daylight would never come," he kept saying like a refrain. Reinoso got up from where he was sitting, walked over to him and put his heavy hand on his friend's shoulder.

"That's all far away now, isn't it?" he said pointing vaguely in the direction of the distant countryside from which they had been uprooted. "What was once Yangana has been left behind over there, very far away. Very far away. And now it is born again here where we are...while what is past is past." As Reinoso was speaking, he clapped Ocampo several times on the shoulder, changing his tone of voice in the most engaging way. For Reinoso was a born master, although a quite unconscious one, of the art of elocution. He gave the dejected man a light pat and asked leave to go outside. "I'm going to pump water," he said and disappeared.

Ocampo seemed to be waking up from a bad dream. He looked up, and finding himself alone with Rosa Elvira, they remained gazing fixedly at one another.

When Ocampo had greeted her that evening and Rosa Elvira had seen him standing there in front of her, she had experienced a deep feeling of pleasure. Their friendship was an old one, pure and disinterested. They had loved one another like two affectionate family relatives who share all their thoughts. They used thee and thou when conversing. When they were both single they had trusted one another with their secrets. To tell the truth, she had always thought that his marriage to his present wife had been a real sacrifice and a disaster for him. He, her excellent friend Ocampo, deserved a different woman.

And here he was. The fact that Joaquín might be jealous, that she was married and belonged to her husband, did nothing to spoil her genuine joy at their unexpected meeting. Nor was there any reason why their embrace should not be a warm and trusting one. But Curly Ocampo had cooled her happy and enthusiastic feelings by merely offering his rough hand, rather cautiously and discreetly!

Now, from where she was sitting, she was sizing him up from head to foot. Here was Curly Ocampo in person and he had talked long about all that Yangana had been and meant. Since he had come, he had told of joy and bitterness. How long had it been since they had seen each other? How old would he be now? Forty? Perhaps. Of course, he was much older than she. He had held her on his knee when she was a child. And as he himself said, he could remember when she was toddling around with a diaper stuck to her bottom and flies buzzing after her.

He was not what could be called a handsome figure of a man. His shoulders might perhaps have been a little higher and not sloping down from his neck "Like a champagne bottle." Although his neck itself was broad and strong. The man's face had a defect, too. It was badly pitted by smallpox, especially on and around his nose. When he smiled, he certainly did not display a good set of front teeth. Two were lacking and another was so decayed that it looked as if it were spotted with lead.

His friend was gazing at that sturdy neck, so handsome and so virile. Its vigorous muscles and well-defined Adam's apple gave an impression of elastic energy every time he moved his head. When he turned to look at something, it was with a quick and resolute air. But, she thought, what really made him exceptional was not that. It was the combination of his eyes, his forehead, his hair, his beard. His eyes were medium sized and expressed a whole range of emotions. They could be lively, sparkling or hard. When speaking face to face with someone, they seemed as quick and sharp and unerring as two arrows. The person whom he was addressing felt an involuntary desire to remain transfixed and submissive, overcome by those eyes.

His forehead was broad, white and imposing to look at. This part of his face had been spared by small pox. It remained perfectly framed between the straight line of his joined eyebrows and his thick curly hair.

His lips were thick and rosy above the fine cleft chin which gave him a kind of faun-like air which women found very interesting. In spite of his rather forbidding appearance, he had only to smile and take off his hat for his whole face and even that gap-toothed smile to seem full of charm.

Then there was his voice. That voice that was so melodious, so deep, with its lingering inflections that perfectly expressed the speaker's feelings. It was one of those voices which echo persistently in one's ears and stimulate a desire, as Rosa Elvira well knew, to repeat over to herself something of what he had said, just as one tries to imitate the melody of a song once heard and liked. Perhaps he himself liked the sound of his own voice, since when talking or telling a story, 'he never failed to emphasize the concluding paragraphs by repeating certain sentences over and over again as if he wanted to make sure that what he had just said had been properly understood before he continued.

Something else. She noticed that although time had passed since she had last seen him, Ocampo was no fatter than before. He was almost slim-waisted. At the same time he had evidently retained his characteristic ability of being able to walk equally well with or without shoes. Or let us say that he could do this better than anybody else. Most men can do only one or the other—walk barefoot or walk shod. When the barefoot ones put shoes on, they walk in the most pitiful and ridiculous way unless they happen to know how. And the others, those who are used to wearing shoes all the time, if they try to go barefoot, find they cannot walk over, for example, a field of freshly cut alfalfa or a muddy road or a path that is more or less stony. Worse than that, they cannot even cross a stream with their shoes over their shoulders. They would sooner walk on their eyes than on their bare feet. Not so Ocampo. Either way he was equally sure-footed and confident.

The hands which he had used to evoke certain passages in the story of the last happenings in Yangana were large, fleshy and broad, the fingers and backs covered with hair. Under this thick hair the veins stood out clearly from wrists to knuckles. His thumbs were disfigured by rough calluses between thumb and forefinger. By contrast to his big hands and strong bony wrists, his feet were noticeably small and arched. He walked in a peculiar way with the heel of his left foot turned out. This may have been the reason why his legs did not touch evenly when he was standing with his feet together. His left leg seemed slightly bowed.

His friend's wife also remembered something else about him. He was unreliable when it came to obligations or engagements and had a bad reputation for fraudulent dealings. His own father, for example, said that Ocampo's word was not worth a pinch of tobacco. His neighbors maintained that his commercial practices were not above suspicion, nor were his barter deals with people from the city. He liked horse-trading and undertaking difficult and hazardous jobs. Ulpiano Arévalo, the veteran of the Concha campaign in Esmeraldas, had blind faith in him, considering him a brave and resourceful man in dangerous situations. This was the only good point about which there had never been any argument. To sum it all up, the general opinion was that his moral character was somewhat dubious; that he was given to cheating in business; that he was generous to a fault, since he was capable of stealing in order to give; that he was capricious and self-centered, overly convinced of his own worth and unable to forgive anybody who implied that he was a second-rate figure in the public life of Yangana; that he had made a foolish marriage when he could have chosen much better.

Nevertheless it was recognized that if he were properly approached, and given preference, he was the first to lend a hand in any public project undertaken in the town. If a contribution was needed, he was the first; if it was a week's work, he was first; if it was a matter of signing a petition, his name was the first. He was always ready to offer his meager resources and his not so meager person. "Of course, he'll try to take advantage of you at the same time," was what people used to say.

He could also read and write well, cast accounts and make calculations. If the occasion called for it, he would undertake to draft a memorandum to the authorities, or a simple petition. Rosa Elvira remembered, however, that her old friend preferred to dictate to someone else instead of writing with his own hand. While doing this, he would walk about briskly, turning his head quickly from time to time toward the writer and almost shouting out the periods however quietly he might have been speaking a few minutes before. He loved to hear himself pronounce a phrase or a sentence. He not only liked the sound of his own voice, he liked to hear the writer reading it back to him. For Ocampo a phrase either sounded well or sounded badly quite irrespective of grammatical construction. When he didn't like it, even if his listeners sometimes begged him to keep it, he would spring at the written sheet like a wild animal, place the wide open palm of his hand on the paper and clinch his fist. Then he would open his hand again and in an almost stately gesture, drop the ball of crumpled paper on the floor. Having done this, he would begin the revised version, speaking slowly as if intoning a chant...

Meantime Ocampo too was full of thoughts and recollections of his old friend Rosa Elvira. There she was, his old friend and distant admirer, looking at his eyes. She had really changed very little. He found her a little broader which was not to be wondered at. After all she had borne a child since he had last seen her. She did have a certain tired look on her face, for the corners of her beautiful curved mouth with its shapely lines drooped slightly—something he had never seen before on those firm and smiling lips.

Her skin, as far as he could see in the evening light, seemed to have lost nothing of its limpid translucency. The only noticeable difference was a change in color, or rather in the shade of pigment beneath the satin transparency of that skin. This, he reflected, could probably be attributed to the limited and insufficient diet obtainable in so lonely and hostile a place, especially in their first months there. "It's a long time now since those people have had any salt in their food," he said to himself, prepared to accept this logical explanation for any change in the appearance of either of the Reinosos.

Nevertheless, it did seem to him that Rosa Elvira's eyes, his old friend and distant admirer's eyes, had lost their mystery. He remembered them as being a little slanted and made even more lovely by the cool shadow of long curved lashes, protected by the perfect arch of her eyebrows. And that the glances from those eyes were always oblique. Whereas now they looked straight into his, steadily and calmly. They were still shaded by the curved lashes and the arch of the eyebrows, still deep set above high cheekbones, but the shadows were no longer provocative and disturbing; they now seemed rather to disguise the oblique sparkle he had once found so mischievous.

As for the dimples on her cheeks, the young mother seemed to have offered them up as a gift to her son, together with the once firm lines of her bust. She now smiled down on young Joaquinillo with all-consuming sweetness and allowed his squeezing and sucking to drain her beautiful breasts.

She was no taller than before and he seemed to be making a mental note, smiling slyly to himself, that in this case the old saying that all women grow until the third child was not true. After all...he calculated...all things considered, she was not exactly a little girl when she married although...she was short, her body was still admirably proportioned at least as far as he could make out under her rough ragged clothes. Her bare legs were the legs that had brought her along the road! Well-fleshed and well-turned, firm, straight as could be and with high shapely heels that when she walked suggested the lively gait of a young mare. Yes, he thought, no doubt about it Joaquín...Reinoso's wife was worth a great deal. And how she had changed! All her tremendous charm turned into friendly neighborliness!

She was still attractive, very attractive. She still had the same sweet quiet way of talking, full of profound reflections which sometimes startled the men, but now her new composure invited trust and confidence. It manifested itself in many little things—the way she quietly rested her hands on her knees, her somewhat pensive look, the tone of voice in which she spoke of her little son, her deep human sympathy when she was listening to somebody. And last of all, those lips which almost seemed parched from unspoken sufferings and privations.

Ocampo felt all this with the most powerful intuition. She was somebody to be trusted with one's most sacred secrets, whose counsel could be sought in the most difficult situations, who could listen to one's sorrows with more understanding and compassion than the closest relative.

Rosa Elvira, this Rosa Elvira Torres, now Reinoso, whom he had met again in her lonely hut in Palanda, had the serene look of a young mother, wise, reflective and discreet. She was still able to love and therefore willing and able to understand the sufferings, the joys, the struggles, the hesitations and the sins of others.

Meantime, Joaquín who had gone outside to "pump water," as he phrased it, was humming a merry little tune as accompaniment to the sound of the stream he was letting fall on the bushes behind the house, spattering and refreshing the luxuriant foliage.

As Ocampo listened to the splashing on the leaves, he felt like saying something about how strong and virile that stream of water sounded and what delights it must promise to its owner's woman. But that same woman was looking at him now, so unsuspecting, so softly, so cordially and innocently, that the words died in his mouth. He realized that he had been on the point of making a stupid joke which she was not called upon to listen to. She who was so willing to hear an anxious or a stammered confidence, to consider an apparently insoluble human problem or terrible suffering.

At that moment Joaquín crossed the threshold, still buttoning up his trousers, and sat down as before, waiting for Ocampo to go on with his story.

One-handed Franco el Manco, who you probably remember, was often referred to as Manco-Franco, Potranco, Blanco, Barranco, Estanco, Cojitranco—had been sent by Don Baltazar Zárate on an errand to the city, taking a string of pack mules to bring back a consignment of dry goods likely to sell well at the Fiesta. Afterwards, Franco' could never properly explain to Don Baltazar how it was that he took so long to return. He told him the craziest, rambling story of how when he got to the city he found that the merchandise he had come for had not yet arrived.; that for that reason he had been obliged to find some farm in the outskirts of the city where he could pasture the mules; that he had problems later because one of the animals had jumped over a low spot in the fence and been found eating the crops in a little farm belonging to a neighboring cholo; and that this cholo was a litigious character who, instead of complaining personally to Manco-Franco-Potranco about it, caught the mule, took it to town and left it in the pound at Police Headquarters where our muleteer had the greatest difficulty proving that he was in charge of the beast and that he came from Yangana.

In the meantime, the days passed and the man might have grown old squatting on the tiled floor of the Town Hall in hopes of softening the heart of the Intendant who wouldn't budge an inch. "You'd be better off, my good man," he said "if instead of warming the cement you were to go and look for two witnesses who know you personally and can vouch for your good behavior."

Unfortunately, our handicapped fellow townsman does not have a very saintly look about him owing to that damned way he has of looking sideways and laughing to himself as if openly making fun of one. This had convinced the Intendant that he was dealing with a thorough rascal, and he even felt like putting him in jail without more ado, shouting that nobody could laugh at him and get away with it, least of all a miserable, insolent country bumpkin.

When our man finally managed to ransom his mule, the Fiesta was almost over and it was only then that he set out for Yangana with his train of well-loaded mules which by that time were pretty thin. Two other Yangana men were with him—Basilio Cuenca, Doña Mercedes' nephew, a very willing lad, and that skinny Nicolás Juela who would do anything to make a dollar. These two were on foot and Manco-Franco-Potranco on a mule, the same one that had very nearly remained in the hands of the Intendant.

The first day out, night overtook them before they reached the shelter of the *tambo*. When they got near to it, they noticed that there was, a good deal of light in the little shack, that there were people inside, and that a number of horses were tethered and stamping outside. Manco-Franco sent skinny Nico Juela on ahead to take a good look and see what it was all about so that they could decide whether it was safe to ask for shelter.

What skinny Nico Juela saw really startled him. The revenue collector and the two policemen, their rifles slung on their shoulders and their trouser-legs covered with mud, were sitting on a bench drinking chicha, each of them with a bottle to his lips. Behind them, Dr. Zapata was lying on a poncho spread over a bed of boards, his head bound up and his hat serving as a pillow, with a blood-stained handkerchief wrapped around his jaws and ears. Lying there as he was, he was asking for some good strong rum and a bandage for his wound...

As for Villaviciosa, with that vulgar pretentious look of his, he was anxiously waiting for the tambo-keeper to prepare a meal for them since, from what skinny Nicolás Juela could hear, they had hardly eaten a bite while on the road. When one-handed Franco heard this he wanted to find out more for himself and crept forward to where he could listen to what the policeman and the revenue collector were telling the tambo-keeper. The story sounded so dreadful that

Franco and his companions did not dare show up at the *tambo*, but took advantage of the dark and went on their way, camping an hour's march further on.

This news, my friends, was the first that any of them had heard of what had happened in Yangana and, as you will see, this chance meeting on the road proved to be important. The Manco, who showed later that he hasn't a foolish hair on his head, thought after leaving the *tambo* that the best thing to do was to press on with his string of tired mules, accompanied only by Basilio who was the stronger of his two companions, while sending Skinny Nicolás back on the road to follow the fugitives to the city.

"He told him to find out what tale they had told and what harm it might do to Yangana." The Manco knew that on another occasion, that time when the Commissioner was treated so disrespectfully, the Governor had dispatched a squad of police from the city with instructions to "impose discipline on a town of savages," and that they had been quartered in Yangana for months.

He gave a little money to Nicolás so that he could be free to listen to what people were saying, hang around the drug stores and read the latest news on the bulletin boards at the newspaper office. The Manco told us afterwards that his motive for moving his mule train forward in the meantime was to placate Don Baltazar Zárate who would certainly be justifiably enraged by further delay, and thus he could still put all the blame on the city merchants for not filling the order promptly.

He knew beforehand exactly what Don Baltazar Zárate would say: "These damned Ecuadorian merchants are the greatest thieves, except for myself of course…It was all my fault since, instead of going personally to Guayaquil to fetch my goods, I did it through these local middlemen...In Germany you won't find businessmen of that sort...Oh, our poor country, in the hands of despotic bankers and businessmen who operate on credit without a cent in their pockets!" El Manco knew that after complaining and carrying on in this way, Don Baltazar would exonerate him from all, blame in the matter and would pay him every penny for his time, trouble and expenses. Since he had himself been a carrier in his youth, and a good one.

As it turned out, El Manco did better than he thought, for the day after he got back to Yangana where he had been anxiously awaited, who should arrive but Skinny Nicolás Juela, half dead from exhaustion and bursting with news. That's the right expression, bursting with news. Yes, bursting with news. And what news!

He first of all told us how he had managed to follow the trail of the bosses and armed police without being seen. He had made his way through the underbrush at the side of the road, slithering and sliding along like a snake behind fences and trees, near enough to see and hear them easily. Wherever they dismounted to rest, there he stopped too. He knew that if he were discovered, he would be in great danger since the police and the revenue officer would recognize him immediately. Nevertheless he continued to stick close to the travelers all through their last day on the road and to reach the city practically at the same time, just as he had hoped and prayed for.

The alarm had already been given, since two hours' ride short of the city they had reached the estate known as The Eucalyptus Grove where there was a telephone and where

Dr. Zapata had lost no time in calling the Governor's office. He reported what had happened and begged him to arrange for them to be met since they were still being pursued by the savages from Yangana. This was about 4:30 in the afternoon and he was on the telephone for a long time. When he came out of the house and mounted his horse again, he was visibly relieved.

By the time the fugitives reached the city, a crowd was already waiting for them at the bridge and showered them with every kind of question. And it was in the city that Skinny Nicolás Juela fully realized the seriousness of the situation. After nightfall he went to Doctor Ventana's drug store to hear what the leading men of the town were saying, and the gist of it was that the Governor had conferred at length with the Minister of Internal Security in the Capital and had given him a full report. Skinny Nicolás gave us further details of what he had seen and heard as follows: "There was a gentleman among those present in the drugstore who must have been related to the squires since he took their side in everything. He had a formidable mustache, was wearing a long frock coat, and sported a cane. This man was telling the others that the Governor had said to him personally that whatever drastic measures might be taken against Yangana would in his opinion be completely justified and in order, since the town was notoriously stubborn and unruly with a very bad record."

"This same gentleman," continued Skinny Nicolás Juela, "then said something which enraged me, ignorant as I am. He declared that just as there are individuals who are born criminals with a natural inclination toward evil, so too there are whole communities that from the very start have been addicted to crime, and that such communities have to be disciplined by the harshest measures including bloodshed. An example of this, the gentleman had continued, is the town of Yangana, it is a criminal town!"

Skinny Nicolás added that the pharmacist did not entirely agree with this reasoning, asserting that the Yangana people that he knew did not seem to be bad characters. "They are good customers of mine," he said, "especially one of them, a certain Torres who buys a great deal of quinine from me."

"There was also another gentleman present, with a high forehead and yellow teeth who kept fiddling with the watch chain on his vest and pushing his hat up on the back of his head every few moments. He simply could not keep quiet and was absolutely against the first opinion, in fact he seemed to be laughing at all the others. He said straight out that the Governor appeared to him to be a stupid man, that those who looked on Yangana as a criminal town were also a lot of fools, and that if the Government gave orders to brutally repress the justifiable rage of a community which was accustomed to freedom, but which the local squires were trying to convert into a herd of cattle, then the Government, too, was not only stupid but downright criminal."

Nicolás Juela told us all this while he was still half-dead from exhaustion. After a while he continued his report and described how at about ten o'clock that same night when the drug store closed and he had drunk his tenth glass of soda water at the counter, he had gone out into the street, belching and with his stomach completely blown up, to look for lodgings in one of the colonnades of Santo Domingo. On the way he saw a group of bystanders in front of a brightly lit saloon where there was a radio on the counter, turned full up and broadcasting the news.

What he heard then almost scared the life out of him. It was a grossly exaggerated and sensational bulletin to the effect that, according to information gleaned from high government sources, a Communist inspired revolution had broken out in one of the most prosperous towns of the Province of Loja and that the Governor of the province had received instructions to suppress unmercifully this introduction of criminal and exotic doctrines. The radio went on to say that the Commander of the corresponding military zone had also received instructions to cooperate with the Governor in putting down this seditious uprising and to employ not only the police but the armed forces under his command.

As soon as the news ended and a program of music came on, Nico Juela went to his lodging, but could not sleep. Next day, very early he went to look at the Bulletin board outside the newspaper office and read there that a special edition would be on sale at 10 a.m. with sensational news of the collective crimes perpetrated by Yangana. Skinny bought two copies of this edition as soon as it appeared and, realizing that there was no time to lose, set off on foot for Yangana, walking and running day and night so that he reached the town almost treading on the heels of Manco-Franco-Potranco.

While on the road he saw several parties of terrified peddlers and hawkers who had been to the Fiesta and were now returning to the city. Skinny Juela took great care not to be seen by any of them. To be recognized at such a time as a native of Yangana might have been extremely dangerous.

"Nobody could say that we had no cause for alarm," remarked Ocampo after a short silence in which he was probably repeating over to himself his last sentence. "Nobody would have dared to say it. We were in terrible peril. Here's the proof, my friends, in this newspaper." So saying, he stood up, put his hand in his right trouser pocket and pulled out a dirty piece of printed paper which had been folded and refolded. "Here's the proof," he repeated once more, handing it first to Joaquín and then to his wife, asking her to read to them the leading articles on the first page. He offered to fetch the little oil lamp that Joaquín had referred to earlier in the day and to light it himself.

By the light of this lamp, which consisted, of a wick of vegetable fiber floating in a cup of palm-oil, Rosa Elvira, who did in fact know how to read better than the two men, began to read aloud. Her husband and their friend sat listening, Ocampo with the look on his face of one who knows the story by heart, and Reinoso showing the eager curiosity that he had felt during the whole tale told by the newcomer.

Nobody smoked since for the moment there was no tobacco left, nor was there a store at the corner where they could send to buy some. They were no longer drinking, either, because when the Reinosos brewed chicha they calculated consumption based on a household of two, so that the arrival of a totally unexpected guest had quickly exhausted their supply.

What Rosa Elvira read was as follows:

"BLOODSHED IN YANGANA—QN THE DAY OF THE FIESTA THE INHABITANTS OF THAT

PARISH ATTEMPTED TO MASSACRE THE
LOCAL SQUIRES—ONLY THE INTERVENTION
OF THE PARISH PRIEST, REV. ARRAU, SAVED
TWO OF THEM FROM CERTAIN DEATH—THE
COMMISSIONER AND THE UNLUCKY YOUNG
IGNACIO GURUMENDI SAVAGELY
MURDERED—DOCTOR ZAPATA, ALTHOUGH
SERIOUSLY WOUNDED, GRANTS US AN
INTERVIEW—NUMEROUS VICTIMS—THE
GOVERNMENT DETERMINED TO SUPPRESS
CRIMINAL EXCESSES WITH IRON HAND—
PUNITIVE COMMISSION TO SET OUT
IMMEDIATELY TO SUBDUE CRIMINALS—
PROVINCIAL GOVERNOR ATTRIBUTES
SANGUINARY INCIDENT TO COMMUNISTS—
YANGANA AND ITS BLACK HISTORY—STOP
PRESS NEWS FROM QUITO."

"Persons who have just arrived from Yangana where they have been attending the well-known annual Fiesta of our Lord of Good Fortune, have brought hair-raising accounts of tragic happenings in that town, situated in a remote area of our province, on the very same night of that celebrated festivity. Eager as we always are to serve our readers, the moment we were informed by the Governor's office that one of the survivors was about to reach the city, after being seriously wounded and barely escaping with his life, we assigned one of our most diligent reporters to cover the story and to interview Dr. Zapata. On Page 4, we are publishing the exclusive information obtained from this source."

"Having gathered and compared the various versions of this dreadful affair, brought by the other fugitives, we are now in a position to give the following complete recapitulation of the true facts."

"Background: Since time immemorial, the religious Fiesta of our Lord of Good Fortune has been celebrated in Yangana every year on the 20th of August. The festivities attract numerous devotees from different regions of the province and even traveling merchants from the neighboring republic of Peru. Apart from the purely religious side of the Fiesta, on this occasion the whole town is converted into a center of active commercial interchange, usually lasting for four or five days."

"This year the Fiesta promised to be especially interesting and lively since the townspeople who, it must be admitted, have some interest in progress, were preparing to inaugurate a new bell for the church and to celebrate its christening with a solemn and well-publicized ceremony. As a result, there were more people there who under ordinary circumstances would not have come, owing to the difficulty of access to the town caused by an almost total lack of roads."

"So it happened that among those present at the Fair in Yangana this year, were three well-to-do landowners, namely Ignacio Gurumendi, a most meritorious young man with family ties in this province, who was brilliantly pursuing his studies in the capital of the Republic; Dr. Zapata, a good friend of this newspaper, and Señor Villaviciosa. All three of them owned estates in the immediate vicinity of Yangana and they had come in good faith to attend the popular games and amusements which by tradition are so picturesque and spontaneous in-the rural communities of this province."

"A Necessary Clarification: There is one significant detail which we cannot overlook. It is that relations between the people of Yangana and the landowners to whom we have referred, were already strained because of something that we reported to our readers at the time it happened. We refer to the bitter legal dispute brought before the Minister of Internal Affairs and the Congress by the inhabitants of the town and the said landowners, concerning the expropriation of the squires estates."

"The people of Yangana maintain that these lands belong to the town and should be returned to the town; and the town is prepared to indemnify the squires for the fair assessed value of the land. Disposition of the case has been delayed up to now by the stubborn opposition of the so-often-mentioned landowners. Without taking sides in this bitter dispute, we will say that perhaps as a result of it, farm land has become scarce in the region and may no longer be enough to provide for future agricultural expansion in this fertile zone."

"From what we have just explained, it seems clear that there was already a quarrel and hard feeling between the squires and the townspeople of Yangana. So perhaps it was unwise on the part of the former to expose themselves to the excesses of irresponsible crowds, always hard to control, by taking part in a fiesta where the populace could be expected to get out of hand under the influence of merrymaking and liquor."

"Another Revealing Detail: Our information would not be complete if we omitted certain minor antecedents which give a picture of the past of this village which has been the scene of the disgraceful events that we are about to relate— antecedents that allow us to say that the behavior of the squires in attending the Fiesta in Yangana can only be called rash and foolhardy. They must have remembered perfectly well that about two years ago the same community had rebelled against the local Commissioner alleging that he had committed certain abuses against the citizens."

"They had then assaulted and ill-treated the unfortunate Commissioner in such a bestial manner that he almost died. It was a miracle that he recovered, considering the disgusting way they defiled his person since, as our readers will also remember, they inserted a number of large tallow candles in his posterior cavity with the intention of killing him. The wretched man hung between life and death for some days and had to be brought to this city where the hemorrhage was finally stopped."

"We cannot help asking if it were not to be expected that a populace capable of such revolting behavior might repeat it in the case of those honorable men of property who were so rash as to mingle with an already exhilarated mob of such character? To tell the truth in the present case we have ascertained from the most reliable and unimpeachable sources that no attempt was made this time to defile any of the victims with large tallow candles in this abominable manner."

"A Disgustingly Intoxicated Mob: The greater part of the inhabitants of Yangana, irrespective of sex or age, taking as a pretext the ceremony of inaugurating and christening the bell—a ceremony presided over by the virtuous Reverend Arrau whose behavior on this occasion has earned him general admiration for his Christian courage and apostolic charity—devoted themselves to getting drunk on great quantities of rum, chicha and fermented cane juice with which they had provided themselves beforehand, disregarding completely the orders of the State Liquor Monopoly which strictly forbids the production and sale of fermented liquors."

"When night fell, a crowd of drunken men disposed to any kind of excess, gathered in the square to witness the customary musical and dramatic performances which, as a time-honored Spanish tradition, are still presented in the towns and villages of our province when celebrating their festivities. It appears that, instead of the usual style of comedy, a group of actors who were either drunk or at least still feeling the effects of drinking earlier in the day, took it on themselves to produce a satirical farce aimed at the squires whom they ridiculed and upbraided, employing insults, nicknames and personal allusions."

"We have been informed that the spiritual father of this monstrous performance is none other than a good friend of this newspaper and we consider it proper not to divulge his name until we have further evidence of the circumstances, since we refuse to believe such an astonishing and unlikely accusation against a man with whose character we are intimately acquainted."

"This attack by words on the stage soon turned into an actual physical assault. The crowd took up in chorus the actors' insulting shouts against the honorable men of property whose names we have already given. Then they launched themselves against them, provoking an unequal struggle in the course of which young Ignacio Gurumendi, heroically defending himself with his revolver, sold his life dearly. Dr. Zapata came out with one ear almost totally sliced in pieces and a number of welts and bruises. Señor Villaviciosa suffered a dislocated ankle and serious bruises on his left arm, while the District Commissioner was killed with machete cuts, being, we should note in passing, the same man who had previously been the victim of the barbarous outrage we have just recalled to our readers. It is also true that on the side of the populace there were several dead and wounded, the number and seriousness of the wounds being still unknown, at the moment."

"Father Arrau's Heroism: The hero of this tragic day's work has been the Rev. Arrau, to whom we have already referred. His calm in the face of danger, and his presence of mind saved the day. He was confronted by the mob of maddened men, drunk from liquor and the sight of blood, who had hemmed in the squires at the very foot of the stage where the play insulting them had been presented, with the intention of cutting off their retreat. His coolness enabled him to save the lives of the remaining victims of the assault, among whom were also two members of the national police assigned to keep order, and the revenue officer from the State Liquor Monopoly. The Rev. Arrau, as soon as he had managed to shelter them in the parish house, contrived their escape and he himself, after administering the last sacraments to the wounded and salvaging the religious ornaments remaining in the church, joined the fugitives."

"Last Night's Statement by The Governor: Although it was very late we found the governor still at his desk. He received us warmly and authorized us to publish the following information: 'am convinced'—and here we give the gist of the governor's remarks—'that the horrible crime committed in Yangana was communistic in origin since I have clear evidence that immediately following the massacre the mob proceeded to carry a red flag through the square and the principal streets of the town. This was reported to me by a completely trustworthy source.'"

"'What is more, they accompanied their march with shouts of Death to the Landowners, and Liberty for Yangana. Then they moved on to the canefields on the neighboring estates and set fire to them and to the manor houses also. This is nothing less than incendiary communism and the worst kind of attack on property. It would be unforgivable blindness not to recognize a close relationship between recent events in the Capital, in the town of Milagro, in Sanagüin (where the Revenue Inspectors were murdered), and the criminal acts which we are lamenting today.'"

"'I repeat that this attack on property shows characteristics of the most dangerous nature. By virtue of the authority which I represent as guardian of the lives and properties entrusted to me, I have sent an urgent communication to the Minister of Internal Affairs and have managed to confer by telegraph with the President himself. I can assure you and your newspaper that the necessary order has already been given to crush at birth this criminal outbreak of contagious foreign doctrines, and that police aided by troops will be on their way to suppress the disorders and excesses in Yangana before the situation becomes completely chaotic and threatens to furnish a fatal precedent for the other towns of our province.'"

"'A primary court judge will travel to the scene without delay in order to initiate the appropriate criminal proceedings, with instructions to take the severest measures against the guilty parties. Finally, the armed force which will be dispatched within a week has been ordered to act with an iron hand and without leniency or clemency of any kind. Ecuador needs peace and it must be imposed, cost what it may. In Yangana there is, you remember, a precedent for this. Here the governor again reminded us of the first revolt against the late commissioner, details of which we have already given to our readers.'"

"We took leave of this zealous public servant after thanking him for his kindness, and a few minutes later he was so obliging as to call us in person by telephone, at our editorial office, to tell us that he had just received a telegram from the commander of the military zone, advising him that he had been instructed to cooperate with him in his pursuit of the criminals by means of direct coordination between the civil and military authorities and by placing at the governor's disposition two companies of infantry fully equipped for immediate action."

"Since another local weekly has also published an account of this much discussed and murderous affair, we must warn the public that our version is the nearest to the truth, as the readers can once again verify by comparing the two accounts and especially by reading the exclusive bedside interview granted to us by Doctor Zapata, one of the principal participants in the tragic events that we have described in this article. The public can read it on page 4, column 2. We promise to keep our readers up-to-date on what happens, publishing, if necessary, special editions during the week. Read our bulletin boards."

"Stop Press: We have just received the following telegram from our correspondent in Quito. 'Quito, August 28 (Oliva). Today's morning papers carry full and sensational accounts of the savage communistic uprising which has broken out in the province of Loja. The government, justly alarmed by the spread of this revolutionary disease which threatens to reach the furthest corners of the Republic, is preparing to request extraordinary powers from the Council of State. The government is receiving widespread support for its policy of mercilessly suppressing the revolt in the province of Loja where it appears, to judge from reports reaching this capital, that a good part of the province is in the hands of the insurgents.'"

"'According to these same reports, all of which are from unimpeachable sources, the red flag of communism is displayed in many places and the news is that the revolutionary hordes tore the national tricolor to pieces. The commander of the corresponding military zone has received orders to move troops to the threatened areas. News of all this has been diffused to the four winds and was heard last night on the North American broadcasting systems. Great apprehension exists in this Capital as to the development and outcome of the situation. Signed: your correspondent.'"

"Stop Press (From our correspondent Oliva): 'Government has just obtained extraordinary powers for 60 days. Infantry Battalion Andinos 27 and a squadron of cavalry moving by forced marches to the disturbed province. Further details follow. Passed by Censor. Correspondent.'"

EDITORIAL

"In another section of this weekly we are giving a detailed account, as a first report to our readers, of the tragic events that have been the cause of bloodshed in the town of Yangana and have spread an ominous stain over its already murky history. While presenting the story of these events we are burdened by a feeling of sincere grief for the victims who fell in the outrageous uprising and we are full of pity for the rash men who, incited by an abominable conspiracy, embarked on a mad and criminal venture which has compromised the present and future of a whole community. At the same time we are fulfilling our duty as journalists by exposing to public opinion the aims and motives which in an evil hour inspired the perpetration of the disgraceful acts that we are now lamenting."

"Once again it is alien political doctrines, with their seeds of hate and violence, spread by the lowest elements of society and obeying dark instructions from abroad, which are responsible for this tremendous collective crime. It is alarming to record that not even the remotest corners of the world have escaped this disease. On the present occasion it has reaped a harvest of blood in a community which, because of its isolation and its lack of communications, we might have confidently assumed to have been far beyond the sinister influence of such doctrines."

"It is no longer only the city, no longer only the factory or the mine, which are the chosen sites of this artful propaganda. Not content to sow the seeds of hate and rancor in the cities, these doctrines are also invading the countryside. The result for the suffering country of Ecuador is that today there is a revolt of Indians on anyone of the landed estates of the northern provinces, a revolt that has to be suppressed in blood; while tomorrow it is a horde of outlaws who cut into pieces the Revenue Inspectors of the State Liquor Monopoly in the province of Azuay; and finally it is an uprising which blindly mows down human lives in the streets of a country town and culminates in a storm of crime. Crime, which sets fire to the homes of landed proprietors, burns extensive cane fields to the ground and plunges the assassin's dagger in the breast and back of those who, by working unceasingly for the prosperity of their native land, have built a fortune for their children."

"And this is how we are living. Under the constant threat, under the ever-growing shadow of fear, under the hidden menace of weapons sharpened in darkness, all to spread chaos, ruin and desolation dreamed of by the sick visionaries of the Red nightmare. And this is how they undermine the very foundations of that peaceful and fruitful harmony without which any social progress is impossible and every collective initiative becomes a vain enterprise."

"This community of Yangana has deserved better fortune than to be burdened not only with the stigma of collective crime, but also with the threat of inexorable punishment in accordance with the instructions received by the provincial government from the central administration. The town has always been known for its enthusiastic desire for betterment and its united effort to obtain it. But for some time lately, the hired assassins of the political terror to which we have just alluded, have for their treacherous purposes begun to turn it to evil ways."

"The town had insistently petitioned to be made a parish and this was finally granted, thanks in part to the fact that this newspaper, convinced of the public benefit which would result, had firmly supported the request. No sooner was the status of the town changed, then the consequences of the agitators' fatal work were clearly evident. The same populace that had unanimously requested to be incorporated as a parish expelled its new District Commissioner in the most ignominious way, abusing his person in a truly loathsome and abominable manner. And now, just when the town of Yangana was perhaps on the point of legally winning its lawsuit and gaining, with the assent and authorization of the Government, the adjudication and distribution of the extensive lands which surrounded the town, the townspeople chose the path of crime. By so doing they place themselves, collectively, outside the law and deserving the fate which will befall them in the form of official armed suppression of the rebels. This will certainly mean, given the violence of what has already happened, that there will be many more casualties before it is possible to restore the order that has been so brutally destroyed."

"Once again we deeply regret the latest happenings, just as we also regret that owing to the overriding urgency of the situation throughout the province, we feel bound to give our approval to the stern measures which the local authorities, with the collaboration of their military counterparts, are hastening to take in order to stifle the revolt in Yangana. They will reinstate the national tricolor where now floats the red and blood-stained flag, thus reestablishing order where anarchy is lord and master, restoring peace where crime is the watchword."

"It only remains for us to demand, in the name of that public opinion which we represent, the pursuit and exemplary punishment of the ringleaders of the infamous and already tragically famous massacre of the 20th of August which has so deeply moved the Ecuadorian family and brought grief and mourning to respectable homes in this city."

"As you can see, Joaquín," remarked Ocampo, "you too have your little part, friend Joaquín, in the newspaper. You, too, have a little part, that part about the big tallow candles." And as he pronounced the last two words he spoke so slowly and sonorously, as if on purpose, that Joaquín asked him rather petulantly, "Listen, Curly, what do they mean by calling them tallow candles?"

Ocampo hesitated for a while and then limited himself to replying, "Hombre, maybe it means candles made expressly to be used as suppositories. Don't you think that's it, my dear Rosa Elvira?" But Rosa Elvira, the newspaper on her knees, did not know what to answer.

"This newspaper drove us out of our minds, my friends," said Ocampo, fanning the flame of the oil lamp which was smoking and smelling badly. For a few moments the room was dark until once again surrounding objects and faces could be distinguished. There was still a weak rosy glow from the kitchen door.

It was this newspaper, my friends, that drove us out of our wits. I do believe that never has a piece of paper been read so many times. Not even a scatter-brained schoolboy, threatened with a beating if he doesn't know his lesson word for word, could have gone over this newspaper as we did. When we all knew it almost by heart, we clamored for a meeting and at this meeting held in the square at Yangana, the newspaper was read once again. You didn't have to be a learned person to understand the danger we were in. We realized quite clearly that troops were coming to fire on us; that the government itself in Quito, which had never paid any attention to our petitions, had now given orders to make us eat bullets; that nobody in our provincial capital was doing anything in our defense; that we were known as flying the red flag instead of the national flag, and as all being communists.

To say that we were panic stricken is to put it mildly. Our fear increased by the minute. There was fear among us, great fear. This was because people remembered how bad it had been that time when the government gave orders to pacify Yangana after that business of the Commissioner and a certain person whom I don't wish to name…The memory of the floggings which even the youngest of our men had to suffer was still fresh. If that had happened over a relatively small matter, what would become of us now that, frankly, we had done something really bad?

But, my friends, I am a man of experience and so I know that however frightened people may be at a given moment, they will sooner or later begin of their own accord to lose their fear. And so it was this time. I remember it was on a Tuesday, already late in the day, very late, when the townspeople began to recover their spirits. It was after the principal men of Yangana had been talking and discussing for I don't know how many hours, in an atmosphere of the basest cowardice, that people's courage returned to their bodies and at last some sensible proposals were heard.

As for me, I kept quiet all this time, listening to what the others were saying, but without taking part in all those arguments and discussions which as a matter of fact disgusted me. As I've already said, I was rather annoyed at Don Vicente and some others report and I didn't feel like getting involved in their stupid talk. However, about five o'clock in the afternoon, somebody finally came up with a very reasonable suggestion. It was to the effect that since, according to the newspaper all the force of the law was on the way to Yangana for the purpose of pursuing and subduing the ringleaders of the revolt and conflagration, that the best way for the townspeople to save themselves was to decide who actually were the ringleaders and to hand them over to the authorities.

If this were agreed upon, then three or four from among the inhabitants of Yangana could be chosen, either by lot or by some other way, to give themselves up as guilty and thus deliver the whole parish from the threatened retaliation by the army. This proposal stirred up a veritable hornet's nest. Many of those present protested in a quiet and reasonable way; others cried to high heaven; others approved the idea in principle; in short it gave rise to the greatest uproar you could imagine. Until Zacarías Fierro raised his fist and bellowed for silence until everyone was quiet. I tell you again that as for me took no part in the hubbub. I watched, I listened and I held my tongue.

Zacarías Fierro, with that great hulking body of his and that quarrelsome bully's face that God has given him, pushed his way through the crowd until he was standing face to face with the principal men of the town, his face all flushed, and what he said was this: "It is I who am the guilty one, since if it had not been for me, nobody would have laid a hand on the scoundrels. It was I who jumped on Gurumendi and gave him the first slap and I don't regret it. A real man should face up to what he has done. They can do what they like with me. When I am called upon to speak, I shall not try to hide the truth. The blame is mine and here I am. I don't deny my responsibility. I, Zacarías Fierro, struck Gurumendi the first blow and would have given him another if I'd had the chance. So what?

What Zacarías Fierro said was very well received, and I think that it was what changed people's minds. I say this because directly afterwards Fermín López the Match came forward with his sickly look, half melancholy and half smiling, and made a similar declaration in front of everybody. "I believe," he said, "that if anyone is to blame for setting fire to the squire's estates and cane fields, it is I because I personally took the first torch and was the first to set fire to the manor houses and the cane fields. And if necessary I would have set fire to my great grandfather's beard.

Maridueña did not want to be left behind in all this, and began to vociferate and wave his arms, saying to their faces that Fierro and The Match were both liars. While the crowd was laughing to hear Maridueña call anybody a liar when he himself is the prince of liars, he made his speech: "The guilty one is I, not they, because when I played the part of the clown in Don Vicente's farce, I changed the script as I felt like, attacking the squires and stirring up the people of the town who otherwise would never have done what they did on the night of the Fiesta. I more than anyone else, provoked the whole affair, and if it's a matter of going to jail to save the town from the wrath of the government, I shall be the first to give myself up to the law."

It looked as if that fat fellow Maridueña was warming up and about to unloose a string of his lies, when that tipsy little Gordillo, the stranger who had stuck himself on to us Yangana people like a plaster, managed to climb up on a bench and interrupt Maridueña. He said that he was the only one responsible and that he was ready to surrender himself as ringleader on the arrival of the authorities. "Because you know," said the drunken little stranger, "that that business of the red flag was all my doing. I tore down the stage curtain and put it on a stick for a flagstaff. I put it over my shoulder and headed one of the groups marching round the square calling for death to the squires and giving hurrahs for Yangana the Free. If it had not been for me, there would have been no red flag, and the government would not have believed that our acts had been inspired by communism and would not have taken this affair so seriously."

As I remember, a light drizzle began to fall about this time, since Don Vicente took shelter under a portico and wrapped himself in his vicuña wool poncho, coughing a little. As you know, the old boy catches colds easily. From the corner of the portico, he looked at me for a long time, with his chin resting on the knob of his cane, gazing at me as if he had never seen me before, as dogs do when they are lying down with their muzzles on their paws. Then he spoke to me very softly, but in such a way that didn't know whether he was joking or serious. "And you, Tobías Ocampo, what do you say to us?" And the sly old fellow's eyes sparkled like beads. And I, who am no fool and don't like to be laughed at and who was rather piqued by his remark, answered, "First I want to know what you have to say, Don Vicente. You who know so much from your books..."

At that, many people there cried out that Don Vicente ought to speak. And finally he spoke. "The things that I have learned from my books have been of great service to me (and here he looked at me so that I understood that he was speaking only to me when he said this). My books have been my greatest friends, except for those present. It must be tiresome to you that I am always reminding you (and again he looked at me) of what have read, but I cannot help it. A man who comprehended these matters once asked God to grant him a corner, a friend and a book. In a way I have all, or rather I should say that I had them, for we are now in danger of losing the corner...and you know that better than I. While listening to the debate on who should bear the responsibility for our situation it has been a source of pride to me, a wistful pride, that nobody hung back."

"Many voices have been raised to ask punishment for the guilty, but those same voices have had the nobility to denounce themselves and to offer themselves as a kind of atonement, in order to save their native town from the infamous penalty which the government's paid assassins will surely inflict upon a justly indignant community which found itself forced to exact, with its own hands, a kind of terrible justice."

"I am very conscious that what those good sons of Yangana and that generous young man who has said that he wants to join his destiny to that" of our town, are prepared to do is nothing commonplace, it is exceptional. It is clear from books, from my books. Zacarías Fierro claims that honor for

401

himself in order to save Yangana…Fermín Lopez declared that he is the one who should be punished in order to save Yangana…a stranger who from now on is welcomed among us, proclaims himself to have been the inspiration of the crimes, the ringleader, in order to save Yangana. Maridueña wants to be the only one to enjoy such a tremendous honor, in order to save Yangana."

"This being so, I have only two things to say; first, if there are those among us who have generously declared themselves to be guilty and therefore ready to sacrifice themselves so that punishment shall be imposed only on those delegated to receive it and the rest of the community shall be saved, then I myself, must declare that I am one of the most involved and responsible. I, too, deserve a share of the blame! You should remember and are in honor bound to admit, that the idea of inviting the squires to the Fiesta was exclusively mine, so much so that Tobías Ocampo for example, (and here again he looked fixedly at me) was firmly opposed to it!"

"Second, it was also I who had the idea of producing for the benefit of the gentlemen from the big estates, a satirical play which would make them understand, by means of a theatrical presentation, the grave difficulties and dangers they were inviting by their conduct. It is a fact that if had not written or presented that piece of work, even without the last-minute changes which the actors made in the script— changes of which I would certainly never have approved— the temper of the crowd would not have reached the pitch of violence which it did and which led "inevitably to an uncontrollable outburst!"

"So you must take two sure things into account. First, that without my direct intervention the squires would not have come. Second, that even if they did come, nothing serious would have happened if the farce about *THE STILL WATERS* had not been presented. But in the same books of mine that some of my friends and also some who are not so friendly are always joking about" (and here the rascal gave me a piercing look with those little eyes of his), "have found an explanation, a very clear explanation of what happened."

"'There are no guilty individuals, not Maridueña, nor López, nor Fierro, nor Gordillo, nor I, nor John Doe, nor Richard Roe. There are some verses that express it very well, and you know them too because they were in everyone's mouth in Yangana some years ago after the performance of a comedy which produced for the Fiesta. Those verses written by a Spaniard, ran as follows:

Who killed the Overlord?
Fuenteovejuna, my lord.
And who is Fuenteovejuna?
All of us.'"

Then the old fellow who is really smart when it comes to talking and can disarm even me with his turns of phrase and pretty words, when he saw what an effect he was having, raised his voice and asked the crowd, "Who killed the Overlord?" and the people cried out in chorus with a great shout, "Fuenteovejuna, Sir." He went straight on and asked, "And who is Fuenteovejuna?" And the people answered with one voice, "All of us." That was all, dear friends.

Between ourselves, with this speech Don Vicente put the town in his pocket.

They all applauded until I could barely stand it. Then they all shouted out "Hurrah for Yangana the Free, Hurrah for Yangana the Free!" "Yes," continued Don Vicente who was, so to speak, visibly bathing in rose water, "We have to look for a way to save Yangana the Free, as you call her, at this critical moment when she is threatened with death. At this point the old villain once again put pressure on me and fixed his gaze on me. "That was why I asked Tobías Ocampo just now, what was his opinion, since he has such an influence in Yangana and has also taken an active part in other places under very difficult circumstances."

"I suggested that his experiences in the mining camps might be of some use to us now. But up to this moment our friend Ocampo has not said a word. In this decisive hour for the town he has refused to express an opinion. I can only think that perhaps the reason is that the invitation to the squires had not first been approved by him."

"Now, however, I challenge friend Ocampo in the name of Yangana, of that free Yangana that we are bound to defend, to let his voice be heard in this agonizing debate in which we find ourselves, and to come up with a formula for saving us which we can then discuss. I warn him, of course, that he must keep calm and not lose his temper if his proposal is rejected."

That was all, my friends, except that in the end Don Vicente caught me in his snare and there was no escape. I've already told you, friends, that all that time I was resentful of the townspeople because they had not taken me into account in anything, and I'm now telling you frankly that I was really fuming about it. From the moment that the Fiesta Committee disregarded my objection to the presence of the squires at the festivities, I withdrew from all active participation and determined that although I would attend all the events it would be purely as a spectator. Perhaps that was how I was able to notice so much that happened. Deep down I was still resentful. I couldn't swallow the fact that the people of Yangana had forgotten me. And I knew that they would be sorry for it later on. But I wanted them to realize it for themselves. And I knew that they would come to me afterwards to make peace and ask for my support.

I thought at the time that I would let them beg me a little, and then I would do whatever seemed proper. But this meeting on Tuesday afternoon changed everything, and before they could come to look for me, to coax me and ask my advice and beg me to be reconciled with them, Don Vicente guided me the same way by a different road. When I finally asked leave to speak, it was already almost night, and I had been touched by how frail Don Vicente looked with his vicuña poncho pulled up over his neck, coughing every few minutes because, as you know, the damp evening air always affects him a little. And, of course, he knew how to strike the right chord with me. The truth is, my friends, he had spoken tome rather grossly, but it was also quite clear to me that they needed my help.

The fact is that I had to stand up on a bench, and what happened then was what always happens to me when I find myself speaking in front of a crowd. I can never properly remember afterwards what I've said. But I have the idea that whatever it was, it was well said, to judge from the enthusiastic applause on all sides. Of course it's clear that I can't say those admirable things that Don Vicente does—he who knows so much about books—but I do know how to call bread bread, and wine wine; and believe, too, that I can see pebbles at the bottom of a stream even when the water is a little muddy. So I said to them in my own style that I could see only one way to save ourselves; that if we were all involved it meant that Yangana as a whole would be attacked, and attacked in its very heart, because we already had a reputation in the eyes of the government for being a community of unruly savages which could only be kept in line by an iron hand and by flogging. That Don Vicente had explained this to us very clearly and there was no sense in having illusions about clemency on the part of the executioners who would fall upon us.

I told them too that I thought that the best way to avoid such a fate was to migrate en masse to some other place far away to the east where nobody would trouble us, abandoning the town after burning it to the ground, so that no trace of us would be found. I said that we should go and join Joaquín Reinoso over by Palanda where there are great stretches of bottom land along the river and where nobody would ever penetrate the area or harass us since no squad of soldiers would dare to risk their lives in those unexplored mountains.

At the same time I outlined a plan for effecting this flight, taking into account that the government forces were already on the march and about to fall upon Yangana and that we must therefore protect our withdrawal until we were well out of reach of their fire. And for this purpose I suggested that it would be necessary to sacrifice some courageous men to meet the enemy on the road, not to attack them face to face but to hold them a little without a pitched battle, so as to impede their advance.

I was so excited and fired up, as I was speaking, that I could see quite clearly how our lads would handle the matter. They would leave the town without a moment's delay, well armed and well mounted, to await the soldiers just on this side of the first ford, and ambush them as they were crossing the river. Next, they would fall back to the narrow gap at Yanacocha where they could mow them down again. Falling back once more, they'll burn the ranch house and its buildings at Uchimba and fell trees across the road, which at that spot is very narrow and full of ruts and ridges. Last of all, they should dynamite the bridge at the entry to the town, blowing it up just as the main body of the troops is crossing.

Obviously I did not openly divulge this plan of action to everybody, since the only ones who should know it were those who were to carry it out, but at that instant I had it all clearly in my head, just as I am telling it to you now. What I did warn them was that if the men of this rear guard chosen by the townspeople themselves, and whom I was ready to accompany even if only as a subordinate, managed to get out alive they had only two choices. They could turn outlaws and highwaymen here in the province, in order to keep the police in check until they could escape over the border to Peru, or they could, some way or other, manage to follow the trail of the migrating townspeople until they caught up with them at Palanda where we would be waiting for them with open arms.

And with this, continued Curly Ocampo in atone of voice full of pride and conviction, and rubbing his hands, I scored a bulls-eye on that sly old Don Vicente and left him behind me, far behind. Because he may know a lot about books, but I know about life. I see things clearly as they are, very clearly. I can see the pebbles at the bottom of the stream, even when the water is stirred up. Yes, even when the water is stirred up.

The narrator then stood up, beat his breast with his open hands, and added forcibly. The crowd reacted favorably to my plan. And that's why we are here. They elected me commander. Don Vicente himself voted for me, although he rejected my offer to go with the men of the rearguard who were assigned to watch the road from the city while the rest of us escaped. When Don Vicente saw that the wind was blowing my way, he followed it along. He said that in his opinion, when a community found itself faced with a supreme crisis, it should submit its destiny to the direction of one man alone. Whether it was decided to stand and fight, or to surrender, or to retreat, the best thing to do was to elect a kind of dictator whom everybody should obey without question.

He went on to say that this man should be still young but at the same time experienced and cool-headed; that he should be energetic and valiant since they were likely to find themselves engaged in a struggle in which no quarter would be given. And finally, he said that when a multitude of people is passing through dangerous moments, instinct will show them into whose hands its fortunes should be entrusted.

But, in his last words he stressed the importance of making it quite clear to the commander chosen by the people for the present emergency, that he would exercise his functions only until the situation returned to normal. After that, we would resume the free and healthy life which we had enjoyed and for which we were resolved to fight. This, my friends, was Don Vicente's speech. And the people, by unanimous vote elected me. Yes, my friends, it was I they thought of when it came to choosing. I turned out to be the man who was still young, experienced and cool-headed, energetic and valiant, to use old Don Vicente's words. I turned out to be the one who would lead all those human beings and their property to this place and this land and I must also be the one who will have to give back the authority vested in me by the people, tomorrow or whenever they request it.

As he said this, his voice changed and took on a slightly somber tone. Give back my authority, he reflected, tomorrow because we have already arrived, or whenever they ask it of me. And who will ask me for it?

He appeared to regain his lively self-confidence and went on in the same exultant tone in which he had spoken when beating his breast with his open hands. This migration to Palanda, to the edge of the river where you live, Joaquín and Rosa Elvira, is the realization of my dream. And I am the chief. The chief. The whole community of Yangana is in my grasp. It is in this hand.

So saying, he clenched his fingers over his upturned palm, and with his thumb doubled over the knuckles of his forefinger, gently undulated his broad fist.

He looked up and surprised Rosa Elvira in the act of yawning. On seeing this he felt a little embarrassed. But for him this woman had always been a peacemaker, so he controlled himself. Suddenly quite calm, he considered what kind of yawn it was that he had caught her in. It was a sleepy yawn, one of those yawns that half loosen one's jaws and moisten one's eyes. Nevertheless, those stares which seemed weighed down by sleep were struggling to overcome it and were fixed with the most intense interest on the masculine clenched fist which her friend was proudly displaying in the pose of a fencing master. Clearly, Rosa Elvira's spirit was still willing...but, her body wanted to sleep.

Ocampo's mind, however, was also occupied by other matters, including his physical comfort. He suddenly found that his belt was too tight even though he had let it out two or three holes after eating and drinking earlier in the evening. It struck him that there were two things to be done right away now that Rosa Elvira had dropped out of his audience. Two things, as he would have said, two things, my friends, raising the index and middle fingers of his right hands to the level of his eyes like a pair of compasses. The first was to take a turn around the camp in order to promote digestion a little, the other was to wet his whistle with a few swigs of the strong liquor he had brought with him, untouched during all the long and painful march.

"Let's take a walk, friend Joaquín," he suggested, stretching himself like a cat that has just woken up, and cracking his joints. "Let's take a walk, Joaquín, my friend of the big tallow candles. I'd like to offer you a drink from Yangana. A cup of that good matured rum that we used to have there, now far away."

Rosa Elvira stood up to watch them go. Ocampo took leave of her with a strong handshake. As the two men were about to climb down the ladder, Rosa Elvira spoke to her old friend as if saying goodbye, in her sweet melodious voice, half tender and half entreating, "Listen, Curly, don't go on being the commander of those people. Go back to what you used to be. You have done your duty. Better to stop now. Better for them and better for you, too."

The two men went out into the night without a word.

A few moments later, as soon as they were clear of Joaquín's hut and could see better in the darkness, Ocampo put his hand on his friend's shoulder and said laconically, "Oh women! Oh women!"

(14)

The fires were dying down in the makeshift encampment. In some of them the smoke was still rising in a dense column, in others it was barely a thin wisp. In yet others it curled upwards in thick spirals, tinting the red glow with streaks of black. The resinous wood crackled in the fire and permeated the air with the pungent smell of balsam. The greener branches burned very slowly, contributing more smoke than flame. The two men stumbled along in silence. They did not speak to each other and it was obvious that they did not want to betray their presence.

They avoided crossing in front of the bonfires, except when they were dying out and shed no light, so that their silent shapes remained invisible. It was easy to understand that the inspection they were making was one of those which was not to be noticed by the people inspected.

From time to time a dog growled and kept on growling in a kind of uneasy sleep, peopled perhaps by nightmares and imaginary fights. He lifted his head drowsily and his moist nose sniffed the night air. Then once more he put his muzzle under his tail and curled himself up like a coil joined by its two extremities. Other sounds could be heard. Pack animals gnawing on the trunk of some tree; the tremulous bray of a jackass; the timid bleat and lowing of tired sheep and cattle. And sometimes the sneeze of a horse in tribute to the cool damp of the night.

And coughs, too, human coughing, resounding in that intermittent silence. From time to time an unusually loud cough would start off a veritable chorus of coughs, all joining in and as it were, supporting one another. Reinoso could not help a feeling of surprise at hearing, in that clearing where he had worked alone for so long, a cough that was not his, that was not Rosa Elvira's, nor was it that thin diminutive little cough from tiny lungs, which sometimes shook his little son while the father and mother listened with alarmed attention.

The two men stopped at one of the fires. It was burning brightly, surrounded by a compact group of campers. From where Reinoso and Ocampo were hiding, they could make out the shoulders of some of them and the firelit faces of others.

"Let's take a look, fellows, and see how the 'señorita' has survived the journey," exclaimed a voice from the center of the group, the voice of a man facing in the direction of the hidden observers. At the same time they could see that he, suiting the action to the word, had got up from the ground and gone over to the fire. He picked out a blazing brand and began to wave it back and forth so as to see where he was going. The señorita, as he affectionately called his guitar, had been obliged to make the trip slung over his shoulder.

By the light of the firebrand, he found a bundle wrapped up in a sheet. He stuck his torch in the ground, untied the knot of the sheet, and took out a shape swathed in a dark-colored alpaca poncho. He took off this covering and the señorita stood out unclothed, shining in the flickering light.

The señorita was varnished in yellow and adorned with fine mahogany inlay. Her owner touched her with a kind of shy delicacy and hesitant joy. The señorita wore a red ribbon on her neck. The strings had been purposely loosened for the journey and rattled on the soundboard like little whips.

When the man had assured himself that the senorita had apparently arrived unharmed, he turned back to the fire. He carried the instrument by the neck in his right hand, holding it high up to protect it from the branches, while the torch in his other hand left a trail of sparks behind him.

When he had rejoined his companions, he tossed his torch on the fire, looked for a large bundle of clothes where he could sit down comfortably with the guitar, touched each of the strings very gently, and then began lightly to strum the music of a song. He had no more doubts. The señorita had had the good fortune to finish the journey with her person and her voice safe and sound.

"Let it be put on record," suggested Betancur, the owner of the guitar, "that this music of mine is the first music that has been heard in this place since the beginning of the world. I should be officially declared the honorary musician of what was once Yangana."

"Take care that the nearest sentinel doesn't hear you," exclaimed a hoarse gruff voice, "because he'll order you to silence the mouth of your señorita and what's more, he'll probably wrap her around your head like a poncho."

To which Betancur replied, "Not even Curly Ocampo would make me silence the señorita. Do you think that Ocampo will be angry on account of a little music? He's not such a beast."

"I'm not saying that Curly Ocampo is a beast, but he has forbidden..."

While Betancur the musician was caressing and softly strumming the guitar, its varnish shone in the firelight. The smoke from the fire mingled with the evening mist over the encampment, streaking it with dark lines, much as when fresh water mixes with sea water at the mouth of a great river. Against this striated silvery background, the head of a young man could be made out, the same head which had just spoken those hoarse gruff words forbidding Betancur's midnight music. Reinoso did not know his face, which had the quick movements of a caged bird, but he could clearly hear what he went on to say.

"I want to play my part...want to be recognized as one of the founders of this new community A charter must be drawn up recording the foundation, and to record also that Marcos Quizpe was among those who came hither...leaving slavery behind them...so that in future times our descendants will remember us with pride...And when I marry and have children, I shall tell them the story, and they in turn will tell it to their children Marcos Quizpe, a founder of this new settlement That is how Marcos Quizpe will be known."

"I'm going to change the subject," it was another voice that spoke, "I think that tomorrow we should all have an uproarious merrymaking to celebrate our relatively happy arrival."

Yet another voice. "Don't be a fool. What we have to do now is to set to work like animals. Then a year from now we can have all the festivities we like in celebration of the first anniversary of the founding of New Yangana."

Moving on to another campfire, the observers encountered and easily recognized Doña Liberata Jiménez, who had gathered round her Juan Vasquez the potter, Don Melchor Celi the vagabond and two of his sons, and Picuita the cobbler—the one who was so fond of blacking his wife's eyes.

Angel F. Rojas

Doña Liberata was saying, "Let me tell you that I'm an admirer of strong characters. That's why I like Curly Ocampo and it seems to me that he ought to stay on as boss. You know that personally I've never put up with him and his ways, but as the priest says, 'render unto Caesar that which is Caesar's.' From what I've heard he has a big mouth and has criticized me, saying that I'm a meddlesome old virago. People say, too, that he does not pay his debts. But in fact all this does not apply here. Most likely that about his criticizing me was quite untrue."

Don Melchor spoke up in answer. "Pardon me, Doña Liberata, but don't agree with you. We must not allow anything in the way of a master. Men should be as free as birds or as Jívaro Indians. If we have fled from Yangana it is to be independent. I would kill or be killed if anybody tried to put shackles on my feet or prevent me from doing what I feel like doing. And I tell you, Doña Liberata, I would sooner have had the three bad neighbors whom we had, sooner those robbers who stole our Common Land, but who left us free, than have a boss over us whose permission we would have to ask every time we wanted to make water."

"It's clear, Don Melchor," countered Doña Liberata, "that you believe in the old saying, 'Lose my temper and make a fool of myself.' But as for me, injustice makes me sick even when I have no personal interest in the matter. If I know that somebody is being treated villainously, or that a robber is going unpunished, or that someone or other is to be punished unjustly, I'm capable of raising a riot and persisting in it at the risk of my life. I cannot bear injustice, no matter who is the sufferer. What am interested in is all Yangana and that's why I want us to be organized and under

416

the direction of one head, so that together we may do something worth while. You yourself must realize that you are no longer free. You have to do what the community asks of you. If you don't think so you can do what you like, but outside this community. And allow me, Don Melchor, to tell you frankly that you are an egoist."

"And you, friend Picuita, or rather Peñaflor, what do you say?" "Hum!" answered the person addressed, quickly collecting his thoughts, "Both things are the same to me. So long as I don't lack work, so long as I can go on stitching my shoes and earning my pesetas to buy a mouthful for myself and my children...whether here or in Yangana, it makes no difference, master or no master. As far as I and my wife and my children are concerned, the only master we have ever had has been this," he concluded, pointing to his stomach. "So long as we have something to put in this, it's all the same to me."

"How gross and ignorant can you be, friend Picuita, and excuse me from saying it to your face," answered Doña Liberata scornfully. "All you think about is filling your belly and your children's bellies, as if that were the only important thing in life," she finished in a biting tone no doubt calculated to silence him. Picuita, that is to say, Peñaflor, was manifestly irritated and made as if to leave, muttering some parting shot which Doña Liberata did not deign to answer.

Ocampo and his partner Reinoso went on through the mist, faintly lit by the firelight, and approached another fireside group with the same stealthy caution.

Here the firelight had rather a strange effect, since one of the men was sitting higher up than any of the others, so that the light shone brightly upward on his broad chin and neck, but left the upper part and forehead in almost complete shadow. This man with the illuminated chin was the only one of the group who was speaking. The words that fell from his dimly seen mouth were intoned in such a way that he seemed to be telling some age-old fable.

"I was the other stretcher bearer, but I had stayed behind a bend in the path to see what happened. So poor Matías Ortega was left alone with Curly Ocampo, just as he had requested in his hollow voice. He put his hand out from under his blanket—a hand which even now makes me tremble when I think of it. It was like a dead man's hand, yet it still moved. Dirty and pale, with nails that had grown long and black and terribly sharp. From a distance it looked almost as yellow as saffron or like a hen's claws. And he used this hand to implore Ocampo."

"'You remember, Curly, when I was fired because the gringo MacGregor found me lighting the dynamite fuse with my cigar, and you stood up for me...and I got my job back?'"

"'Yes.'"

"'Do you remember when we four from the same town— Shameless Carlos who was still new to the work, Joaquín Reinoso, you and I, joined the strike and were fired on and I was almost killed?'"

"'Yes.'"

"'Well then, Curly. Isn't it true that you are still my good friend?'"

"'Just as always, Matías!'"

"'In that case, Curly Ocampo, kill me.'"

"Curly sat down on his heels by the roadside and covered his face with his hands. He could not do it. Poor Matías had raised his head with a great effort and was smiling to himself since Curly was not looking. And I can no more forget that smile than I can forget that yellow hand. It shone in the sun. The teeth were white, exceedingly white. You could see that those teeth were bones, just bones…Other men's teeth, healthy men like us, have never looked to me like bones but in Matías' case they were dried bones. And he was smiling so sweetly."

"'Curly Ocampo!' he called. 'Kill me!'"

Ocampo continued to shake his head in refusal. It was for this that every day the poor sick man had wanted to be alone with Curly Ocampo, who had done his best to cheer him up.

"Ever since we set out from Yangana, Curly had carried a revolver in his belt, and a machete to clear the path. Poor Matías never took his eyes off the belt and kept looking at the pistol butt, except when his gaze shifted to the machete in Ocampo's left hand."

"'You really are my friend, aren't you, Curly?' he asked between those painful fits of coughing. It seemed as if he wanted to complain, but was afraid that Curly would feel too sorry for him, or perhaps as a man he was ashamed to complain. 'You really are my friend, aren't you?… Then don't deny me this favor. I can't go on…'"

"Curly didn't say a word, but with eyes full of pity followed poor Matías' gaze. And poor Matías' gaze only shifted from the pistol to Curly's face and back again. Whenever their eyes met, Matías made slight but insistent motions with his head and his hand. From time to time he coughed and spat in the most horrible exhaustion."

"In one of these paroxysms his head slipped off the stretcher and remained hanging over the edge. Curly Ocampo jumped up in an instant and bent over to lift Matías' head back on to the stretcher. The poor sick man seized the opportunity to stretch out that same yellow hand and grasp Curly's revolver. By the time Curly realized what was happening the gun was pointed at his chest and those yellow eyes were glittering like a madman's."

"'Kill me or I'll kill you,' he cried in a hoarse voice. Curly Ocampo sprang on him, as agile as a tiger, meaning to strike the weapon from his hand with the flat of his machete, but before he could do it a shot rang out. Ocampo was momentarily confused by the violence of the attack and threw himself on poor Matías with all the weight of his body in the hope of disarming him. The stretcher collapsed immediately under the impact and both men fell to the ground, one on top of the other. I heard Matías' bones crack the way a full grown cassava plant cracks when you tear it up by the roots, like this: truc, truc, truc; and Matías' last smile for his friend bathed his bone-white teeth with a bloody froth."

The narrator with the firelit chin paused a moment and then added. "It was the first time I had ever seen Curly Ocampo weep."

"'He tried to kill me,' he said to us stretcher bearers while we were shaping a cross with our machetes to put on poor Matías' grave—the first man we buried on the road..."

"Let's get out of here," Ocampo said to Reinoso, tugging him convulsively by the arm..."let's move further on...to that fire over there." They moved forward.

They passed several almost extinguished fires, where the flames seemed to be sleeping under a cloak of ashes. They could hear human sighs, an occasional snore, the sound of a sleeping body changing its position, hushed lullabies and they could smell the cool night air, in places so pure and fresh and in places tainted by acrid smoke or the exhalations of the mass of human bodies.

On their way, they overheard a snatch of languid conversation, "So we'd better get married, darling. You can count on it. I give you my word of honor..." "What I'm afraid of is that I may get pregnant and that my parents will find out... What'll I do then?"

They could not see the young lovers hidden in the thick mist. All that reached Ocampo and his companion was their whispered voices seemingly wrapped in cotton.

"I'm thinking about setting up a wooden cane grinder to make coarse sugar," an invisible man was saying further on. "I wonder how long it takes in these parts for cane to be ready for harvesting. Will it be a year? A year and a half? I believe that with this soil, which is virgin and damp, eighteen months will be more than enough."

But the man he was talking to was thinking about something else. "Reinoso," he said, "who has been here so long, has told Baltasar that neither he nor his wife nor the little boy have suffered from malaria. According to Reinoso, the climate here is very healthy. If there is no malaria here we will be in good shape. It seems that Don Salvador asked him about dysentery too, and Reinoso gave the same answer, 'Neither I nor my wife have had it!'"

"'And what about the grippe?' Don Salvador is said to have continued. "'I assure you there is no trace of it here,'" said Reinoso. "And ticks in the pastures?" ""But, Don Salvador,'" said Reinoso, "there are no pastures here. You'll have to make your own pastures, and as for ticks, the cattle you have brought must have brought their ticks with them!'" Apparently Don Salvador was not very happy about all this and said "that if the climate of Palanda was so healthy, he would die of hunger for lack of patients."

Still further on the mist was impenetrable and seemed to have its own voice, a voice muffled by walls of cotton and saying at that moment, "I'm not a greenhorn...I've properly hoodwinked the watchman. I've eaten fruit all along the way. And I've stolen any amount of eggs. I've got here with a full stomach and it hasn't cost me a cent. Why ration myself as stupid dolts do? The fact is that I'm no fool. I'm smart, very smart. And I have a bellyful of dainties. Let others fast! Nobody orders me to do anything and least of all to fast!"

Reinoso and Ocampo found it strange to listen to these conversations carried on almost under their feet, as it were. It seemed as if they came from the very ground they were treading. We are used to hearing people converse standing up or at least sitting down and even then some, distance from the ground. But here, threading their way through the thick mist which shrouded the dead or dying fires, they imagined that the voices came from bodies lying under the ground and that the words were being pushed out by the pressure of their footsteps.

One of the voices from ground level, a voice well known to both of them, was expressing a profound wish concerning the new life which would begin for the adventurers on the morrow. The voice kept on saying over and over again,

"Starting tomorrow, I want to be a pimp...starting tomorrow I want to be a pimp...starting tomorrow I want to be a pimp."

It was the voice of Camilo Isidro, the most foul-mouthed man in the whole neighborhood.

They turned to one side to avoid meeting one of the armed sentinels, and cautiously continued their tour.

Now they could hear women's voices round an almost extinguished cooking fire. The sibilant notes of the S's rose and fell softly.

"The children will have to learn differently now. We must realize that they will belong to a world unlike the one we have left. We shall have to educate them according to the conditions in which they will be living. The first thing I mean to request at tomorrow's meeting is that we build a good schoolhouse. And just as we'll have to clear the woodland to raise the schoolhouse, we'll also have to cultivate a new spirit in our children. It is important to explain to them what has happened to us and why we have come here, so that they can learn the story of their parents and know their enemies."

"They should also learn to love the earth and their country in a new way. Without this new appreciation of the country which has treated us so unkindly, they will not be able to survive...I propose to say all this and other ideas of mine at tomorrow's foundation ceremony, to make sure that from the very start a good schoolhouse is built..."

The next voice was milder and interspersed with an old man's little coughs. "The same old story, daughter...cof, cof, cof...you've always prepared pretty little speeches for graduation day, cof, cof, cof...then the day comes and all you can do is stammer…cof, cof, cof…and the result of it all is that you make yourself ridiculous and nobody pays you any attention…cof, cof, cof. You've been a schoolteacher for years and years and still don't know how to manage yourself…cof, cof, cof. So who is going to believe in your ability?"

Next Ocampo pointed out to Reinoso another poorly lit spot. "Here's a gang of young fellows who have been a real headache for me, but in the end they have worked, too…They knew when and where we were cutting a new section of road and our scouts took special precautions always to be within shouting distance of the crazy kids. You could see they were capable of all kinds of mischief. For example, they tossed pieces of burning wood all up and down the line of march, and took the greatest delight in skipping out of the way with incredible twists and turns and jumps, apparently feeling no fatigue from the interminable walking. They couldn't stay quiet for one moment."

These rascals were a special torment to other boys who tried to huddle up in some corner to get some sleep. A shrill whistle would announce the attack. The whistle was followed by a shoe hurtling like an arrow through the dimly lit space, or a broken branch thrown by a hidden hand as if from a catapult. Or a daring aggressor would give a heartless tug at some sleeping boy's mat, leaving his shoulders on the damp leaf-mold and the mat in the hands of the assailant. Whenever a sentinel approached on his rounds, the noise and laughter stopped short and serious conversations on important matters were again heard.

A young lad was asking the boys of the gang a question, and Ocampo recognized him as the younger brother of the bird-faced adolescent who had been carrying on so confidently and forcefully at one of the other firesides, about wanting to be considered one of the historic founders of the new community.

His question was received first with silence and then with hoots. "But tell me now, I want to know what's all this about Communism? Do you know, Abdón?" The person thus addressed finally deigned to answer, "Leave me-alone. I don't know a thing about it."

In spite of this rebuff, the younger brother of the bird-faced boy repeated his tedious question. "And you, Juan de Dios, do you know about it? Because," he explained, while the sentinel observed the group of young rascals with suspicious curiosity, "the government says that we are communists. Can it be because we wanted to defend what belonged to us?"

But Juan de Dios was evidently one of those who wanted to sleep at any price. "Listen, do me the favor of not bothering me with your nonsense at this time of night, d'you hear?" And he wrapped his head up in his blanket under a hail of jokes, laughter and random projectiles.

"You are older than I and ought to know. The only thing that my father has told me about it is that it's an idea of the gringos, who want to take away from some people what they have in excess and give it to those who have nothing. But if that were the case, we were not communists since what we were doing was to claim what had been stolen from us. Or is it communism to refuse to let those robbers steal the Common Lands?"

"Carajo!" exclaimed another, "Why don't you ask Don Vicente Muñoz who knows everything about it, or go let yourself be led astray by Juanita Villalba who also understands these things, instead of coming and pestering us with your questions as if we were an oracle or King Solomon himself?"

Another bad tempered grouch tried to shut the inquisitive boy's mouth by adding, "All that I know, you Tom Fool, is that it's about something that people do when they're hungry."

"In that case," added a voice, as if in explanation, "at this moment I am a communist."

There were a few more random words, abruptly cut short by a warning whistle, by a projectile in the form of a shoe sailing through the air, and by the sound of its impact on some unguarded shoulder.

Further on, Damasio Sánchez was singing in a very low voice in the almost palpable darkness. His voice was one of those that seemed to rise out of the ground itself. It was a voice that was growing out of the grass, and it seemed really strange to hear a song at ground level. There was no musical accompaniment beyond the resonance of the damp night, vibrating like a taut drum, and the whisper of the wind swishing against the familiar trees and the strange travelers who had not been there the night before.

But that concert of natural sounds, rendered doubly resonant by the night; that low and indistinct sound of restless herds; that unwonted chorus of coughs—all merged together in a rich harmony in which the song sung gently by Damasio Sánchez came through like soft background music.

Betancur the musician looked on Sánchez the singer as his arch-rival and would gladly have seen him dead.

The song which Ocampo and Reinoso overheard was an old one and full of nostalgia.

> When I left my native land
> I said goodbye to no one...
> The clouds were weeping blood
> And the sun refused to shine.
> You begged me to leave you!
> What I left you was my heart.
> Now you will miss my shadow
> When you are exhausted by the sun.

Piled up nearby was the immense store of seeds that Don Eliseo Aliaga had brought with him in spite of his stiff-jointed old legs. The two watchers could just distinguish the rounded shapes of the stuffed saddlebags, the half hidden leather pouches, the haphazard mound of bursting sacks. From time to time, men who were still awake and watchful passed between the lined-up loads and the fire, casting their sudden leaping shadows on seeds and tree trunks. One or two sleeping bodies could be made out as they shifted position on the pile.

Here in this part of the damp, the night scents were compounded of new ingredients. They vividly recalled the homelike smell of stored provisions, of harvested fruit, of groceries, or a market place. One thing was certain, there was nothing of a city market place about this makeshift granary set up in a wild open space, with no roof or shelter against the threatening night. Undoubtedly that flagrant rum-drinker who, to quote his own drunken lyric, "had joined his destiny to the destiny of Yangana," was lurking somewhere near, but the two stealthy observers saw no sign of him.

The group conversation at this spot was different from any of the others. It was composed of a series of painful reminiscences expressed in the form of questions, each man asking his own question which nobody answered. In this way the whole group recalled and lived over again events which came to their minds at that moment.

"D'you remember how those same forty men set fire to the houses in the Square, as soon as we were all on the other side of Destruction Creek?"

"And d'you remember that the fire spread immediately to the Leones section, jumping over both Don Pedro Matías' house and Don Tomás Ramón's, and starting again with the oldest one there, where apparently it caused the most dreadful confusion because that idiot Serafín Armijos was to have been buried that day in a big funeral and nobody could get there?"

"And d'you remember that Papá Lisandro Fierro's house caught fire of itself before its turn?"

"And d'you remember how sad we felt when Don Baltazar Zárate's house began to burn, and then Don Vicente's, and that two-story house that the cholito Presentación Quille had in the town?"

"And d'you remember that after that the men received orders to destroy the seed beds and young growing crops and crops ready for harvest that could not be taken with us, and that only Don Eliseo Aliaga's nurseries and orchard were spared?"

"And d'you remember that the parish house, old as it was, remained almost intact except for a wing of the roof that caved in on the side next to the church?"

"And d'you remember how we almost all sobbed and snivelled when we looked back from the pass at Caranango and saw the valley of Yangana and the Common Lands and the fields all black from the fires?"

"And do you remember how Papá Eliseo Aliaga began to weep there on the spot, more than anyone, and to callout after his trees as if they were dogs that could follow him to Palanda?"

"And d'you remember how Ocampo who is so bold, when he reached the same spot, shook his fist at the Cross at the head of the Pass?"

"And do you remember how the bell that Papá Taro had cast for us remained forlornly in the middle of the destroyed town, and there was no way to rescue her?"

"And d'you remember the first night we slept in the open, how José Clemente Piedra misbehaved with that disheveled wife of the Chino's, making love to her under the Chino's very nose?"

"And d'you remember poor Matías Ortega, and how Curly Ocampo gave him a quick passport to the next world?"

"And d'you remember the bridge at Yangana, where when we were kids we all used to write our names in chalk on the wooden structure at the risk of falling off the beams into the river?"

"And do you remember the day the newspaper reached Yangana with the news that the government troops were about to attack us for being Communists?"

By now only a few fires were still burning. The inspection was almost ended. The two men found themselves nearly back at their starting point, where the fifth sentinel guarded the narrow winding path leading to the river, a path established months before by the daily passage of Joaquín and his wife. The sentinel was sitting on a tree trunk, so motionless that he seemed to be half asleep with his rifle between his knees and behind him the firelight, the smoke and the mist of the campsite. Every so often the lighted end of his cigarette, an inch or two from his lips, glowed like a firefly or a tiny lantern. Except for that little spot of fire so close to his copper-colored face, the sentinel gave no sign of life.

"The most important thing is ahead of us," whispered Ocampo. Don Vicente is still awake in his tent and he has some others with him, too.

"The old fellow stays up late;" remarked Reinoso, "could he be reading one of his books?"

"No doubt he's arguing against something or somebody, that's my guess," answered Ocampo with a touch of irritation. "We can't do a thing about it even if we can't stand it."

The bonfire here was burning brightly and they had no difficulty identifying the speakers and following the conversation.

"The only thing I like about Don Vicente is that he's not a hypocrite," Ocampo admitted after a pause, "he says and does things to your face."

Curly Ocampo was right. At that very moment the old man was talking about him.

"We cannot deny that he has behaved well," went on Don Vicente Muñoz. "He has brought us here and has managed the matters that we entrusted to him with energy and honesty. It took great fortitude to carry out his idea about abandoning and destroying the houses and he proved himself admirably competent. He has been a strict disciplinarian and has allowed no food to be wasted, which is what we have to guard against more than anything else if we are not to suffer hunger in the coming months, since our corn, beans, rice and cassava still have to be planted. Thanks in great part to him, the animals and the seeds have all arrived safely, undiminished and unharmed."

"He has paid a high price. He has got up before dawn; he has often gone without sleep or rest, watching both vanguard and rearguard, supervising transportation and trail cutting. He had to forget that he had a wife and children to look after. He was forced to shout much and swear more. He could not avoid making secret enemies who will not forgive him the penalties he had to impose, since there were times when some of the more unruly ones tried to stir up trouble for him and have their own way in everything."

"Nevertheless, he will not do for authority in the new town. That is another matter. Everything in its proper place. Just as in wartime it is suitable that the military should take command because a time of war is a time for men of war, so also in peacetime it is civilians who must rule. Ever since we set out, we have been in company like a band of soldiers. But now, today, we have reached our journey's end. All this time Ocampo was our undisputed leader. What we have to think about now is what authorities will govern the community in the daily tasks of peacetime construction. And these authorities must be honorable people who are well trained and prepared for civic leadership, people who know what is best for the town."

Ocampo, hidden there in the dark, grasped his friend Reinoso's hand with a violent gesture. "Did you hear that, Joaquín? Did you hear it? I'm not honorable…"

Meanwhile Don Vicente continued his discourse: "Military authority rests on valor, on daring, on the gift of commanding and inspiring others in the face of danger…What we can call civil authority must rest upon trust, on skill, on tact, on honorable record and behavior. Ocampo who proved himself to be an excellent leader for our migration to the promised land, would be a failure as civil authority. He has too little equilibrium and too much imagination. And he has been guilty of errors in the past which he may not be able to avoid in the future…"

Reinoso could still feel, from time to time, his friend's sharp fingers convulsively grasping his arm.

Don Vicente went on: "At our meeting tomorrow I shall propose that Ocampo's duties be terminated and that civil authorities be elected. I should like to offer the name of Don Baltazar Zárate for our principal official. You have expressed your fears to me that if we elect anybody but Ocampo we shall have a problem on our hands, owing to his fury and the dissatisfaction of his admirers and supporters. But I can tell you that to my way of thinking there is a very simple solution to this problem. We shall appoint Ocampo as chief of the organized security force which we will in any case have to establish here. On the understanding, of course, that he will be directly subordinate to the principal civil authority. To Don Baltazar, for example. Let us understand the situation. We have never had such an organized force because there has been no need for it. And that was because we have never before faced the kind of perilous circumstances in which we now find ourselves."

"Ahead of us we have the work of constructing a whole town, a whole community. And it certainly will not be accomplished by isolated effort. 'All as one' will be our motto so that when we are asked, 'Who built New Yangana?' we can answer, 'All of us!' Ocampo under the direction of Don Baltazar—this is an acceptable formula."

"No, not that!" muttered Ocampo indignantly to his companion. Chief of Police and subordinated to Don Baltazar…never! I'll turn back from here, or be lost forever in obscurity before I accept that. So I've just been a worthless fellow who has only served to bring everyone here where they're safe and sound, and once here, I'm to be kicked out with 'we don't need you any more!'"

Meanwhile, Don Vicente continued to speak to a profoundly attentive audience.

"I think, of course, that we owe our most fervent thanks to Ocampo. From beginning to end, he has been the hero of our march. This has restored his reputation even in the eyes of his severest critics. I mean to propose tomorrow that, as a testimony of our gratitude, we name one of the public squares in the town which we are about to found here 'Plaza de Ocampo' in his honor. In this way the people he led will always remember him as they will also remember with pride their own rebirth. Doesn't this seem to you to be a way to win him over and at the same time pay honor where honor is due and also to insure him a place in the memory of future generations? Besides, as Montalvo said…"

Ocampo tugged at his friend's arm and said with thinly disguised excitement, "Let's go. This old fool is about to start on his quotations from Montalvo. I'm inviting you to drink with me and I want us to have a talk. We've got to talk, Joaquín. I need you and I need to talk."

They moved on again as stealthily as before. The nearest sentinel, noticing two men passing close to him, put his rifle at the ready and caned out, "Who goes there?"

To which Ocampo replied with all the tone of command he could muster, "Yangana The Free!"

And he felt like reprimanding the sentinel severely for taking so long to notice their presence, and for not even recognizing his commander. But it struck him that there were not enough words in the human language to express himself properly on this point. He preferred to stifle his anger and go on his way.

Suddenly, he didn't know how, he thought he heard a soft sweet voice, a voice which he loved, saying to him as if giving him advice, "Don't go on being the leader of these people. Go back to what you used to be. Better to leave them. Better for them and better for you, too…"

He turned to his friend Reinoso and exclaimed, "The things that women say and do sometimes!" And he felt a little comforted.

It was time to change the guard and from the different corners of the Camp, the watchword was heard, repeated ten times, "Yangana The Free!"

"We shall improve the breed of our horses and mules, since for that purpose we selected and brought with us the best that we had."

"On this side of the river—the right bank—there is an immense expanse of bottom land well above water level. The land on the other side is subject to seasonal flooding, and there we shall plant our rice. On this side we shall plant large areas in plantains and sugar cane. The very first clearing we make will be for corn."

"Tomorrow—not a day later—we must look for suitable earth and clay for making adobes; tiles and bricks. The lumber we shall need for building houses is here under our noses; it gets in our way. What we are about to undertake will in time become a big city, Joaquín, and we shall grow old watching the growth of the community that we are founding here."

"When a long time has passed, the guilty town will have been pardoned, and then our children will build a road to the provincial capital—one of those roads so hard to construct that even the government would never attempt it. And on this road the people of our reborn town will bring their first automobiles."

"While all this is taking place, it will be our duty to cherish the memory of what we were and what we did, to continue free but disciplined, to bring up and teach our children to feel proud that they are our descendants. And in the end they will make their peace with the Ecuadorian state and will enjoy the glory of belonging to a spirited town which chose collective exile rather than their own degradation."

Joaquín Reinoso, also with the drinks that he had taken, felt an impatient urge to discover without further delay just what intentions lay behind his friend's words. He was sure that he, was not mistaken in believing that the long preamble had been meant to build up a state of mind, an ambience favorable to certain profound and far-reaching confessions, and that he must lose no time in forcing them out of Ocampo.

Following these thoughts and assuming a cold manner which perhaps he did not feel, he protested to his friend, "Can't we get to the point? Because I'm sure that you haven't brought me here at this time of night just to discuss what kind of town you and your companions mayor may not found here, nor to make me listen to what these people who are sitting up around the fires are talking about. I've heard your account of the march here and I've obviously been very happy to listen to everything that my old friend has told me. But why can't we now, without beating around the bush, talk about whatever it is that you really want to say to me? Because remember, when we were close to Don Vicente's little tent, you said that you had to talk to me about an urgent matter and also that you needed my help. All right then, how can I be of use to you?"

Reinoso pronounced these last words with a kind of studied courtesy, half aggressive and half mocking.

Ocampo, however, persisted in talking about his vision of the future. "We must also aspire to be in better condition than we were before. After all, what was Yangana? A town that for many years had remained backward, stagnant and out of touch with the world. For the time being, the same conditions are bound to prevail in this new land. We will have to be backward, abandoned, solitary, given over to ourselves and incommunicado. But we must not stagnate for long without beginning to move. Impossible!"

"As I see things, Yangana was in a state of decay. It had run to seed, or you might call it over-cooked. It had not grown in any way for a long, long time. But this new town of ours must grow under our eyes. We will allow no swarm to break away from the hive; nobody will be able to leave. We must increase and multiply, we must be prolific and populate the land. We will undertake an anti-malaria campaign with all our energies, war is a time for men of war, so also in peacetime it is civilians who must rule. Ever since we set out, we have been in company like a band of soldiers. But now, today, we have reached our journey's end. All this time Ocampo was our undisputed leader. What we have to think about now is what authorities will govern the community in the daily tasks of peacetime construction. And these authorities must be honorable people who are well trained and prepared for civic leadership, people who know what is best for the town."

Ocampo, hidden there in the dark, grasped his friend Reinoso's hand with a violent gesture. "Did you hear that, Joaquín? Did you hear it? I'm not honorable...:

Meanwhile Don Vicente continued his discourse: "Military authority rests on valor, on daring, on the gift of commanding and inspiring others in the face of danger. What we can call civil authority must rest upon trust, on skill, on tact, on honorable record and behavior. Ocampo who proved himself to be an excellent leader for our migration to the promised land, would be a failure as civil authority. He has too little equilibrium and too much imagination. And he has been guilty of errors in the past which he may not be able to avoid in the future..."

Reinoso could still feel, from time to time, his friend's sharp fingers convulsively grasping his arm.

Don Vicente went on: "At our meeting tomorrow I shall propose that Ocampo's duties be terminated and that civil authorities be elected. I should like to offer the name of Don Baltazar Zárate for our principal official. You have expressed your fears to me that if we elect anybody but Ocampo we shall have a problem on our hands, owing to his fury and the dissatisfaction of his admirers and supporters. But I can tell you that to my way of thinking there is a very simple solution to this problem. We shall appoint Ocampo as chief of the organized security force which we will in any case have to establish here. On the understanding, of course, that he will be directly subordinate to the principal civil authority. To Don Baltazar, for example. Let us understand the situation. We have never had such an organized force because there has been no need for it. And that was because we have never before faced the kind of perilous circumstances in which we now find ourselves."

"Ahead of us we have the work of constructing a whole town, a whole community. And it certainly will not be accomplished by isolated effort. 'All as one' will be our motto so that when we are asked, 'Who built New Yangana?' we can answer, 'All of us!' Ocampo under the direction of Don Baltazar—this is an acceptable formula."

"No, not that!" muttered Ocampo indignantly to his companion. Chief of Police and subordinated to Don Baltazar never! I'll turn back from here, or be lost forever in obscurity before I accept that. So I've just been a worthless fellow who has only served to bring everyone here where they're safe and sound, and once here, I'm to be kicked out with 'we don't need you any more!'"

Meanwhile, Don Vicente continued to speak to a profoundly attentive audience.

"I think, of course, that we owe our most fervent thanks to Ocampo. From beginning to end, he has been the hero of our march. This has restored his reputation even in the eyes of his severest critics. I mean to propose tomorrow that, as a testimony of our gratitude, we name one of the public squares in the town which we are about to found here 'Plaza de Ocampo' in his honor. In this way the people he led will always remember him as they will also remember with pride their own rebirth. Doesn't this seem to you to be a way to win him over and at the same time pay honor where honor is due and also to insure him a place in the memory of future generations? Besides, as Montalvo said…" Ocampo tugged at his friend's arm and said with thinly disguised excitement, "Let's go. This old fool is about to start on his quotations from Montalvo. I'm inviting you to drink with me and I want us to have a talk. We've got to talk, Joaquín. I need you and I need to talk."

They moved on again as stealthily as before. The nearest sentinel, noticing two men passing close to him, put his rifle at the ready and called out, "Who goes there?"

To which Ocampo replied with all the tone of command he could muster, "Yangana The Free!"

And he felt like reprimanding the sentinel severely for taking so long to notice their presence, and for not even recognizing his commander. But it struck him that there were not enough words in the human language to express himself properly on this point. He preferred to stifle his anger and go on his way.

Suddenly, he didn't know how, he thought he heard a soft sweet voice, a voice which he loved, saying to him as if giving him advice, "Don't go on being the commander of these people. Go back to what you used to be. Better to leave them. Better for them and better for you, too..."

He turned to his friend Reinoso and exclaimed, "The things that women say and do sometimes!" And he felt a little comforted.

It was time to change the guard and from the different corners of the Camp, the watchword was heard, repeated ten times, "Yangana The Free!"

EPILOGUE

The Horizon of a New Tomorrow

(1)

Tobías Ocampo, alias Curly, with the drinks he had taken, felt a kind of curious lucidity. He was slightly exhilarated, in that stage when incipient tipsiness can sometimes be illuminating. It seemed to him that he could see everything clearly—"the pebbles at the, bottom of the pool even when the water is muddy," as he liked to say of his own perspicacity. He could feel a growing resolve to talk to his friend freely and without any preamble about his secret dream.

"I have a vision of what the future city will become, friend Joaquín," he said, with a sweeping gesture toward the river bottom. "We shall lay out the square taking this little house of yours as a point of reference. The streets will be broad. We shall construct the public offices and buildings round the square. The river runs a short distance away and is navigable for rafts; it will carry us to sell our produce to the foreigners living downstream. Our fields and orchards will cover the river banks."

"There will be many pastures where our cattle will graze freely, without finding a fence between them and the watering place. We will care for these cattle that belong to all of us so that no disease—no disease of any kind! will destroy them. As for new or unknown diseases, we will order our herb doctors and medicine men to search for and discover appropriate remedies. Once our cattle are grazing freely and healthily in the spacious pastures we shall make for them, our herds will increase and prosper."

"We shall improve the breed of our horses and mules, since for that purpose we selected and brought with us the best that we had."

"On this side of the river—the right bank—there is an immense expanse of bottom land well above water level. The land on the other side is subject to seasonal flooding, and there we shall plant our rice. On this side we shall plant large areas in plantains and sugar cane. The very first clearing we make will be for corn."

"Tomorrow—not a day later—we must look for suitable earth and clay for making adobes; tiles and bricks. The lumber we shall need for building houses is here under our noses; it gets in our way. What we are about to undertake will in time become a big city, Joaquín, and we shall grow old watching the growth of the community that we are founding here."

"When a long time has passed, the guilty town will have been pardoned, and then our children will build a road to the provincial capital—one of those roads so hard to construct that even the government would never attempt it. And on this road the people of our reborn town will bring their first automobiles."

"While all this is taking place, it will be our duty to cherish the memory of what we were and what we did, to continue free but disciplined, to bring up and teach our children to feel proud that they are our descendants. And in the end they will make their peace with the Ecuadorian state and will enjoy the glory of belonging to a spirited town which chose collective exile rather than their own degradation."

Joaquín Reinoso, also with the drinks that he had taken, felt an impatient urge to discover without further delay just what intentions lay behind his friend's words. He was sure that he was not mistaken in believing that the long preamble had been meant to build up a state of mind an ambience favorable to certain profound and far-reaching confessions, and that he must lose no time in forcing them out of Ocampo.

Following these thoughts and assuming a cold manner which perhaps he did not feel, he protested to his friend, "Can't we get to the point? Because I'm sure that you haven't brought me here at this time of night just to discuss what kind of town you and your companions mayor may not found here, nor to make me listen to what these people who are sitting up around the fires are talking about. I've heard your account of the march here and I've obviously been very happy to listen to everything that my old friend has told me. But why can't we now, without beating around the bush, talk about whatever it is that you really want to say to me? Because remember, when we were close to Don Vicente's little tent, you said that you had to talk to me about an urgent matter and also that you needed my help. All right then, how can I be of use to you?"

Reinoso pronounced these last words with a kind of studied courtesy, half aggressive and half mocking.

Ocampo, however, persisted in talking about his vision of the future. "We must also aspire to be in better condition than we were before. After all, what was Yangana? A town

443

that for many years had remained backward, stagnant and out of touch with the world. For the time being, the same conditions are bound to prevail in this new land. We will have to be backward, abandoned, solitary, given over to ourselves and incommunicado. But we must not stagnate for long without beginning to move. Impossible!"

"As I see things, Yangana was in a state of decay. It had run to seed, or you might call it over-cooked. It had not grown in any way for a long, long time. But this new town of ours must grow under our eyes. We will allow no swarm to break away from the hive; nobody will be able to leave. We must increase and multiply, we must be prolific and populate the land. We will undertake an anti-malaria campaign with all our energies, in case we have brought it with us—since you who live here have told us there is no malaria here now."

"But we have to live in a new way, in a better way, and never forget for a moment that we are a world apart, that we can hope for nothing from outside. And being the masters of this new world we will have to determine our own destiny. And so Joaquín, that destiny is bound to be a great one. There is no other way, it has to be great."

Ocampo's voice was gradually rising in, pitch and growing declamatory. Although at the beginning his phrases had come out slowly and carefully, they now began to pour out in a hurried and emotional stream. Nevertheless, Joaquín persisted in trying to find out why his friend had brought him to that place at that hour if he, were not going to speak frankly and openly. So he insisted on bringing up the subject again.

"Very good, my friend. Give me another drink because I am going to turn in. You don't want to say why you need me, and I'm sleepy. Give me that drink, brother. I see that you no longer trust me and in that case we're just wasting time. Tomorrow we can talk again at our leisure."

No, thought Ocampo. Joaquín can't leave before it's time. I'll give him another drink, or several drinks, as long as the bottle lasts, and glad to. But that he should pack up and go just like that…I'll come clean with him, absolutely clean.

"So you want me to tell you why I need you? Can't you understand it yet, Joaquín, or don't you want to understand it? I was getting to it, but you're too impatient. Come on, drink up."

Joaquín put the bottle to his lips, tilted his head toward the treetops, took three loud swallows, and wiped his mouth with his hand.

"I need you, Joaquín, because this plan of mine to build a city here, this plan to lay the base of what tomorrow will be a real city, to work together in unison without faltering, with all our hearts and minds, in order to provide ourselves with much more than the mere necessities of life, and thinking always of our future growth…this plan calls for an administrator capable of overcoming in every way the indolence or indifference of others, of the lazy ones who will only want this to be the same Yangana transplanted to a new site, and nothing more while on the contrary, as I see it, we shall have to work here until we burst. If our uprooting and flight was painful, it will be slower and harder to struggle for year after year to create something not measured by what we are now but rather by what we ought to become when this is greater, immensely greater For all this I need you, Joaquín Reinoso, because I mean to be that administrator."

"But..."

By now Ocampo was completely carried away by his own words. He cut his friend short impatiently. "You've already seen, Joaquín, what's going on in the camp. There are those who want me to stay on as that person in sole command, and those who don't want me. Nobody is more against me than Don Vicente. He is working to deprive me of my command at the end of the march and to set up what he calls a civil administration with Don Baltazar Zárate as chief authority and a group of doddering old men who will serve as what Don Vicente calls councilors. He even wants to catch Don Leandro Fierro himself in his net, that poor dried up old fungus."

"While, as for me, I swear by my dead father that out of pure pride and loftiness of mind I have not taken a single step to garner the good will of a band of men. I have considered that what I did for the people who in their hour of greatest danger put themselves under my command when I least expected it, was proof enough of my courage and competence. As a result of this attitude of mine, I have lost ground and lost supporters. There are murmurs that I mean to seize power and apparently that's what they most fear. That's why Don Vicente is trying to make a deal and give me a piece of candy to suck and make me think that I'm being thanked and honored."

"They want to make me Chief of Police, that is to say, they want to reduce me in rank as a reward for my efforts. But I tell you in confidence, Joaquín, that I think that it's not yet time for anything but the system of sole command. Are we or are we not under campaign conditions? Of course we are. In a campaign there must be one commander and only one. We are still on a war footing and on a war footing we shall be living for a long time until we carry out our plan for building a new life where at the moment there is nothing. For that reason we need a single director and a single will capable of ordering and accomplishing. Up to now, brother, that direction has been mine."

"To be frank with you, I mean to keep my position, and what is more am determined to defend it, in whatever way, against any person or persons who may try to take it from me. I am sure I can count on all the armed men who marched here under my command, and also on the survivors of the rear guard suicide squad who, according to my secret information, had almost caught up with us yesterday."

"That's why I said that I need you, Joaquín. I need your support tomorrow in the first meeting where the question of suspending or terminating my powers will certainly come up. It's not in my character to sing my own praises and tell everybody what a stress and strain the march has been for me and how I have given ample proof of my worth. Can I count on you, brother Joaquín?"

Obviously Reinoso was far from convinced. "And why do you persist in wanting to be that sole administrator even if you have to use force? Would you be prepared to shed blood if they don't agree amicably?"

Ocampo made an impatient gesture but controlled himself in the face of his friend's unexpected stubbornness, and continued.

"I'm going to give you an explanation which under other circumstances would never have given you. Besides, I've started to tell you my innermost feelings and now I have to tell you every one of them. To tell you the truth, brother Joaquín, up to now I have been a stray bullet, a madcap adventurer. I've never been of any serious use, and now I'm growing old. The best years of my life have slipped away without anything worthwhile or noteworthy to show for them. Opportunities like this one don't present themselves every day. You don't always come across a hundred and sixty families who have decided to go into the wilds and found a new community. Nobody has ever believed in me except possibly one person, only one. Not even my own mother."

"My fellow townsmen have looked on me as an audacious and roving adventurer and dishonest to boot. When I feel like drinking, I drink conscientiously and neglect to pay my debts because—so it is said—I'd sooner buy booze with other people's money. I engage in shady business deals And now when I've reached an age when I've no time to lose I feel an urge to demonstrate to my town— that town that has always looked on me as worthless—what I can finally prove to be for it—the one indispensable man. That's why I want to continue bearing on my shoulders the weight of its present and future. That's what I want, Joaquín, that's what I want." And here he beat his breast with both hands.

"And if in the tale of what was once Yangana, in the tales of those hundred and sixty families, there figure both the stigma of a crime and the heroic feat of a courageous flight, then I want to be the one mainly responsible for the glory or the disaster of its resurrection. That's why, my brother

Joaquín, I have need of you very great need. Can you help me?"

But Joaquín, with his dogged stubbornness, returned the question, "Is that the real reason? Isn't there another? What's the point in all this?" Reinoso was implacable in his emphasis on the word "point."

"There's also something else, and I'll tell it to you straight," replied Ocampo, putting his hands in his pockets and speaking gravely. "I hate to give an account of my actions, not even to God. I won't allow anyone to question me. I've been that way all my life. Don't you know that I'm a professional swindler?" (There was a touch of bitterness in his voice). "I know perfectly well that some of those damned conspirators of the other party want to ask me how Matías Ortega died, since with good or with bad intent they have spread a rumor that I murdered him with an ax-blow on his head. They also want to ask me about the violation of Medina the Butcher's eldest daughter, a piece of news that they artfully made sure would reach the ears of my wife."

"And the reason for all this venom is that I had to ration some of them during the march, or I made them work hard, or I punished them for stealing provisions to fill their own bellies. These are the ones together with some pious old humbugs, who have stirred up this barefaced opposition to me."

"But tell me, brother, what was the arrangement that all of you made when you left Yangana?"

Again Ocampo was disappointed by his friend's avoidance of a direct answer to his plea. Again he controlled himself and calmly explained, "It was very simple. Just that I should lead them to the river lands at Palanda and that I should be the only one to order and direct, with full power and authority. They handed over to my care everything that they had, and bound themselves to obey me. Until the end of the last day's march. But the point is, brother, that this isn't the last day. We haven't arrived yet. We are still on the march and the end is far off. I believe that I can do a great deal for my town."

"And when the task is finished, then I myself, without anybody asking me, shall of my own free will, call together the people who from the start placed their trust in me, in order to say to them, 'What I am handing over to you is something that I have accomplished, with your cooperation. Now that the hardest part is over, the most painful part, the interminable labor of beginning everything, I am returning to you what you once put into my hands there in Yangana on that terrible day.'"

"Will you help me? Because if you won't help me, brother Joaquín, I shall have to do it without you. Whatever the consequences. I don't believe my enemies would ever persuade you to join them. In any case, have got to do what I've just told you. If there is opposition, I shall overcome it by force with the help of my supporters. Either they elect me or I shall elect myself. There is no other way. It would mean eliminating someone. That would then be their affair, and they can settle it…"

"Now, why don't we have some more drinks of that good liquor?…"

So the exhilarated Ocampo, the practiced drinker, and the impassive Reinoso who from long abstinence was very much out of practice, again took turns lifting the bottle toward the treetops.

(2)

Although both men had drunk more or less the same amount, it was Joaquín Reinoso who was the more affected by it. A drowsy, almost numb feeling was slowly spreading over his back and shoulders. His tongue seemed stuck to the roof of his mouth. And when Reinoso appeared tongue-tied…

Nobody knew better than Reinoso himself how to loosen his tongue when it got stuck. His remedy was to start talking in the awkward way that North Americans do when they are learning to speak Spanish. So when he found himself in this predicament, he decided to cure himself, and began to play the part of a "gringo." At the same time he felt wonderfully at ease and full of affection for his old companion in mischief whom he had obviously enraged only a short time before by refusing to answer a single one of his questions.

"You understand, Cholo, I much happy with you…no matter me if Yangana take cassava have planted…Nor matter me be hungry in company with my Yangana friends. So Commissioner not die when I stick him candles?"

In the mine he had learned to swear in English. His knowledge of that language was confined to a few bad words and interjections. The fact is that the gringo MacGregor himself spoke to them in no other way. He was the foreman in charge of the tunnel at the level where Reinoso, Ocampo and poor Matías Ortega worked. He was a huge man, 'five stories high,' who always wore immense rubber boots and blue denim pants hitched up ridiculously high. The miners used to say to his face that they must be good for jumping over mud holes and that he probably crapped standing up. The miners knew him well since he visited the tunnel four times a day to inspect progress while they were cutting rock with pneumatic drills.

"All right! Son of a bitch!" continued Reinoso, "You come take what have to eat. But bring animals and I must feed son tomorrow. True? God damn! No food for cattle, because no pasture here. Understand me? Fell trees is hard work…Remember Mr. MacGregor? Remember big-belly Mitmann? Remember big-belly Mitmann have glass eye and we fool Matías Ortega to believe gringo Mitmann have not one but two glass eyes? O.K.!"

He had lost his reserve of an hour before and was slapping Ocampo's shoulder.

"Curly Ocampo! You tell me ungrateful people want change you for others; you angry because people say Curly Ocampo good to bring them here but no good for directing foundation. Curly Ocampo, I believe yes, you are good to command here. I ready, God damn! to help you against anyone. I good friend of yours as before, but I think no more bloodshed. Understand? No more blood. All right!"

In spite of his drunkenness, Joaquín was to a certain extent still vigilant. So many nights and days of waiting and watching had sharpened his instincts for being on guard whether asleep or awake. In the almost hypnotic situation in which he found himself all his senses were extraordinarily alert. The cool night air and fitful whispers of the woods were speaking to him. As he listened aimlessly to this mysterious language, he became aware that something was happening beyond the blanket of mist which surrounded them.

Then he stood up, weaving a little, laid a heavy hand on Ocampo's shoulder, shook him out of his state of suspicious attention, pulled him along and made him stand up. The two men began to walk forward slowly, Ocampo supporting his tottering friend on his left shoulder.

"Where are you trying to take me, Joaquín?" he asked. "Cholo, I want to take you lookout place, is very close, understand?"

The lookout he referred to was a knoll, a hillock which looked like an immense Indian burial mound, surrounded by palm trees and crowned with an enormous black rock. It was not difficult to reach the top, since the surface was all rough and rugged.

After a quarter of an hour's slow climb, panting and puffing, the two friends arrived at the summit and could see at their feet the waving fan-shaped plumes of the palm trees half hidden in the mist.

"Curly Ocampo!" exclaimed Reinoso, momentarily taking his right arm off his friend's neck. He took several turns on the rock to get his bearings, and finally pointed his sharp forefinger straight ahead. "Attention, Curly Ocampo, God damn! Look there, yes. Look there...All right!"

And he pointed out to him with jabs of his forefinger a faint light through the mist, a barely perceptible light which seemed to be coming from very far away.

By this time, Tobias Ocampo, alias Curly, felt himself a little clearer in the head. He breathed deeply, delighting in the cool moist air from the mist, rubbed his drowsy eyelids and looked...

(3)

Before him lay the vast savannah, still white in the mist. To right and left he could see a few scattered hilltops, their dark blue shapes rising through the white foam that blanketed all the bottom land. They were smoother, lesser offshoots of the Andes, that had come down to rest far away at the headwaters of the Amazon. The mist swirled round them, in places a dense fog and in places a light gauze. The two men could hear the deep roar of the invisible river thundering in its gorge like a beast in its lair.

And now from the direction where the curtain of mist seemed thinner, a light began slowly to spread, very slowly, as if huge half-shaded lanterns were being lit one by one. As the patch of sky grew clearer and clearer, like a recently wiped window pane, a shining torrent of mist streamed out to reveal the outlines of the palm trees and the features of the beholders. Ocampo felt dazzled by the vision and faced it with his arms crossed proudly on his chest.

It was a splendid vision but a tranquil one, and Ocampo, realizing that nobody had to be defied, that it was neither a provocation nor a threat, relaxed his chest, unfolded his arms, and remained quietly gazing.

"What does it mean, Joaquín?" he asked in a wondering voice.

"It's the dawn," answered Reinoso softly, with the sweetness that only drunks and women in love can sometimes put into a phrase or a look. He turned and pointed to the immense square of sky where the sunlit mist continued to pour out like dammed up water when the floodgate is opened.

"So that's the dawn?" repeated Ocampo.

"Yes, cholo...that's the dawn. You understand? That is daybreak," replied Reinoso, stumbling a little. "We let day catch us, cholo, we drinking all night...Now turn round, look here behind, cholo. Understand? See where our people are...That, too, be a dawn and daybreak."

Up there on the peak, Ocampo felt dimly that a new life was beginning all around him. For the migrant group that had just found shelter in this piece of jungle—this group with its voices, its customs, its fears, its seeds and plants, its flocks and herds, the sad past was already far behind, the present had not yet taken shape, the only road was the road to the future. And before anything else, he must make up his mind about that future. Would it be with him or without him, or against him?

Should he use force if he had to in order to take command of the people who had trusted him as their leader during the migration and who were now people about to cast him aside like a piece of worn out rubbish? Should he put an end to opposition with an iron fist, leveling all obstacles if there were real resistance to his personal commands? Should he destroy the group headed by Don Vicente? Would it be best to seize power by taking advantage of the fact that the armed men were still under his orders and respected his courage and gift of command?

Would the town which was to be founded down there be able to survive without him? Which would be better for the real interests of the town—his resignation or his proclamation as leader? Wasn't his spirit full of hope and fervor? Hadn't he only just found a goal for his life? A field of endeavor worthy of his superabundant vitality? Would he have to give up his position just at the moment when it had made him realize how fitted he was to be leader and supreme authority?

What would Rosa Elvira, his dear confidante and the wife of his best friend, say in that soft voice of hers, so sweetly persuasive? Wasn't there an old saying to the effect that a woman's advice is short and he who doesn't follow it is crazy? Could she have been right when she said that he had better give up the command and return to what he had been?

The mist was now dissipating in a gentle dew which fell on the blankets of the people sleeping in the open, in the wide clearing which Reinoso had made single-handed when he lived there alone in the jungle.

"And the dawn," went on Reinoso, "is white, much white in these parts...the dawn here has no blood...You understand? Pay good attention me...Ready? All right, son of a bitch! The dawn here much white, and the dawn is also the New Town you come leading...God damn! Listen, cholo, just as dawn here no have blood, so New Town too no shed blood. Understand? All right! Should be like this daybreak...white...much white...without blood! Damn it!"

"I don't want bloodshed, Joaquín," answered Ocampo after a moment's pause. He spoke in a firm voice and it was clear that he understood all the significance of his friend's obstinate insistence on dragging him up to the lookout "don't want bloodshed. And there won't be bloodshed. I shall be what I was before; I shall get drunk whenever I feel like it and I'll cheat and short-change my neighbors. You are right, brother Joaquín. You have convinced me. The dawn should not be bloodstained. It should be white, very white, just like your wife Rosa Elvira said last night, Joaquín. That's what she wanted."

And with this sudden disinterested outburst characteristic of warm-hearted drunks, he leaned on the column of black rock and looked with eyes smarting from the night air at the dammed up light spilling over to the east. He saw the whispering palm trees below him, and the mist moving up and away among the tree tops, and the sharp outcroppings of hills still wrapped in damp wreaths of cotton, and the swathes of bonfires and blankets, and the rows of men and animals in the clearing, and a friend's face all bathed in new light, a friend whose arm was linked to his and who imitated a gringo when he talked.

Exultantly Ocampo took a deep breath and shouted:

"Viva Pueblo Nuevo!"
Long live Our Town!
FINIS

www.ingramcontent.com/pod-product-compliance
Lightning Source LLC
Chambersburg PA
CBHW030748030726
47497CB00001B/181